Fossil Lake

An Anthology of the Aberrant

Edited by Christine Morgan
Cover art by Kirsten Maloney

Published by:

Sabledrake Enterprises
2401 Chestnut St.
Everett, WA 98201
http://www.sabledrake.com
sabledrake@sabledrake.com

Copyrights ©

"A Letter from the Lake" by Ramsey Campbell from The Inhabitant of the Lake and Less Welcome Tenants, originally published in 1964

"Revolver Concert" by Spencer Carvalho, originally published in Barcelona Review issue 70, 2010

"Malicious Intimacy" by William Andre Sanders, originally published in Carnage Conservatory e-zine, June 2012

"The Last Revelation of Gla'aki, an Excerpt" by Ramsey Campbell, from The Last Revelation of Gla'aki, 2013

"Eat Yourself" by Michael Shimek, 2014

"The Varmint of Fossil Valley" by Lewis Unknown, 2014

"Road Kill Angel" by Dana Wright, 2014

"Silver Screen Shadows" by Mathias Jansson, 2014

"C-C-Cold" by Ken Goldman, 2014

"What's Your Beef?" by Mark Orr, 2014

"Alchera" by D.J. Tyrer, 2014

"The Dank" by Doug Blakeslee, 2014

"Dark of Madness" by Tanya Nehmelman, 2014

"All That Jazz" by Meagan Hightower, 2014

"Thick" by Melanie-Jo Lee, 2014

"The Ziggurat of Skulls" by Joshua Dobson, 2014

"Apartment B" by Stinky Cat, 2014

"Pretty Girl" by Deb Eskie, 2014

"Come Fly With Death" by Wesley D. Gray, 2014

"The Horn of Plenty" by Russell Nayle, 2014

"The Lost Link" by Carl Thomas Fox, 2014

"Nat Poopcone vs. the Beast of Fossil Lake" by Jerrod Balzer, 2014

"Where Lost Ones Dwell" by Tony Flynn, 2014

"Lana Doesn't Get Lucky" by Kerry Lipp and Emily Meier, 2014

"Gothicism on Trial" by G. Preacher, 2014

"Finding Miss Fossie" by Melany Van Every, 2014

"Arkham Arts Review: Alienation" by Peter Rawlik, 2014

"Mishipishu: The Ghost Story of Penny Jaye Prufrock" by Mary Pletsch, 2014

"Beneath" by Michael Burnside, 2014

"Passionate in Chicago" by John Goodrich, 2014

"Mr. Winter" by Jeremy Terry, 2014

"Impressions" by Christine Morgan, 2014

"Make Me Something Scary" by Patrick Tumblety, 2014

"The Day Lloyd Campbell's Mama Came to Town" by Scott Colbert, 2014

"The Rack" by Mike Meroney, 2014

"Beautiful" by John Claude Smith, 2014

Dedication

This book is dedicated to the memory of Janrae Frank,
the King of Daverana.

Copyright © 2014 Sabledrake Enterprises
All rights reserved
2nd Edition – Spring, 2014
Cover Design by Kirsten Maloney Copyright © 2014
Footprint/Dinosaur images by KeithBishop © 2007

ISBN   978-0-9844032-5-7

All rights reserved. No part of this publication may be reproduced,
stored in a retrieval system, or transmitted in any form or by any
means – electronic, mechanical, photocopy, recording or any other,
except for brief quotations in printed reviews – without prior
permission of the publisher.

This is a work of fiction. Names, characters, places, and incidents
either are the product of the author's imagination or are used
fictitiously. Any resemblance to actual events or persons, living or
dead, is entirely coincidental.

"A mix of horror and humor, the frightful and the bizarre, this darker than dark anthology is transgressive and fun. FOSSIL LAKE is truly and "literary" an eye in the shadows, a glimpse of terrors big and small in all their horrific forms as they make a home in Fossil Lake. Readers are sure to fear the dark of grandparental basements – this anthology is better than the best of Norwood's Discoveries!"

– Mary SanGiovanni, author of *Chaos* and *The Fading Place*.

Table of Contents

Editor's Introduction

Fossil Lake is a real place.

Actually, Fossil Lake is several real places. There are Fossil Lakes in Wyoming, Oregon, Colorado, North Dakota and Montana. Professor Edward W. Barry of the John Hopkins Institute published a paper on a Fossil Lake in France in 1917. A Fossil Lake was discovered in Darfur, Sudan, in 2007. There's a Fossil Lake in Australia.

For any one person to attempt to lay claim to it is preposterous. Fossil Lake belongs to us all. It belongs to the world.

And what about the other Fossil Lakes, the ones that exist within our minds? The Fossil Lake of the psyche, of the soul? What might be found buried in those subconscious, sedimentary layers? What might drift in those deep, dark undercurrents?

In this book, you will visit many different Fossil Lakes. Some are overt, some subtle. Some share certain common themes and threads while others visit their own unique landscapes of the transgressive and surreal.

You'll find stories to amuse, arouse, disturb, enlighten, entertain and perhaps sicken, in various turns and measures. You'll find stories from seasoned pros and talented beginners, all of whom it was a genuine honor and pleasure to work with. You'll find original tales as well as reprints, and stories inspired by or in the tradition of masters of the genre.

It is my hope, Dear Reader, that you enjoy this anthology in the spirit with which it was intended.

Christine Morgan
Seattle, WA
October 2013

A Letter From the Lake
Ramsey Campbell

The following is a letter from Thomas Cartwright to his friend Alan Kearney, dated 30 October 1960 . . .

Last Friday I made a special journey down to Bold Street, and found out quite a bit about my lakeside street. The agent wasn't particularly pleased to see me, and seemed surprised when I told him I hadn't come for my money back. He still was wary of saying much, though – went on a bit about the houses being built "on the orders of a private group." It didn't seem as though I'd get much out of him, and then I happened to mention that I was having dreams like the earlier tenants. Before he could think, he blurted out: "That's going to make some people a bit happier, then."

"What do you mean by that?" I asked, sensing a mystery.

Well, he hedged a bit, and finally explained: "It's to do with the 'haunting' of your lake. There's a story among the country people – and it extends to them in the suburbs around Mercy Hill, which is nearest your place – that *something* lives in the lake, and 'sends out nightmares' to lure people to it. Even though the nightmares are terrifying, they're said to have a hypnotic effect. Since the place became untenanted, people – children particularly – in the Mercy Hill area have been dreaming, and one or two have been admitted to the Hill hospital. No wonder they have nightmares around there – it used to be the site of a gallows, you know, and the hospital was a prison; only some joker called it 'Mercy Hill' and the name stuck. They say the dreams are the

work of what's in the lake – *it's* hungry, and casting its net further out. Of course, it's all superstition – God knows what they think *it* is. Anyway, if you're dreaming, they'd say *it* won't need to trouble them any more."

"Well, that's one thing cleared up," I said, trying to follow up my advantage. "Now, why were the houses really built? What was this 'private group' you're so secretive about?"

"It'll sound crazy to you, no doubt," he apologized. "The houses were built around 1790, and renovated or added to several times. They were put up on the instructions of this group of about six or seven people. These people all disappeared around 1860 or 1870, apparently leaving for another town or something – anyway, nobody around here heard of them again. In 1880 or so, since there'd been no word from them, the houses were let yet again. For many reasons, people never stayed long – you know, the distance from town; and the scenery too, even if that *was* what got you there. I've heard from earlier workers here that the place even seemed to affect some people's minds. I was only here when the last but one tenant came in. You heard about the family that was last here, but this was something I didn't tell you. Now look – you said when you first came that you were after ghosts. You sure you want to hear about this?"

"Of course I do – this is what I asked for," I assured him. How did I know it mightn't inspire a new painting? (Which reminds me, I'm working on a painting from my dream; to be called *The Thing In The Lake*.)

"Really, it wasn't too much," he warned me. "He came in here at nine o'clock – that's when we open, and he told me he'd been waiting outside in his car half the night. Wouldn't tell me why he was pulling out – just threw the keys on the counter and told me to get the house sold again. While I was fixing some things up, though, he was muttering a lot. I couldn't catch it all, but what I did get was pretty peculiar. Lot of stuff about 'the spines' and 'you lose your will and become part of it' – and he went on a lot about 'the city among the weeds.' Somebody 'had to keep the boxes in the daytime,' because of 'the green decay.' He kept mentioning someone called – *Glarky*, or something like that – and he also said something about Thomas Lee I didn't catch."

That name Thomas Lee sounded a bit familiar to me, and I said so. I still don't know where I got it from, though.

"Lee? Why, of course," he immediately said. "He was the leader of that group of people who had the houses built – the man who did all the negotiating . . . And that's really about all the facts I can give you."

"*Facts*, yes," I agreed. "But what else can you tell me? I suppose the people round here must have their own stories about the place?"

"I could tell you to go and find out for yourself," he said – I suppose he was entitled to get a bit tired of me, seeing as I wasn't buying anything. However, he went on: "Still, it's lucky for you Friday is such a slack day . . . Well, they say that the lake was caused by the fall of a meteor. Centuries ago, the meteor was wandering through space, and on it there was a city. The beings of the city all died with the passage through space, but *something* in that city still lived – something that guided the meteor to some sort of landing from its home deep under the surface. God knows what the city would've had to be built of to withstand the descent, if it were true!

"Well, the meteor-crater filled with water over the centuries. Some people, they say, had ways of knowing there was something alive in the lake, but they didn't know where it had fallen. One of these was Lee, but he used things nobody else dared touch to find its whereabouts. He brought these other people down from Goatswood – and you know what the superstitious say comes out of the hill behind that town for them to worship . . . As far as I can make out, Lee and his friends are supposed to have met with more than they expected at the lake. They became servants of what they awoke, and, people say, they're there yet."

That's all I could get out of him. I came back to the house, and I can tell you I viewed it a bit differently from when I left! I bet you didn't expect me to find all that out about it, eh? Certainly it's made me more interested in my surroundings – perhaps it'll inspire me.

Excerpt from: "The Inhabitant of the Lake," 1964

Eat Yourself
Michael Shimek

Josephine Kline felt as if her every hair stood straight as an arrow, bats flapped wildly in her stomach, and her heart had started its own drum circle.

She was going to go through with it, though.

Maybe.

How could she not? It was the experience of a lifetime. She and her husband had somehow won tickets to the most exclusive restaurant in the world: Eat Yourself.

The reviews, signs, and advertisements spoke for themselves:

Top notch . . . frightfully entertaining! – George Fannelli, *The New York Times*.

Treat yourself to . . . yourself!

Five thumbs up! (attached to a billboard with five human hands giving the thumbs up sign, the last one with a bite taken out of it)

The restaurant was one of a kind. Only A-list celebrities were invited – yes, it was invitation only. No one who wasn't rich or famous was ever invited.

Until now.

"Paul, I'm nervous."

"Jo, there's nothing to be worried about. This is exciting!"

"I don't know . . . We don't belong here. We're not these type of people. I mean, look."

Outside their limousine was a mass of paparazzi, lights flashing at anyone entering and exiting the upscale restaurant. It was a two-story building with no windows, painted all black. Somehow bypassing fire codes, it had only one set of doors, which were so large an elephant could stroll through. A red carpet ran from the entrance to the curb, velvet rope keeping back the gawkers.

Jo's husband was nothing but wide eyes and smiles as he stared at the glamour that was so foreign to them.

They were from a rural town in Minnesota. She was a schoolteacher, and he was an accountant for a local hardware store. They had never been to New York City, maybe traveling to Minneapolis once or twice a year for fun. They were small city folk; the big city was a whole new experience. They'd immediately found themselves lost at the JFK airport, even with a man stationed to greet them.

"It's *amazing,* Jo! We've never been pampered like this before, and I don't think we'll ever get another chance. We're living like celebrities! How can you not be enjoying yourself?"

He ignored her pleas of concern, too caught up in the spotlight. She sulked back into the leather seat. Their vehicle was second in line. She couldn't see who had exited the limo in front of them, but the flashbulbs popped wildly for whoever walked down the carpet. Their chariot rolled forward. It was their turn.

All of Paul's teeth could be seen. Jo faked a smile.

The door opened. Cameras blazed with blinding twinkles. Paul grabbed Jo's hand and pulled her into the craziness. Her dress sparkled, and his suit shone. He waved for the cameras; she did, too, but quickly and hurrying toward the entrance. When the giant door opened, she darted inside, losing her husband's grip in the process.

Paul came in soon after. "Whoa," he said, his smile never faltering. "That was intense."

"I'll say," she said, hoping he would get the hint.

He did not.

Jo tried to ignore his ignorance and breathed a sigh of relief. The new surroundings helped her relax.

The room they were in was quite fancy: leather couches, ultra-modern art and décor, water cascading down the entire side of a wall. Although it was more elegant than anything she was used to, Jo still found the room calming.

"Welcome to Eat Yourself." A voice came from the only other doorway in the room. The woman was tall and svelte, prettier than most models. "My name is Teresa, and I will be assisting you with the preparations. Please, sit."

They sat on one of the couches.

Teresa handed them each a stack of papers and a pen. "These are the waivers. You *must* sign these before going any further."

Paul immediately began skimming and signing next to the red tabs.

"There's so much of this," Jo said, hesitating. "What does it all say?"

"Basically, that you know what you're getting yourself into," the hostess said. "You can't sue if something goes wrong, we're not liable if you die or are unsatisfied . . . minor legal things like that." She raised an eyebrow, the implication clear. Sign, or leave.

"Honey, come on," Paul said. "Just sign the papers."

She caved. Without even reading what was written, she signed and dated all twenty-three lines. Paul grinned at her and pulled her close.

"Excellent," Theresa said as she took the waivers. "Now, if you follow me, we can begin with the drugs."

Jo's worry increased. "Drugs?"

"Of course," the hostess said. "You don't expect to be operated on without any drugs, do you?"

"Um, no, I guess not."

Theresa smiled and winked at the couple. "Don't worry, it's a good cocktail of stuff. It'll help calm you down, too."

She brought them into a large and noisy room filled with tables and reclining chairs. At several tables were diners in various stages of their meals. Many were awake, drugged and laughing, and trying to hold conversations with those around them. Some were passed out, the doctors in the middle of the operations. Those with bandages either ate in quiet, or loudly to proclaim their achievement. Jo saw rich politicians, famous movie and television stars, athletes, and many people who belonged to royalty.

"Oh, wow!" Paul grabbed Jo's arm and pointed. "Is that the queen's son? We can see right into his chest. And so can he!"

Depending on what was removed, the surgery could be done on someone who was fully conscious. The prince had apparently opted to be awake, and he stared in horror and excitement at the open cavity in his chest. Jo looked away from the gruesome sight.

"Ribs," Paul said. "He must be having ribs. I hear that's a popular choice."

Jo avoided looking at anyone else's table, focusing on the hostess and the empty chairs she brought them to.

"Here you are. If you two will have a seat, I will inform a nurse to come and hook you up. Congratulations on winning this once in a life time opportunity. I hope you enjoy the rest of your evening." With a smile, the woman was gone.

"She was nice," Paul said.

"You mean pretty," Jo said. It was a joke, but with her nerves it might have sounded a little harsh.

Paul blushed and was about to say something, but a very good-looking man approached the table, pushing a rolling tray equipped with various medical instruments.

"Hello, my name is Daniel, and I'll be your nurse tonight. Are you two ready?"

"We sure are," Paul said.

Jo nodded but kept silent.

"Good. There's nothing to worry about. First, I'm going to take a quick blood sample and attach these IVs to you. Lay an arm out on the table, either arm works."

Both Jo and Paul complied. With professional care, like they were at any hospital or doctor's office, the nurse pricked their arms, filled up two small tubes of blood, and then attached them to the IV bags.

"The saline will feel a little cool as it travels through you. Next, I'll inject the mix of drugs that will help mellow you out and prepare you for your surgery." He pulled out two syringes and injected a purple liquid into the bags. "While that circulates, I'm going to go and test your blood, just to make sure there's nothing to throw off the operation."

Jo stared at her arm in disbelief. *I can't believe I just let that stranger do that,* she thought. *What am I doing? I'm really going to let them hack a part of me off so they can cook it and feed it to me? How is this right?! How can this be the "in" thing?* She wanted to scream, but her mind and body felt as light as a cloud. She was nervous and angry, but it didn't matter anymore. Nothing mattered much anymore.

"Say, these drugs are working pretty fast, huh?" Paul lifted his arms and waved them across his face. He giggled and put them back down. "Can you feel it?"

"Oh, I'm feeling something," she said. She wanted to sound upset, but it only came out in a mumble.

Paul giggled some more, and before she knew it, Jo was laughing right along with him.

Daniel returned. "Both of you are good to go. I've got some menus for you, and in about ten minutes Chef Baron LaVour will be out to take your order. Any questions?"

Jo had one. "How long will it take to regrow the limb, or whatever part is removed from the body?"

"That depends. A finger usually takes an hour. Nothing takes longer than a day, though. With the highly trained scientists, geneticists, and doctors we have here, Eat Yourself has the most advanced technology involving medicine and health in the entire world."

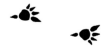

After the nurse left again, Jo opened the leather-bound menu and glanced at what the restaurant had to offer. It all sounded fancy, and oh-so gruesome: blood bisque, fillet of tongue, roasted thigh. If she hadn't been hopped-up on drugs, she might have either fainted or puked all over the table.

"Paul, I'm really having second thoughts about this."

He scrunched his eyebrows. "Are you serious? You want to back out *now?*"

"Well . . ."

Two men walked up to Jo and Paul's table. The larger man was tall and thick; he looked ex-military. With strong arms crossed over his barrel chest, shades tinted so his eyes could barely be seen through the lenses, and a black toque resting on top of his head, Chef Baron Lavour was indeed an intimidating person. The smaller man reminded Jo of a remora, the fish that hangs onto a shark through suction. Dressed with a black bowtie and holding a high-end electronic tablet, he never wavered more than an arm's length from the boss.

"Good evening, and congratulations on your winnings. I am Troy, Chef Baron LaVour's personal sous-chef and assistant. I will be speaking on his behalf. Any questions before we begin?"

They shook their heads.

"Good. Before you order, I will need to ask a few questions. First, what are your names?"

Paul spoke for them. "Paul and Josephine Kline."

The assistant pecked away at the screen and continued on. "Ages?"

"I'm thirty-nine, and she's thirty-seven."

"Had you heard about Eat Yourself before receiving an invitation?"

"Yes, of course. Who hasn't?"

"You'd be surprised, Mr. Kline. Do either of you have any food allergies?"

"Nope."

"Good. Now, have you decided what to order?"

Paul smiled and winked at Jo, and it was then that she realized what dish he had chosen. *No, not that one,* she thought.

"I want the Suicide Feast," he said.

A hush fell among those seated nearby. It was the most dangerous meal in the entire world. Choosing the Suicide Feast involved the aorta, a section each of the carotid and radial arteries, and both corneas. It was prepared only one way, and that was Chef Baron LaVour's way.

The chef's gaze bored through the tinted glasses, narrow slits studying Paul as if taking his measure. Then the large man nodded. He turned to Jo and waited for her order.

"Um, I'm not really sure . . . can I just have, like, a couple of fingers fried? Like, only one, maybe two?" Her voice quavered. She didn't want to do it, not even with the drugs pumping through her system. She hoped the chef would see her unease and dismiss her from this gruesome trend that was somehow acceptable in today's society, but she could tell he would have none of that in *his* restaurant.

The chef's eyes glowed with a fiery anger. He hissed something to his assistant and stormed off.

"Chef Baron LaVour has little patience for indecision," Troy told Jo. "He will decide for you and return when he is ready."

Before she could argue, Troy snatched the menus from their hands and left the table.

"Geez, Jo, way to embarrass me," Paul said.

Her face flushed. *"I'm* embarrassing *you?"*

"Shh, honey, don't raise your voice –"

She cut him off. "I've been telling you how uncomfortable this whole thing has made me, and you've ignored every bit of it. *You* just ordered something that could potentially kill you. Remember when that actor ordered it and died from complications?"

"That was when Eat Yourself first opened. It still had its bugs to work out. Nothing like that has happened in months."

"Right, *months,*" she said.

"It's perfectly safe, Jo. They have scientists and doctors on standby just in case. I bet they're always updating their procedures to keep up concerns. A business can't continue if the customers keep dying." He paused and added, "I won't let you ruin this experience for me. We'll talk about it later. Sit back, and go along with the ride. When it's all over, you'll be happy you went through with it."

Divorce had never been a thought in her head until now. Paul had never acted so stern toward her before. *Never.* This whole experience had changed him, and not into someone she appreciated. She wouldn't divorce Paul, of course; she loved him, but they were *definitely* going to talk when the night was over.

The sous-chef returned and acknowledged Jo. "Chef Baron LaVour has chosen your meal, but he wants it to be a surprise." He then turned to Paul and said, "You, sir, did select a meal that requires heavy sedation. I'm afraid you will have to be put completely under for this operation."

"Oh," Paul said with a frown. "Will I be able see when I'm eating?"

"Yes. Although your dish involves the corneas, those only take a few

minutes to regrow. Any other questions? No? Good. Ah, here comes the nurse now to prep you for the surgery."

The handsome nurse – *they must only hire models,* Jo thought – approached the table again. His rolling tray now held two syringes placed on top. "Are you ready? I've been informed that both of you will be under for the procedure. Is that correct?"

"Yes," Paul said.

This was it. The last second to drop out had arrived, and Jo no longer wanted to eat part of herself at Eat Yourself.

"No," she said. "I don't want to go through with this anymore. It's despicable, and I cannot believe I ever set foot in this horrid establishment."

Anger flared in Paul's face. "Honey –"

The nurse cut him off. "I've got this," he said. "Mrs. Kline, many people have doubts at the last second. It's perfectly normal. I'll give you a little something extra to help calm you down, and then you can decide after that. Sound good?"

"No. I want to be unhooked from all of this right now. I – hey! What do you think you're doing?"

Without her consent, the nurse had picked up one of the needles and plunged it into her IV. She tried to sit up, but he pushed her back into her seat. She would have struggled, but in her weakened state it was no use.

Jo felt even lighter than before. Her eyelids hung heavy, threatening to close and darken the world. She wanted to stay awake, but whatever she had been given was too strong. Her eyes closed, and before sleep claimed her, she heard the comforting words of her husband.

"Don't worry, Jo. Everything will be perfectly fine when you wake up."

*   *   *

Everything was *not* fine when Jo woke up.

She opened her eyes to blurred vision. When she went to rub them with her left hand, bandages scratched at her face. Clearing her eyes with her right hand instead, she saw in horror what had happened.

She was in the same chair. Set on the table in front of her was a plate. In the middle of the plate, arranged on a bed of greens, was a human hand. It had been cooked and grilled, the grill marks adding a fresh reality to the otherwise preposterous image.

That's my *hand.*

Jo's eyes went wide. She was dimly aware of Paul, sitting across from

16

her, chewing happily on a section of artery, beaming with excitement and pride.

"That's my hand," she said. "That's *my* hand. That's *my* hand!"

"Jo? Jo, settle down. Jo! Help! Somebody help her!"

Her mind melted into mush. She screamed for escape, thrashing and flailing at anyone who reached for her. After three men pinned her down and another jabbed a syringe into her neck, she felt herself slump to the floor.

*   *   *

"Get her out of here. Take her through one of the underground emergency exits. We don't want someone to capture a picture of her like this."

Troy sighed as he watched several of the nurses run off. It was another potential media nightmare. The woman hadn't died, but it was just as bad. She would most likely never regain her sanity, just like the television star and politician who currently resided in a mental institution.

They should probably count themselves lucky only three people had gone insane.

Not everyone could handle the genius of Chef Baron LaVour. Not everyone could handle Eat Yourself.

But, the couple had signed the waivers, so it didn't really matter. *Thank God for the legal system,* Troy thought and then headed back to work.

The Varmint of Fossil Valley
Lewis Unknown

Eugene Verner shifted in the saddle, pain flaring briefly in his old joints. Not for the first time did he regret hiring his services to the wagon train, but he'd been low on liquor money. 'Sides, it was easy work compared to bounties or herding cattle at his age. Hell, the settlers even had a map to this new Eden of theirs. All he had to do was see them through a thousand miles of Indians, bad weather and the odd bandit gang.

A task he had now completed, as his horse cleared the top of a rise and he gazed for the first time upon Fossil Lake.

It took up a third of the valley, its deep blue waters looking cool and inviting. The reeds at the edge formed a pattern that seemed like a welcoming smile from a folksy old uncle, just itching to tell you a story and share some moonshine.

So why did the sight of it send a cold shudder down Verner's back?

He was still staring at the lake when the lead wagon caught up to him. The driver, a big red-bearded man with a bald head and hands like ham-hocks, pulled his team to a halt and gazed out across the valley with admiration.

As well he might. The gentle hills tapered to good flat land, tall grass perfect for grazing. It would make for fine fields once spring came. To the north was a stand of woods, amber and crimson leaves blowing in the breeze. There'd be ample timber for good sturdy homes, and game to hunt to help them get through the winter.

"Beautiful place isn't it, Mr Verner?" said the red-bearded man. "Just

right for a good God-fearing community to take root."

Verner scratched his own beard, mostly grey. "It's your community, Pastor Campbell, not mine. And I've told you before, it's just Verner."

A friendly smile shone from his open, honest face. "Ah sorry, my friend, force of habit. Though I've told you, it's only Pastor Campbell when I'm in church. You call me Hugh and I'll call you Verner, deal?"

Verner nodded, not bothering to fight the wry half-grin that was the closest he came to smiling. They'd had this same conversation a hundred times since setting out for the Montana Territory, and he expected they'd have it again.

Campbell might be a man of God, but he wasn't afraid of hard work, and was even willing to dish out a little tough love to get lost sheep out of the saloons and into church on a Sunday. More than a few such joints back in Chicago had come to the conclusion that it was cheaper stay closed until after the Sunday service rather than deal with the broken fixtures and furnishings after Pastor Campbell came to collect his wayward parishioners.

"Still we're finally here, God be praised," Campbell said. "Before we enter the valley proper I believe it would be only right to hold a prayer meeting in thanks to the Lord. You're welcome to join us."

The prospect of yet another prayer meeting finally shook Verner's attention from the lake. "I wouldn't want to intrude," he said. "Tell you what, you do that, and I'll find us a spot to camp tonight." He nudged his horse away before the other man could answer.

Soon Campbell's voice was booming out over the valley, thanking the Lord for protecting them on their journey and mourning those lost along the way. Of which there had been plenty, and Verner himself hadn't seen much of God's hand at work there. A family of five dead of a pox, their wagon set ablaze to prevent the infection spreading; children desperately reloading rifles while their parents fired at charging Indians; a collapsing bridge that dropped oxen and wagons into a swollen river; a little boy breaking his neck in a fall.

All that, he had seen on the trail, but no God. Maybe He'd popped round to offer everyone tea and cake while Verner had been scouting ahead. Still, most of them had managed to make it, and that was something worth celebrating.

He chose a likely spot about halfway between lake and woods, next to a stream. Firewood and water, without having to get too close to the –

Why he felt that unease, he couldn't reckon, but it preyed on him enough so that when he swung down from the saddle he managed to jar his bum

knee. His spate of cursing bounced off the nearby boulders in an echo, startling up a flock of birds that scattered in all directions.

Almost all directions. Even rubbing his knee, he noticed how it seemed even they avoided the lake. Come to think of it, though he'd noticed animal spoor and even some rabbit warrens, there wasn't much in the way of tracks of any sort along the shore. Weren't even any bullfrogs croaking in the lazy autumn sun.

He told himself he was being foolish and did his best to put it out of his mind, but he watered his thirsty horse at the stream instead of leading it to the lake.

As he marked out the campsite, pausing several times to massage kinks in his back that he wouldn't have noticed even ten years ago, he wondered why he saw no sign of the tribes. This place was practically perfect – water, hunting, farmland, the hills providing shelter from the winds – but as far as he could tell, no one had settled hereabouts in ages.

The folks from Campbell's wagon train proved eager enough to make up for that lack, happy families grateful to have arrived. It didn't take long for them to set up their camps, making fires, sending children to fill water-buckets. Everything was lively, noisy activity as they went about preparing for their dinner.

The cooking was done by the Capriones, an Italian husband and wife who'd had themselves a fine restaurant back in Italy. Somehow, out of the goodness of their generous hearts, they'd become burdened with a useless nephew who claimed he was just about the heir of Dante in terms of poetry. He could be a bother, so they sent him out searching for mushrooms and other edibles to get him out from underfoot.

The McAllisters opened up their stash of Scotch, under the disapproving eye of Hugh Campbell . . . until, that was, he winked at them and asked for a double. Arthur Connolly pulled out his fiddle, his young wife Alice singing along, while Michael and Sarah Thompson danced as they hadn't since their wedding day. Horst, the stern and serious German, spun yarns for the children of ancient castles, snowy mountains, and ghostly lords who led packs of wolves.

It was a good night, a night none of them would forget. Their first night in their new home . . . and their last night of happiness.

*   *   *

Deep in the lake, something stirred, its slumber broken by the sounds of celebration. It glided through the water until its snout broke the surface and drew in the scents.

Black, dead eyes reflected the burning fires. A long tongue licked around a mouth full of yellow fangs. A cold heart beat faster in excitement.

Two-legs! With their soft skin and tender meat!

How long? Too long.

Too long, but here they were. To stalk, to catch, to rip limb from limb and finally devour.

But, not yet! First the meat must be ripened, ripened by fear. Then, only then, the feast could begin.

* * *

Cries of horror and discovery woke the rest of the camp to find some of their oxen messily slaughtered.

A horde of black flies lifted from the cooling bodies and the blood stained grass as Verner knelt. He waved them away, trying to ignore the stench of blood and ruptured intestines, and examined the wounds. The throats had been ripped open, the bellies slit to spill entrails over the ground. The throats must have gone first, otherwise the screaming of the beasts would have woken the settlers.

That, Verner thought, was worrying. It suggested intelligence. And it wasn't the only worrying thing. Verner leaned in closer, using his hunting knife to lift flaps of ragged skin.

"Good God," Hugh Campbell said. "What did this? A bear? Wolves?"

Grimacing at his complaining knees, Verner stood up and shook his head. "Ain't been eaten on. Near as I can tell, whatever did this just butchered the poor beast and left it to rot. Only creature I know that kills like that is man."

Campbell wiped his anxious brow. "Indians, then? You said you hadn't seen any sign of them before."

"If it's an Indian, then it's a damn big one." Verner pointed at the ground. "Look there at those tracks."

"Looks like . . . foot-prints and hand-prints," Campbell said. "But the size! That hand-span is twice mine!"

"And whoever he is, he runs on all fours." He followed the trail of reddish-brown smears with his gaze, unsurprised to see that they led inexorably toward the lake. "I'll take Horst and Connolly. We'll circle around, see if we can find where the bastard's hiding. Meanwhile, keep everyone else close to camp. Stay on watch. The son of a bitch might not be alone."

Horst and Connolly, having come to trust Verner on the long journey, had no problems with the plan. The other settlers were frightened, but agreed

it had to be done.

In fact, the only one who took issue with it was Albert Caprione, who felt insulted at being left behind with the women and children. He pouted behind his sparse greasy beard, wiped a strand of lank hair from his eyes, and started in whining as his aunt and uncle sat in embarrassed silence.

"Why aren't I going with you fuckers? Not only am I a poet of some fame, I learnt to shoot from Davy Crockett! I can kill an Injun dead at 100 yards!"

Verner just stared at the podgy, callow youth. At first, Albert tried to look away, but his eyes were constantly drawn back to the older man's. Then he began to sweat, his lips trembling. Not until it looked as though he was about to faint did Verner speak.

"Son, you're full of shit. You can't rhyme for shit and you sure as hell can't shoot for it either. I saw you when the Indians attacked. You just cowered up behind a wagon and cried like a baby. So I'm gonna to tell you what's gonna to happen here. You're gonna stay with the camp, and if you give anyone any problems, I'm gonna take you out back and whip you like the cowardly dog you are. Do you understand me?"

"Yes, sir," Albert squeaked. He scurried away as Verner climbed into the saddle.

Small as it was, that confrontation proved to be the only success he was to have that day. He, Horst and Connolly circled the entire lake but failed to find any further tracks or any sign of Indians. Far as they could tell, the entire valley was uninhabited.

*　*　*

It watched from beneath the surface as the two-legs rode around the lake on the four-legs.

They were looking for it, just like the others in the past, but they would never think to look here. That's why it deserved to eat them. Such weak and silly creatures could only ever be prey, after all.

It had planned to leave them be for another night, to let the fear build. But now, it could no longer resist the temptation.

Tonight the feast would begin.

*　*　*

All they could do that night was keep watch and hope for the best. Men walked patrol, shouldering guns. Nervous women kept the fires burning.

They were all unsure whether they hoped their attacker would return so they could put an end to it, or that whomever – whatever – it was had fled far away.

Albert Caprione tossed and turned in his bedroll, hidden beneath his uncle's wagon. He clutched a pistol and prayed that if the Indians came back, they would overlook him for more obvious targets.

The longer the night went on, the greater a stroke of genius his plan seemed. He began to imagine, even look forward to, the attack. The Indians killing the watchmen, only for him to then emerge from his hiding place and shoot them dead like the hero he was.

After all, what did that broken down old trail boss know? He was Albert Fucking Caprione! The greatest epic poet since Dante or Homer! Sure, he might have exaggerated a little when he said Davy Crockett taught him to shoot, but he'd read a story with Crockett in it once, and that was enough for a genius like him to grasp the basics.

It was at that point Albert felt huge hands seize his lower legs, sharp things like knives or claws digging into his calf muscles and hamstrings.

Before he could gasp in a breath to scream, he was dragged bedroll and all out from under the wagon. Dangling upside-down, gazing into a maw of yellowed and impossibly sharp fangs, all he could think was what a great poem this would make.

*　　*　　*

A wide red blood trail led from the Capriones' wagon to the edge of the lake, flanked by more of the same large tracks.

They found Albert's body floating, half devoured, his skull crushed, one eye gone and the other dangling on his cheek. His ribcage had been ripped open and most of his organs were missing. All that remained of his genitals was a bloody, indiscriminate mess that couldn't have been identified as either male or female.

Some of the searchers, unable to contain themselves, were violently sick off to the side. Others held back Matteo Caprione, who would have otherwise plunged into the water to cradle the grisly remains. His wife wept and wailed and babbled in Italian. Unpleasant, burdensome and bothersome though Albert may have been, he was still their nephew, and no one deserved an end such as this.

Verner stared at the corpse, a cold rage bubbling inside him.

He'd led these people here, through storm and fire, past Indians and bandits, to a place where they should be safe. Now they were in danger of

dying at the hands of some beast, for he couldn't imagine any man capable of such brutality.

No, he wasn't going to stand for this. He swore that no more of his charges would die here. Tonight, there would be a reckoning.

"Hugh," he called.

The pastor came over, his face pale. "What is it, Verner?"

"Need you to take everyone out of the valley. Today, while it's still light. Leave the wagons and livestock. Camp up at the top of the hills, but don't light any fires. That murderin' devil is bound to come back again, but this time I'll be the only one here. And I'll be waiting."

Campbell appeared ready to dispute this course of action, how there was no way one aging trail boss could stand against such a beast, but then he must have seen that cold rage in Verner's eyes and known it was pointless to argue. "I'll get right on it."

"Soon as we bury his body. Albert might have been a worthless little shit, but he was our worthless little shit and we take care of our own."

The service was quiet. Few tears were shed besides those of Matteo and his wife. Most of the settlers were more concerned with which of them might be next. Still, Hugh Campbell gave a good sermon before telling them the plan. A few of the men immediately volunteered to stay, but Verner talked them down. This was his fight.

Once they were gone, he started making his preparations.

*   *   *

Within the lake, it turned and writhed, stomach a roiling pit of agony.

The runty two-legs had seemed plump and juicy, but the meat must have been bad, tainted with dirt and sickness.

It considered leaving the other two-legs be for that night, but it needed something to take the foul taste from its mouth. If the next one proved as vile as the last, though, it would just slaughter them all and leave them for the crows.

Powerful arms and legs propelled it shoreward, skimming beneath the surface with the speed of a loosed arrow. Cautiously raising its head, it sniffed at the air.

Alarm gripped it upon finding its prey had seemingly vanished, the two-legs gone from the valley while leaving their four-legs behind. Then it detected a single two-legs still there, by the burning fire. The two-legs smelt old and tired, not the best meal, but it would have to do.

It crept from the water, staying low in the grass, closing in on the circle of wagons and the fire where its prey sat unaware. It lurked for long moments, watching. The old two-legs seemed to be dozing.

Splashes of steaming drool hit the ground as it ran its tongue over its fangs. Its muscles tensed, pushing it forward in a great leap. A mighty arm struck at the unsuspecting back.

The beast let out a confused snarl as its clawed hand smashed through a coat and hat draped over a bundle of sticks shaped like a two-legs. The snarl changed to a scream as a wire snare hidden among the sticks snapped tight, cutting deep into slimy flesh. The other end of the snare was affixed to one of the wheeled contraptions the two-legs used, so heavy that even with all its strength the creature could barely budge it.

As it shrieked, as it roared its pain and fury into the night, something that smelled of the manure of four-legs appeared.

*   *   *

Eugene Verner thought he was ready for what he'd face when, covered in ox-shit, he rolled out from under the wagon with a gun in each fist. Some kind of deranged cannibal giant, perhaps.

And, struggling against the snare was a giant, yes. Ten feet tall at least, and with the basic form of a man . . . but there the similarities ended.

Its spine was twisted and misshapen, more suited for running on all fours than standing straight. Its skin, glistening in the firelight, alternated between patches of scales and sodden fur. Each toe and finger was capped with a razor sharp claw. On its neck, gills flared in gulping anxiety. Two batlike ears poked through the strands of a long, tangled mane.

The face was almost human, almost. Beneath a wide flat nose, the bellowing mouth bulged into a snout. A snake-tongue flicked through rows of yellow fangs

The eyes, though, the eyes were the worst. They were not the eyes of a mere animal, but contained a baleful intelligence, a cold cunning, and a hatred of everything that walked, swam, flew, or crawled beneath the great blue sky.

Verner froze at the sight of those eyes, the blood draining from his face. A heavy tightness clenched his chest. His arms lost their strength, the gun barrels tipping down.

The monster lunged toward him with such force that the wagon wheels skidded sideways across the ground. The snare cut deeper into its trapped arm, thin blood flowing. Its deadly jaws snapped the air. Its claws flailed just

short of Verner's stunned flesh.

It uttered garbled sounds that, though barely recognisable as words, were some dialect of the Indian tribes. Hearing that, hearing this abomination trying to speak, Verner jerked from his stupor. Fighting the hot ache in his chest, he put forth a Herculean effort to raise his leaden arms.

The guns rang out again and again, each shot hammering home into the monster's chest. Flowers of blood bloomed on its skin, though the impact barely seemed to slow or affect it.

All too soon, Verner's guns were empty. Still the beast stood, hauling itself and the wagon ever closer. Resigned to this final struggle, Verner let the guns drop. He clung to the side of another wagon, supporting himself with one hand while drawing his hunting knife from his belt with the other.

The beast lunged again. Verner leaped to meet it, despite the protesting creak of his joints. He caught hold of its ropy mane and swung himself up onto its broad, scaly back. He locked his legs around its ribs. It bucked and thrashed, trying to shake him loose, but he'd broken more than a few wild broncos in his days.

He stabbed the sturdy blade into the side of its thick neck. Yanking it out, he slammed it in again and again, perforating its hide.

Eventually, between man, snare and beast, something had to give. Surprisingly, it was the beast, as the snare's sharp wire sawed through bone and its arm hit the ground with a sickening thump. Voicing an ear-piercing screech, it pitched over backwards.

Its full weight smashed down atop Verner. He felt his ribcage crush, felt a snap and the loss of sensation in his legs. He couldn't even hitch in a breath to cry out. On the brighter side, his other aches and pains were no longer a bother.

He waited for the end, for the beast to finish him off. But that end was slow in coming. Agonized and disoriented, wanting only escape, it blundered haphazardly away into the night.

Verner hitched himself up enough to lean against a wagon wheel and shut his eyes.

*   *   *

That was how they found him in the morning, when Hugh Campbell came with a small group of men into camp, guns at the ready.

After the ruckus they'd heard the night before, they weren't expecting it to be pretty. Nor was it. They found a large, scaled arm lying in a pool of blood, with a generous blood trail leading towards the lake. Then they found

Eugene Verner, slumped against a wagon wheel, his face pale, half his chest caved in.

Hugh Campbell edged forward, his hand reaching out respectfully to the dead man, only to start as Eugene's eyes flickered open. Though they were clouded, he peered at the men. His face contorted into a grimace of effort as he inhaled.

"That you, Hugh?"

"Yeah, it's me, Verner," Hugh said, tone solemn. "Bad night, then?"

"I've had worse." Verner said, the last of his breath seeping out in a rattling chuckle, and then he died.

Road Kill Angel
Dana Wright

"God, I *hate* this damn road."

Jessica slapped on her blinkers and jerked the car door open, slamming it closed with a huff as she got out. She stalked down the darkened street, lit only by the steady stream of her car's headlights, and stifled an oath.

Another dog lay by the side of the road, hit by a speeding motorist. This was the third one this week.

Fossil Lake. Yeah, right. It was more like a fucking graveyard. Fake scenic wonders, fake transplanted trees, and now a nice nifty hole in the earth that they tried to pass off as the stock name for the new subdivision.

The area used to be a nice patch of woods with a real lake, years ago, but the drought had taken care of that. Now the developers had decided it was time to recreate one of nature's wonders.

Fossil Lake, version 2.0. What a crock.

The main road was turning into a drag strip, and Jess despised it. The builders promised speed bumps and street lights, but so far none of it had happened. All the new construction had gotten her was an unfortunate new hobby, and it was starting to get on her nerves.

The little furry body lay there, twisted. Jess peered closer. This one was some kind of beagle mix. She leaned in and checked for tags on the collar under the blood-matted fur.

"Why do those assholes have to aim for every animal they see?"

This was somebody's misplaced baby. Cute as hell too, or at least it would have been if it wasn't covered in blood and viscera. And dead.

Jess closed her eyes and sent a prayer over the critter, as she always did. She had grown weary of burying dead things, but there was no one else to do it. She went to the back of her car and hit the button on her key fob, opening the hatchback.

She would carefully tuck this one into the earth just like she had all the others. It made her happy to at least do that. Well, maybe happy wasn't the right word. It just felt right. Jess knew it made her a freak but she didn't much care. Rifling through the equipment, she unearthed a tarp and shovel. Dragging the equipment from the vehicle, she set it on the ground next to the animal.

Movement out of the corner of her eye drew her attention. An engine roared. Headlights cut the gloom with white hot menace.

"Damn it!" Jessica froze in the middle of the street as the car barreled toward her. "Slow down!" She waved her arms at the motorist, but the car just kept coming.

It slammed into her, and everything slowed down to a crawl. Air rushed from her lungs as her eyes met the driver's startled gaze. Her body crumpled against the windshield and bounced off the hood, landing on the pavement. The loud crack of her skull hitting the pavement barely registered.

Jess lay in the street watching the red tail lights speed by and fade into the distance. Was this how the dog felt as its life drained out? Wracking pain turned to blinding numbness as cold crept into her body, dragging her down into the darkness. Into silence.

*   *   *

"I don't know, Virgil. She's kind of a mess."

"We need someone to do the job. Unless you're volunteering."

"No."

"I didn't think so."

"Is this protocol?"

"She doesn't belong here. Send her back. She'll do it."

"Fine." The voices stirred Jessica from the quiet warmth and she snuggled in deeper. "Dad . . . turn down the TV. I'm trying to sleep."

"Jessica. Time to wake up."

Irritation spiked through her. "Dad, come on!" Jessica growled, sitting up. "Please, just let me sleep . . ."

Blinking, her eyes becoming adjusted to a cold bright light, she found herself staring at an imposing gray haired man in white robes. A younger man with a shock of dark hair, in similar garments, stood next to him.

"You're not my dad," she said.

"No." The older man smiled.

She rested on a white bed of something that looked suspiciously like clouds. *No freaking way.* She raised her sore arm and gingerly touched the back of her head. It hurt. A lot.

"Ow." When she drew her hand back, it was covered in blood.

"Don't worry," he told her. "You won't feel it for long."

Jess frowned. "What happened? Where am I?"

"Time to go back. Good luck."

She barely had time to register his words, and then she was falling.

*   *   *

The wind whipped through her hair. She screamed, gravity pulling her down. Faster. The pavement rose to meet her, coming closer and closer. Inches before she would have connected, something froze her fall.

Her back began to itch and burn. "Ow!" She flexed her muscles and something shifted behind her. She turned, expecting to see someone.

Nothing. Wiggling her back, she rotated her shoulder blades to try and dislodge the uncomfortable pressure. Out of the corner of her eye she saw muddy gray feathers expanding into huge fans. "What the fuck?"

"Nice wings," said an unfamiliar voice.

"What?" Jess looked around and saw she was on the same lonely stretch of highway next to Fossil Lake.

It was almost like she had never left. Her car was still there, lights carving a path in the darkness. The body of the beagle rested next to the tarp. She trudged back toward the dead animal and tried to shake off the uneasy feeling that her world had completely shifted off its axis.

The sudden sharp memory of the car hitting her made her gasp. Horrified, her eyes scanned the street and found her own body lying in a heap on the concrete.

Am I dead? She reached down and pinched the pale flesh of her arm. Pain radiated across her skin.

"Okay, not completely," she said. "Um. Okay."

Now she was hearing voices and blacking out with freaky visions. *God, that's my body on the street!* She stood there, gaping. This night was getting better and better all the time. God, she just wanted to go home, pop a bag of microwave popcorn in the nuker and have a beer. A really big one.

A fine mist began to fall and she shivered as the tee shirt and jeans she was wearing dampened. Her sneakers squished as she stepped into a puddle from the earlier rain.

Great.

Dead body. Deserted road. Middle of the night. Wings. Oh wow.

Her mind folded in on itself. Why the hell was she standing out here in the middle of nowhere? This was not going to end well. She was pretty damn sure of that.

Where'd I leave my phone? I need to call Dad!

He was probably home by now, wondering when she was going to get off her shift at the diner. Or fallen asleep on the couch.

She didn't see her phone, but saw the shovel and bent to pick it up.

At least I can still touch things. That's good.

The unfamiliar voice spoke again. "Are you going to help me, here? Or am I supposed to wait for the next one?"

"Who said that?"

"Down here." A light touch of cold went down her leg as something brushed against her jeans.

Jess jumped. Standing at her feet was the translucent, silvery form of a beagle. Or, rather, two parts of a beagle. And one was talking.

"Is this a joke?" she asked.

"Seeing as how I'm dead and so are you, I wouldn't say that it was a joke. No." The beagle glanced over at his body by the tarp. "You need to send me home, okay?"

"How do I do that?" Jess snorted. "Look for some red shoes and click my heels together?"

The beagle gave her a cross look. "Didn't they teach you anything while you were gone?"

"Um, no. I woke up, I fell, and now I have these ugly gray wings." She shook her shoulders and said wings flexed and retracted against her back. "Oh, and apparently I'm just as dead as you."

The beagle rolled his doggy eyes and dragged the bottom half of its spectral body so it could sit down next to her. "Well, not quite as dead. You're holding the shovel, aren't you? That's something." At her baffled expression, the beagle cocked its head. "Look, maybe you're here for a purpose."

"What? Wiping up carnage for all eternity. Nice." Jess scowled and kicked at a rock in the road.

"What am I supposed to do now? My body is lying in the street! Should

I call someone? What the hell would I say?"

"You really are a smartass for an angel."

"Angel?" Jess laughed harshly. " Now that is funny. Sorry. I'm a little cranky. Dying will do that to a girl."

"Someone's coming." The beagle squinted at the bright but distant lights speeding down the deserted street and mewled deep in his throat.

Jess's fingers began to tingle. She looked at the headlights and something deep in her gut tightened, fierce and visceral.

"It's the same car," she whispered, awareness flooding through her. "I feel it. The blood. It's calling me."

She flexed her fingers and made a fist, nails cutting into her palm. The freakishness of the moment should have alarmed her, but instead it solidified everything that had happened.

"Yeah. You can wash the blood away, but it still connects with you, you know?" The beagle growled under his breath, gazing out into the darkness at the ghostly shapes dotted along the stretch of highway. "He hit me. Most of the others too. Can you see them? Every time he comes this way, we're drawn to the road. We watch, but there is nothing we can do." He looked up at her mournfully. "Until you that is."

The center of her back itched and her wings grew heavy, aching to fly. She wanted to catch the fucker and make him pay. Rage filtered through her, powerful and sudden. She stalked toward the road, her stride brisk.

Her newfound connection with the dead alive in her being, she called to the animals and they came. All shapes and sizes, they crept onto the forbidden territory of the road, the place that had been their unfortunate demise. Their ghostly forms flickered in the darkness, a sea of ghost lights.

"God, how many are there?" she whispered.

"Too many," the beagle said. "He comes this way every day at least once. He aims for them."

Jess's mouth curved in a terrible smile. "My turn."

She reached out to the dead, their blood mingling on the advancing unholy car.

"Come," she called. "We take what belongs to us."

The animals converged. Their forms solidified, becoming flesh for a wild hunt. Howls rent the night air as the hissing of cats and barking of dogs merged with the trumpeting of deer and the chattering of squirrels and raccoons. Their eyes glowed red in the darkness, staring with malicious intent at the vehicle barreling down on them.

Jess heard music blaring from the speakers, the sound stabbing through the quiet night.

Why'd he come back? To make sure I was dead?

Anger coiled inside her, hot and vicious. Clenching her teeth, she opened her wings and took a step forward. The hunt followed, powerless victims no more. The hunted had become the hunter, and their prey approached.

Headlights washed over Jess's body as the car came closer and closer. He had to see her. There was no way he didn't. Uncharted rage spread through Jess and she broke into a run, meeting the car at full speed, her new powers giving her strength she never knew she had. Her sneakered feet pounded the pavement. As the car roared down the highway in her direction, Jess snarled and leaped, using her newfound wings as leverage. She landed on the hood.

She saw the driver's wide eyes meet hers through the windshield, read a silent, "What the fuck?" on his lips.

Her wings spread to their full span, blinding him, blocking his view.

There was nowhere to go. He jerked the car to the left and Jess held on, her wings acting like sails in the midst of a storm. As the driver stepped on the brakes, the car went into a spin and collided with a tree close to the side of the road. Jess sprang high from the impact. The front of the car merged with the massive oak, accordion-style.

She hovered above, wings supporting her. The driver, hollering in pain and anger, struggled in the wreckage. It held him fast. Jess descended again onto the crunched hood. He stared at her with disbelief, then at the horde of animals surrounding the car.

"Oh, God!" he cried.

"Exactly." She brought the shovel down onto the cracked windshield with full force. Glass shattered, a shower of fragments exploding inward.

The driver screamed. "You! You bitch! I killed you!" His voice was high and full of terror. He gave a futile swipe at his eyes. "You're dead. So are the rest of you. Fucking road kill!"

Jess smiled a terrible smile and let her wings open to their full expanse.

"Come and get him."

The wild hunt converged on the car, their rotting bodies crowding against the sides of the vehicle, mouths gaping in want. Teeth and claws ready to dispense justice, they moved forward, a mass of ghostly energy turned feral and very, very real.

A half-skeletonized buck gouged at the driver through the open window and several points connected with the man's bloodied face. The buck let out a satisfied bellow. Undead squirrels and raccoons swarmed inside to scratch and bite at tender flesh. The beagle howled and the dogs and cats joined the fray.

The sounds of ripping and tearing rose into the night. Jess hummed as the flood of creatures that had been wronged took their vengeance. In minutes the passenger door was dislodged and hanging open, the driver's lifeless body spilled out onto the dirt.

With their terrible task completed, the animals began to drift again into a spectral state. Soon, they had returned to where they lay in death, waiting for Jess to find them at last. Only the beagle remained by her side.

She flicked her damp hair out of her eyes and surveyed the mess, then looked down at him. "I need to bury you, I guess."

"Can you send me home first? I really don't want to watch."

Jess bent and patted the ghostly dog. "You got a name, boy?"

His silvery tail wagged. "Bernie."

"Thanks, Bernie." Jess smiled and fluffed his ear. "You were a great help. I couldn't have done it without you."

With a deep sigh, he rubbed his head against her leg, then vanished into the eternal night.

She sucked in a breath and blinked against the tears that threatened to fall.

Alone again.

Something in the distance drew her gaze, tearing her from her melancholy. She saw several more flickering wisps along the lake and highway.

The others were waiting. This wasn't over. Not by a long shot.

The blood of the innocent called to her from the long and winding road around Fossil Lake. Jess brushed off her jeans and ruffled her wings.

She walked with purpose toward the lights, an avenging angel, shovel in hand.

Silver Screen Shadows
Mathias Jansson

Shadows are moving on my wall
Characters moving and falling
Behind the shower curtain
Blood stains flows
Black feathers snows
In my isolation cell

The wall a rear window
To a place of insanity
On the hill the house
In the window my mother
Waving to me

That night I sewed my first
Lampshade of lips
Nitrate was burning
In the projector light
And shadows danced on the silver screen
Only for me

C-C-Cold
Ken Goldman

Just past the Busk Ivanhoe Tunnel, where the slim road practically disappeared, Matthew turned to Sharon. "The Snowcats will plow through this fucker. They'll be by any minute, just wait and see."

Three days spent shattering his marriage vows (again) had given Matthew the assurance that Mother Nature herself would happily bend over for him, too.

Sharon did not seem as assured. "I don't see any Snowcats. Or any tire tracks. I doubt anyone's crazy enough to come out here in this mess."

Bitter cold air from the north filtered through Colorado's mountain canyons into its basins and valleys to the south. It spilled over the mountain range, funneling through gulches and ridges, gathering strength. Wind speeds reached 75 mph, shredding even the sturdiest cabin roofs while taking down power and telephone lines. Fierce gusts conspired with thick snow squalls creating one bastard of a blizzard.

It had somehow managed to sneak past local forecasters and their meteorological charts to say howdy to the handful of dumbfounded weekend skiers attempting to maneuver jeeps and SUVs through the tricky passes that snaked their way through the Rockies.

"How well do you know this road?" she asked.

The 'road' was not really a road at all. Anyone having a passing familiarity with the mountainous terrain knew this half paved rock ridden passage was more of an elaborate trail. And during the winter months when the snow flew, it hardly could be called that.

"Hey, I know this region like the back of my hand – or your magnificent cooch, lover."

The truth was that this rampaging storm had transformed the terrain into an unrecognizable moonscape an Arctic expedition would have difficulty maneuvering. Matthew turned on the weather station.

"... *vehicles can get only about a mile past the water tunnel above Fossil Lake on the Leadville side. Deep snow has fallen up high so it will be awhile before the road opens. First heavy snow warnings have been posted along the trail at 11,510 feet before the ski hut*..."

"We're past that marker, Matthew. Damn!"

He already knew that much. Punching off the radio, he also knew that what threatened to bury his Trail Blazer was no longer snow. In under an hour's time, it had become deep shit.

"We're into a full white out here, babe. I can't even see the moon. I think we may have to pull over and wait this out." He reached for his cellular to inform his wife he would be late, but quickly decided against making the call. What was happening outside proved difficult enough. He didn't feel like starting another storm inside.

"If we get stuck here ... I mean, if anyone finds us together ..."

To the world, Matthew's professional relationship with Ms. Sharon Weist had lasted a mere fifteen minutes the previous winter, when she had shown him and Andrea some Arvada lake front property. What followed was pure serendipity, a chance meeting with the lovely young realtor at Starbucks that escalated into innocent flirtation, a stolen kiss or two eventually paying off with some nooners.

For almost a year, they had managed to pull off the occasional clandestine weekend. If he were caught in the middle of nowhere sharing this covert rendezvous with her, Matthew would have some clever explaining to do. But Sharon specialized in closing the big deals, and after months spent banging bones, maybe she figured their getting discovered might not prove such a bad thing after all.

Matthew's cellular chirped. His attention remained fixed on what he could see through the windshield, but he felt Sharon's stare boring in on him.

"Aren't you going to answer it?"

Having no choice he put the cell to his ear.

"Hi, honey ... Yes, I'm just heading home now. Hit a little snow, is all, so I'll be late. No, babe, don't wait up. I'll warm up whatever you've got in the fridge. Yeah, skiing was really great. Kiss Derek goodnight for me, okay? Yes, I'm fine, really. Driving's not so bad. Listen, you're fading a bit. I'll see you in the morning. Love you."

Sharon's silence turned deafening. Without looking, Matthew knew the expression that had crossed her face, a face that did not remain beautiful when she felt pissed. Hoping to deflect the elephant in his Trail Blazer, he went for the fake-out.

"I can phone my sports column in to the office tomorrow —"

"Maybe you should call your wife back first, tell your Andrea about those other slopes you've been hitting while she's been home changing diapers, hey?"

"Very funny. Let me drive, okay? I can't see for shit."

"No, Matthew. You really can't."

Recognizing his no-win situation, he didn't want to make an uncomfortable moment worse. But if Sharon were testing him to determine just how much testosterone he had, then he would have to show her.

"You want to discuss that block of hot ice you're sitting on? I mean, you might have picked a better time to bitch. I'm a little busy here trying to save our asses."

"A better time? You just spent three days fucking me. I figured that might put you into the proper disposition to discuss what's happening with us. But your loving Andrea has her pot roast waiting back home for you in the 'fridge, doesn't she? It's all about you again, isn't it? I don't even ski, and I hate snow. Damn, you can be such a prick!"

"That's cold, Sharon. That's just plain cold."

Frosty pellets smacked the Trail Blazer like buckshot. Caked with compacted ice, the wiper's blades slapped uselessly across the smeared glass, reducing visibility to near zero. The headlights revealed a billion dense flakes filling the world.

Sharon rubbed a circle on the windshield. "The defroster isn't doing anything. Maybe you were right about stopping. Maybe we should pull over, wait this out. "

"Yeah. Then, when someone comes along, *wham!* There's no visibility, in case you haven't noticed. A Snowcat rounding a curve could turn this vehicle into a waffle. Good plan. Stick to selling your condos, sweetheart."

"It was *your* fucking idea! Would you rather we spin off this godforsaken road where no one will find us until the spring thaw?"

Matthew pounded the steering wheel. *"Shit! Piss! Fuck!"* He breathed hard, managing to rein himself in. "Let's not do this, okay? Let's —"

. . . and then he shut up fast.

He noticed the charcoal eyes first. Sharon leaned forward, again swiping the windshield while squinting to see through the glass. Matthew turned on

the brights. Illuminating mostly the flying snow, the fog lamps reflected off something in the road directly in front of them, some living creature hidden amid the snow bursts.

"Look out!!"

Matthew pumped the brake while the Trail Blazer veered crazily. It struck the creature dead on with a sickening crack as if they had collided into solid ice. The vehicle spun out, its steering impossible to steady. The SUV thumped sideways into a deep ravine, plummeting down the slippery slope like a wild amusement park ride. It came to rest in a snow bank, rear wheels still spinning in the drift.

Unfastening his seat belt, Matthew reached for Sharon. "You okay?"

For one awful moment she didn't respond. Then, "I think so . . . a little shaken. No bones broken, no teeth missing. Look . . ." She indicated the steam hissing from the section of crumpled hood not buried in the snow. "What was that thing we hit? Sasquatch?"

Matthew turned the key, but the engine only sputtered. "Don't know. It's too dark. It could have been an elk or stag. Maybe a big horn sheep."

"Those eyes were looking down on us, not up."

"I don't give a shit if it was Frosty The Snowman. In case you haven't noticed we've got a problem here." He reached for his cellular, punched an emergency number. The screen indicated no signal.

Sharon thumbed the keys of her cell and shook her head. Matthew tried the ignition again but the vehicle gave only a dull click. The head lamps flickered like an old-time movie, then went dark. The battery had shorted out, and no engine running meant no heat. Frigid mountain air was one merciless bitch, and it would take only hours before her pals frostbite and hypothermia visited to claim a few fingers or toes.

"You're a writer, Matthew. How would you write a character out of this mess?"

"I'm a sports writer. Ask me why the Nuggets suck this season."

Sharon tried to smile but gave it up. "Will anyone find us here?"

Matthew knew the snow could completely bury their vehicle in only a few hours, but someone would find them, all right – in April or May, when all that survived of their sorry asses were two piles of skeletal remains. Assuming the wolves didn't find them first.

"By morning, maybe the storm will clear. We can go for help. I have supplies back here. A kit. Emergency stuff like blankets and flash lights, matches. There's a tow rope, too, in case another car comes by, or a Snowcat. And there's some peanut butter and crackers. Water bottles, even some beer left in

the cooler. We'll be okay, Sharon. Really. We'll be okay."

He hoped he sounded convincing. A cold beer wasn't exactly the ticket in sub-zero temperatures, and they weren't going to build a camp fire inside the car. He handed Sharon a thick blanket and took one for himself. They huddled close in the darkness, so close Matthew felt unsure whether his shivering was his own or an extension of Sharon's.

In a long silence they waited.

"It's still out there, isn't it?" she asked. "That thing."

"I don't know. Maybe we killed it, or hurt it. Don't fall asleep. Body temperature drops when you sleep. We have to stay awake to keep warm, okay?"

"I'm not warm. I'm nowhere near warm. I can't feel my legs."

He pulled her closer. "We'll be okay," he said again.

She looked at him. "Or maybe we'll die."

Something thumped hard against the rear bumper. Matthew grabbed one of the flashlights. The high powered beam scanned the white landscape, but he saw only a galaxy of flakes swirling in the light. Whatever had been there had gone.

Sharon clung to him. "An animal maybe?"

"Had to be. Christ knows what."

"Maybe it's that thing we hit."

"I didn't see it clearly. All kinds of creatures live in these mountains."

"Hungry creatures? Bears?"

"Bears would be hibernating. But food is scarce during the winter. Just about everything wandering around here is hungry."

"I didn't need to hear that."

The quiet returned and stayed, an uneasy stillness not to be trusted. Matthew inspected the terrain, what the high powered lamp could see of it. Nothing stirred, but he couldn't shake the feeling they were being watched. Several times he shook Sharon to keep her from dozing off. The snow had not let up and the cold seemed much worse.

By 2:00 a.m., he realized they could not remain much longer where they were. If he could climb the slope back to the road, he might get some reception on his cellular. Considering they had little choice before the blowing snow obstructed the vehicle's doors, the idea seemed worth a shot.

"Stay here. I'll see if I can get a signal from the road, maybe find a passing Snowcat."

"I'm not staying here alone."

"It could be dangerous. Something is out there."

"I'm not staying here!"

That ended the discussion. She managed to get the door opened enough to squeeze through, sinking into snow waist deep. Slipping on his back pack of supplies, Matthew pulled her out. Together, they'd slogged maybe fifty feet when a sloshing sound came from behind, a thick dripping noise like saturated trees following a heavy rain. Matthew aimed his beam back toward the Trail Blazer, the lonely beacon exploring an Arctic world drained of color.

Something was there, all right. Matthew recognized those dark eyes. Caught in the lamp's glare, the creature seemed the size of the Trail Blazer itself, as if some mammoth ice sculpture had badly melted. It turned to avoid the harsh wash of light, a sopping glob of frozen liquid that impossibly breathed with life.

"That thing," he whispered. "Jesus, it's . . . it's *ice*."

"It doesn't like the light. Let's go, Matthew. Let's go right now!"

Running, even moving at all, seemed impossible. They did not look behind, just kept pushing through the snow as best they could. Twice, Sharon disappeared into drifts. Matthew pulled her out, feeling his lungs might explode. Eventually exhaustion overtook them. Soaked, their breaths heavy, they found no place even to collapse. When Sharon finally managed to speak, her words seemed the ramblings of a fevered mind.

"Tell me you love me, Matthew. Tell me you love me enough to die for me."

"What?"

"Say it. You never really told me in so many words. I need to hear you say it."

"Jesus, Sharon . . ."

"Please . . . please . . ."

The thick white pines rustled. Matthew aimed the lamp towards the cluster of trees. Concealed in darkness, lacking even shadows, the creature had overtaken them. Now it stood dripping in ambush only paces away, a monstrous Hollywood special effect chiseled in ice. Close up, its mouth appeared the size of a coffin, revealing misshapen teeth that hung from its maw like thick icicles.

No, that wasn't correct . . .

Its teeth *were* icicles!

Matthew pulled at Sharon's arm but she wouldn't move. Maybe she couldn't move. He kept the lamp on the creature's eyes, hoping to blind it long enough for them to get away.

"We can't stay, Sharon. We can't –"

She wouldn't budge. Her lips formed unintelligible gibberish while a whisper escaped her throat. The predator shambled through the drifts toward them, cavernous mouth opening wide, black eyes fixed on its quarry.

"... love ... you ..."

"Sharon, come on, dammit! We have to – I can't ..."

She seemed a dead weight immersed in the snow, impossible to extract. Matthew left her there, panicked flight propelling him through the thick snow. Behind him, Sharon shrieked. Slamming fists to his ears did not deafen the sound reverberating inside his head. He turned, aimed the high intensity light.

The creature must have seen him but selected the easier prey, spilling over Sharon like some cascading polar waterfall. Icy mandibles punctured her throat, reducing her screams to weak gurgles. She was a fighter, Matthew always knew that about her. Her arms flailed and her legs kicked, but she proved no match for this thing. She had fallen into some mutating frozen pond that kept reshaping and moving around her, swallowing her whole. In the wash of light, Matthew saw Sharon's flesh go blue, as if she had been refrigerated inside her own casket. Masticated in thick blood-drenched clumps, her flesh shredded like slabs of raw meat inside a blender.

Matthew fled. His lungs felt about to blow a hole through his chest, but he would not stop until he found a way out of here or until he was dead. If the road had not become completely hidden beneath the snow he knew it lay somewhere ahead. He slogged through the freezing drifts for what seemed hours, but it could have been only minutes. Matthew no longer could tell.

He heard the familiar sound before he noticed the lights. There was no mistaking the thick growl of that machine. A Snowcat was plowing its way just up the ridge from where he stood. He climbed towards the road and snapped on the high beam of his lamp, swinging it wildly over his head. The bright lamps of the Snowcat illuminated the landscape like a Christmas tree, and the tank-like behemoth came to a squealing stop.

"Had an accident?" the bearded man shouted from behind the large wheel. "You're not the first tonight. Been picking up stranded folks all around here the past twelve hours."

A man half conscious, Matthew climbed on board. He pulled off his wet gloves, wiped thick chunks of ice from his face. He warmed his hands near the blowing defroster.

"People, they get lost in these parts every winter," the driver said. "Blizzards, they just sneak up on folks all the time. Hell, you're one of the lucky ones. Sometimes we never find 'em."

"Thank Christ you're here. I thought I was a dead man for sure."

"Anyone else in your party?"

The question came like a sucker punch. Matthew managed to feign a momentary disorientation that fortunately required little acting.

"No . . . Just me. I was headed home to my wife. My SUV ran off the road."

The bearded man started the Snowcat moving. "Here's not a real good place to be wandering alone at this hour in this mess, let me tell you. I'll get you to the lodge at Hagerman Pass. In the morning, if this bastard storm lets up, you can call for a tow for your car. It's maybe an hour down the ridge."

The driver's attention remained focused on the road.

That was good.

* * *

Later, in a room at the lodge, Matthew lit a fire and sat by it, his mind racing. Then he made the call.

"Andrea? Sorry, honey, I didn't mean to wake you. Listen, I had a little accident coming back. No, nothing serious, but I have to be here in the morning to find a tow and I may have to stay a few days. I'll call tomorrow when everything's a little more settled, okay? No, I'm not hurt, just tired. Go back to bed. Love you."

He did love Andrea, he loved her very much, and Sharon must have known that. But he always tried to be fair with Sharon, had even tried loving her. What happened tonight was terrible, but it was over. Now he needed to get a grip, he had to think. There was Andrea to consider now.

Tomorrow, he would retrieve Sharon's bag from the SUV, then burn everything. It might be touch and go for a while, a hairy situation when Sharon did not show up and the media posted her photo everywhere. If he were somehow linked to her, people would have questions. But they had covered their tracks for months, telling nobody about their stolen weekends.

In a few days, he would go to his office at the Denver Post. He would pour himself a hot cup of coffee, then phone to arrange the Carmelo Anthony interview, ask the Nuggets' offensive how Rick Camela managed to wipe the court with him for 33 points when his team played Minnesota. Business as usual, no hurt, no foul.

He could get through this because he loved Andrea, beautiful, loving Andrea, the mother of his child.

The wife of his bosom.

The cunt.

His wife had spent this entire weekend without him, never once complaining. She didn't protest the other weekends when he had decided to pick up and go skiing, or fishing, or whatever other horse crap he told her.

She was the ideal wife who never nagged or bitched. Who said nothing when he left her alone for days with the baby, while he was off plowing Sharon six ways from Sunday. Normally, a man would think that was strange, but Matthew didn't consider it strange at all.

. . . not since the night last winter when he'd stolen a peek at his wife's e-mail and discovered that his good neighbor and golfing buddy, Dick Habersham, had been fucking Andrea's eyeballs out for months. The bastard even wrote something about wanting to stick it into her ass their next time together. Andrea probably had been riding Habersham's cock this entire weekend while Derek slept in his crib in the next room.

Thinking more clearly now, Matthew smiled. Suddenly the night's events made perfect sense. Even an ice monster roaming Fossil Lake's snow covered woods made sense, an insatiably hungry beast hunting those poor fools who found themselves lost among the fir trees and white pines on a cold and blustery winter's night. Those lost souls must have proved such easy prey.

"Easy prey." Matthew said the words aloud.

["Sometimes we never find 'em."]

He stoked the fire, sipped his coffee.

He would wait a respectable amount of time. Maybe a month or two, when questions regarding Sharon had died down and the media moved on to other stories. Plenty of winter remained, and the mountains along Fossil Lake got hit with blizzards well into the spring.

"The iceman cometh," he muttered.

He climbed into the bed, pulling blankets over him and savoring their warmth. Speaking to Andrea had cleared his head. His world again had righted itself, again had meaning. He understood what to do now. Tonight he would sleep well after all.

Because there was no telling when another blizzard might hit these Rocky Mountains.

And because he knew that, unlike Sharon, his wife Andrea loved to ski.

What's Your Beef?
Mark Orr

It wasn't the first ride Bert Granchi took in a car trunk, but it was the longest.

The car bounced, driving the rim of the flat spare tire into his ribs. Bert grunted behind the duct tape gag. How far out into the country was the asshat going to take him before turning him loose and letting him walk back to town? They must be halfway to Fossil Lake by now, if not beyond it.

That she-male bitch Connie Maxon! This was all her fault!

So he sent her a few e-mails calling her a cunt for her bad reviews of the stories he scattered online like brilliant, beautiful stars across the skies. So he posted nasty things about her and her sicko lesbian lovers all over his blogs. So he called her house and cussed her out, and her asshole mother, too.

So what? She didn't have to go and sic her uncle-fucking brother on him –

A sharp turn rammed Bert's head into the tire well. He tugged at the ropes holding his hands behind his back and lashed to his ankles. No use. Jerry Maxon must have been a fucking Boy Scout. Bert usually got loose before getting dumped in the fucking middle of nowhere, but not this time. It would serve Maxon right to have to lift him bodily out of the trunk before cutting him free.

From the sound transmitted through the tires to the chassis, they were on gravel now. Bert didn't know there were still roads left in Illinois that weren't paved. Maybe they were in Indiana, or Michigan, or even Wisconsin. How would he get back from there? He thrashed around, but only tightened the knots.

Even the gravel gave out eventually, and dust from a dirt road drifted into the trunk. Bert sneezed, and waited. There was nothing else to do, except plan the story he would write about redneck cock-suckers who kidnapped darkly Gothic writers for ridiculously long joyrides.

He would call it "The Dark Ride," and have Jerry Maxon get devoured by a creature from the Outer Darkness. Or maybe have him swallowed whole by the huge cunt of his lesbian sister. Then she would drink bleach and die, and Bert's revenge would be complete. He would publish it in one of the fifty or sixty blogs and online journals he kept, and his fans would know of the horrors inflicted upon him by his enemies. That would be a sweet revenge, indeed.

Let her give *that* story a bad review, if she dared. He would show her he was capable of writing a truly frightening tale, worthy of his literary heroes. Not even Lovecraft or Poe could describe such a horrifying end for the asshat and the cunt.

Who cared about grammar or spelling, or the restrictive conventions of so-called literature? His work was unbound by the formulas of lesser writers, a new style that was beyond the petty concerns of plot, characterization, or theme. Only Bert Granchi was the true successor of the masters of his genre, and only he could tell the terrifying tale of his unearthly vengeance.

Bert shaped the gruesome demise of the Maxons in his mind as the big Ford Crown Victoria hurtled on through the night. He had gotten to the point where Jerry was being engulfed by the vast vagina when the car slewed around and stopped suddenly, slamming him against the back of the trunk, jolting the exquisite prose out of his mind and replacing it with the fear of what would come next.

Bert Granchi, heir to the grand tradition of Lovecraft and Poe, wet his pants.

The lid opened, framing his tormentor in the light of the full moon behind and above his rangy frame. Bert blinked until his eyes adjusted. Two other figures moved into view, one of them holding a flashlight. The hands of these others reached in, dragging him over the edge and dumping him on the grass, where his nose was assaulted by a horrific stench. He gagged behind the duct tape, and thrashed against his bonds.

Maxon reached down and wrenched the gag away from Bert's mouth. Bert screamed at the pain of losing a healthy portion of his skimpy mustache and beard to the adhesive.

"Sorry 'bout that, Bert," Maxon said. "Did you enjoy the ride?"

"Fuck you, asshat," Bert said. One of the others kicked Bert in the ribs. He sucked in a big lungful of putrid air, then retched on the ground.

"I don't think he cares for the way old Bossie smells, Jerry," a voice said.

Bert wriggled away from his vomit. He saw a dark mass on the ground ten feet from where he lay. It looked like the carcass of some large animal. He spit the last of the puke from his mouth and said, "What is that? A cow?"

Jerry Maxon laughed. "Of course, you idiot. Why do you think we call her 'old Bossie'?"

"She stinks."

"Well, naturally. Bossie's been dead for, oh, a week or so."

"All right, fucker. I've smelled your fucking cow. Cut me loose and go away."

"Cut you loose? Why would we do that?"

"Because you have to, asshat. You can't just leave me tied up out here in the fucking country, next to a dead cow!"

"Wouldn't dream of it, Bert, old pal. We've got something a little more interesting in mind."

Laughing, Jerry's friends picked Bert up by his elbows and dragged him closer to the rotting carcass. He tried to puke again, but there was nothing left.

"Don't you hate the dry heaves?" the man on his right said. "I know I do."

The other one agreed. They stopped beside the cow. Maxon reached down and pulled on its ribcage. It opened up like a giant clamshell.

"We cleaned your new home out as much as we could," Maxon said. "You won't have to move in with a bunch of guts and such. Just well-seasoned beef. Does that suit you?"

"What the fuck are you talking about, you cock-sucking uncle-fucker?"

Maxon grabbed Bert by the face. "I'm talking about sewing you up in the corpse of this fucking cow, you son-of-a-bitch. I'm talking about protecting my sister from your shit. I'm talking about making sure you keep your fucking mouth shut from here on. Is that clear enough, asswipe?"

Darkly Gothic writer Bert Granchi shit himself.

Maxon wrinkled his nose. "That doesn't help the aroma around here any."

"You can't do this! Hey, I didn't mean anything by it. I was just being, you know, who I am."

"Yeah, I know you were, Bert. You think you're the bad boy of the new Gothic revival, and you've just naturally got to piss off anyone you feel like, and they don't get to say squat about it. Fuck that. It's time you learned that there are some people you just don't go around pissing off. I'm one of them. Drop him boys."

Bert hit the ground hard.

"Okay, let's get this over with." Maxon said.

Bert heard the snick of a switchblade opening. The rope holding his bound hands to his ankles was severed.

"Can't stuff you inside all bunched up like that," they told him. "That wouldn't be very comfortable, now would it?"

Next he felt his clothes being cut off. "Hey, what are you guys, faggots?"

"You wish, mother-fucker," Maxon said. "We're just concerned about your health. It's going to get mighty warm in that cow tonight. We wouldn't want you to get heat-stroke, or something."

"We ain't gonna wipe you ass for you, though," one of the others said. "You're just gonna have to lie there in your own shit."

"Fuck you, you cuntboy faggot!"

Someone kicked him in the crotch, doubling him up.

"That wasn't very nice, Bert," Maxon said. "In fact, I don't think I care to hear anything else come out of your pie-hole." He tore loose a long piece of duct tape and wrapped it several times around Bert's face and the back of his neck, not being very careful about Bert's long, greasy hair. Some wound up taped into his mouth.

That chore done, Maxon held the cow's body open while the others picked Bert up and placed him inside the corpse.

"I wouldn't wiggle around too much in there," Maxon said. "The ribs are exposed. You might impale yourself on one, if you get too frisky."

Bert tried to scream.

"Sorry? I didn't quite catch that. If you want out, you just say so and we'll pull you free right away."

He tried again, choking on strands of hair, breathing rotten cow-stink and his own shit-stink above piss and sweat and other indescribable odors.

"How's that? Still not getting a clear signal. Well, boys, doesn't look like Bert minds too much. Let's sew him up."

Bert thrashed around, poking himself on the cow's ribs.

Maxon leaned over him. "If you're worried about air? Not a problem." He pointed. "Good thing cows come equipped with assholes, isn't it? You'll get all the air you need through old Bossie's butt. Considerate of us, wasn't it?" Maxon glanced around at the others. "You guys got the sewing kit ready?"

The taller of the other men held up a spool of fishing line and a large needle. "Ready when you are."

Maxon smiled down into Bert's face. "You just relax, and we'll have you all nice and cozy in a few minutes." He dropped the clamshell side of beef closed.

The corpse jerked and twitched as the men sewed the halves together. It took a while, but eventually they had old Bossie back in one piece again. Bert heard the big Ford engine fire up, and the car drove away.

48

He lay still a long time, willing his pulse to slow down. He stared out of Bossie's ass. The moon illuminated the small opening, not that there was anything to see but a few weeds just beyond. Bert flexed his arms and legs, unable to loosen the ropes.

They'll come back in a while, he thought. *This is just a big joke, and they'll get me out of here soon. I've just got to be calm until they do. Ha-ha, very funny, Maxon. We'll see how funny the law thinks this is.*

Bert felt a tickle along his side and belly. Something was moving around inside the cow, something that wasn't Bert Granchi. Or maybe a lot of little somethings.

How long had the cow been dead? Maxon said a week. Bert shivered. Something dropped onto his face from the decaying meat above, something small and wiggly. More fell on him, and still more. Had he been able to scream, he would have, for Bert knew what he shared his new abode with.

Maggots. Thousands and thousands of maggots. Above him, below him, all around him, the wriggling larvae of a thousand flies were slowly devouring the carcass. How long until they started in on his very much living flesh?

Bert writhed and pushed his feet against what had been old Bossie's shoulders. The only way out was through that very small hole, but he might be able to force himself far enough through to get someone's attention.

If there was anyone around. If he could get the duct tape off of his mouth.

He looked up at the narrow circle of moonlight just as something partially blocked it, and he froze, forgetting all about the maggots.

A large rat stared in at him through Bossie's bung hole, nose twitching at the unexpected scent of very frightened human inside the rotting corpse. Bert's fingers dug into the slimy, decaying flesh above him as he tried to pull himself back with his fingertips, away from the open anus.

The rat crept in after him.

Another followed.

Bert lay very still as the vermin twitched their nasty little noses around his. One crawled up into his hair, while the other checked out the duct tape gag.

That's it, little friend, Bert thought. *Gnaw the tape away, and I'll be able to get someone to come get me out of this.*

But the rat decided there was nothing edible there. He felt it slither down his arm to where his hands were tied over his ass. It nipped at a fingertip. Bert jerked his fists closed, but the rat backed out before he could get a grasp. It sank sharp little rodent teeth into the meat at the base of his thumb. Bert twitched and wriggled, unable to voice the scream clogging his throat. The rat slipped down his hip, and he felt it poking around his groin, trying to get

underneath him.

The uncle-fucker is trying to get to my balls! Bert turned his head to look down, hoping to glare the rodent away from his genitals.

The rat on his head, which he had forgotten about, slipped off and dangled in front of his eyes, one little paw tangled in his matted mane. Bert's eyes crossed as he focused on the rat. Puffs of air from his nostrils ruffled the vermin's fur. Its mouth opened wide, and sank its teeth into Bert's nose.

Oh, God! he screamed internally. *Rats carry rabies, don't they? I'm gonna get fucking rabies! Oh, Jesus, get me the fuck out of this!*

If Jesus heard, He did nothing.

Bert shook his head, dislodging the one rat, but in the process tilted his lower body up enough for the explorer down south to slip into his loin area. He bucked his hips, trying to smash the monster before it ate his balls.

It didn't eat his balls, but it did take a healthy bite from his penis. Bert arched his back and shivered with the exquisite pain. His scalp scraped across the upper ribs and parted like the Red Sea. A wave of blood flowed down into his eyes, and nose. He snorted, blowing red snot and tears out of Old Bossie's asshole.

His wet nasal assault connected with the snout of a creature much larger than his tormentors, lurking just beyond his air hole. It hissed, and turned, and lifted a brushy tail.

The skunk sprayed a full load of stench into Bert's face before it waddled away. Bert coughed as best he could, shaking his head and snorting the odor out of and away from his nose.

That didn't help the stink, but there was one blessing. The aroma drove the pair of rats out of the carcass and into the night.

Bert was finally alone in his new home. He cried, the whimpers stifled behind the duct tape but the tears running freely. He didn't want to think about how much of his dick the rat carried away in his gruesome little belly. He didn't want to, but he couldn't help it. He knew he was maimed for life. Even if he ever did get a girlfriend, he would never be able to have sex with her. He would die a virgin.

He would die a thirty-six year old virgin, if he didn't get out of this cow corpse soon and get himself some medical attention. God only knew how many diseases he'd been exposed to already. Rabies, for sure. Possibly cholera, plague, typhoid, whatever else one got from exposure to long dead bodies. Plus, he'd been bitten several times, and was probably bleeding to death. And he was very hungry and thirsty. Getting sprayed by the skunk was the least of his worries. His room in Grammy's basement smelled almost that bad anyway.

He whimpered until he ran out of breath, rested, then whimpered some more. When would they come to let him out? How long was it 'til morning? Didn't they say that's when they'd come back for him?

Bert froze. He ran the conversation with his kidnappers through his mind over and over again. He tried to remember at what point they said they'd come back, and realized against his deepest desires that they never had.

They were going to leave him there forever. There would be no rescue, no opening of the cow's dead body at sunrise, accompanied by hearty laughs all around at Bert's expense. He was going to die inside this cow, and no one would ever know what happened to him.

Bert Granchi wet himself again. And shit himself, again. Then he fainted.

* * *

The tight beam of sunshine coming in through Bossie's asshole pried Bert's eyes open.

He looked out on the totality of his world beyond Old Bossie, a patch of weeds still reeking of skunk. His body ached in ways he could never have imagined. He flexed and wiggled, trying to work the stiffness out of his limbs, but there just wasn't enough room inside the cow to unkink himself. He stopped moving. A crazed giggle escaped through the thick curtain of duct tape.

His grandmother was peering down the cow's butt, her thick glasses reflecting the light of the new day back into his. "Well, sonny boy," she said. "You sure got yourself in a pickle this time, didn't you?"

Bert couldn't answer except to nod his head.

"What, can't ya talk, you loser?"

He shook his head.

Grammy snorted. "Don't know what I expected, but this isn't good. I should've known you'd wind up like this."

Bert whimpered. He wanted to promise her he'd be good from now on. He couldn't, though. Even if he hadn't been wearing several loops of duct tape around his face, he knew it would be a lie. Lying was bad.

She scowled at him. "At least I won't have to bail you out anymore. No more visits from the sheriff or the F.B.I., or whoever the people you piss off sic on us. That's just plain gotten old, sonny boy. Good riddance to bad rubbish, that's what I say." She snorted again, and her face drifted from his view.

No, Grammy, I'll be a good boy! he thought. *I won't cause you any more problems.* No more big phone bills from calling people he hated and leaving threatening messages on their voice mails. No more lawsuits, no more flame wars, no more anything.

But Grammy didn't come back. Grammy didn't set him free. Grammy didn't fucking care if he died inside this cow.

Nobody cared. Nobody cared. Bert cried silently.

Another face intruded into his line of sight. That lesbo bitch, Connie Maxon, grinned in at him. "Serves you right, you bastard. I hope you're enjoying this. I sure am."

He tried to communicate remorse with his eyes, but she just laughed.

"Gotta go, Bert. There's a long line of folks out here you've pissed on and pissed off. They're all here to spit in your eye. I hope a few off them do more than that. I know most of them. They're nice folks, except when it comes to you. In fact, I met my new very best friend because of you. You made her life a living hell. When we met and I mentioned how much grief you'd caused me, well, that turned out to be the basis for a pretty intense relationship." Connie laughed. "I should feel grateful to you. It's all to your credit that I've found someone so wonderful to spend my life with. Wish us luck!"

She moved away, and the interminable parade of Bert's enemies began to file past his air hole. Some reminded him of what he'd done, some just laughed, some actually spat. After a while, they were coming in pairs, then threesomes, then in legions, vastly more faces than could fit into the little window of Bossie's rectum.

They were all so chummy, so happy to be there together. Bert was almost envious of the camaraderie of his enemies. Almost.

Eventually the faces faded away, and all that was left was sunlight and silence. Bert stared out the hole, wishing for them to come back, pleading for just another few seconds of human contact, even if it was only to pile shit on his head and rub it in his face.

He'd take it, and gladly, if only they wouldn't leave him to die alone.

They didn't return.

All there was for a very long time was the stink of death, the faint caress of the maggots and flies, and the light.

And heat. It was getting hard to breathe inside Old Bossie. Steam from the dissolving corpse obscured the light. Bert's hair hung down in greasy braids before his eyes, the blood from his scalp wound plastering it to his face like the wallpaper in Satan's den.

No, not den, Bert thought with a giggle. Dens were usually paneled, weren't they? It was probably his living room. Yes, that was it. The devil's living room was decorated with the bloody hair of men who died inside the week old bodies of cattle.

The day floated by. A long series of insect invaders joined Bert inside Old Bossie, beetles and slugs and worms and centipedes and doodlebugs, but he didn't pay them any attention. He just stared out her ass, waiting for Grammy to show up again and tell him what a loser he was, how much trouble he'd caused her.

Grammy didn't come back, either, and after a long while, the light began to dim. Not much, just a little.

Something stirred in Bert's brain. It was like waking up, but not exactly. It was more like coming out of a thorazine haze. It was like the slow return to conscious thought after the shock therapy and the drugs they gave him at the mental health center.

Ha! Mental health center, my ass, he thought. *They tried to break me, that's what they did. They tried to make me sick. I was fine when I went in, it's only since I got out. . .*

He shook his head and concentrated on the light, clinging to it with his eyes.

The light can't go away again, he thought. *If it does, I'll lose my mind for sure, what's left of it.* He moaned.

Voices floated in with the fading light. Voices!

Someone is out there, he thought, *someone will surely get me out of this fucking cow!*

Bert worked his jaw, trying to loosen the duct tape enough to scream for help, but that asshat Maxon had put too much around his face.

Along with the voices, Bert heard an engine, the deep thrum of a truck. It drowned out the individual words until the source of those voices got closer, and even then, he could only make out an occasional word. Something about a damned cow, and a winch, and a fire. Surely Old Bossie was way too far gone to cook, he thought. Even stuffed with long pig.

He threw himself back and forth against the inside of the carcass, bloodying his arms and legs and back on exposed ribs. There was no reaction from outside that he could discern. How could they not see Bossie shake? He paused and panted through his snotty nose. How to make the men outside realize he was inside the cow? How much more of this torment did they expect him to take?

Maybe it was Maxon and his pals out there. Maybe they'd come back to release him after all, and this was just more of their idea of fun, to get in that last bit of torture before slitting Bossie open along the seam they'd created with the fishing line. Bert smiled behind the duct tape, sure that it must be them, and that it was only a matter of moments before they'd cut him loose.

And Grammy would be out there, and so would all those asshats who'd stopped by to make fun of him. He'd give Grammy a swift fucking kick in her support hose, and tell Connie Fucking Lesbo Bitch Maxon and her new cunt girlfriend and her uncle-fucking brother and all the rest what he thought of them.

The clanking of a chain drove those thoughts from his brain. Shadows moved across the beam of light entering through the anus. The engine was closer, louder, obliterating any possibility of hearing the men outside. On top of the growl of the V-8, there was a high whine. Bossie shifted, moved, lifted. Bert slid back down towards her head as she was raised into the air.

He stood on the thick, rancid beef of Bossie's shoulders and peered at the now distant bung hole that was his only view of the world. Past it, he saw a chain wrapped around her back legs, and beyond that, the winch hanging from the John Deere green painted crane that had lifted him and Bossie from the ground. The carcass swung back and forth, making the light dance around him. The whine of the winch stopped, and Bert heard one last thing before his mind gave up on reality.

"Got no choice, Stu," a man who didn't sound at all like Jerry Maxon said. "You find a cow that's died of anthrax, you just gotta burn her before she can infect the rest of the herd. Don't even want to get close to her, poor thing, except to loop that chain around her ankles. Poor Old Bossie. Okay, boys, swing her around, into that fire pit. Gotta douse her with gas and burn her up."

Bert's mind gave up its tenuous hold on reality, leaving only one marginally sentient thought echoing in his tormented brain, a line from Poe that should have occurred to him hours before.

For the love of God, Montressor.

For the love of God, Maxon.

For the love of God.

The cow spun as she was positioned over the fire pit, but Bert didn't care. He didn't notice when she was dropped six or eight feet, even though the shock shattered both his legs and one side of his pelvis. The aroma of Texaco was just one more insult to his olfactory, not worth noting.

The blazing heat that baked him in the oven of Bossie's body couldn't reach the place he had retreated into, which was the first merciful thing that had happened to him in almost twenty-four hours.

*　　*　　*

A few hours later, a bulldozer shoved a ton of dirt onto the bovine and human ashes mingled together.

Grammy reported him missing, and suggested the names of a few suspects, but there was little enthusiasm on the part of the police over Bert's disappearance. His enemies were so many, none stood out as potential culprits. After a while, even Grammy realized how much better her life was since he'd gone away, and the world went on just fine without him.

Every so often, though, an e-mail might pass between one or another of the legions of Bert's victims and foes, a sly "asshat" or "cuntboy" between friends, just to remind each other of the *infant terrible* who had brought so many people together in their common hatred of him.

Not the best legacy anyone could hope for, but neither is it the worst.

Alchera
DJ Tyrer

"Sometimes, when the weather is just right like this, the lakebed will trap a layer of mist and it will seem as if the lake is there as it once was."

Cammie listened as Rob told her all he knew about the old, dried-up lakebed that lay just a little distance from the house. He, of course, had lived here for years, knew all about the place. Outback-born and bred, Rob was an old hand in the sun-baked heart of Australia. She, on the other hand, was a 'Pom Sheila', as he delightfully put it, and everything about the land of the kangaroo was novel to her.

Here, at a place with a name she couldn't pronounce, they were right out in the middle of the desert. There was nothing here but rocks and the occasional piece of dead-seeming scrub. Rob told her that when the rains came every few years the area would briefly erupt into a bright and luscious riot of life. But, the rest of the time, it was about as dead as anywhere on the planet could be.

To the untrained eye, the deserts were of no use to anyone, except the boffins who used them to test the efficacy of A-bombs to vitrify the flesh of Mother Earth. Rob had told her of the great mushroom clouds tall enough to rise above the distant horizon and the ash clouds that had blown in on unexpected winds after the tests.

Of course, the desert concealed something of worth, or there wouldn't have been such a good-sized house here. Even had an eccentric been taken with the remoteness of the spot, nothing more than a shack would've been plausible this far from civilisation. But, there was gold in the hills – or, had been, 'til the mines played out – and her grandfather had built this house here on the wealth he gained from the mining operations.

Rob had been the foreman at the mine and had received a half-share in the house from Cammie's grandfather, just as she had. Cammie suspected the old man had hoped the joint-inheritance would inspire them to marry. Rob had laughed at the suggestion, but, secretly, she found the prospect not entirely unthinkable; she rather liked him.

In return for her share of the surrounding lands and a decent bank balance with which to manage them, Cammie had come to Australia to fulfil the stipulation that she spend at least a quarter of the year in the sandblasted, once-yellow, gothic-inspired wood-board house. There wasn't exactly much to do out here, but she guessed that with inherited wealth she could afford to fill her time with books and records, or hosting soirees for the society friends she was certain she would soon make. Three months a year, especially if divided up, would pass easily. Particularly if things developed with Rob.

Back in England, Cammie had been a shop girl on low wages in a nation still slaved to rationing, one that had won a war only to lose the peace. Down Under, everything seemed plentiful and she had the money to afford it. Just as her grandfather had done half-a-century before, she had abandoned everything she knew to start a new life on the far side of the world.

Unlike him, she hadn't abandoned a young family and left them destitute whilst building a fortune: James Atheling might have started with nothing, but he had soon climbed the greasy pole to wealth and power. Not a single penny had seen its way to her mother or aunt. She supposed this inheritance was a belated apology of sorts. Or, maybe some kind of 'I told you so', given his requirement that she emulate his relocation to Australia in order to inherit.

"Your grandfather was a strange old coot," Rob told her, "a good boss, decent and fair, who knew mining inside out, but strange, nonetheless."

He'd often told her that, but had never been too clear on why he said it: "It was his manner, how he was, you know?"

She didn't. The most she could establish was that he had been inordinately fascinated with the lakebed.

"Used to sit out here on the veranda staring at it for hours," Rob said. "Not sure why, it doesn't look much different to anywhere else around here, just flatter."

He was right, yet she could almost understand her grandfather's obsession with it. She couldn't explain it, but there was something about it that called to her. Perhaps it was because the hard-baked ground was a lighter colour than the land around it so that it reflected the light of the moon and stars, giving it an ethereal quality by night. When the mist gathered upon it, a rarity in these parched, scorched lands, it looked even more magical. As Rob said, it looked as if the lake was actually there: a cloud lake.

Sitting on the veranda in the swing-chair where her grandfather had once sat, the long-dead lake filling her view, she asked Rob why the lake and the others like it in the region had dried up.

He looked up from his bottle of beer and said, "Well, that's hard to say . . ."

"Don't you know?"

He laughed. "I don't think anybody knows, not for certain. I guess the climate just got drier. I read that it's dry out here because of the mountains back east, so maybe the lakes were here before the mountains. I have heard folks say that there was a great drought or some disaster that just dried them up. Your grandfather used to say there were cities out on their shores that died when the lakes died, but I can't say I credit it. Although there were some odd towers, like enormous termites might have built, out by where they were doing the tests. They looked a bit like buildings, I guess. But, really, they were just natural outcroppings. Maybe those were what he was thinking of."

"Seeing it like this, I could imagine there is a city on the far shore." Cammie paused, staring intently for a while. "It almost looks as if there is one out there, as if I can see lights. I guess the moon is reflecting off something."

Rob's only reply was a snore and, then, the sound of his bottle slipping from his fingers to roll across the floorboards and out onto the sand.

Cammie gave a little laugh to realise that he was sleeping. She supposed he found her notions silly and boring; Rob was not the sort of person to view the world romantically. He was practical to the core. Appreciating the unusualness of these conditions was about as far as he was likely to go. She couldn't see him imagining cities in the desert night.

Only, the strange thing was that, the more she looked out across the lake, the more she got the impression that there were buildings out there with lights in their windows. She even thought she could hear the distant sounds of nocturnal city life echoing through the silence across the lakebed.

"It can't be real," she murmured to herself. The problem was that denial only served to crystallise her doubts about what she was seeing. It really did look like there was a city out there, regardless of how impossible it seemed. It had to be a trick of the light, or maybe she was asleep, too, and dreaming.

Yes, there were definitely lights out there across the lake. There was a

58

house, a large house.

There wasn't one there, not really, she was certain of that, had walked all around the fossil shores of the lakebed and seen no other buildings anywhere in the area.

Nonetheless, she could see one now. Could it be a reflection of the mansion on the mist? Maybe. That made the most sense. More so than some ghostly building. Yet, the longer she stared, the more solid it seemed, the more real.

Then, she realised that she was no longer sitting on the veranda, but standing on a quayside, beside a lake with cloudy breakers bursting mistily against the shore. The building opposite had to be the mansion itself; the more she looked out across the foamy lake, the clearer she could see it. The peculiar outline was unmistaken. How had she got over here; over to this place that didn't exist? She had to be dreaming!

Slowly, Cammie became aware that she stood in a city beside the lake of clouds. Was this place Alchera? She recalled Rob using that word when talking about the lake, but couldn't recall the context. Was this a memory or a dream? It seemed more real than her dreams usually were, yet had a numinous quality that reality lacked. She couldn't recall an experience quite like this. It was strange and intoxicating.

"What is this place?" she asked herself.

"This is Carcosa, the greatest city in the world," a voice replied and she turned in surprise to see a young woman in a flowing yellow robe of some diaphanous material, also staring out across the lake.

"How did I get here?" Cammie asked.

"You were always here on the lake shore," the woman repeated in the nonsensical way characters so often did in dreams.

"But, I was in the mansion across the lake." Was it foolishness to quibble in a dream?

"There is nothing across the lake but empty fields," the young woman said. "Although there are those who claim to have seen a phantom city out there, like our own, only a shadow."

"I don't understand."

"What is there to understand? This is your home and has always been. What more need you know than that?"

"No, it isn't. I've never been here before." Yet, even as she said that, Cammie felt uncertainty creep over her. Surely she had dwelt here forever? Or, had she been here in her dreams? After a short pause of confusion, she went on. "No, no, that's right. I lived in the mansion across the lake. I've never been here before. This place doesn't exist. This is just a dream."

"Cammie, why do you say such things? You've always lived here with me."

"No, I haven't! I don't even know who you are!"

"Cammie!" the young woman gasped in shock. "That's a cruel thing to say!"

"Who are you?"

"It's me, Cassie! Honestly, what is wrong with you?"

"I don't know . . ." Where did she belong? Here or across the lake in that phantom mansion? Which was real and which was not? Was either real? She shook her head, attempting to clear it, recall her past.

"Come walk with me . . ." The woman held out her hand and she took it, walking with her through the shadowy city of soaring towers.

It was like the freakish offspring of London and New York as she had seen them in photos and on the movie screen, possessing the great age of the former and the skyscraping buildings of the latter. It was a bizarre amalgam; bizarre yet strangely familiar. The towers seemed so great of height that they passed behind the swollen belly of the ivory moon.

"I can't stay here," Cammie said, at last, her voice plaintive. She knew she had to leave, yet part of her was pained at the thought.

"Oh, Cammie, there's no need to be this way."

"I have to leave; I have to go home."

"There is nowhere else; this is your home."

"It isn't, Cassie. Oh, I wish that it were, but it isn't; it isn't . . ."

"Well, decide not now, Cammie. Let the red dawn surmise what we shall do, when the twin suns sink beneath the lake and all life is through . . ."

She was silent for a while as they walked through the empty streets of the funereal city, attempting to make sense of that. Eventually, she had to ask, "What does that mean?"

"That is how our passion play ends."

"What do you mean?"

"When the twin suns descend and boil away the lake in a coruscation of flame, this city shall cease to exist and all life here shall end.

"I don't understand . . ."

"You shall shortly. See, there to the north, the twin suns burst into fiery dawn."

She turned her gaze northwards and, amidst the towers, she did, indeed, see two fiery red suns blaze into existence. With a horrific inevitability, the two balls of flame fell towards the lake as waves of heat rippled out towards them. Cammie felt her skin blister and bubble and slough away, just as the cloud lake boiled away in a hiss of steam, the rising clouds joining ash and dust to form twin mushroom-shaped plumes.

"We die in Lost Carcosa," she thought she heard Cassie say before her consciousness evaporated in flame.

*　*　*

"Now, where has that dopey Sheila got herself to?" Rob wondered.

He'd woken to find himself on the veranda alone and her bed unslept in. It was now noon and he was beginning to worry.

"I guess I'd better go looking for her . . ." he muttered, and headed for the battered old skeleton of a Model T that served him for transport. He was trying to imagine just how far she might have gone since last he saw her. He'd have to spiral out from the house and hope he could spot her.

Finally, Rob spied her, spread-eagled upon the lakebed on the far side of the sunbaked expanse. He hopped out of the car and ran to her side, then recoiled in horror as he saw her burnt and blistered skin. She must have lain there beneath the burning sun all morning. He had never known someone to be so badly burnt this quickly.

Cautiously, he checked for pulse or breath, but there was none; Cammie was dead.

He sighed. It was a crying shame, she'd been a real nice Sheila, for a Pom. The weird thing was that the blistering reminded him of a geezer he'd once seen who'd been badly burnt in a fire. If he hadn't known better, he'd have said she had died in a blaze. Bizarre!

Behind him, to the north, a distant mushroom cloud stood sentinel on the horizon, another test underway. Before him, Cammie was as dead as the lake on which she lay.

The Dank
Doug Blakeslee

You know there's trouble when a gnome hands you a mysterious package. "What's up with the mystery gift?" I asked. "My birthday isn't until January." "It's a delivery," said Bernie.

He wasn't really a gnome, at least not that he would admit to. A bit over four feet tall, with a mop of messy white hair and long sideburns . . . the only things missing were a long nose and jaunty cap to go with his wizened features.

"I don't recall anything on the schedule," I said, wracking my brain to see if I had missed any last minute changes.

That was our business, here at Rogue Transport and Logistics. Part of it, anyway. The job board showed everyone else out on various calls, leaving me – Theo March, changeling and man in charge – the only one available.

Crap.

"It's a personal favor for a few friends," Bernie added. A small bag hit the desk, clinking and clacking. "They paid in rimestone. Enough to cover expenses and twice the usual markup."

I raised an eyebrow at that. "What's the job and what's the catch?"

"You wound me, Theo. Why would there be any issues with a simple drop-off?" His face held a neutral, innocent expression perfectly.

I held my hand up to stop him. "Where does it need to go? And what sort of trouble can I expect?"

"Just an easy drive to the lava caves near Bend," he assured me. "Some spelunking to an underground lake, drop the package into the water, and

leave. Simple."

"What's in the package?"

"A leather pouch."

"Containing?"

"Restorative juju." He grinned at me. "Open it up, dump it out, and let it disperse. Piece of cake."

I sighed. "Uh-huh. That's a long haul to Eastern Oregon."

"Motel's reserved in your name." Bernie slid a sheet of paper across my desk. "All the details are here, including the shortest route through the cave. Even taking your time, you'll be in and out in a couple of hours."

A hand drawn map showed way-points marked in a clear cursive script. "I hate caving," I said.

"Tough."

Had I mentioned I was the boss around here? Yeah, right.

Bernie went on, gesturing towards the garage. "I've packed you a kit to take along. It's in the van. Everything you'll need."

"You've gone to a lot of planning for a simple, piece-of-cake job."

That got a chuckle. "Theo, my lad, you're the reckless, irresponsible son that I never had. Writing everything out is the best solution to keep your ass out of the fire."

"Thanks. I think."

"Don't stray from the path and don't kill anyone," he said, and tossed me the keys. "Seriously, no shooting or stabbing."

*   *   *

"Easy drive, my ass." I climbed out of the van several hours later, stirring up a cloud of dust that hung in the still air. My ass indeed, and it ached as much as the rest of me.

Sweat beaded on my forehead. Being a changeling with an affinity for fire and earth doesn't make me immune to nature's laws. Back home in Portland might have been cool and pleasant; way out here, the summer heat lingered well toward dusk.

One other vehicle occupied the parking lot, an older model Ford station-wagon with fake wood panels. Two harried adults shepherded a gaggle of kids towards it with the desperation born of exhaustion and low blood sugar. The last stragglers leaving the park, heading towards air conditioning, food, and sleep.

Rough wooden signs and directional arrows proudly proclaimed

'Newberry National Volcanic Monument – Fossil Point Lava Caves' in faded white lettering. I pulled out the park map and ran a finger along the path highlighted in yellow marker. *Half mile hike, turn left, take the service trail for a hundred feet to the cave. Time to get this show on the road.*

Bernie's particular cave entrance was not the gentle slope that map indicated. A safety rail surrounded the steep descent, keeping the curious away, warning, "No Trespassing" in red.

I hopped over, went to the edge of the drop-off, and peered down. The fading sunshine showed the cave floor less than ten feet below. Cool air blew up from the depths, a respiration that resembled the breathing of a great beast.

Enough with the imagination, it's just a cave with a draft.

I free climbed down the side of the wall, landing heavily in the loose rocks and assorted garbage; bottles, cigarette butts, and food wrappers.

What a mess. Tourists must use it for a trash pit, not a scenic attraction.

Turning on my head-lamp, I started to pick my way deeper inside. Dry stone walls engulfed me with poor footing threatening to twist an ankle and send me spilling to the rocks. The temperature dropped to around forty as I progressed, feeling uncomfortably cold compared to the heat outside.

Further in, it stank of sour guano. Bats whirred and flapped, heading out for their nightly feeding. A rummage through the kit Bernie had provided me revealed no breathing mask or face covering. I found heavy leather gloves, rope, climbing harness, spare batteries . . .

. . . a fluffy pink bath towel, a couple of chocolate bars, and a change of underwear.

The hell?

"Not a great packing job, Bernie," I muttered out loud. "It's like you expect me to fall in the lake."

It struck me that this might be a glorified snipe hunt, but the rimestones had been real enough. An expensive joke, if it was one.

More guano, white and sticky, covered the floor, moving under its own volition. I squatted for a closer look and immediately regretted it. Worms and crickets, blind and pale, fought over the bounty of waste material. Locked in a struggle over the best feeding spots and choicest pieces of . . . crap. The carcass of an expired bat must have been manna from heaven.

I could hear Bernie laughing as I straightened and continued picking my way forward.

* * *

"Son of a . . . what the hell, Bernie? Your map sucks."

An ice cold mist sprayed as water splashed over the rocks, into a small pool, then burbled off into the darkness. I pulled out the instructions and scanned them again. Turn right at the first fork, keep left until the long drop, crawl through the gap to the right, and then straight until you get to the underground lake.

Simple, he'd said. Total bullshit.

The map had to be wrong. Or the passages shifted. Something.

I traced the alternate route. *Dammit, going the long way around.* I wasn't lost, but this wasn't a three hour tour anymore. *I'll be lucky to get out here by morning.*

The path sloped sharply downward, slick with water, moss, and mud. I grabbed the closest rock, tested it for security, and eased over the edge. Cold water ran over my hand as I moved from purchase to purchase, pausing to check and double check that I wouldn't be flung into the darkness by a loose stone. Fatigue crept into my arms, but I reached the floor before my grip gave out for good. The burbling creek vanished at the edge of my light, rushing towards the lake that lay ahead.

Theoretically.

"At least the path is marked," I said.

"Marked? Not marked. No signs. No signs at all," something croaked in the darkness.

Since I'd been talking to myself, the reply came as a surprise.

The long knife snapped into my hand and I crouched, whipping the light around. "Who the fuck are you?"

"I'm me. Prince of the Dank. Dweller in the Shadows. Lurker in the Cave." A shape hovered at the edge of the light, eyes reflecting and glittering.

"Are you some kind of cave troll?"

"Perhaps not troll. Perhaps troll. Here for a long time. No longer matters. Powerful and mighty and wise. Many followers." A grimy, moss covered hand tested the pool of light, carefully, as if expecting to be burned. It grunted with satisfaction.

"What do you want?"

"Talk. Long time. No visitors. Just bats and rats and mice. No men." The shadowed head turned towards the darkness behind it. "Sister no longer welcomes me. Hides when she bathes now. Fleeting pleasure gone. No more soft skin and white hair."

"Uh . . ."

"But Mother loves us. She loves all her children."

And I'm done with this thing. Person. Whatever. I nodded down the side

passage. "Love to talk, but no time. The lake's that way?"

"Fossil Lake? Kingdom of the Dank. Yes. Yes. That way. Long and dangerous. My home. You shall not pass."

"Why not?"

"My home. Not for others."

"Please?" I held the knife, and it was unarmed, but Bernie's words etched in my head. I didn't need to antagonize some critter that decided to be territorial. Being polite and talking worked on occasions.

"Trade for passage. Riddle gift." The man-thing crawled into view, pale from years of darkness, perhaps since birth. Covered in moss and mud, wearing not a stitch of clothing. "Yes?"

"Riddle gift? You mean a riddle game?"

"No. Riddle gift. You solve riddle and give me a gift. I let you pass." The thin mouth of sharp teeth pulled into a rictus grin. "Fail and you must serve me."

He doesn't look like a sphinx or a fighter; probably could take him with a quick move. "Fine, riddle away."

The thing scratched itself, flaking off bits of mud and other . . . stuff. "Riddle . . . what riddle should I pose to you . . ."

Jesus, this is going to take forever.

It raised a finger. "Soft when new, hard when old. Jewels to hold, holes I behold."

"Uh . . ."

"Come. Come. Not difficult."

Great, underestimated the opposition again. Let's see. Old. New. Holds, but has holes. That's a poor container. Colander?

"You have answer?" It sat down on a flat stone, legs spread wide. "Or do you wish to serve a master? The dank calls and many answer. I know others. Many others. They praise me. Mother says so."

"How about a minute to think." *Ugh, I don't need to see that. He really needs a pair of . . .* "Underwear!"

"But we have none."

I tossed him the change of fresh undies from the kit. "Put these on."

"Intriguing." He sniffed them, wrinkling the flaps that passed for his nose. "Smells odd. Not like the dank."

"It's spring fresh. Not like you'd know that, living in this basement."

"Bounty soft."

"Or maybe you do." I studied him again. He *looked* human. Sort of. Nasty and unwashed. Spoke English, after a fashion. Acted human, in a stunted and regressive way. "Good enough answer?"

"Yes. Clothing fine." The troll thing struggled into the briefs, wearing the garment like a onesie pulled up to the chest. "Good fit."

I'm going to get you for this Bernie. So help me god.

"Follow water," he told me. "Safe passage."

"Thanks. I'll be on my way."

"Say hi to Sister. Beware of Mother's love." Then he slithered through a too-small crack and vanished.

Right, the pervert mentioned watched his sister bathe. This is going to be a special trip.

* * *

I found her crouched on a boulder in the middle of a cavern. Six passages led out from it, unmarked on Bernie's map, the underground creek disappearing into a small crack in the floor. A single, milky-white eye in the middle of her forehead followed me with an eerie accuracy. Long flowing white hair covered her body, clinging in strategic places.

She gestured to a smooth stone in front of her. "A man. So long since I've seen a man. Come and sit with me."

"You must be the sister."

"The pretty one. Mother says so. You're a charmer. I can tell." A warty, green tongue slathered over her pale lips, leaving a thin brown slime behind. "Sit. Sit. We can talk."

"I'm in a hurry."

"Just like a man. Always in a hurry. Never time to talk. Always on the go. Never stays and plays." She sniffed. Her mouth turned down and a single tear leaked from the corner of her eye.

"I guess I can stay for a bit."

Damn it, Theo, I chided myself. *Always such a sucker for the ladies. Even the weird cave-dwelling ones.*

She smiled, showing three blackened teeth. Her hands rubbed together. "Oh good."

I eased onto the smooth stone. "So, come here often?"

A shrill laugh echoed around the cavern. "Oh, you're a slick one. Are you trying to pick me up? My boyfriends will be jealous!"

"No. No." I waved my hands at her. "I didn't expect to find . . . anyone down here."

"You are in luck. Not often we have visitors. New people to meet and greet. Not like brother. Nasty. Creepy. Crawls and whines and begs. Mother sent him away." She spat on the ground.

"I've met him."

"But forget him. What's your name, sweet man? I'm Krynee the Ocular. Princess of the Dank. Sitter on Stones. Eye in the Shadows."

"Theo. You're an oracle?"

"Wise for a changeling. Handsome too."

"You're the first person that's ever called me wise."

"Wisdom comes with age. Youth is foolish, the old are wise."

"So they say."

"Would you like to know your future, Theo? I can tell you . . . for the answer to a riddle."

"No thanks. I'd like directions to the lake, though."

"Then answer my riddle, and I will tell you the way."

I was sensing a theme here. "You wouldn't rather trade?"

Her eye shifted toward an alcove. A crude bed of rags, dirt, and other stuff lay within. "If you wish."

"Ask the riddle." *Please ask the riddle!*

She cackled again. "Spread on sand or hung on a line. Warm when dry, cold when wet. A hiker's need, even threadbare. Don't leave home without it."

Okay, think about this. Something a hiker would need for sand, but on a line? Tent? No, no. Wait a minute, Bernie's packing job. "Towel?"

That produced a chuckle, one of mirth and amusement. "The towel, yes, warm and soft and fluffy. And spring fresh."

I'm so docking your pay for this one, Bernie. I dug in the pack and handed the pink towel to her. "Here you go. Enjoy."

She snatched it with a flash of pale flesh and hooked fingers. Krynee rubbed the towel against her face. "Oooo, soft."

"Soo . . . directions?"

She pointed to the third passage on the left. "That will lead you to the lake. Say hello to Mother Dear, Theo March. Beware of the water, it'll be your death."

She knows my last name. Figures.

* * *

The hemp rope vanished into the darkness as I let out the final length. I gave it a tug, testing the anchor around the slick stalagmite. It dug into the groove I'd carved out of the limestone, bracing it with rocks for the illusion of security. The flowing water trickled down the side of the cliff face, little more than a damp dribbling.

I wrapped the rope around my hand, letting it bite into the heavy leather gloves. I belayed down, holding the other end to arrest my fall. The soles of my boots scraped against the wall, the treads keeping me from slipping as they tore off wet moss and slime. Below, the floor rose up, illuminated by the fading lamp light. I had swapped out the batteries an hour ago, only to find them little better than the original pair.

I fell despite my precautions. The rope went slack, maybe slipped, maybe cut. Luckily, it was a short fall and I landed butt-first in muddy sand that squished and oozed. A wet cold seeped into my jeans. Next to me, the rope coiled down in a heap. I saw the loop had come undone.

"Dammit!" My voice echoed loudly in the cavern.

I flashed the waning light around, seeing it glimmer across the surface of a large body of water. The ceiling lay hidden in the dark, but the walls drew my attention.

Bones. Dozens and dozens of bones, sealed and preserved by time. Large ones, small ones. Femurs. Ribs. Vertebrae. Skulls. Not dinosaurs but beings of the imagination. Goblins, griffins, and the like. Fantastic creatures found only in storybooks and legends.

"Fossil Lake," I murmured. "Not what I expected."

"None do," someone replied, in a syrupy and cloying voice.

I hung my head, sighed, and turned around.

A plump figure rose up, half submerged, from the lake. Pale green skin, scaled and wet, glistened in my light.

"Hi. You must be Mother."

"A visitor. How delightful." She smiled, warm and welcoming, the emotion reflecting in her all-too-human eyes. "I am Mira of Cetus. Pleased to meet you, young changeling."

"Theo."

"What brings you here, Theo?" The water rippled as she walked out of the lake, clad in a dress of seaweed that hung to her knees. Finer strands of kelp sprouted from her scalp, woven into a single, long braid.

"Dropping off a package for someone. Am I going to have to answer a riddle before I can?"

"Aren't you a quick learner! So clever, and so handsome, too!"

"Thanks," I said, though after the previous two encounters, I didn't have to be that clever to put the pieces together.

"Does Mother need to ask the riddle? Or do you already know the answer? Or does Theo need a hintsie?"

What sort of game is Bernie playing at? I hate being kept in the dark.

"Is the answer chocolate bars?" I dug into the kit for the last of the items Bernie'd packed, items that had seemed odd before but made sense now. Not that he'd bothered to let me know.

"Very good! Such a good boy. Someone prepared you well. That is the answer and I will claim my prize." She held out a scaled hand.

I gave her the bars. "Here you go."

She sniffed them, looked at the wrappers, and nodded. "Dark chocolate from Switzerland. A fine quality and more than adequate price. You may approach the lake."

I did so, though I had the proverbial bad feeling about this. All I had to do was dump the contents of the pouch Bernie had given me into the water. Piece of cake, he'd said. Yeah, right.

The wet sand, still squishing beneath my boots, was very gritty and pale. Calcified. Less like sand, more like . . .

"But," said the lake-woman in a lilting tone, "what will you give me for the next boon?"

And here it comes.

"Next boon?"

"I told you that you may approach. How, though, do you plan to leave? Your light is fading and your rope lies unsecured. Without my help, you'll never escape this cave. They will find your bones, gnawed and scattered."

And, eventually, pulverized into sand, like the stuff I was walking on.

Great, I found Grendel's mother. "Rock and a god damn hard place. What do you want?"

She tutted reprovingly. "Mother would only like a kiss on the cheek."

Okay, she's not hideous. A bit scaly, wet, and smells like seaweed. You've kissed worse, Theo. "Just a kiss?"

"Is that so much to ask? After all that Mother's done for you?" Grendel's guilt-tripping mother . . .

"That sounds reasonable enough," I said.

Mira glided toward me, leaving a groove in passing in the bone-meal sand. She turned her head, presenting a finely-fishscaled cheek.

Just like duty-kissing a weird old auntie. Nothing big.

I puckered up and gave her a quick peck. Her skin was cold. I tasted salt on my lips. *Salt?*

Before I could pull back, a gush of water filled my mouth. Like her skin, it was salty and cold. It flooded in, choking and gagging me. I pushed away, falling backwards in the sand, vomiting up silty greenish water in heaving gasps.

She gave me a scolding, disappointed look. "You resisted my affection.

That makes me unhappy, Theo. That makes Mother very unhappy. My children need another brother, a strong and handsome brother like you."

"Children?" I coughed out another lungful, my eyes watering and nose burning from the acidic fluid.

"All who come here are my children," she said, gesturing around. "So many children in the past, each a treasure upon which I showered my love. But then they'd grow up and turn from me, from their own dear Mother. They'd want to go away forever."

I glanced again at the bones embedded in the cave walls. Gnawed and scattered, she'd said.

"So you ate them, to keep them with you?"

"Consumed them with the sorrow of a mother's sacrifice." She heaved a watery, mournful breath. "Now Mother has only two . . . a useless worm and a wicked girl. Not a fine, strong, handsome son like you."

"I'm not your son." The long knife appeared in my hand and was slapped away almost as fast, a stinging blow as something hard and scaly smacked it from my grasp.

"Tut. Tut. No weapons, young man!"

But the touch of the blade had shattered her illusion. I saw her as she truly was. A long serpentine body stretched back to the lake, following the groove in the sand. Thick scales covered her torso. Dozens of tentacles sprouted from her shoulders, ending in sharp claws.

Bernie, what the fuck were you thinking? No violence, my ass!

"Mother will have to punish you for this impertinence," she gurgled, through a mouth now more suited to a large eel.

"Good luck with that," I said, still backpedaling, groping for anything I could use to defend myself while scanning frantically for the knife.

"Join my family," she said, undulating closer. "In time, others will come along. Perhaps a bride for you. Mother would love grandchildren. Strong and healthy and loving."

"That's not happening."

"Disobedient boy!" More of the massive, tentacled body flowed out of the water, growing thicker and thicker with each revealed foot. A phosphorescent glow throbbed from some large mass submerged in the lake.

What the fuck is beneath the water? Sand slipped under my heels as I scrambled backwards. A dizzying nausea threatened to spill more of my stomach onto the floor.

My hand fell on the kit, almost empty now except for the leather pouch. *Restorative juju, Bernie said. For her, I'm betting.* I thrust my hand in, wrapping

my fingers around the leather bag just as her cold, fishy tendrils wrapped around me.

"Come to Mother!"

She lifted me into the air.

"Go to hell!" I tossed the pouch past her. The tie unraveled, spilling out tiny metallic shavings that scattered across the surface like rain drops. *Please let this work.*

Smoke billowed up from the lake, a swirling cloud that hung on the surface. Her shriek echoed off the walls as she convulsed, squeezing me with a sudden force, expelling the last of my breath and the choking water. Then I went tumbling end over end, hitting the beach, skidding into the rock-and-bone wall, shattering the miner's lamp.

In the darkness, I heard her wail and splash, spitting out words in an unknown, guttural language. Then the noise faded away, leaving only the soft sounds of diminishing ripples lapping on the lake shore.

Well, that job's done, I thought, letting my aching head sink onto my crossed arms. *Guess they'll find my bones some day.*

*   *   *

"Get your ass up, boy," said a familiar, gruff voice.

Bernie?

I squinted at sunlight streaming through blinds, blinking rapidly at the sudden intrusion. Sunlight . . . blinds . . . a window . . . a motel room . . . and a wizened gnome at the bedside, giving me the hairy eyeball.

"What the hell?" I rubbed my face. "How did I get here?"

"Marcus and Steve found you in the van," he said. "Soaked to the bone, bruised as hell, but alive. I'm guessing that you took a wrong turn. You never could follow directions."

Something about this didn't add up, but I latched onto the last part. "That map of yours was shit," I said.

"No it wasn't."

"It was. And no wonder you packed all that extra crap. Could have goddamn warned me."

"You took care of the pouch?"

"It's deep-sixed, along with whatever lurked in that damn lake."

He grunted with satisfaction. "Good. That's been a bother forever. Did you find anyone else?"

"Her children. I think." The thought brought back more disturbing

memories.

"Captives, not children," Bernie said. "She lured the unwary to serve her. I guess they hauled you out as thanks for freeing them, and then disappeared."

I wasn't too sure about that, but what other explanation could there be? I'd gotten from that bone-embedded cave to the van somehow, after all.

"Now what?" I asked.

"We're done." Bernie grinned at me. "The cave collapsed, we got paid twice, and everyone's happy."

Everyone? I let it go for now. "What do you mean, paid twice?"

"I'll explain on the way home." He pointed toward the motel bathroom. "After you take a shower. You smell like the dank."

Dark of Madness
Tanya Nehmelman

The dark can be damning. You never know what's hiding within it. The senses are heightened. Every little noise, creak and crack sends shivers, tingling down the spine. Every moving shadow plays a horrific image in the mind. Maybe if the guilt didn't linger, the darkness wouldn't be so bad.

The wind howls, and you hear her whisper, "Why? I did everything for you." Those were her last words. Why did you do it? The question dwells in your mind. You lost it for a second, but a second was all it took. After all, you did it with a smile, didn't you? Didn't you? So why is it bothering you now?

Was it the way the tears rolled down her cheeks? The way she begged for your pity? Or the simple fact that she just plain trusted you? No, it's not any of that, is it? You've wanted her dead for a long time now, ever since you were children. Haven't you?

You dressed like her, acted like her, and wanted to be her. Somewhere in your small mind, you believed you'd grow up to be her, didn't you? Even as adults, you tried to be her. But when everyone continued to praise her, and not you, that's when you snapped, wasn't it? With her out of the picture, you are free to be her. Isn't that right? So what's the problem?

Darkness surrounds you. Strange sounds of the night buzz in your ears. Her body is gone. You made sure of that, didn't you? Of course you did. You tied the sack of bricks firmly around her ankles, and knocked her body off the pier. Then you stood over, watching, glug, glug, glug, as the body sank. She's with Papa now. This was his secret fishing spot, and every time he brought you girls out here, he warned you to stay away from the brim. He claimed it was so deep, that if you fell in, he'd never be able to find you. So why are you on edge? There is no way she's slinking out in the darkness now, is there?

Your heart bangs in your chest in that ridiculously fast manner now. What's that, you hear footfalls in the distance? Nah, it's just another sound of the night. So you tell yourself. Why are your hands shaking? You damn well know if this would've been the other way around, her hands wouldn't be shaking. This angers you, doesn't it? Even with her gone, you can't be her. Maybe it's because she's not gone. She's out there in the dark, watching, waiting.

Was that a scream, echoing out in the distance? There it is again. Wait, that's not screaming. It's just a loon. You're losing it, aren't you? A small, senseless thing like murder and you can barely keep your pants dry, can you? You're pathetic.

Your heart is racing again. Are those beads of sweat I detect on your brow? Why, sure they are. And you thought this was going to be easy, didn't you? Of course you did. You didn't seem to have a problem with it, when you wrapped your fingers around her scrawny neck, did you? She spotted the burlap sack of bricks at the end of the pier, and turned to question you. That was your chance. You pounced on her, taking her by complete surprise.

You actually liked it at the time. The way her eyes bulged from their sockets, the blue tinting her lips as she tried to gasp for air, and way the vessels broke in her eyes, pooling them red. When her body fell limp in your arms, ecstasy swept over you, didn't it? You let her body plop to the boards, and kicked her with your foot, making sure she was out.

To think, that was your own sister, your flesh and blood. I'd hate to know what you would do to a stranger who crossed your path. Using, your own hands, not even a weapon, to squeeze the life out of her. You didn't feel guilty then, so why the change of heart?

Click clack click clack click clack ... The sweat tickles, as it dribbles down your face. You don't dare move to touch it. Someone's coming, and it sounds like they're wearing heels. Wasn't your sister wearing heels, when you heaved her body into that cold, murky darkness?

Was your chest hitching with that last breath, you took? It is! What, are you gonna cry? Worse, are you gonna piss yourself? Man up already. What can this broad possibly do to you, you big bad sister killer? That's right, you weren't even sure if she was dead, when you shoved her defenseless body into the abyss, were you? So it could be her, lurking out in the darkness, seeking revenge. Revenge against a sister she assumed loved her. After all, you were an expert at faking that, weren't you? How else would you have gained her trust enough to get her here, alone, out in the middle of nowhere?

That's right, you're in the middle of nowhere, so who else could be clacking about out here, besides her? You can picture her now, can't you? Her clothes sopping wet, and clinging to her perfect body, that long blonde hair matted to her face. Her skin sagging, and wrinkled from waterlog, and her bright red eyes glaring, looking for you!

But that's the kind of stuff that only happens in movies, right? So there's nothing for you to worry about. Click clack click clack click clack ... except for that, of course. Who could possibly be out here, in the middle of nowhere, with you, right now? Maybe it's the devil himself, coming to claim your wicked soul.

Nightly insects buzz, and you're crouched behind a tree. Your breathing has picked up. You place a hand over your mouth to stifle the sound of your breath escaping your slightly parted lips. Your entire body trembles, as loud puffs of air withdrawal through your nostrils.

Click clack click clack click clack ... it's getting closer. Your heart frantically raps on your chest, it feels like it's trying to escape its bony prison. Why oh why did you push her in, without getting the keys from her pocket first? Now you're trapped, out here, all alone. Click clack click clack click clack ... except for who ever that is, stalking about the night. There's one word for your situation, isn't there? Karma.

Ah, yes, karma. The one word you liked to throw around, isn't it? "Karma," you'd say with a sinister smile. You didn't much believe in it yourself, did you? You just liked to throw it in everybody else's face, like it was a curse. Well, you God damn hypocrite, KARMA!

Your chest is hitching much, much faster now. It reminds you of something, your sister's did the same, as she couldn't stop the life from escaping her. You close your eyes, as your lungs fill with pain, unable to suck in enough oxygen, in your panicked state. Is this what she felt like, before she fell limp in your arms?

Click clack squish click clack squish click clack squish, the sound is so loud, it has to be right next to you. Is that a fishy odor in the air? You don't want to open your eyes, to see her standing over you, her sagging swollen face, in yours?

But you can't resist can you? Even though your heart feels as if it's going to jump right out of you chest, you open your eyes. You gasp, choking on your own breath, although you see nothing, but darkness, and the silhouettes of trees. Yet that strong fishy odor hangs, heavy in the air. She has to be out there. Watching, tormenting you, payback for unsuccessfully killing her.

You would think something like that, wouldn't you? After all, you'd go after her if she tried, and failed to kill you, right? Crunch click clack squish. What was that? It's right behind you! One hand on the rough tree bark, to balance yourself, you turn with a loud gulp.

A strong whiff of fishy lake stench slaps you in the face. You see nothing but the darkness, and the sliver of the moon's reflection on the water. Leaves wrestle to your left. Your head pivots. Click clack squish . . . A large, wet, raccoon scurries by. Something shiny is clamped in its mouth. You let out a sigh of relief, and turn back towards the tree.

There's something on your neck! It's leathery and damp. The pressure sends your heart into madness. There's no way she can be alive! That was only a foolish thought you had, right?

Full panic has swept over you. It's ever so hard to breathe. You can't move, paralyzed with fear. You just know, your dead sister's hand is wrapped around your throat. Gagging chokes escape your lips. You try to force in air, but the grip is too tight. Overwhelmed with terror, you don't even realize the warm, wetness seeping through your pants.

You know, you really are pathetic, when you let the guilty voice in your head scare you to death.

All That Jazz
Meagan Hightower

Almost every night I stay up late, and I wonder . . . What if I'd tried harder? Sooner? Could I have changed what happened? Could I have avoided the sadness and heartbreak? And was it even possible or unavoidable to do so?

I have no means of answering those questions. I can only guess, and sometimes even guessing is wrong.

I remember the day she and I met. Back then I went by the name of Seth, and she called herself Ruby. She was dolled up in the latest trendy threads and hair style, and I can still recall the scent of her favorite perfume from all the time we spent together at that speakeasy in Fossil Lake.

The summer of 1925, and how it changed my life.

To this day I will never forget the way she used to dance with me when the jazz band played, and how we would always laugh over the silliest things over drinks.

But then Nick had to start getting possessive over her for a reason we could never really understand. It's things like that that really break my heart.

It was one of the rare times I was off of work, so Ruby had invited me over to talk. She figured that with the band being in town, it would be the perfect time to talk without Nick noticing. Even though he rarely left the bar, he always gave me the evil eye when she spent time with me.

For almost thirty minutes we cut a fine rug. Nick never stopped staring at us the entire time. It seemed like the more we danced, the more he had gotten angry. Though if I was in his place and some mac was dancing with my kitten, I would be just as angry.

"I'll order the drinks," I told her when she picked a table far away from the bar.

Once again I got the evil eye from Nick when I walked up to the bar. As usual, he was in his ugly suit and wearing his disgusting eau de toilette. His face was so fixed up in anger it didn't seem like the face of the cool fake-loo artist gangster I worked for.

"I'll have two Bronxes."

"What are you doing with her?" Nick asked, pouring.

"Just dancing," I said.

"Stay away from my woman."

Nick placed the drinks on the bar. When he turned away, I took the drinks over to Ruby. From the look in his eye, I did not want to find out what he meant by those words. I'd rather be on the nut that have a belly full of lead poisoning. It would not surprise me if Nick was packing heat with an intent to harm.

"I wish we could just blow this town," Ruby said, sipping her Bronx lightly. "I told Nick that I'm not his woman. I am not a thing to own."

"Why don't you and me go dust ourselves out of here? And see the world?" I whispered in her ear.

"I'd love to. But how? Nick will blip us both for leaving."

And that was the thousand dollar question. How to leave Fossil Lake without my boss and her unwanted admirer finding out?

I got into the business since I wanted a way to earn fast cash, and Ruby was at the wrong place at the wrong time. Ruby always did believe that I did carry a torch for her, and that in itself was a very dangerous love; I knew better but still couldn't be helped.

"I know the roads very well. He'll never find us," I said, with a strong surge of confidence. From driving the hooch routes, I knew I could leave without much of a trace. Only problem again was trying to get her out.

"Really?" The tone of her voice was tense and excited, but she tried to not look overly ecstatic.

We talked a little more at the table before finally deciding on the plan. Ruby was a little uneasy about it, but we both agreed that it was for the best if we left town and never came back. Anywhere we would go would surely be better than living in this dump. At least, that's what I was hoping for.

"Hey, Ruby-baby. Why don't you lose the boob and be with a real man?"

We looked up; sure enough it was Nick.

"Go away," Ruby said, frowning.

"You come with me," Nick said, leaning menacingly over our table.

No one else in the crowd of dancers seemed to be paying attention, which was not surprising. We were all the way in the back. I got up, wishing I'd thought to not sit in the corner so that empty chairs stood between me and him.

"Nick, leave her alone. She does not belong to you."

"Yes, she does."

"I think I'll be going now," Ruby said.

She started to leave, but Nick pawed at her with his greedily greasy hands. I tossed my drink at his face. It had no effect. I'll have to hand it to Ruby, she did fight back. Nick tried to overpower her, but she slapped him. The only problem was that he hit back, harder.

"You will learn to obey me!" he screamed, pulling her by the arm down a short hall.

I tried to follow. He kicked a chair at me. I stumbled over it, and by the time I recovered my balance, he'd dragged her into one of the storage rooms.

I heard things being thrown and broken in there. Something thumped the wall violently. Ruby cried out, audible even over the music, and it filled me with a strong feeling of dread. It was so unreal with her cries mingling in with the dying whispers of jazz . . .

When people said that Nick had a short temper, they weren't joking. Some told me later that Nick only did the right thing, putting his woman in her place, but I don't think Ruby deserved his wrath.

Bursting into the storeroom, I entered a scene worse that could ever be described. I saw Nick holding a gun, and Ruby cowering in the corner. She had too many cuts, gashes and bruises to even count, and her dress was torn wide open.

I don't even remember what I yelled; the shot covered my shout. I was already too late. Brains splattered the walls. A spray of blood landed on Nick's face. He just laughed.

He didn't notice me standing right there in the doorway. I had never felt so full of hatred and bitterness in my life until that moment.

Would anyone blame me for wanting to fill him with sunshine until he just bled out? Before, I just hadn't liked him, but I'd tolerated his presence. After what he'd done, I just flat out hated him.

I picked up a bottle, and I stepped up behind him. He still hadn't noticed me and didn't know what hit him when I slammed the bottle on his head.

The blow didn't knock him out, but it did shut up his laughter. He whirled and pointed the gun at me. I knocked it out of his hand.

He punched me, but I punched back. I hit him with a one two combo, and he fell down. I grabbed something sharp from a shelf and stabbed him. Even then, with the claret flowing, he had plenty of sass left in him.

His hand tightened on my wrist, but I was not going to give up. My rage and pain rose to a fever pitch. I had to finish it. I had to do it for her. Ruby's destruction had to be avenged, and I had to do it for her. I couldn't help it; I'd been dizzy for that dame ever since we met.

All the love in the world was enough to give me the strength to go on stabbing.

Nick's grip gradually weakened. He barely moaned as I ripped the sharp point across his throat. Blood rained down like a storm of red confetti.

Out in the main gin-joint, the jazz-band and the dancers hadn't missed a beat. They kept on jitterbugging as I left by way of the back door.

I skipped town without telling anyone. Changed my name and occupation. Tried to start my life over. I don't much recall what I did in the following months, but I never bootlegged liquor or worked in a mob ever again.

The thought of Ruby never did leave me.

Sometimes I wonder what would have happened if we'd gotten out earlier.

My mind has continued to eat away at itself, and run itself into insanity. Even now, almost eighty years later, it's never made any sense.

I still smell her perfume. I still hear her voice.

And I still hear the music . . . all that jazz . . .

Revolver Concert
Spencer Carvalho

A long line of people wait outside, hoping not to die tonight.

Lucy Cooper huddles close to her fiancé, James. She inhales cold air and exhales steam. Further up the line, above the concert hall entrance, she can see the marquee lights showing the words DAVID WILDE and below that in smaller letters REVOLVER CONCERT TONIGHT ONLY.

A reporter and cameraman are interviewing people. A man in a black security jacket, wearing a headset and holding a clipboard, is going down the line talking to people. Lucy is unable to hear him yet.

James says, "Don't worry. We'll be in soon."

The man in the black security jacket finishes talking, moves to where Lucy can hear him, and starts again. "All right, the show's going to be starting soon, so I'm going to explain a few things and then get you guys inside as soon as possible."

The crowd cheers.

"For most of you, this is probably your first Revolver Concert. What you're gonna do is once they let you inside is, you're gonna proceed to the security checkpoint. There, they're gonna check your ID to make sure you're at least eighteen. Then you're gonna sign the life waiver and then they'll let you into the main hall. Any questions?"

No one says anything.

"All right. Good." He moves forty feet further down the line and starts talking to them, same spiel.

Lucy looks to James. "Life waiver?"

"Yeah, it's just some legal thing so no one goes to jail."

"I'm still not sure what's going on here."

The guy and girl in line in front of them turn around. The guy has his arm wrapped around the girl's shoulder.

The girl smiles at Lucy and says, "I've been to a Revolver Concert before. You wanna hear about it?"

"Yeah, sure."

"Okay, my name's Joan. My boyfriend's Ted."

"Hey," says Ted.

"Hi," says Lucy.

"Before the show starts," Joan continues, "this guy in a black suit comes out carrying an old wooden table about two feet wide and places it by the microphone stand. Then he opens the drawer of the table and removes the revolver." She smiles wider upon saying the word *revolver*. "He places the revolver on the table, closes the drawer, and walks away. Then later, David Wilde comes out. At random points during the show, he fires the gun into the audience."

"So at every show six people die?" asks Lucy.

"It's not always six," Ted says. "Sometimes a bullet goes through someone and he gets more than six. Or sometimes people only get wounded." He laughs. "And this one time, Justin Carter, the leader of the boy band *Back Degrees,* went to a show and David Wilde comes out, sees him and just shoots the guy six times. It was great."

Lucy looks to James again and asks, "So, we could die tonight?"

He grins and says, "Babe, it's like a six in ten thousand chance."

Joan chimes in, "Hey, I look at it like fate. If it happens then it's meant to be."

Lucy ignores her comments. "Six in ten thousand, but there's still a chance we could die?"

James shrugs. "Sometimes you have to take chances in life."

Lucy looks down and is still pondering this idea in silence when the line begins moving forward.

"Finally," James says. He cranes his neck up as they pass under the lighted marquee.

The line moves quickly as people start filling the concert hall. As soon as Lucy enters the two large double doors to the building, the heat hits her. They continue to the security checkpoint. She hands a guard her ID, which he swipes through a machine. A green light flashes and she is allowed to pass to the next station. James goes through a metal detector and she follows. Then they approach a desk. Joan and Ted sign the forms and then pass through.

Lucy and James both approach the desk. He quickly signs his form while she starts reading hers.

"Um, excuse me?" she asks one of the guards.

"Yeah?" the guard says.

"What does this mean when it says the participant forfeits his or her life for the duration of the concert?"

"It's just legal stuff."

"Yeah, but what does it mean?"

James, impatient, says, "Just sign it, okay."

She looks at him for a few seconds and then picks up a pen, and signs her name. The blood-red ink disturbs her. She puts down the pen and James grabs her hand as they move past the security barrier.

Around them are various concession stands and merchandise booths. She sees Joan and Ted looking at shirts and posters. Behind her she hears someone talking really loudly, and turns to see that the cameraman and reporter from outside are now inside interviewing people. James also turns around to watch them.

A young, smiling girl wearing a David Wilde shirt says to the camera, "He's just so handsome! He's really great!"

"Yes, but what about the fact that he kills people at all his shows?" asks the reporter.

"Well, it's kind of like a spiritual experience because there's all this like life all around you and when someone in the audience dies it's like, like their life leaves their body and like spreads out into the other people in the crowd. It's really amazing!"

"What do you say to the people that say that David Wilde is only doing this because he can? That he's using his celebrity status to legally kill people?"

"Well, they don't understand him the way I do. He wouldn't do that."

A guy wearing another David Wilde shirt walking by stops and yells at the camera, "David Wilde rules!"

The reporter quickly moves from the girl to the new guy. "Excuse me, but why are you a fan?"

"Because he rocks!"

"Are you worried about getting shot tonight?"

"No way. My friend, who's like really good at math told me that, like, David Wilde usually shoots people towards the front, so like, if you're in the back then you're fine and there's a less than one percent chance of being shot and I'm in the very last row."

Lucy tugs on James's arm and says, nervously, "We have seats up front."

"Of course. I'm not going to a David Wilde show to sit in the back. Besides, the seats up front are cheaper."

"James, I'm not so sure about this."

"Babe, we've been through this already. If we're going to spend the rest of our lives together we need to share our interests. You'll see. You'll love the concert." He goes back to watching all the different people moving around the crowd.

Lucy looks at the reporter, who is talking to another person now.

"What is your name and what is your favorite David Wilde song?"

"My name is Gene, and I love the song *Try It.*"

"And why is that?"

"Uh, well, 'cause I've got my own band called *Violent Thunder* and I'm the guitarist so I like *Try It* because it's the ultimate guitar song."

The reporter faces the camera and says, "For those viewers at home who don't know, *Try It* is an entirely instrumental song. It's supposed to be the hardest electric guitar song in the world. In fact, David Wilde has said that the first person to be able to play it properly will get a million dollars." The reporter glances from the camera to Gene. "And how are you at the song?"

"Well, I can play it but it takes me too long. The song is three minutes, so, to get the money you have to play the song in three minutes or less. I'm down to twenty-seven minutes. But I'm getting there."

The reporter turns to the camera again. "A testament to how fast David Wilde truly is."

An announcement blares over the loud speakers: "You may enter into the main hall now. The show will be beginning shortly."

"I'll take that as my cue," says the reporter. "From KIS news, this is Bonnie Benatar reporting, live, at the David Wilde Revolver Concert."

"And we are out," says the cameraman.

Lucy gives James a worried look.

"Come on!" he says as he pulls her with him into the main hall.

They get to their seats, which are very close to the stage. She feels her pulse pick up frantically as all the other seats get filled.

A man in a black suit appears on stage carrying an old wooden table. Upon sight of him, the crowd begins cheering. The man is wearing white gloves that match his white hair. He places the table by the microphone stand. He opens the drawer and removes an object, which he places on the table. The crowd cheers again. Lucy is unable to see it but knows that it is the revolver. He then closes the drawer and walks off stage.

The stage lights dim and out comes David Wilde. The audience screams

with joy. His long hair partially obscures his face. He has an electric guitar with a strap around his neck and holds an acoustic guitar in his right hand. He leans the acoustic guitar against the old wooden table and adjusts the strap of his electric guitar. The crowd continues their cheering.

David Wilde carefully looks out at them. His gaze scans over the different people ready for his music. His eyes lock briefly with Lucy's, and he smiles.

He then leans toward the microphone and says, "Let's start this show with a bang!"

Picking up the revolver, he fires once out into the crowd. If anyone screams with pain or horror, it's drowned out by the cheers.

"Now who's ready for some music?" The crowd cheers even louder.

David Wilde gives the greatest musical performance Lucy Cooper has ever seen.

The sad songs make people openly weep. The uplifting songs make Lucy feel as if she's riding a roller coaster. He switches from electric to acoustic guitar depending on the song. One, called *Different Ways*, is first played electrically and then acoustically. Lucy loves it each time and has trouble deciding which one is better.

Despite her enjoyment, she is distracted by trying to keep track of the number of times David Wilde shoots out into the audience during the show. When he plays *Try It* she sees his hands move faster than she thought was possible. The song finishes and she cheers as excitedly as anyone.

He looks across the audience again. His eyes linger on Lucy as he says, "One more song."

The crowd collectively says, "Awww."

Wilde plays the song *Farewell*. When he finishes, they give him a roaring standing ovation. Lucy stands and roars with the crowd. He removes his guitar and places it by the old wooden table.

"That was amazing!" says James, clapping like crazy.

As the applause continues David Wilde locks eyes with Lucy. He maintains the gaze until the applause dies down. She is mesmerized by him. The applause eventually stops completely, with David Wilde still standing by the old wooden table.

The crowd just stares at him, as if expecting something more to happen. Encore? But he just stands there quietly staring at Lucy.

Lucy hears a guy behind her say, "Weird. I only counted five shots."

David Wilde picks up the revolver, points it in her direction, and fires.

James's entire chest seems to explode as the bullet hits him. The crowd starts cheering again. Now the show is truly over.

Lucy hovers over James's bleeding body. The concert hall starts emptying. She yells for help as the people leave. Most of them ignore her. Some take pictures with their cell phones. No one helps her. The concert hall empties except for Lucy and James.

"James, I'll go get someone, okay? Okay? James!"

His eyes are lifeless. A strange smile is permanently left on his face.

From behind her, a soft voice says, "Miss?"

She turns around and sees the man in the black suit with white gloves.

He calmly hands her a red rose.

"David Wilde was wondering if you would like to accompany him for dinner tonight."

Thick
Melanie-Jo Lee

During the three hour drive to Fossil Lake, Lana and Marcella did nothing but argue. At points heartfelt and loving, at others hurtful and bitter, both women refused to back down.

"I want to be married in my parents' back yard, Marce. You know this, you've always known this!" From their first date, Lana had been describing her dream wedding. It should not have been a surprise.

"I'd rather it just be us and James and Daniel at the JP's office, but when it comes down to it, that isn't the problem, Lana, and you know it." Marcella's hands gripped the wheel so tightly, the blood all but drained from her fingertips.

Lana did, but she tried anyway. "Your father seems to like me —"

"Like to watch you and Alexa go at it, probably in green Jell-O."

"She's your brother's wife!"

"She's that two-bit hooker my brother married, and ever since their wedding, my pig of a father's been undressing her with his mind."

Lana gagged. Sure, Alexa had worn a dress so short guests could see her underwear as she walked up the aisle, and so tight her generous chest all but spilled out. Hell, in one of the pictures, Marcella and Lana actually had spied nipple.

But would Marce's dad actually be thinking . . . ?

She had to admit, shuddering and swearing never to eat green Jell-O again, he probably was.

"I don't want my family involved," Marcella said. "They're vicious, manipulative and toxic. My mother calls *you* all sorts of horrible things, but she's fine with Grant and Alexa. Why? Because they're straight, that's why."

Lana remained silent.

"I know what you want, Lala," Marcella continued, using her pet name. "It's not that I don't, or that I don't care. We can have at it in your parent's back yard, with the barbeque and all your family if you want. I just do not want my family involved. They won't accept us, they won't accept you, and they certainly won't accept any marriage of mine unless it's done in front of Father Anthony at St. Michael's . . . and to a *man*."

*   *   *

In silence, they unpacked the car, shouldered their backpacks, grabbed a cooler each, and headed down the trail to their campsite.

Marcella's mind and emotions were in overdrive. She knew how Lana felt; Lana knew how *she* felt. She'd told Lana all about her parents, about how Father Anthony condemned her to hell when, at fifteen, she'd announced her interest in witchcraft . . . and again at eighteen when she stepped out of the closet in jeans, hiking boots and a flannel jacket.

Quite the butch you were, Marcella. And now you're quite the bitch. She sighed.

As they set up the tent, she attempted to start a conversation, but the fire-laced glare she was rewarded with shut her down. Deciding to let Lana stew in her own juices a while, she made some cursory excuse and headed down to the lake with her fishing gear.

The canoe was exactly where the ranger had said it would be. The water was calm, and the setting sun lingered just above the ridge. Good time to fish in peace, catch some dinner. Even the loon calling across the lake didn't break her concentration as she rowed to the center of the lake, fixed a lure to the line, and cast out.

*   *   *

Lana unrolled the sleeping bags and zipped them together. When she'd spread them on the floor of the tent, she paused, rocking back on her heels. Changing her mind, she unzipped the bags, and closed them up separately.

Even if we zip 'em back together later, for now this'll show her I mean business.

Knowing full well she was being childish, Lana finished prepping the tent. She grabbed the small cooler, and climbed the tree-ladder to the shelf built across a heavy branch. Similar shelves dotted the campground; safe places to put coolers or other valuables that campers didn't want wildlife scrounging through.

A glance at the lake showed her Marcella out there, sitting in the canoe. A twinge of guilt tightened her chest, but only briefly. She was right, and Marcella had to know that.

After a handful of tries, she got the fire going, thankful that the ranger had provided them with several nights worth of dry firewood. Lana hated chopping wood; that was more Marcella's thing. Just like fishing, camping, hunting . . .

. . . and the lack of real wedding plans . . .

Twigs snapped. The little hairs on the back of her neck stood up, and not just because the French-braid exposed them to the air. *Something* was behind her. She rose, spinning around to see . . . nothing. All she heard was insect chitter, the sound of the fire crackling, and an occasional bird call.

Chiding herself, she turned back to the fire. Soon she had two foil-wrapped potatoes slow-baking in the coals, perfect to have with whatever fish Marce brought from the lake.

She had been out there an awfully long time, though, and Lana felt a bit of worry crawl up from under her anger.

What's taking her so long? I'm starving . . .

SNAP.

She spun around again, this time catching a glimpse of a dark figure ducking behind a tree.

"Hello? Who's there, who are you?" At her feet was a stout length of firewood. She leaned over to pick it up, losing sight of the tree for a moment. When she straightened, she gasped, startled.

A man stood there, a man with long, stringy black hair and a dirty goatee. His eyes glittered with something that made Lana's skin crawl. His smile looked deranged. When he spoke, his voice was whiny and high-pitched, the words coming so fast they tumbled over each other.

"Hi. I'm Nick. I'm sleeping a couple campsites over. What are you doing?" He stepped forward, holding out his hand like he wanted to shake.

She took it, not able to control a shudder when his stubby fingers wrapped around hers. Rage flittered in his eyes, though he maintained his smile.

"Lana. I'm camping here with my fiancé." She eased back, trying to distance herself from his smell. *Has he ever showered? He smells like the guys' locker-room at work.*

"Oh. Where is he? Where's your food, you gonna just eat fish out here? There's nothing in that lake ya know, except monsters. You got anything to drink? I could kill a beer." The giggle that snorted from his nose was as bad as his voice.

"We didn't bring any alcohol. Marcella's out in the canoe, I'm sure she'll be back soon. You should probably go." Lana gripped the branch, pretending to lean on it like a walking stick.

"Wait, what did you say? Did you say *she*? What the fuck, you a fucking dykecunt?"

Lana backed up, stumbling over an exposed root. "Y-yes. No. No. I'm a lesbian."

"You *are* a fucking dykecuntqueer bitch! Well, I'll fucking be." He took another step toward her. When she raised the piece of wood as a threat, it only brought another gurgling giggle from the grimy man in front of her.

"You get away from here!" she cried. "*Now!* I've got a Sat-phone, I'll call the ranger and have you ejected from the park!"

"I was just being friendly, you bitch cuntlicker. Freak of nature, sinning whore. How dare you come here and ruin my place with your filthy sin? God's gonna smite you, bitch, if I don't first!" With that, he turned and fled back into the brush where he'd come from.

Lana stood, open-mouthed, until she heard the canoe scrape on rocks. Moments later, she caught sight of Marcella coming up the path.

"What the hell, Lana? What happened?"

Relating the incident brought on the shudders again. It took ten minutes for her to calm down, her arms wrapped around Marce's waist, finally feeling safe.

"He's gone now, love," Marcella said. "He's gone. I'm here. If he comes back, I'll lay it to him. He won't bug you again, okay?"

She nodded, turning her face up for a kiss. Moments later, Marcella was filleting a nice pike she'd pulled from the lake, and Lana was checking the potatoes. By the time they'd cleaned up, stoked the fire for the night, and gone to bed, the incident was well out of their minds.

Especially *after* they'd zipped the sleeping bags together again.

* * *

Outside of the campsite circle, hidden in a particularly thick patch of underbrush, Nick crouched, watching, as the silhouettes of the two women in the tent moved against each other.

His right hand went into his pants, rubbing, rubbing, rubbing . . until his breath caught in his throat and he grunted.

He'd made a mess in his pants. *Goddamn cuntlicking dykewhores will pay for that!*

He slunk away while their cries of pleasure echoed across the water.

*   *   *

Marcella was gone when Lana woke up, having left a note on the tent flap to tell her she'd headed out fishing again, hoping to get a walleye for breakfast. That made Lana laugh out loud.

A walleye? What kind of name is that for a fish?

Deciding a fresh start was in order for the day, she pulled her hair into a ponytail, grabbed the nature-friendly soap and her towel, and walked down to the private beach in her swimsuit. She fought the urge to squeal until she was shoulder deep in water so cold it made her teeth chatter, and pulled the straps of her suit to her waist for a quick wash.

It shouldn't be so hard to plan the wedding, she thought as she scrubbed. *I just really want her family there.*

But Lana knew she'd give in eventually. She always did.

The cold had either numbed her body or she'd become used to it, so she ducked under to rinse herself off, then swam out a little way.

When she surfaced and brushed the water from her eyes, *he* was there.

The grimy man from the night before stood on the edge of the water, staring out at her. She wasn't sure, but it looked like he was grinning far more widely than a human should be able to. And he had his hand down his pants.

Her heart skipped a beat. Paddling in a frantic circle, she looked across the lake, but didn't see the canoe. She panicked. *"MARCELLA!?"*

As she splashed back around to face the shore, Lana saw he was gone. She stayed out in the water what had to be another twenty minutes anyway, until she was shivering so violently she didn't think she could swim, let alone walk. Finally, she made her way to shore. Wrapping her towel around her waist, she ran up the path to the tent.

She stripped out of the wet swimsuit, threw on a pair of yoga pants and a sweatshirt, and slid into the sleeping bag to wait safe inside until Marcella returned.

"Babe . . ." said Marcella, finding her there a short time later.

Lana tried to talk, but fell apart. Marcella crawled into the sleeping bag with her and held her while she waited for Lana to calm the emotional storm and tell her what had happened.

Marcella held her a few minutes more, then rose to leave the tent. "You need something warm inside to help with the cold. I'll leave the flaps open and be right outside at the fire, okay?"

Lana nodded, curling on her side to watch as Marcella prepared breakfast.

Soon, she was presented with a bowl of hot oatmeal and a mug of steaming coffee, which she took gratefully.

"Maybe we should call the ranger?" Lana asked, after she'd warmed through and calmed down. "I know it was stupid, going down there on my own, but I . . . I guess I just forgot. We've never had a problem here before."

"Honey, we're supposed to be alone out on this side of the lake. The ranger said there was no one else out here. I'm going to call him, yes, if only to bitch him out about that. But, I don't think this guy is here legally. I think he's one of those what do you call 'ems. . . squatters. Crazy homeless shits that live in the forest until reality finally catches them and throws them in the looneybin."

Lana nodded, sipping the coffee held tight between her hands. "I just want him to go away. This was supposed to be our vacation, our stress-free getaway. A no crazies time." She smiled weakly. "Hot sex in the woods time."

Marcella winked. "I think we had that covered last night, but I might need a refresher . . ."

Tempting as it was, Lana shook her head, her smile stronger now. "Later, lover. I want to go on that hike today, get some more photos, remember? I need twenty more for my last assignment, and then I'm done!"

Next year at this time, she would have her own show at the gallery in the city. Inspired by that, Lana stood, stooped, and ducked out of the tent. Her stomach fluttered when she thought she saw a familiar dark shape in the woods, but she realized it was just a shadow.

Play of light. Just like my show will be.

She was determined to push all thoughts of Icky-Nicky out of her mind. She would not allow some stranger, some creepy twit, to ruin her weekend with Marcella.

"All right, babe, if you're sure?"

Lana turned to Marcella, smile bright and shining, and snapped a picture before she could argue. "Oh, I'm quite sure. Grab your stuff and let's get moving."

*　　*　　*

He watched, waiting patiently. He hadn't meant to get caught at the water this morning, but what was done was done. Now he had plans; once the bitchdykes were gone, he was going to mess with their stuff. Maybe leave them a little message.

The bull-dyke and the crybaby were out of sight when he finally edged his way out of the brush and into their campsite. He kicked the wood around, just for starters, then pulled five of the ten boards for the ladder off the tree, and threw them in the remains of the fire. That took a bit of time; he wasn't as in shape as he'd thought. It was worth it though, they wouldn't be able to get to their food.

He began mumbling out loud, giggles interspersing with the inane babble. Finally, pictures of Lana's body in his mind, he pulled his pants and shorts down, masturbating violently until he spunked all over their little bed.

A man is what they need, someone to teach them better. I'm gonna fuck that little crybaby until she bleeds.

Ten minutes later, he ejaculated again, crying this time, thinking of the mother that had abandoned him so long ago.

*   *   *

They stopped on the side of the trail for a late lunch, cheese and crackers complemented with cold water from a spring. It smelled a little, like minerals and salt, but it tasted wonderful. Lana wanted to go on hiking, even though she had her shots in. Marcella wanted to go back, so they wouldn't be caught in the woods in the dark.

"Even with the path, we could get lost out here," she said. "We didn't bring flashlights. And if there are bears out here, I don't even have the pepper spray. It's back at the site."

Lana raised an eyebrow. "Really? You?"

Marcella flushed. "Yeah. I was distracted by your ass." That caught Lana off guard, she saw. So, smiling wickedly, she went on. "Babe, I want to get you back to the tent so I can slide your clothes off, run my hands over your body, and . . ."

"And . . . ?"

"We'll have to go back to see what comes next." She set off at a sprint, leaving Lana behind, laughing and calling foul.

Marcella only made it a couple hundred yards before slowing down to catch her breath. She stopped at the next picnic area to wait for Lana, and finally saw the top of her head crest the little hill.

"Took you long enough!"

"I wasn't running. And I was taking pictures as I went along." She sat next to Marcella on the picnic table.

They sat in silence for a bit, listening to the birds and insects do their bird and insect business. Soon, Lana was nuzzling Marcella's neck, and she turned to slide her hand into Lana's shirt. After some more easy flirting, Marcella slid down, kneeling between Lana's legs on the bench, easing her onto her back across the table. She pushed Lana's shirt over her belly to expose her breasts, trailing kisses across the smooth skin. Circling her tongue around an already-distended nipple, she moved her hand to rub between her lover's legs.

Lana's hips rose, as did her moans. Shifting her focus, Marcella tugged at the yoga pants, drawing them down over her hips and thighs. As she wasn't wearing underwear, Marce got right to business.

Neither of them paid attention to the noises coming from the shrubs behind the water pump, but when stones and chunks of bark and sticks began hitting them, they jumped. Lana yanked her pants up while Marce pulled the shirt down, and they ducked for cover.

"God sees you, you bitches! *Cuntlickingmotherfuckingdykes,* you'll be sorry!" More stones pelted down on them, one hitting Marcella close to the eye. "You'll burn, bitch, you'll burn! He'll start with your snatch, fire you up good and proper!"

Marcella leaped up on the picnic table, yelling violently. She caught a glimpse of Lana's creeper running away as fast as his stumble-bum legs could carry him. "That's right, you little coward, you fucking worm, you better run!"

"Marce, let's just get back to the site, okay? I don't feel safe now."

"Okay, babe. And when we get there, I'm calling the ranger."

*   *   *

The ranger couldn't come out to investigate until morning. Since it was already getting dark, they reluctantly made the decision to stay one more night.

Marcella built a fire while Lana went into the tent to change. At her sharp squeal, Marce pulled the flap back so hard the corner tore. "What is it? What happened?"

Lana held a hand over her mouth, gagging. Marcella noticed the smell then, and saw what Lana was pointing at.

Cum. All over their sleeping bags, spread around like some twisted fuck had rolled in it. *And the smell!* It smelled of more than just cum, it smelled *bad.* Like apricots that had been left to rot in milk.

Her own gorge rose as she pulled the ruined sleeping bags out of the tent. "We've still got the blankets, right?" She hoped so; she didn't fancy a trip back to the car – in the dark and with that creepoid who knew where – especially if it meant leaving Lana alone.

"I've got one in my pack, and there are two in the tent. I don't think there's any of that crap on them." Lana held them up so Marcella could inspect them.

"Nope, they're clean. Okay, we'll use these tonight, and tomorrow morning – no matter what – after the ranger gets here, we're heading out."

"I just want to go home, Marce. This wasn't how our week was supposed to go."

"I know, babe. I know." Marcella gathered Lana into her arms again, squeezing her briefly before grabbing the sleeping bags and jamming them into a garbage bag. "We're not even going to take these home. We'll get new ones, doubles. Maybe we'll even ditch the tent, what do you think? Get a new tent after the wedding? We'd talked about it before –"

Thunk. Her world went black.

*   *   *

Lana saw the branch connect with the back of Marcella's head just a second too late to warn her. A scream caught in her throat. A dirty, stubby-fingered hand grabbed her ponytail and yanked her backwards.

"You filthy little rugmunching bitch, you're going to love my dick rammed into your squeaky tight cunt. You're gonna swallow my spunk and love it. You're gonna grind your ass into me and beg for more. *I'm gonna fuck you straight, cunt!*" Nick whisper-grunted into her ear, humping at her ass like a dog. The smell of his breath, his clothes, everything, made her gag again.

He spun her around and pushed her to her knees, waggling something she supposed was his penis. The limp piece of flesh barely poked out past the fly of his jeans. The smell of it . . . the odor of piss and sweat and rotten fruit and death; finally she *did* throw up.

"You pussysucking whore!" he screamed, kicking her in the stomach, knocking the wind out of her.

Lana lay on the ground, cradling her ribs, trying to force her diaphragm to work. Between gasps of air, she was still retching, water mixed with bile making an encore appearance as drool down her chin. As she struggled to breathe, he kicked her over so she was on her belly, arms trapped beneath her, then grabbed at her pants.

This spurred her into action. Breathing or not, scrambled away through the leaves. A knee landed on her kidney, the burst of pain a rainbow of colors behind closed eyelids. Finally, she was able to scream.

"Shut your dirty cakehole, cunt. You're gonna take this like the man you want to be." Nick repositioned himself, knees against her thighs, one hand on the back of her head, the other still trying to pull her pants down, humping at her ineffectually.

She squirmed, trying to get away from his poking, semi-hard choad. The more she fought, the limper he got, it seemed. It wasn't until she screamed at him that his mother would be ashamed of him did his flaccidity turn around. Suddenly he was rock hard, still too small to actually get anywhere near her back entrance, but it disgusted her even more.

It also made her laugh.

Furious, he flipped her over to attack her from the front. His little fists pounded at her belly, her crotch, her thighs, assaults easily warded off as Lana continued to laugh. He spit on her face and attempted to bite her nipples through her shirt. This fresh attack with teeth renewed her anger; she stopped laughing and struck at him, scratching and punching as best she could with him straddling her, but he seemed impervious to the blows.

Somehow, he managed to get his knee between her thighs, and both her wrists into one of his hands.

"My mother left me to live with my grandparents when I was just a kid!" he growled, fumbling his jeans to mid-thigh. "She has nothing to do with this, she wouldn't care anyway, she hates dykes just as much as I do!" He'd maintained his erection through the beating, but still had nowhere to go with her pants covering everything.

Lana laughed again.

Nick began to grunt in little squeals like a pig, still thrusting incompetently, ass bopping up and down, apparently thinking he was actually succeeding in raping her. "Mama would be proud of me now!"

Suddenly he stopped, frozen above her. His eyes nearly bugged out of their sockets. He shrieked, face twisting into a visage of pure terror. Trying to leap up, he tripped and plowed face-first into the dirt.

The acrid stench of burning hair reached Lana's nose. She pushed herself up on her elbows, and saw Marcella – the piece of wood Lana had herself raised against Nick the night before – in her hand. Tonight, though, its end had been on fire.

"It'll hurt to shit for a long time to come, won't it, you greasy little retard?" Marcella's voice was low, simmering with rage. "Who the fuck do you think you are, attacking us like this, trying to attack Lana like this? What kind of man are you?"

Seeing Nick dancing back and forth from foot to foot, ass smoldering, Lana's giggles returned, unable to help herself despite the situation.

Marcella stuck the end of the tree limb back into the fire, bringing it to a blaze again. "Oh. Stupid question. You're not a *man*. You're a little boy looking for your mama. Aren't you?"

Once again, when his mother was brought into the conversation, the smallest dick Lana had ever seen rose to its limited attention. She burst out in howls of mirth. "You really *are* a mama's boy, aren't you, Nicky? Widdle Nicky need a diaper? How about a bottle? Oh, no, I bet your mama *breastfed* you, didn't she?"

Lana held out her hand to Marcella, who helped her get to her feet. They turned to Nick. It looked as though he were about to make another foul-mouthed remark, but thought better of it as he regarded them.

"You should never mess with lesbians, Nicky," Lana said.

"Especially lesbian *witches*," Marcella added. "We have short tempers."

Smiling now, the two women advanced on him, backing him onto the path that led to the lake. Each step he took, he winced and whimpered. Lana imagined it hurt, *burned like fire* perhaps, each time his ass cheeks met. He stumbled into the water.

Marcella and Lana followed.

Nick went waist-deep before he began pleading for them to leave him alone, to stop bullying him. Couldn't they see he was scared?

Of course Lana could see he was scared. About as scared as she had been the first time he'd grabbed at her. She took Marcella's hand in hers and together they raised their fists high.

For a moment, all was silent across the lake except for Icky-Nicky's sniffling. They watched as he took another step backward, right into the center of the full moon's reflection.

Now.

"Aradia, look upon on the one caught in your gaze. He has harmed your daughters, he has defiled your world. We ask you, bright shining one, take vengeance on his flesh, his mind, his spirit."

The water swirled around the wanna-be rapist. As it touched his skin, it made a *squicking* sound. His face practically shone in the moonlight, and Lana saw his confusion turn to fear and then to horror.

Speaking as one, they stepped forward once more. "*Socraigh ár biotáillí saor in aisce bheannaithe, a bheith!*"

He turned, trying to swim away, but the water grew heavy around him, pulling at him, sucking him in. With each useless stroke he took, it became thicker and thicker, until it was nearly solid. His arms were trapped at his sides. As he opened his mouth in a panicked scream, the water surged over his face. It poured down his throat, pudding-like, cold.

His body convulsed, trying to cough it out. The liquid substance invaded him. Each small amount he managed to expel was quickly replaced. Waves slapped violently at his face. His head thrashed back and forth in a struggle for breath. His eyes bulged. Water flooded his nose and ears.

"Mmmpgh! *MMMMPGH!*"

Standing on the shore, safe from Aradia's rage, Lana and Marcella watched as the small, greasy little man was sucked under. They stood and watched until the water became supple again, and Aradia's face had traveled away from them.

Then they returned to their campsite and made love in Her name.

The Ziggurat of Skulls
Joshua Dobson

Squatting in the center of the abandoned city deep in the heart of the jungle, the mountainous step pyramid dwarfs the surrounding vine-choked ruins. For some mysterious reason, the vines and banyan trees devouring the ruins refuse to so much as approach the cyclopean ziggurat, therefore the details of its construction are more apparent than those of the crumbling structures that encircle it. From a distance the massive pyramid appears to be constructed of small round stones of some many-hued, crystalline rock, but as the gargantuan temple looms nearer one can make out the eye sockets, the nasal cavities, the curving mandibles and rows of shining teeth they house.

Petrifaction has turned the skulls to crystal, (or rather petrifaction has replaced the original skulls with near perfect crystalline copies) supplanting the yellows, whites, and browns of aging bone with whirling rainbows of pink, red, blue, purple, yellow, and orange that glitter brilliantly in the glaring tropical sun.

The riot of brilliance that is the lower levels of the ziggurat of petrified skulls eventually gives way to the monochrome upper levels, stained the glistening reddish hue of the ordure deposited by the crown of carrion birds that halos the lightning lashed apex of the pyramid. (Though the horde of winged scavengers that endlessly circles the top of the temple of bones may seem immense it is merely the meager remnants of the once vast flock whose beaks flensed the flesh from the skulls.)

The ziggurat of skulls bears the marks, most in the form of scorches and burns, of repeated attempts to destroy it, but the attacks of the temple's enemy or enemies were meaningless in the face of the pyramid's vastness.

The fossilization of the skulls of the lower levels was the result of one such attack. Legend holds that forces hostile to the pyramid contrived to bury it. Reports vary as to whether this attempted entombment was to be accomplished by way of a torrential flood or an apocalyptic earthquake. However, all reports agree that the burial was a failure, the obscuring agent, whether water or earth, being volumetrically insufficient to swallow the immense ziggurat. Perhaps the forces hostile to the ziggurat realized the futility of their attempted entombment, and the flood waters receded, or perhaps the pyramid somehow dug itself free of the shallow grave endeavoring to devour it. Whatever the case, when the obscuring agent disappeared, it was found that the skulls had fossilized. There are some who say this petrifaction represents the temple growing stronger, armoring itself to gird against future hostilities. Others insist the petrifaction was the work of the pyramid's enemies and was meant to stain the temple with brilliant hues such as poisonous organisms wear to advertise their lethality.

The fossilized skulls that make up the bottom step of the ziggurat were quarried from australopithecines, both robust (with their mohawk-like saggital crests) and smooth-domed graciles. Some of the skulls found here on the lower tiers represent species completely unknown to science. Whatever their species, all these apes had smaller brains than those of the species comprising the genus *Homo* and were therefore much easier for that which began construction of the pyramid to catch, with the result that the lowest tier of the ziggurat is by far the tallest of the thirteen steps, stretching hundreds of cubits into the air.

One who places their hand against the wall of fossilized australopithecus skulls at ground level will be able to dimly feel vibrations rumbling through the walls of the temple. Some say it's just the bone wheel endlessly turning, some say it's that which began construction of the pyramid snoring as it slumbers in a bottomless pit beneath the ziggurat of skulls.

The only access to the labyrinthine guts of the ziggurat is via a door at its apex and the only access to this solitary door is by way of a spiraling ramp that ascends the temple level by level from base to summit. (Though the upper levels are booby trapped, the architect who constructed these lower levels had no use for such trifles.)

The first petrified *Homo habilis* skull appears halfway up the second tier of the titan ziggurat. *Homo erectus* and *Home ergaster* begin to appear towards the bottom of the fourth step. *Homo heidelbergensis*/*Homo rhodesiensis* occupy the fifth step and the lower portion of the sixth. The ziggurat of skulls was a little over six and a half stories high when the first Neanderthals fell prey to the mysterious architect that constructed the lower levels.

The tremors that tremble through the temple steadily increase in intensity as one nears the middle of the pyramid. Here, in the center of the sixth step, the shuddering vibrations are so forceful they sometimes knock climbers from the narrow spiraling causeway that ascends the ziggurat. One need not place their hand against the wall of Neanderthal skulls to feel the wheel in the center of the temple rumbling as it revolves; one can feel it in their bones.

The shudders lessen as one ascends higher up the ziggurat to the seventh step, near the top of which, the first *Homo sapien* skull quarried for the pyramid grins out at the empty sky.

Numerous rumors hold the ziggurat's mysterious architect responsible for the extinction of a good number of the species represented amidst the skulls that form the walls of the temple. Other innuendos attribute creations as well as extinctions to that which built the lower levels of the ziggurat of skulls. Proponents of this theory insist that many of the species whose skulls we tread upon as we climb the ziggurat were created (or at least modified) within the osseous walls of the temple before the architect released them into the world as one might release game into a game park. Even those who refuse to believe the architect created humanity will concede that the mysterious builder may have provided a nudge here and there along the path of evolution.

The transition from species to species in the masonry of the ziggurat is not clean and definite with the appearance of one species precluding the later appearance of earlier more primitive species. However it's clear that who or whatever built the lower, pre-human levels of the ziggurat loved *Homo sapiens* from its first taste of them. And this love was not unrequited.

Homo sapiens were unlike any previous quarry the architect had hunted. Whereas previous species of hominids had fought tooth and nail (as the many chipped and/or broken teeth of the skulls attest) against the subsuming of their skulls into the temple, *Homo sapiens* (some of them anyway) willingly submitted themselves to the power of the ziggurat and its mysterious architect, becoming thralls of the pyramid before which they prostrated themselves.

Somewhere around this time, the ruinous city that surrounds the temple sprang up.

At some point something happened, something terrible no doubt. This is as precise a statement as one can honestly make about the matter. Some insist the mysterious enemy or enemies who constantly tried to thwart the architect of the lower levels succeeded in launching an assault of unprecedented fury that resulted in the wounding or maiming of that which built the lower steps of the ziggurat. And then there are those, and I count myself among them, who believe that the worship inflicted on the architect by man left the mysterious builder, fat and lazy, pampered and weak. (Some say it was this weakness that allowed the hostile forces to wound the architect.)

For whatever reason, the architect was forced to retreat from the world. Some say it went back from whence it came. Others insist it is still here only sleeping, waiting and dreaming beneath the ziggurat of skulls in a pit whose mouth its servitors sealed with a gate made of bones. And there are others still who claim that which built the lower levels was killed in the last assault launched by it enemies. ("There is no god but the wheel" proponents of this theory are often heard to insist.)

When that which built the lower levels ran away, went to sleep, or died, responsibility for the ziggurat fell to its human servants. Exactly how tall the ziggurat was when construction duties passed from the hands of the mysterious architect (if hands it had) to those of man is not known.

Many experts contend that the levels of the ziggurat stained red by the waste of the carrion birds are precisely those that were raised by the hand of man. The carrion birds, some insist, came only after man took over management of the temple; birds, like all other forms of life save man, shunned the ziggurat of skulls when that which began its creation was still in residence (and/or awake.)

The blanket of bird droppings may or may not be exclusive to the manmade steps, but it's well known that the booby traps (which begin atop the ninth step) are most certainly confined to the human-authored portions of the pyramid.

Ascending the lower levels of the ziggurat is merely grueling and tedious, but from here on up, the way is fraught with numerous perils. The air at these heights is so thin it's hard for one to breathe. The lightning that lives in the clouds above the rain forest finds the pyramid irresistible and constantly licks at it, like a tongue compulsively probing a sore tooth. The raging gusts of wind that buffet these heights conspire with the slippery blanket of bird guano to hurl pilgrims over the side of the ziggurat. The road of bone that spirals up the ziggurat of skulls is miles wide in certain spots and no more than a guano-slicked ribbon of bones mere cubits wide in others. In certain spots, almost all of which cling to the dark side of the ziggurat, (eternally veiled in shadow due to the pyramid's orientation relative to the sun) the tapering off of the road occurs quite suddenly. And then there are the booby traps. Stepping on the wrong bone can lead to one being dropped into an inescapable oubliette, crushed beneath huge balls of bone that roll down the ramp, skewered and/or slashed by blades and/or spikes that suddenly shoot from walls and/or floors, or killed in any number of ways by even stranger mechanisms.

In addition to the booby traps, the elaborate labyrinth of blood gutters that spirals down from the sacrificial altars atop the pyramid are everywhere in evidence on these upper steps. At certain places, if one places an ear against a wall of bone at just the right spot, one can feel the warmth within and hear the roaring blood rushing through the osseous walls. There are also fountains of a sort, where blood pours from the eye sockets and nostril cavities of the skulls only to be collected in other gutters that channel it back into the walls of bone to continue its descent to the heart of the temple.

The labyrinthine network of blood gutters and the immense wheel of bone which it serves are humanity's greatest contribution to the ziggurat of skulls. (Unless one believes those who say humans didn't really build the blood wheel, rather that its construction was already underway when the architect disappeared and humans merely completed their master's work.)

At some point, the human servants of the ziggurat of skulls divided themselves into two castes. The primary responsibility of the higher 'priestly' caste was to perform the sacrifices in order to provide provender for the slumbering architect and skulls with which to grow the ziggurat. The duties of the lower 'slave' caste were to have their heads chopped off and to perform the menial labor associated with building new steps atop the ziggurat with the skulls of their brothers and sisters.

The skulls which were given willingly to the ziggurat are identifiable by the trepanation holes bored into their foreheads. Both slaves and priests drilled holes in their skulls (to allow that which built the lower levels to enter into them some claim.) The priests distinguished themselves from the slaves by way of binding the squishy soft, not yet fully formed skulls of their infants in order to elongate their craniums.

The thirteenth level of the ziggurat is built entirely from the deformed skulls of priests. There are conflicting theories regarding the meaning of this fact. One school of thought holds that some vague doom (perhaps brought about by the ancient and ever-scheming enemies of the ziggurat) befell the people of the city in the shadow of the pyramid. The priests, proponents of this theory insist, offered their skulls as sacrifices in an attempt to ward off the doom. Those who believe this hypothesis say the priests knew the doom was coming and built the elaborate mechanisms of the temple in preparation for a day when the humanoid servants of the pyramid would cease to exist.

Adherents of a conflicting theory refuse to speculate on why the priests built the intricate network of clockwork gears (except perhaps to say they may have been bidden to do so by their slumbering master). But once the mechanisms were built, proponents of the latter theory insist, so impressed were the priests with their handiwork that they considered it the highest of honors to be devoured it. And then there are others still who insist the priests were somehow accidentally devoured by their machines. Yet another school of thought holds that a schism amongst the priests split them into two sects and bloody warfare erupted between those who remained loyal to the architect and those who, believing the architect dead, worshipped the wheel. (The wheel is older than the ziggurat that houses it, those who kneel before the wheel insist.) The internecine squabble theory is highly controversial in part because many people find the very notion of enmities between the wheel and the architect deeply and profoundly offensive. They are one in the same, or at least in close collusion with one another.

Whatever the cause, the priests are all long dead, and with them died whatever esoteric knowledge of the ziggurat and its enigmatic architect they may have possessed.

As we near the summit of the ziggurat of skulls, I'm afraid, dear reader, that I have a confession to make. Earlier when I described the ruinous city that huddles around the base of the pyramid I used the word "abandoned," an apt word for describing the city but not the temple itself. For you see, the descendants of the ziggurat's slaves still dwell here. The breeding chambers deep inside the pyramid continue to spawn slaves. Whether or not these devolved specimens, albinos with shiny pink eyes, completely hairless bodies, and squishy cartilaginous bones actually qualify as human is not so clear, the shape of their soft jelly-like skulls appearing closer to those of *Homo floresiensis* than those of *Homo sapiens*.

Though traces of an unfinished fourteenth step, no more than a single rank of skulls high, can be found atop the temple, no new construction has taken place in eons. The devolved slave spawn have long since forgotten the techniques of osseous architecture given to their ancestors by that which built the lower levels of the ziggurat. Nor are their cartilaginous bones, soft gelatinous things prone to skull-rot, suitable for construction purposes.

Though construction has ground to a halt, the sacrificial altars atop the ziggurat of skulls are still in operation. The temple is essentially a giant machine that runs on blood. The blood of the slaves beheaded on the altars courses down through the raveled maze of blood gutters until it spills upon the immense wheel of bones in the exact center of the temple. As the blood wheel turns, it drives an elaborate system of gears (whose teeth are made from real teeth). These gears in turn power the automatons atop the temple, clockwork priests made of carved bone, whose rusty, heavily nicked blades lop the heads off the slaves and set the blood flowing down the gutters. What's left of the bloodless bodies of the beheaded, after the carrion birds have claimed their due, drops down chutes lined with spinning blades that grind the remains up into a paste which provides nourishment for the inhabitants of the breeding pits. The severed heads that used to be collected, stripped of skin, and placed atop the ziggurat, now simply roll from the pyramid and splatter against the bones below to be feasted upon by carrion birds.

If the blood wheel were to cease turning the entire world would end, or so say those who kneel before the wheel. The universe's entire existence is predicated on a thin trickle of blood spiraling down a pyramid of bones. And this flow of blood is dependent upon the blades of the automatons shearing the heads from the devolved slave spawn queued up before the altars patiently awaiting their deaths. The deteriorating blades that hold the world together are magnets for the lighting that lashes the top of the temple. These rusted, heavily nicked bits of steel sometimes require upwards of three strokes to slash the head from a sacrifice. If the bones of the devolved slave spawn were not so soft and pulpy the whole machine would have broke down long ago.

Although the devolved slave spawn have a primitive vocal apparatus and even a crude language, they retain no cultural memories of their forebears. They know nothing of the mysterious architect who constructed the lower steps of the ziggurat. Nor do they seem to know much at all about the priests or the blood wheel, nor why they queue up before the sacrificial altars to offer their heads to automatons that run on blood.

Some slave spawn escape from the breeding hives and wander the guts of the temple. These escaped slaves never dare leave the pyramid in which they were born, but they often linger at the edifice's only opening, gazing out with their pink albino eyes at the world beyond the ziggurat of skulls. All we know of the interior of the temple of bones derives from the strangulated whispers of escaped slaves. From these fugitive slaves, one capable of deciphering their primitive tongue hears whispered accounts of strange happenings inside the ziggurat of skulls.

Many of these accounts concern a vast black pit beneath the bottom of the ziggurat. A pit so deep as to be, for all intents and purposes, bottomless, into which the blood of the sacrifices trickles after the wheel has drunk its fill. The pit, the escaped slaves contend, is covered by a gate of bones which is bound to the blood wheel by a chain of gears.

Recently, if the reports of the escaped slaves are to be believed, the cyclopean gate of bones atop this bottomless pit has begun to slowly inch open.

Apartment B
Stinky Cat

I don't expect you to believe a word of this.

In fact, I wish it weren't true. Four years later, there are still nights I lie awake in bed, unable to escape the memories of the horror I encountered in Apartment B.

I wish I could tell you just what it was. Maybe identifying and understanding whatever it was could help me forget about it, but I have never been able to offer an even somewhat satisfying explanation for what I saw that night.

Consequently, I hold out little hope of you believing me when I say that every word of this is true.

It began when I rented a room in a dilapidated home with a couple of friends I'd met on Craigslist. I could hardly afford my share of the rent, as I was barely scraping by on my disability check. But the price was right, no background check needed, and, honestly, I had nowhere else to go.

It was a great place though, an imposing Victorian row house, tall and narrow with a turret rising three stories above the street. Just seeing the weathered brick façade, stained almost black by a century of Chicago pollution, gave me a chill. Even on the warmest day, that building seemed to have a cold wind blowing through it. For lack of a better word, there was a *heaviness* in the air – an oppressive atmosphere over the whole place.

Now, I've neglected to tell you the really unnerving part. Directly across the street was the old Resurrection Cemetery, infamous for its many reported hauntings – too numerous to recount here. Needless to say, I must have heard them all before I moved into the house, so whenever I looked through that rusty black iron fence through the forest of tombstones, I expected to see Resurrection Mary darting between the monuments. The thought of seeing her, even for a second, terrified me, but I couldn't help looking. I'd find myself transfixed on that landscape for hours. Conveniently enough, our apartment overlooked it, and I came to memorize it from my worn-out chair in the living room, located on the second floor of that turret.

My roommate Meghan cleaned bedpans in a nearby nursing home, and my other roommate Dave stocked shelves in a bookstore. I really didn't see much of them because they got up early and went to work before I got out of bed. Their alarm clocks were really loud and annoying. When you're disabled, you really don't have anywhere to be, so I'd stay up late writing and sleep until noon. This gave me plenty of time to work on my novel when they were either asleep or at work, but I have to admit I spent most of my days staring out that living room window, scanning the graves for any anomalous movement.

Sometimes I'd waste so much time this way that I was barely able to post hate-filled rants on my blog or send death threats to idiots who one-star my books on Amazon. I knew they'd never even read my books before rating them because I hadn't sold any yet. Between my reputation and my disability, you can understand why I still haven't finished that novel.

Directly across the room from this window was the kitchenette, and between it and the living room was a small round table with a chandelier hanging over it in what passed for a dining room. A door in the kitchen area led to a hall, down which could be found the bedrooms and bathroom. Since my bedroom was in the very back, a windowless space barely big enough for my bed, I usually set up my laptop at the kitchen table.

I think it was a Monday night more or less like any other that Dave joined me at the table with a fish taco, a can of PBR, and a Ouija board.

"Hey, whatcha writing?" he asked.

"It's a novel about a monster living in Lake Michigan."

"Like the Creature from the Black Lagoon?"

"No, a big sea creature like the Loch Ness Monster."

"That seems a little implausible, Ricky. Don't you think it would be kind of hard for a monster that big to hide in such a busy lake with twelve million people living along its shores and all the commercial fishing, tourist steamers, and . . ."

"Trust me. It will terrify you."

"I dunno. It sounds kinda stupid."

"Shut up, you pile of baby batter that should have been aborted!"

Meghan sat next me, trying to calm me, "It's okay, Ricky. He's joking."

By this time, Dave was having a good laugh at my expense. "Move that crap out of my way, so I can show you something that will really terrify."

I closed my laptop and placed it under my chair as he unfolded his Ouija board and put the pointer on top.

"What the hell is that?" I asked.

"It's our Ouija board. We use it to contact the dead," said Meghan.

"I don't mess with that sort of stuff. I'm a Christian," I told her.

"You don't go to church, and I'm pretty sure Jesus wouldn't approve of you making death threats to people all day long," Dave answered. "Have you read your blog? I'm pretty sure you're not a Christian."

"It's okay, Ricky. It's just for fun," said Meghan.

Dave instructed us to put our fingers on the pointer and concentrate. He asked the board, "Is there a spirit with us?"

The pointer pointed to the word "YES" on the board.

Meghan asked, "Can you give us a sign?"

It was then one of the bulbs in the chandelier burned out, plunging the room into somewhat less brightness.

My body stiffened. I staggered backwards from my chair, tripping over my laptop and crashing to the floor. The collapse stunned me. Writhing on the linoleum, I whimpered uncontrollably, unable to rise, helpless to flee. Suffering as I was from a disabled pinky toe for which I got a monthly check, I was powerless to resist the dark force which had made its presence felt through that single light bulb.

I could see only blurry shapes through my tear-filled eyes. I could hear nothing over what sounded like a young girl sobbing.

How long I lay there I don't know. Meghan and Dave were apparently so horrified they were unable to rise from their seats. They were frightened so senseless they even appeared to be laughing and pointing at me.

I have no idea how Meghan managed to summon the strength to walk to the kitchen cabinet and return to the table with a little light bulb. With Herculean fortitude, she twisted the dark light bulb while battling the invisible demons which were undoubtedly tormenting her. Then, as if by magic, she screwed the new bulb into the socket, flooding the room with light slightly brighter than the light had been before she replaced the bulb.

Having defeated the demonic entity, my savior laughed with joy and called out, "Get up, you pussy. It was just a burnt out light bulb." She was obviously delirious, since we had no cat.

Trying to take his mind off the terrors we had just experienced, Dave bravely changed the subject to my writing. "How do you expect to be a horror writer when you're afraid of your own shadow?"

Though his question puzzled me, I appreciated his attempt to distract us from the awful scene which had just unfolded.

Having survived this inexplicable and traumatic experience, we seldom spoke of it afterwards. In fact, my brave roommates usually pretended to have forgotten all about it. Unable to accept the true terror of what happened that night, Dave sometimes even pretended that I had scared myself and that the light bulb had somehow burned out just because it was old.

Though I have studied page after page of Wikipedia, I have never been able to explain what happened to that demon-possessed light bulb in Apartment B.

Pretty Girl
Deb Eskie

Everyone wants to be the pretty girl.

We are conditioned to strive for beauty from our earliest years. Our parents, with the best intentions, tell us just how pretty we are when we are two years old, and they accentuate that innocent doll-like adorability with bows, lace, and light pink lipstick so we can make ourselves up like Mommy.

But what we didn't realize, at that oh so tender age, was that Mommy used makeup to hide her true face, her sad face, a face that struggled to maintain the very same smoothness of youth it possessed when she first met her husband, and they were in love, and he paid her the least bit of attention. My mother saw the opposite of beauty as death, and she wanted me to know love and experience joy, and love and joy, of course are the benefits of being attractive. Without attractiveness there could be no fulfillment, no reason for existence.

Thankfully, I was pretty; a dimpled-face cutie-pie with long blond hair that my mother enjoyed styling into different dos. I was primped and curled and danced onstage in baby beauty pageants. It didn't matter how much I cried or stamped my foot, Mommy never listened. Those pageants were important to her and my success was hers as well.

So I did what was expected of me. I dressed how beauty queens are supposed to dress and I surrounded myself with only pretty people or people that were jealous of me and therefore easily taken advantage of.

Like Lizzy Kay, head of the school newspaper and the events committee at school. She worshipped me and constantly complimented what I wore, as if being nice to me would somehow make us alike. I knew what she said behind my back, though, words I was all too familiar with: bitch, slut, whore. Girls use the same terminologies boys do when they want something they can't have.

In spite of my social reputation, I learned early in life that not everyone was on my side. I had plenty of friends, but trusted no one. Plenty of boyfriends, but was backstabbed by them all. I was a cheerleader and model, dated only jocks and upper status high school boys, and still sought out this happiness my mother claimed was in store, but had yet to find for herself.

Of course, she didn't know about my little secret. Nobody did. How could I tell my pretty, perfect mother that her pretty, perfect little girl was somehow imperfect, different, abnormal?

At puberty, it kicked in. I would masturbate constantly, trying to eliminate the hunger, the empty feeling in my stomach I would get, even if I had already eaten a big meal. For some reason, only orgasm would help, but then I'd be hungry again, just an hour or two later.

I started having sex with my first boyfriend at thirteen. He was a senior and it did not take long for him to convince me we needed to share our love under the sheets. I was scared at first, but sex felt good and I quickly adapted to it. However, James didn't like me on top because he said I took too much control and had too much passion for a recent virgin. He said I looked at him funny when we did it, like I was someone else, like I was insane.

He ended up breaking up with me, and I encountered this dilemma again with other boys. Many claimed I wanted sex too much. I was too into it, too much for them to handle. Something in me would emerge when I was aroused and it scared my boyfriends; the hunger, the desire, the need to fill the emptiness in my gut. I liked to taste them with my tongue, their every part. I delighted in the flavor of sex, the salt of sweat, the hot, sticky sensation of mouth upon flesh.

It didn't stop with just sex either. I loved food and loved to eat. Like my father, I was an avid carnivore. After shows, Daddy would take me to Burger King and we'd have ourselves giant Whoppers with everything on them, and Mommy would get angry and tell me I'd be too fat to ever win the Little Miss Darling award. But I always won. The food I gorged upon never affected my body. I remained as skinny as ever, no matter what I inhaled and digested. My dates would watch in amazement as I'd indulge in large quantities of red meat as rare as the restaurants would be willing to make it. My friends hated me as they'd nibble upon their bland salads and raw tofu.

And so I suppressed whatever it was that lingered inside me, whatever sick, depraved urges I felt. The idea of my mother, or anybody, discovering my secret was a terrifying one. I imagined Mommy would never look at me again, and my friends, as two-faced as they were, would abandon me for good. I researched fetishes on the internet, but could not find my own identity among even the most bizarre categories. I believed I was alone, a hyper-sexual freak of nature with a ferocious and dangerous appetite.

My parents had a new friend over for dinner one night, a man named Thomas Berlin whom they knew through business. It was obvious to me that he and my mother were sleeping together, although, my father was most oblivious. Surely, my mother was hoping he'd notice, but that was asking a lot of Daddy. He didn't even notice Mr. Berlin's gaze upon me.

But I did. It was a familiar gaze, one that said "I would shove my dick in you so hard the gods above would hear you scream." I received that gaze all the time, wherever I went. I received it even as a child in pageants from the judges, hosts, and regulars. I knew that gaze from teachers, doctors, and strangers who'd pass by me and turn their heads twice to get a better look.

Although Mr. Berlin was sleeping with a married woman, he had daughters of his own and did not condone pedophilia. Nor was he used to being attracted to someone as young as I was. He was polite to me and listened attentively when I spoke, or when my father bragged about my school accomplishments, mentioning of course that I wanted to be a biologist. To this, my mother always scoffed and rolled her eyes. Science was a silly and unnecessary interest for a pretty girl to have.

I rinsed the dishes after dinner and put them in the dishwasher. Mr. Berlin handed me his used plate and when our fingers accidentally met, he jerked his hand away and dropped the plate, cracking the side. Mommy apologized and blamed my clumsiness, but Mr. Berlin defended me and accepted the blame instead, to which Daddy made some wise crack about having too much wine. My parents' friend nervously helped me gather up the pieces. When we caught eyes, I smiled at him and he smiled back. He was nice, and charming, and sweet. It didn't faze me much when men acted weird around me, but I was rather fond of Mr. Berlin's humility.

The next time Mr. Berlin was over I found a gift wrapped box sitting on my bed. Inside it were a pearl necklace and a tiny note that read "To Margery: A string of beauty for a beautiful girl. Thomas." I placed it around my neck and wore it shamelessly in front of my mother, who asked me where I'd gotten it.

"A boy from school," I lied, without skipping a beat.

"I have one just like it," she told me, and she paused. "From your dad."

My mother was also a good liar, but not as good as me.

The gifts became more frequent. Usually, I'd come home late from a party and hear my mother moaning in her bedroom. That is how I knew Daddy was still at work. Then I'd find earrings, roses, and scented letters written in fine cursive on my bed. Mr. Berlin soon confessed that he was in love with me, but was hurt and upset that I had a boyfriend and didn't think I'd want anything to do with someone three times my age. In one letter he faulted me for giving him such awful, sinful thoughts that he couldn't bear to sleep.

My new boyfriend, Sasha, told me that by accepting the gifts I was leading the old man on, and that made me a tease. I didn't like when he called me names. He wasn't very nice to me, not like Mr. Berlin was, but he was good looking and let me ride on top.

Still, the hunger pains were unreal, sometimes to the point of nausea and dizziness, and I spent quite a bit of time in the nurse's office. I had numerous hospital visits as well, and was checked for anemia, but the results were negative. My friends decided I must be bulimic, what with my meat affinity and thin physique. Perhaps they weren't that far off the mark. Perhaps I did have some sort of eating disorder, if not bulimia, than one that had me contemplating horrific sexual scenarios. The more these images plagued me, the less I let Sasha touch me.

After a particularly dramatic fight with Sasha about my apparent sexual dysfunction, I came home to find my mother rummaging through my desk drawers and jewelry boxes. Inside my special princess music box that my father gave me were all of Mr. Berlin's love letters.

Mommy read them and smacked me hard across the face. "You slut!"

I didn't know what to say. I suppose part of me wanted her to find them. She sat at my vanity table and examined her face and bleached salon styled hair. Then she lit a cigarette and glared at me through the mirror.

"You have no idea what it's like to be hungry," she said through the smoky air, "to wanna devour every last bit you can get because you are so starved. You won't know what that's like until you are my age." She stood and got close in my face. "What the fuck are you?" she demanded, and I could smell the booze on her breath.

She left me in my shock and humiliation, and I wanted so badly to answer her, but I didn't know what I was. I did know hunger though. I did know the need to devour. I also knew something was terribly wrong with me, and now Sasha knew it too.

After weeks of no sex, we had tried again, but I bit his chin and drew blood, and he responded in absolute dread and fury, throwing me out of his house. I was most worried about what would happen the next day when everybody'd know that the prom queen was a sadistic psychopath.

Now my own mother despised me. I had tried so hard to be the better, more improved version of her. I thought that that's what she wanted, that she would be proud of me, but this whole being beautiful thing felt more like a curse than a blessing. Mr. Berlin told me I had been put on Earth to torture him and make him do bad things. If that were the case, if I indeed was a villain, then I wasn't being true to myself, or to my nature.

In biology class, I was fascinated by the cruelty and brutality of nature. The food chain was a violent, murderous bloodbath among beasts and humans. Instinct was ruthlessly unforgiving. It didn't matter how domesticated a tiger was, she was still capable of mauling the shit out of people if need be.

This made me think of my girlfriends who desperately tried to fix and idealize themselves by shaving or waxing every last bit of hair below the neck. I too was guilty of this, but recognized the absurdity. It didn't matter how much work went into being pretty, hair would always grow back. I had to stop suppressing.

I emailed Thomas Berlin and begged him to see me. He refused at first, and ranted in an email about how much he cared about my family and respected my father, and didn't want anyone to get hurt including his wife and kids. But I knew he'd show up. It was the same kind of bullshit rant Mr. Whitman, the school janitor, gave me when I seduced him.

Mr. Berlin and I met up in a parking lot overlooking South Beach. I'd called my father to let him know I'd be sleeping at Callie's house, the most responsible and smartest of my friends, so there'd be no concerns. Mr. Berlin had flowers for me, but he wouldn't look me in the eye.

I spoke softly to him and giggled and put my hand on his knee and he rubbed my wrist as if he couldn't believe I was truly sitting beside him. We kissed heatedly, knocking his glasses right off his face. I undid the buttons of my shirt and Mr. Berlin kissed my breasts, like he'd never seen anything quite as full and succulent before. His hands rubbed up and down my body, and I fell back against the car door as Mr. Berlin licked me and put his fingers inside me.

My stomach began to growl and saliva dripped from the corners of my mouth. He was the hardest I'd ever felt a man be, as he fucked me with all the energy and fervor he could muster at fifty years old. He started to breathe heavier and my hunger increased as my vaginal muscles flexed. We both began to reach orgasm. Then his gasps became woeful howls of immense pleasure and tears filled his eyes as he let out a great sound of release.

Slowly my mouth stretched open and enlarged to the size of Mr. Berlin's head. As I enveloped his head inside my mouth, Mr. Berlin's eyes popped open to darkness. He screamed, and thrashed, and struggled, but it was too late. I bit down. I chomped through the bones, vessels, and arteries in his neck, munched and swallowed.

A morning jogger found Mr. Berlin's headless body once I was gone. My mother sobbed for weeks after she learned of the news and though she never said anything, I know she somehow suspected my involvement.

Daddy still didn't seem to realize that Mr. Berlin meant more to his wife than just a friend, but he did express interest in the peculiar circumstances of Mr. Berlin's death. The police, he said, could not understand how a man's head had been bitten right off. The papers had yet to report it, but I was certain the findings of human bite marks were unfamiliar territory for the pathologist who performed the autopsy.

I felt amazingly at peace for the first time ever and relished in a satisfaction I had never had with any other man. Or any other meal, for that matter. I knew what I wanted now, and what I was. In biology my fetish was revealed to me, as I began to study up on a strange little insect called the praying mantis. This remarkable creature cannibalized its submissive mate once fertilization took place.

I was pleased to learn I wasn't alone in the world. There was something in nature just as beautiful as me, just as powerful, sexual, and vicious. It felt good to know I was so much more than what people thought of me, more than what my mother wanted me to be, more than eye candy, more than just a pretty girl.

Mr. Berlin had said I made monsters out of men, but he was sorely mistaken. It was men who made a monster out of me.

Come Fly With Death
Wesley D. Gray

Come fly with Death
and feel the splitting as you come apart
with turbulent screams bifurcating bones.

Flee further from this life –
unfurl your wings and soar
with tangled feathers cutting the night.

Join his skeleton beak,
slicing stabs at airless wind,
and wield its dashing spine.

Stay near to glinting shroud and glide,
knowing tattered wings will guide,
as whispering scars are left behind.

Go now into that hollow abyss,
but do not pass the dark in calmness;
break the barrier with raging clamor!

Do not scrape or merely crawl.
Come fly with Death –
and swoop, and yawp, and bawl.

The Horn of Plenty
Russell Nayle

The sound of the neighbor's rooster woke Jack. After an hour and a half's sleep, he was in no mood to be nice to anyone – or anything. Even his hamster shied away from him. He couldn't go back to sleep, but it was just as well. He hadn't packed his gear yet for the day trip to Fossil Lake, and the bus was supposed to leave from the mall parking lot in an hour.

Jack had taken this trip many times. He usually sat in the back seat, where he spread out his baling twine and safety pins – for insurance purposes. A man once tried to sit next to him. Ever since, Jack came prepared.

He dodged the granny spies to cut through the back yard of his apartment complex. It was the fastest way to the mall. The safety pins in his backpack jabbed him between his shoulder blades with every stride, but he didn't have time to rearrange his gear just yet. Getting to the bus was his priority.

Jack made it to the parking lot, elbowed his way to the front of the line, and proudly displayed his ticket. The bus driver recognized Jack, and grudgingly let him board. He'd accused Jack of trying to rook him before, but Jack's ticket was kosher this time, so there was nothing he could do.

The others boarded the bus with no problems. They all took seats near the front.

After half an hour's ride to the lakeside, Jack wanted to be first person off the bus, which wasn't so easy to do from the back seat.

Another passenger, Greg, slid his 300 pound bulk halfway into the aisle.

"You're not getting in front of me, boy," he told Jack. "Wait your turn."

"Da fuck?!" growled Jack. "No way is some fat guy going to make me miss five minutes worth of fossil hunting!"

"Yeah, well, *I* am. Deal with it, Shortcakes."

"I am *not* short! I'm five-foot-ten-inches!"

"No you're not."

Jack fumed. He'd figure out a way to get back at Greg. Overpowering him was out of the question. The safety pins he'd packed would have to do. A kilt pin would have been useful.

The moment he hopped down from the bus, Jack pushed past Greg, and ran to the shore.

*   *   *

The bus driver and Greg looked at each other and shrugged.

Greg asked, "Do you think he came for the fossil hunting or the food?"

"If I knew that, I'd dress in drag and do palm readings instead of drive a bus."

"He looks familiar. Have you seen him before?"

"Lots of times," replied the driver. "He tries to board the bus once a month or so. A couple of times he handed me a counterfeit ticket. You should have seen the tantrum he threw last time. My two-year-old nephew takes it better when he can't have a cookie."

Greg laughed. "Well, I'm here for the cookout, and the scenery. Fossils don't really rock my socks. I'll help you set up, if that's okay."

"Thanks. I appreciate it. Can you grab one end of this table?"

Twenty minutes later, there was a commotion by the edge of the lake.

Greg pointed to where Jack was splashing around in the water. "What is that he's doing? My grandpa told me a story about catching fish with some twine and a safety pin on a stick, but I always thought it was one of his tall tales. That boy is going to scare off the fish."

Jack bent over, and reached down into the water.

Greg's eyes widened. "Oh, lord, I did *not* need to see his plumber's butt. Is that a tat on his tailbone? Can you read it?"

The bus driver replied, "It looks like a comment cloud, but all I can make out is 'WOOF.'"

They continued to watch Jack, fascinated.

Jack's jerry-rigged fishing line had gotten caught on something. He was in the water up to his crotch trying to un-lodge it. Mud and all, he emerged, and approached the picnic table with a twisted looking horn.

"Take that, bitches," he screamed while running circles around the table, waving his find. "Yeah, take that!"

One woman who was sitting at the table asked, "May I see that? It looks like part of a narwhal tusk. But what's it doing in a fresh water lake?"

"It's a unicorn horn. I just *know* it is."

The woman tried to keep a straight face. "Send it off to a university in the Maritimes. Get a biologist to look at it."

"It's a unicorn horn. I don't need some fool from a college to tell me that. I know what it is."

"Okay, okay. Just don't wave it in my face."

Jack paused, looking stunned as it visibly dawned on him he was talking to a woman. An actual woman. Clearly, not many women would engage him in conversation. Opportunities like this seldom presented themselves.

Greg and the bus driver, still watching, winced in unison as they saw him suave up and try to make his best move.

"Ma'am, would you like to go to dinner with me sometime?" Jack asked her. "You'd have to drive, though."

She'd managed to keep the straight face before, but this time proved to be a bigger challenge. "No thanks."

"Geez. Some women are so picky."

The cookout had barely started when Jack announced that he was ready to go home. Greg reminded him that they weren't due to leave until 4:00.

"Sit on that horn thing you found until then, okay?"

"I will not! It's a fossil. It's from the lake. It's fragile."

Greg shot back, "Yeah, like you."

The cookout went well, with brats and some burgers. Almost everyone enjoyed the day trip, except for that one woman, who seemed to have lost much of her appetite and only picked at her food. For the rest of them, Jack's antics were an amusing sideshow to a gorgeous day spent poking around among the rocks.

*   *   *

All Jack wanted to do was get home with his twisty horn. He persisted in telling anybody who'd listen, but they sided with the fat guy and made him wait until 4:00.

After three agonizing hours, which gave his clothes time to mostly dry out in the sun, he reclaimed the rear seat on the bus for the return trip. Nobody else wanted it.

During the ride, Jack kept fondling his fossil. Others returned with some trilobites. One woman found an ammonite. Nobody else found a unicorn horn!

Once off the bus, Jack raced home with his precious find. He sat down at his computer and googled "unicorn horn," and "narwhal." None of the results really looked like his fossil. Frustrated, he hung his fossil off his headboard with baling twine, and went to sleep.

The mirror shook. His dresser shifted a little. He rolled over, and pulled the covers over his head.

The next morning, his wallet was missing, and everything that had been on the dresser was scattered across the floor.

Throughout the next month, plenty of other strange things happened. His beloved Empyrean Sky t-shirt was shredded. Things kept getting knocked off his dresser. Several times, he saw a black cloud behind him when he looked in the mirror. Lights flickered, and he occasionally got ear piercing feedback from his speakers. He heard demonic laughter at night.

Jack still had the name of a guy he'd seen on TV who investigated this sort of thing, Don Zoofus, written on a post-it that he had stuck to his fridge. He looked up the man's number, and called to explain the situation. The answering machine picked up, so he left a message.

Zoofus returned his call that evening. He could not come investigate for a couple of weeks, he said, because he had several urgent cases pending, but he expressed his interest.

Jack endured the weird happenings for two more weeks, until Zoofus arrived with his equipment. The cameras looked nice, but what really caught Jack's eye was the voltmeter. Zoofus called it a K2 EMF meter, or something that sounded high tech. It had pretty lights.

Zoofus spent two days on his investigation. When he finished, he proclaimed that the twisty horn was the cause of the strange occurrences, and recommended that it be removed from the premises. He explained that it was Jack's decision, of course.

Reluctantly, Jack allowed Zoofus to take the horn. Zoofus promised to bring it home with him, do a purification ritual, and encase it in a bell jar, so that any remaining evil couldn't escape.

Despite that, Jack continued to experience weird phenomena.

And three weeks after Zoofus left, he logged onto eBay, where he saw his unicorn horn for sale, for $300.

The Lost Link
Carl Thomas Fox

If Francis didn't get there in time, *he* would not be happy. *His* time was precious. There was so much to tell *him*, and only Francis would be the man to do it.

It was his right, after all. He had found the irrefutable proof.

Fuelled with his knowledge, Francis raced through the empty rain-slicked streets in his rental car. It was the middle of the night, a dreary British night with the rain cascading down. In the gloom, everything had a sleek black sheen. So sleek and slick that, in his excitement, he fought to maintain control of the car, doing his very best not to die with this knowledge.

He tried to remain calm by remembering the events that led him to this kamikaze errand.

Fresh out of studying for his Ph.D for palaeontology, Francis had been keen to begin his first dig and add something new to the world's knowledge of prehistory. There had been so many changes lately! Such as the concept that dinosaurs had evolved into birds, rather than being lizards, as the original translation of their name meant. No, they were of the bird genus, to the point many had feathers, not scales as popularly believed.

For all these reasons, he'd wanted his first dig to be something special.

Fortunately for him, he did not have long to wait.

Millionaire George Vermis, a genius who owned the southern stretch of England and Wales through the numerous businesses he had in his pocket, was considered by many to be an eccentric. He was also considered a benevolent presence, submitting much money for charities, and supporting the development of people's history. When an attempt was made to remove the great Red Dragon from the Welsh flag and replace it with the golden cross of St. David, Vermis had been the one to put a stop to the act. Though Italian by birth, it was said he felt a strong kinship with the infamous Ddraig Coch, as the dragon was known, which was why he had set up his mansion in the blistering wilds of the Welsh countryside.

Two years ago, there'd been news of a new dinosaur find in Central Italy, in an old dried up lake called Lacfossile – literally, and ironically, translated as Fossil Lake. Vermis, whose family came from and still owned land in the region, managed to gain control over the area. He'd then needed an expert he could trust.

Sensing his opportunity, Francis Drake approached the millionaire, dressed in a crisp, smart suit and bearing a list of his credentials.

Impressed, even seduced by the young man's innocence, enthusiasm and theories, Vermis put him in charge of the dig, and paid for everything: the handpicked team, the hardware, passports and transport.

Fully funded, Francis headed off for Southern Italy, not sure what he was going to come across. What he did uncover, after two months of digging and sifting through endless earth samples, he knew would change everything. His own hypothesis, those belonging to endless experts around the world, and even the ideas of the general public.

What he found would change the world.

That was why he was risking life and soul to get to *him*, his benefactor, on this rainy night.

Dragon's Keep, the home of Vermis, was a large stately mansion on top of a tall hill, looking at stretches of fields and wooded areas. High walls of white stone surrounded the estate, which in turn were topped with hedges cut and trimmed to look like waves, or monstrous wings. Dramatic lighting intensified the effect in the darkness outside.

Francis had called ahead, and was expected. The grand gates stood open and ready for him. As he drove through, he noticed another car leaving, an expensive red sports car full of beautiful women. They were dressed up as if for a party. Francis was briefly hypnotised by them, unable to look away. However, as he looked, he noticed how all five of the women glared at him with deadly venom.

No matter, they drove off.

The grounds of Dragon's Keep were breathtaking. Large, lustrous gardens filled with oceans of flowers, winding rivers of gravelled paths and towering sculptures forged and carved from bushes and hedges. The curving sweep of driveway led up to the house, in front of which was a fountain with a statue of a rearing dragon. Probably to show Vermis' love of living in Wales.

Coming to a quick stop, Francis sprang out, making sure he had his bag, and rushed up the stone steps. Before he had a chance to knock, the mahogany doors opened, revealing a tall, elderly gentleman, with thinning white hair.

"Good evening sir." The man spoke in a calm, collected English accent. "Mr. Vermis is waiting for you in the office. I will take you to him."

"Thank you," Francis said. His own voice was strained with the weariness of tension and pent-up adrenaline.

He followed the butler into the foyer, with high ceilings, tiled floor and arching staircase. There were doors all around, leading off to several different areas of the house. The butler led Francis through one such door, into the private office of George Vermis.

Like all other rooms in the house, it was elegant and spacious, with large windows. This room had a rich green carpet and dark bookcases filled to the rim with old, worn volumes of books in several languages. A big fire blazed. A large projector screen on one wall faced a mammoth desk of intricately carved mahogany, topped and studded with green leather. The carvings consisted of loops and twists. Books, inkwells, old fashioned quills and a large metal dome covered the surface. Worked into the desktop itself was a computer keyboard, sockets for USB connections and CDs, and a touchpad mouse.

The man sitting at the desk was tall and handsome, dressed in black trousers and a burgundy shirt, under which a strong, chiselled body could clearly be seen. His hair was finely cut, with a modern styling to show he was with the times. His face looked youthful and sincere.

The moment Francis stepped in, the man stood up to greet him, clasping his hand in a strong handshake. Although he felt warm, there was an instant's dry chill of his skin the moment their hands made contact. No sweaty palms here.

"Francis, how good to see you," he said in a deep, booming voice. "God, man, you look terrible. Have a seat."

Francis took the offer without question. The stress and exhaustion had begun to catch up with him, and he knew his appearance showed it. When he'd last been here, he'd been young and fresh, with smart clipped hair and a smooth, unblemished, clean shaven face. Now, he was worn and haggard, his hair overgrown and dishevelled, weeks of stubble marking his rough, sun baked face.

Examining Francis' new look, Vermis reached for the small knob on the dome and pulled up, revealing a porcupine of cigarettes. Taking one, placing it casually between his lips, he gestured towards the others. However, Francis declined the offer. It was straight to business.

"Well," said Vermis, closing the lid, "what brings you back so quickly?"

"The find of the century, Mr. Vermis. I have all the photos here."

From his bag, Francis pulled out a black iPad. Opening it up, he selected the picture menu. Vermis indicated he should send it wirelessly to the projector, which he switched on. Looking at the screen, Francis synced his iPad and turned back round to face Vermis, who looked on, smoking and full of interest.

"This is what we found." Francis selected an image of a dinosaur skeleton in dusty earth.

It showed a winged beast, unlike any that had been found to date, with a crown of horns upon the pointed skull.

"A new species?" asked Vermis.

"A dragon, Mr. Vermis. Evidence that dragons existed in prehistoric times."

"Dragons," Vermis echoed.

"We unearthed a total of six skeletons. One was that of a tyrannosaurus. The others were decidedly not."

As Francis spoke, he shifted through the photos, showing what he was saying.

"This one, the larger specimen, with the horns pointing up, I am assuming is a male. Four others, smaller, have curling ones, which I propose are females of the species. Their bones appear to be of a honeycombed structure, making them both strong and light. We also discovered the fossilized remains of a nest filled with eggs."

Vermis said nothing, staring intently at the screen.

Francis continued. "One of the females appears to have been injured . . . you can see the broken limbs and crushed ribs. From what I can determine, the tyrannosaurus must have killed it while attempting to raid the nest. The females fought back, judging by how they were positioned around the dinosaur. Note the breakages in the tyrannosaur's teeth . . . the dragons seem to have had scales thick enough to be like armour."

He glanced to Vermis, who nodded for him to go on.

"These female dragons are about the size of elephants, but the male is almost twice that. It was this one that killed the dinosaur. See the scratch marks on the dinosaur skull? They match the male's talons. But look at the charring on the bones. It looks like they were blasted by some intense heat. We took samples, which proved to be primarily methane, oxygen and hydrogen. In addition, there were traces of platinum. We did some experiments, and this mixture creates an intense fire."

"Volcanic? Something in the environment?"

Francis shook his head. "There was organic matter in it as well. DNA. These gases and metals were biologically formed."

"So you are telling me that dragons used to exist?" There was a curious note of apprehension to Vermis' question, which was not the reaction Francis might have expected.

"Oh, no," Francis replied with a grin, preparing to deliver the rest of the news. "We found more eggs. Many more. In a cave just south of this site, a cave recently revealed during an earth tremor, we came across a series of eggs that show the dragons in progressive stages of change."

"Change?"

He didn't understand why Vermis failed to share his own thrill, and moved rapidly through the images, talking faster, sweating as much from excitement as from the overpowering heat of the fireplace.

"As you can see," he said, "with each stage, the dragons changed. Over several successive generations, they lost their wings, going from six limbs to four. Then, becoming bipedal. The tails disappearing. Opposable thumbs and toes developing. The face flattening."

"How do you know this isn't some sort of a hoax?" Vermis challenged.

"Because the cave was sealed, all eggs were the same size, about twice the size of a rugby ball. All preliminary tests show they are of the same structure, the skeletons retaining the honeycomb structure." He zoomed in on an image of several skulls arranged in a row. "Observe these bizarre markings. They follow sequential patterns. Almost like numbers. As if in a series of successive experiments. They were breeding, changing –"

"Evolving," Vermis said.

"At an impossibly accelerated rate." With that, Francis showed a photo of a final egg, but the fine-boned skeletal remains inside barely resembled a dragon at all.

"It looks almost human," said Vermis.

"Yes! But look at the skull . . . the backswept forehead, the elongated conical shape . . . just like the classic depictions of gods and aliens as seen in the art of Central American civilizations, and Egypt during the reign of Akhenaten."

"Are you suggesting dragons lived alongside mankind?"

"More than that . . . they evolved to look like us!"

Vermis fell silent and snubbed out his cigarette. He moved closer to Francis, deeply focused on the images.

As he did so, Francis noticed that his host had no eyelashes, and wondered why he'd never been aware of that peculiar characteristic before. He then noticed that, despite the roaring fire, Vermis wasn't dripping in sweat as Francis himself was. There was a sheen to his skin, but Vermis wasn't sweating.

He remembered, for no reason at all, that although Vermis had smoked that cigarette down to the butt, there'd been no flick of a lighter or flare of a match that he could recall.

Vermis reached over without asking and took the iPad from Francis' hands. As he moved, Francis thought he smelt something . . . a hint of methane?

"Who else knows about this?" George Vermis asked. "Have you shown anyone?"

"Only the team you gave me." Still perplexed by his benefactor's reaction, Francis tried again to drum up some enthusiasm. "What do you think, isn't this the find of a lifetime?"

"It is."

Then Vermis threw the iPad into the fire.

'NO!!!' shouted Francis.

In disbelief, without thinking, he rushed to the fire to save the evidence. But Vermis grabbed his shoulder in a grip that almost shattered the bone, and threw Francis across the room. He roared like an animal as he did so.

Stunned, Francis stared up at the man walking closer to him. He saw Vermis' eyes alter, the whites and the blue of the irises splitting vertically, parting, opening as if they were eyelids themselves. Revealed beneath them were reptilian eyes.

He touched a remote, which switched off the lights so that only the crackling flames lit the room.

"You're right, we have evolved," he said. His words seemed to hiss. "We needed to, in order to survive what was coming to destroy the dinosaurs. It took us centuries to alter our DNA to become what we are. But I cannot let you reveal our existence."

Francis knew he was going to die. He tried getting up, throwing his fist into the thing that was Vermis, aiming for the face. It felt like he hit solid metal, his fingers cracking and locking.

Smiling, Vermis sent an iron fist into Francis' stomach with the same force as a hammer. Then, without giving him a chance, Vermis picked him up and threw him at the door. Through the door. It shattered and he skidded across the foyer floor.

Survival instincts kicking in, Francis scrambled up the main stairs, ignoring the pain raging through him. Upon reaching the landing, he was forced to stop, not knowing where to go.

He heard another roar, even more monstrous. Turning around, he saw a laughing Vermis stride into the foyer. Vermis held out his arms and blew out a deep breath. Strangely, as he did this, his body seemed to inflate and expand . . . then the scientist in Francis understood. The expelling of heavier oxygen and carbon dioxide allowed the natural internal methane and hydrogen to . . .

A push of his feet sent Vermis shooting straight up the stairs as if flying. He landed in front of Francis, still laughing, only to seize him and throw him into the wall.

Francis hit with so much force that his entire spine shattered. He barely felt it when Vermis picked him up again.

"What are you?" he wanted to ask, even if it had been in only a whimper, even if he didn't already know.

His benefactor answered him anyway. "We are the past, and we are the future."

As Vermis inhaled again, the sides of his throat swelled. His mouth opened wide. In his dripping saliva, Francis thought he glimpsed the faint sheen of metal. Fumes of hydrogen, oxygen, methane and platinum washed over him.

In his last second of life, Francis found it ironic that his death would come in the same way as his greatest find.

Then the raging fire rushed out, engulfing him.

*   *   *

George Vermis returned to his office, licking his lips and fingers, leaving only bones and scorched bloodstains upstairs. As he went, he reached up to his face and peeled off the faux eyebrows held on by a sticky side. Next he tugged off the wig, revealing a flawless head of smooth, hairless skin, and the very apparent conelike shape of his skull.

Throwing away the props, he went to his phone and dialled a number. It only took a moment for the call to be picked up, but it was Vermis who started speaking.

"Master, it was as you feared," he said. "The site in Italy was one of our ancestors' lairs, where they worked in creating the new generations . . . Yes, Master, I have dealt with him and destroyed his evidence. Just before he arrived, I informed my hunters and sent them to keep an eye on the rest of the team. I shall now contact them with the order to kill . . . Yes, Master, thank you . . . No sir, they didn't find the second cave and the evidence that we evolved first."

He hung up the phone, then grasped his lips and pulled. His skin wrenched from him, pulling and stretching. Not one rip appeared; the skin was unbreakable after years of improvement. However, they still were not able to have a kill and feast without needing to shed it afterwards. Although strong, it started to sag and detach.

Widening the gap that had once been his mouth, he worked his face and head through. The new skin beneath was covered in a slick, viscous, almost amniotic, fluid. Next came his shoulders, then his arms, one at a time. His torso and hips followed, then his legs. Finally, he was able to step outside his old skin.

It was already drying out and turning to ash. Vermis kicked it away and went to his desk. He was wiping away his wet birthing fluid with tissues when he became aware of the butler standing in the shattered doorway.

"I shall inform the builders and cleaners tomorrow morning, sir," said the butler, in a droll voice. "I assume you will not be needing supper tonight, after all?"

"No, thank you, Manfred."

"Shall I return it to the pantry?"

"Take her to the guest bedroom," Vermis said. "Let her be treated like a princess for the night. Then, when I wake up in the morning, I will have a nice dose of breakfast in bed."

"Very good, sir."

As the butler departed, Vermis began readying himself to play the part of the prince . . . before ending the fairy tale, and dealing with the princess, as he saw fit.

Nat Poopcone vs. The Beast of Fossil Lake
Jerrod Balzer

It was another busy Friday night at the Romeo Diner. Carry was finishing her fried mushrooms and diet soda at the counter when a short, greasy man with long hair and a goatee approached her.

"Hi, I'm Nat Poopcone," he said. "Can we date?"

She stifled a laugh, then nearly vomited when his stench reached her nose. *What is that? Broccoli?*

"I'm serious!" His spittle struck the exposed skin around her skimpy, black outfit, which caused her to flinch and inch her food farther away from him, but he continued to talk. "I'm a publisher looking for models. You might be perfect for my next issue of *Ethel's Real Gazette.*"

This caught her interest. *That explains it,* she thought. *He's the eccentric, creative type!*

"Well, you know," she said, and offered her usual lie: "I happen to be a very popular model, but I do have some free time coming up. What qualifications do you require?"

The little man looked up at her with bright eyes as a grin crept across his face. "Only two things. First, I need enough money to buy a beer."

She nodded. "Okay."

"Now!"

"Oh!" Carry fished in her purse and handed him a five dollar bill.

He accepted it, ordered his beverage, and then took a few swigs before continuing. "Okay, next I only need to know your age."

"That's easy! I'm eighteen."

Nat spit a cloud of beer at her. "Fuck off, then, cunt! You're too old."

Astounded, she reacted with what would have normally been a kick to the groin, but it struck his chest thanks to his abnormal height. There was no problem punching him in the nose, however, and he was quite the bleeder.

He pinched his nostrils closed and yelled as he ran out the door, "You're a horror target now, bitch! I'm hardcore!"

*   *   *

Nat scurried next door, past a long line of fans waiting for The Brass Hole to open for that night's live heavy metal show. He walked straight to the front and began to explain who he was, but, being downwind, the bouncers already knew and let him inside.

They often agreed to allow him to set up a book signing table during shows. It served two purposes: it made him feel important, imagining all the people outside were waiting to see him rather than the band, My Dying Fart; and it offered everyone else some comedy relief. The gothic club down the street had a guy who practiced humiliation with his wife by showing up each night in teddy lingerie and standing near the dance floor with a big smile. The regulars looked forward to him as a humorous addition to the scene. The same went for Nat. Though no one ever said it to his face, Nat was the infamous "Brass Hole Asshole."

Nat rushed to his foldout table and began going through his trade paperbacks.

Someone noticed the coagulating mess covering his hands and face. "Hey, are you okay?"

"I'm fine," he replied. "I can't waste this blood." He proceeded to stick his finger up his nose like a quill to an ink well and smeared his name on the first page of the books. As he began to run dry, he pressed his entire face into books.

Curious, the guitarist of My Dying Fart picked up a copy of *Tabloid Porpoises IV*. He opened it, then flinched. "Dude, there are boogers in this!"

Nat grinned. "Nah, that's my pulp! I should probably charge extra, huh? Well, it's mostly my blood, but other fluids might make it on the page, especially when I'm signing at home. It's all part of what makes me so hardcore. Other people are afraid of me because I'm too dark. I'm surprised you can even see me right now because I'm so dark *and* hardcore like Lovecraft, Poe, Matheson, Berenstain, and *The Twilight Zone*. I'm also dark . . . and hardcore. That's my blood."

The guitarist's eyes began to cross, but then he caught sight of something shining under Nat's black ball cap. "Is that . . . aluminum foil under your hat?"

Nat nodded. "I have to wear it at signings so I won't shit my pants. Damn faggots think they'll ruin my career with brown rays but I'm always one step ahead. And, hey, speaking of careers, I can help yours! I'll mention your band in my next story so everyone will know how cool I – er, you are. You'd be in great company because I've done the same for Metallica, Obituary, Cannibal Corpse, Entombed, Nelson, Grave, Cradle of Filth, Wilson Phillips, Ozzy Osbourne, Rammstein, Hanson, Corrosion of Conformity, and Megadeth. I cuss a lot, too. Check this out: fuuuck. I bet you don't hear that from many Christians, which I am. I also drink beer on YouTube. I'm hardcore. That's my blood."

The guitarist needed some hard liquor to wash this all away before the show started. "Cool, whatever. I –"

"I'll remember you said that!" Nat blurted. "I'll tell everyone how much you love my work. Thank you for your support. All the faggots will be so jealous now! I'll tell those cunts, and you'll be right up there with Trivium, Opeth, Napalm Death, Bee Gees, and Bathory."

"Yeah, um . . ." The guitarist opened the book in his hand and turned around so that his rear end was against it. "Here, this is my way of offering good luck." He passed wind on the pages before replacing it on the table and leaving.

It ended up being a busy night for Nat. Despite the laughs and finger pointing, he sold several books. No one had the heart to tell him this was because the club had a strict rule on no re-entry and the bathrooms were out of both toilet paper and paper towels. If someone was to leave to clean up and come back, they would have to pay another twenty dollars, or they could pay ten dollars for one of his books and share it with their friends – all but the first few pages.

As he left the club at closing time, he counted his money. He'd made enough for the bus trip home and another special one that he had been planning for a while now. This weekend, he finally had the funds for both the trip and a six-pack of beer, so he had to strike while the time was right. He would leave first thing in the morning.

His destination was the dreaded Fossil Lake, a place that carried the same name as his company, Fossil Lake Press. Even though the lake had been around for centuries, it just wasn't right for that fucker to have the same name. He hadn't known of it when he created his company, but when it showed up on a Google search, and above his own website to boot . . . well, that lake was clearly trying to ruin his career. It was time to confront it once and for all.

By the time he stepped off the bus just before noon, he had finished off

the six-pack and filled two cans with urine, which had spilled under the seats. So, thanks to being dropped off a tad early, he had to walk a few miles to reach the lake. By then, he had been rushed to the hospital three times for exhaustion and dumped back on the side of the road. The third time took longer because the EMTs had accidentally picked up a dead opossum, instead.

So he reached Fossil Lake the following day.

It was a gorgeous site. The clean, blue water sparkled and, if one was patient enough, a unicorn could be spotted emerging from the lush woods surrounding it for a drink. *Funny,* Nat thought, *there don't seem to be any dark, indescribable secrets here. What's so scary about it?*

As he walked closer, he saw something that made his blood boil. "I should have known you assholes would have some part in this!"

In front of him was what appeared to be a makeshift lemonade stand, but the board nailed above read "Skullvines Bate 'n' Tackle." Behind it stood a tall, broad-shouldered man with a dark beard, and next to him was a John Lennon clone with tinted glasses and a mischievous smile.

Nat barked at them. "Jerrod Balzer and S.D. Hintz . . . You faggots call yourselves editors and you can't even spell your sign right."

"Hey, Nat!" Jerrod said. "What brings you here? Could we interest you in a unicorn ride?"

"Yeah!" S.D. said. "You'd look totally goth."

"Fuck you! I just want to know what's so mysterious about this lake so I can deal with it. Why is it called 'Fossil Lake' like my press?"

"Oh, that's easy," Jerrod said. "It's because of the big bone."

"Where?"

S.D. pinched one of his own nipples while Nat stared. "You have to row a boat to the center if you want to see it. Give us ten dollars."

Fortunately, Nat had the money. He took out his wallet and began digging through the lint.

"And," Jerrod said, "if you want the added Bate 'n' Tackle, it's an extra five dollars."

Nat wrinkled his nose and mumbled, "Yeah, whatever." He paid them and suddenly S.D. disappeared.

"Hey! Look up here!" Hintz was sitting on top of the stand with his pants dangling around his ankles while he masturbated furiously. Nat couldn't help but gaze, so he was caught unaware when Jerrod tackled him to the ground and gave him a wet smooch on the cheek.

Nat squealed like a pig until Jerrod let him stand up. Then he screamed at them, "What the fuck? How does that help me find the bone in Fossil Lake?"

S.D. was dressed again and back behind the stand. "I don't know, but it was awesome!"

"Aargh! Where's the fucking boat?"

Jerrod pointed toward the nearest edge of the lake. "It's right there, but grab it while the old man who owns it is still asleep or he'll be pissed."

"What did I give you ten dollars for?"

"I don't know, but I sure as shit hope it wasn't for a blowjob."

Nat stormed away and hurried to the boat, where he got in and rowed to the middle of the lake, then collapsed from exhaustion for four hours. After he was roused by bird droppings, he found an old cupcake under one of the seats and was energized soon enough.

He looked around but saw nothing.

"Hey!" he called. "Wherever you are, I'm here to tell you that the name 'Fossil Lake' belongs to me and my press! Stay away from it or I'll make you a horror target!"

Large bubbles rose to the lake's surface directly in front of him, which he took as a response.

"That's right. I'm hardcore like Lovecraft, Poe, Matheson, *Twilight Zone*, and *Blue's Clues*. If you want to fuck with me, you'll need to take it to YouTube and show me what you've got. I'll always beat you, though, because I drink beer when I record and sometimes I use sound. Just fucking remember that!"

More bubbles rose, enough to push the boat back.

Nat steadied himself and continued. "That's right, bitch! It's on now, huh? This is for pink slips! Get up here so we can talk face-to-face!"

With a low rumble, the water foamed and churned until the massive beast of the lake rose high above him. He looked up in awe at first, and then his face turned beet red. His teeth gnashed and his eyes bulged.

The creature consisted mostly of a long, thick neck with pulsing veins running throughout, and its mushroom-shaped head lacked eyes or a nose, but had a large mouth on the top.

"No! *No!*" Nat shouted. "This is *my* story! I will *not* have giant cocks in my story or anywhere *near* something called Fossil Lake!"

In response, the monster spit something gooey in his face.

Nat cried. This was all too much for him. But then he remembered all the happy faces at the recent book signing. He had to keep going for his fans. They needed him to keep writing and being hardcore. He had to do it for Lovecraft, for Poe, for Metallica, for *The Twilight Zone*, for *Kissyfur*, and especially for My Dying Fart.

He picked up an oar and smacked the monster with it. It flinched and moaned, so he hit it again and again. He could hear Jerrod and S.D. cheering from the banks, "That's it, Poopcone, beat it harder! *Harder!*"

Ignoring them, Nat continued his assault until his arms could hold the oar no longer. "All right," he said between gasps. "Give me your best shot."

The monster shifted to one side and a giant scrotum emerged from the depths. A testicle reared up and knocked him to the other side of the boat. During the fall, Nat's pants dropped to his knees, making it all the more difficult to stand back up.

At the sight of his nudity, the monster suddenly shuddered and went limp.

Well, shit, Nat thought, *whatever works!*

He left his pants down and took a few more swings at the weakened creature with his oar. All was almost lost but it still had a lot of spunk left. It spun around to build momentum and smacked Nat hard, slamming him to the bottom of the boat and nearly capsizing it. However, something else happened – something unexpected. The force of the blow caused an object to be pushed from Nat's anus, an old toy that had been stored there for years. The original 80s Tranny-former toy oozed at first, then shot out as the pressure was released with geyser force. Pent-up gas and feces from his high school years were finally seeing the light of day in what could only be described as a shitty ghost tornado.

Once fully released, Nat looked up and found the monster floating dead in the water, along with everything else that once thrived in the lake. The boat was also sinking thanks to the weight of all the Poopcone poo, so he had to quickly leap onto the beast's corpse, with oar in hand, for safety. He managed to ride the giant cock to shore, but the effort was more than he could handle, especially after everything he had just endured. After sliding away to the ground, he fell unconscious.

The Skullvines boys tried to revive him. They guzzled cough syrup while urinating on him, but to no avail. Our poor hero had slipped into a coma. Friends came to the hospital from all around to offer their support. His room was plastered with rainbows and hair band posters. Interestingly enough, he no longer carried a stench or wore a greasy film. It seems that all the waste and gas built up inside him over the years had seeped through his pores, and he was rid of it at last.

Then, one mysterious, indescribable day, Nat Poopcone awoke and disappeared, kind of like Darkman, or Lovecraft, Poe, a *Twilight Zone* episode, Matheson, or *Too Close for Comfort*. Would he ever be heard from again?

*   *   *

It was a pleasant autumn day for visiting the cemetery, so Lisa and Leslie caught the city bus after school to do just that. It had only been a few months since their father passed away, and they weren't ready to leave his side yet. Though thirteen and fifteen, they were often mistaken for twins, more so when they both wore black, like today.

They approached the large marble tombstone and placed flowers on the ground. After a brief moment of silence, Leslie began to say something when they both heard a click. They turned and saw a ratted sleeping bag a few yards away with what looked like hands sticking out of the end, holding a camera.

There was another click and a flash.

"Don't mind me," a voice said from within the bag. "I'm a publisher. I'll make you famous! You know, like Cindy Crawford, Vanna White, Punky Brewster, and Lovecraft."

Enraged, the girls ran up to the bag. Ignoring the shouts of "Fuck off, cunts!" and "I'm hardcore!" and especially, "I'll make you a horror target!", they proceeded to kick and stomp the shit out of it.

Where The Lost Ones Dwell
Tony Flynn

There is a place, so deep in Hell,
Where they say The Lost Ones Dwell.
And in this place, a tree does grow,
From Fossil Lake, where blood does flow.
And the captives here will not know peace.
Their sufferings will never cease.
The blood flows forth their awful crimes,
And flow it will, for all our time.

And from this blood, the Tree draws strength,
And with more blood, it grows in length.
And from the branches of this tree,
Not leaves do grow, but Souls, you see.
The Souls, whose actions blood did spill,
Now a place upon the tree they fill.
Like fruit they grow from on the branch.
To escape from here they have no chance.

Because food are they to those in Hell,
In the Forest where the Lost Ones Dwell.
For beyond the tree, there stands alone,
A mountain The Harpies call home.

They know no mercy; nor pity; nor grace.
They hunger always in this place.
And only one thing can their bellies, satiate:
The souls of those put here by hate.

And so they fly from up on high,
And plummet forth down from the sky,
To envelop in their monstrous wings
Those put here for terrible things.
They pluck them whole from off the tree
And carry to their lair to see,
A nest of Harpies: Young and old,
But hungry all, and bitter and cold.

Yet even after, no peace resumes,
For every year, the tree does bloom.
And forth the tree, they rise again,
The souls of those condemned as men,
And plunged down to the icy pit,
To wait until Harpies see fit
To take them, and their Souls devour,
Those foolish men, seduced by power.

Lana Doesn't Get Lucky
Kerry G.S. Lipp and Emily Meier

Lana carried the severed head by the hair as she walked toward Fossil Lake.

The head belonged to Bart, recently deceased. So recently, in fact, that the blood still dripped from the jagged cut that separated his head from his body.

She arrived at the bank, popped a beer, took a sip and set the can down. Then she lit a smoke. Dusky purple light sprayed across the horizon, sky as smooth as the calm water. The sky and the lake mirrored each other.

Bart's blood still dripped and his skin still felt warm. His dead eyes illustrated that age-old cliché of the silent screaming death, but Lana found it impressive. Clichés and stereotypes existed for a reason, and Bart's eyes both defined and justified that reason. She could stare at them all day and see something new, like artwork. Pure and unsettling.

His eyes told the story. Maybe it hadn't happened until the last second or two, but he'd figured it out just before he died. She hadn't seen his life flashing before his eyes as she removed his head, but they sure told the story of his death.

And what a story it was.

Bart, like every other guy, had one thing on his mind . . . and that thing was between Lana's legs. Though she was old enough to know what guys were after, it still angered her each time she gave it to a guy she liked and in return he reduced her to a midnight text message.

I want to cut him into pieces, she'd thought the first time, sobbing, staring at her phone, willing it to light up with his name.

It never did.

She ended up hunting him down and cutting him into pieces. She loved every second of it. And that was how it started for Lana.

Reminiscing about the recent kill, she tossed Bart's head and then caught it. Just like a ball. It weighed about ten pounds. Not too heavy, but heavy enough. Lana tossed it and caught it again. She stared out at the deserted lake as darkness descended.

Fossil Lake was perfect. It was surrounded by swamp, so no one wandered out this way often. Dragging the bodies this far would be more of a workout than she wanted, so instead, those got buried or burned.

But she always kept the heads for this little ritual. She'd relax by the peaceful lake with a six pack, some smokes and her iPod, before disposing of the heads in the secret place.

She tossed Bart's head and caught it in between sips from her beer and drags from her cigarette. Toss. Catch. Sip. Smoke. Toss. Catch. Sip. Smoke. Toss.

Oh fuck. Slip.

Bart's head fell. Lana just couldn't bend her fingers in the right way, and the crown of his skull hit a chunk of driftwood. His eyes looked at her for a final second before he rolled, bounced, and submerged deep into the dark water.

Lana rushed to the edge, but his head was gone, eaten by the abyss of Fossil Lake. Not good. She had to get it back and put it in the other place. The secret place that no one knew about.

"Sheeeeeeeiiiiiiit, that head sunk like a rock," said a burbling voice. "Nice work, butterfingers."

Lana jolted, and looked all around. All she saw was the forest, the lake and dusk. No lights, no people. Cold sweat burst on her brow and her stomach dropped. Had she been caught? And by who? She looked around again. Still saw nothing.

"Down here, toots," the voice said.

And Lana looked down and saw the ugliest fucking creature she'd ever seen.

Small and bulbous and scaly, the frog squatted in perfect frog pose between her feet, right in front of her and looking up her skirt.

"Nice," he said.

His throat throbbed and his pulsing fire-red eyes looked her up and down. Spiky horns protruded from random places on his head and body. Lana didn't know if frogs were supposed to have dicks, but this thing in front of her had a fat lumpy one, all chunky white and green. He looked like an acid trip concoction of frog, dragon, and porcupine. While she wanted to look away, she couldn't help but stare at his little froggy dick. Pus-colored saliva dripped from one corner of his mouth as his flaming peepers bored into Lana's eyes. Even in the dusk, his eyes lit like dancing candle flames. The kind you'd see at a cult sacrifice.

"Don't stare, bitch, it's rude," the frog said. His lips somehow twisted into a crude grin, teeth looking like a grenade blew up in his mouth.

Her jaw fell open. Lana gaped at the frog, entranced not only by his ability to talk, but by his sheer ugliness.

"You dropped that head, toots. You want it back?"

She knew she couldn't just leave it in the lake; someone would find it for sure. She had to put it with the others.

"Yeah," she stuttered when she could speak. "Can you get it for me?"

"I'd be happy to," the frog said. "You've done so much for me. I guess it's only fair that I fix this for you."

Again, she had no words.

"Don't look so stupid. I'll explain it all when I get back. But here's the deal. I do this for you, and you owe me."

She wanted to kick the frog, punt him straight into Fossil Lake too, but she couldn't.

"Calm down, bitch," he said.

Now she found words. "Call me bitch one more time and I'll stomp your spiky toad ass."

"I'm a frog, don't get it twisted!" He paused. "I'm sorry, I'm not used to conversating. Didn't mean to piss you off."

"My name's Lana."

"Let me get that head, then, Lana, and we'll talk. But first, the deal."

"And what's the deal, you froggy prick? It's like you forget that I can kill you and get that head myself."

"Don't underestimate me, bit . . . beautiful lady," he said.

Lana smiled. "Better. What's the deal?"

"That water is nipple-freezing cold. It makes my horns even harder. Might shrink my . . . well, whatever, don't judge me. You don't wanna go in there. I'll get this for you and then you'll owe me."

"Owe you what?"

"Your company, some food, a place to stay, and maybe even a kiss."

She cringed. But the frog was right, she needed that head.

"We'll see," she said. "Don't push your luck. Go get it and we'll talk."

His red eyes flared. He turned, splashed through the water and dove deep. Lana waited, sipping a beer and smoking a cigarette. The frog was gone a long time, but eventually, he broke the surface with a big tangle of Bart's hair clamped between his crooked teeth. He hopped up the bank, dragging the head. Lana stepped forward and grabbed it.

"Got him," the frog said. "Fucker had a heavy head."

Lana set it snug against some driftwood so that it couldn't roll back into the water. "I don't know how," she said. "There couldn't have been much in it."

"Brains and heads, regardless of how well they are educated, generally weigh the same."

"Oh, so now you got jokes? Lana asked.

"I'm just glad you're finally getting them, bi . . . beautiful."

"I don't know what the fuck is going on here." Lana said, sitting on a rock. "I'm so confused."

"Give me a beer and a smoke and I'll give you the skinny." His fire-red eyes looked her up and down. "Looks like you could use a little skinny," he added.

Lana ignored him.

"Hey," the frog said, "I just did you a huge favor toots, and we agreed to a deal. Beer and cigarette please."

"And just how the fuck am I supposed to give you a beer and a cigarette?" Lana asked.

"Jesus, we gotta smarten you up," he said. "Pour the beer in that divot in the rock and light the smoke and wedge it right there."

She did.

The frog took a big slurp of beer, then hopped over to the burning cigarette and took a mighty puff. When he exhaled, some of the smoke billowed through his amphibian skin.

"Nice," he said. "Now let's get down to business."

"Thanks for getting that head, I appreciate it. So what happens now?"

"First, I thank you, too," the frog said. "I pretty much owe you my life."

"I don't understand," Lana asked, puzzled. "And what's your name anyway? That would make my life a lot easier. I'm still not even sure this is real."

"My name is Lucky," the frog said.

"Lucky?"

"Did I stutter, bi- Lana? That's my name, and actually it's completely justified. I've been lucky to live at this lake. I've lived at a lot of lakes and never been as lucky as I've been here."

"What do you mean?"

Lucky rolled his eyes, drank from the pool of beer, hopped over, and hit the cigarette.

"You've made me Lucky, Lana. I've been a frog for a long time. A lot longer than most frogs. They usually die, a lot of them from starvation. Do you have any idea why I'm this fat?"

"No?"

"From the heads you hide," Lucky said. "Do you know what human heads attract as they decompose?

"Flies?"

"Any idea what my favorite food is?"

"Flies?"

"Pretty much," Lucky said. "Other bugs too, but the flies are my favorite Especially corpse flies. Greedy, bloated corpse flies. Fat and lazy and full of all kinds of juices. Delicious." Lucky licked his lips. "When you dump a head, the flies swarm, and I eat big and easy all day long. So thank you, Lana."

"That's fucking disgusting," Lana said.

"Uh, you're the one that kills people," Lucky fired back. "I just feed off of that."

She nodded, sipped her beer, and stared at the fat horny frog named Lucky that twitched in front of her. "So what's our deal, fatass?" she asked.

"Easy, bitch, I'm sensitive about my weight. I can't help it that you've killed so many people it's like I eat at Golden Corral every single meal. Have you ever considered moderation?"

"Have you?"

"Fuck off. Let's put all this shit aside and talk about what we can do for each other. You've fed me and made me fat and happy for a long time now; I appreciate it. Have the cops ever found a piece of a head you've left over here?"

"I don't think so," Lana said.

"And that's because as a thank you for you feeding me so well, I make the skulls disappear. You turn down the attitude a couple clicks, and maybe we can help each other out." Lucky drank and then smoked, hopped around a little bit, and looked up at Lana.

"What do you want?" she asked.

"I want a partner," Lucky said.

"I don't care what we've done for each other, I'm not letting your lumpy dick anywhere near me!"

"If I was a poison dart frog, I'd blast one right in your eye," Lucky said. "That was hurtful."

"Look, I'll admit, I'm a little crazy, but I draw the line dark and thick well before frog fucking."

Lucky rolled his flaring red eyes. "I'm not actually a frog."

"Well then . . ."

"And I'm not a toad either, before your smart ass says it," he cut her off.

Lana puffed out the smoke and her cheeks before taking a sip of her beer. "Okay, you fat lumpy-dicked asshole, thanks for getting that head, and

144

you're welcome for the smorgasbord of meals I've unknowingly provided you with. Maybe I'll even stop by the pet store and staple a baggie of live crickets to the next guy's forehead."

"Don't condescend me; I don't need pet store crickets," Lucky said. "We had a deal. If this is how it's gonna be, I'll just show up at your house. We can settle things then."

"Good luck finding out where I live, you fucking toad." She stood up. "Thanks again for getting that head. Eat, sleep and be merry. I'll be back to make sure that it's gone before anyone can find it."

"Fine, bitch," Lucky slapped his tongue out, hitting her ankles. "But I have a feeling we'll be seeing each other soon. And shave those things, would ya? That stubble is disgusting."

"I just . . . You know what? Fuck you," Lana said, and she turned to go.

* * *

When she got home, the paranoia set in like it always did.

As she settled into bed, she tried to push away the strange experience with Lucky and regain the calm that helped her sleep at night. Just as her hand began to help her relax, a noise at her window startled her.

It wasn't a knocking – more of a splashing. She turned on her lamp to see bits of blood splattered on her window.

"What the . . . !"

Grabbing a knife out of her nightstand and running to the window, she shoved it up. Out in the yard was Bart's head, with Lucky crouched on top, the frog's toes dipping into the pulpy remnants of Bart's severed neck and his frog legs flicking Bart's blood onto Lana's window.

With the window up, the next splat hit Lana in the face.

"Told you we'd be seeing each other, bitch!" Lucky yelled, loud and high enough to shatter glass.

Lana ran outside, scooped up Lucky by the legs and Bart by the hair, and pulled them into her kitchen.

"Finally!" Lucky said.

"How the hell did you get here? What the hell are you doing?" Lana demanded, dumping the head into the sink.

He gestured to some bloated black flies lying dead in Bart's neck stump. "Nabbed a few flies for you, too. I'll have a sandwich. Got any bread?"

"You fucking frog!"

"We had a deal. I got you the head, and now you owe me. You have to help me."

Raging red, Lana struggled to think things through. Bart's head in her sink, and his blood on her window, would certainly not be good when the cops showed up. And they would show up, if her neighbors heard Lucky's shriek.

"How am I supposed to help you?" she cried. "If you haven't noticed, you brought me quite a mess to clean up!"

"Doesn't matter," Lucky said, nonchalant. "We're not sticking around. Let's go."

Lana crossed her arms. "Where are we going?"

"You kiss me, I'll turn into a prince, and we'll go get married," Lucky said.

"Just like the story?"

"God, you can't fucking tell when I'm joking. Life's not a fairytale, princess. Let's go. You have to drive. My legs aren't long enough. And don't forget that sandwich."

Lana hesitated, but realized he was right. They had to move. Her, Lucky and Bart's head had to get gone.

She grabbed her keys and followed Lucky to her car. He hopped as fast as she could walk. As soon as she opened the door, he hopped into the passenger seat. Lana got in and put Bart's head on the seat beside the frog.

"Where to?" she asked

"Back to the swamp, dummy," Lucky ordered, then cleared his throat.

"I hate you," Lana said and put the hastily-slapped-together fly sandwich on the seat in front of him.

"Thanks, bitch," Lucky said, his crooked, pointed teeth twitching. He smacked his lips, munching and moaning in gluttonous pleasure. "Not bad, not bad at all. So . . ." He croaked, paused, burped, then added, "what'd these suckers do that pissed you off anyway? Call you fat? Try to rape you?"

Lana sighed. She'd been trying to contemplate her options while he ate, but he'd finished the sandwich in three bites.

"Truth told, I see the fat thing," he went on. "I really do, and you make a hell of a sandwich, you really do, and looks like you enjoy your own food. Rape thing though? I don't really get that." He eyed her up and down, then stopped, fixed on her boobs. "Well, maybe, but probably not sober."

Lana sighed again, "I only weigh . . ."

Then she stopped. Even though she wasn't that heavy, logic would never work on Lucky. She just wanted him to go away. So she tried to explain how the guys had used her. How she knew their intentions. How the murder, the decapitation, became her crusade –

She was interrupted by Lucky's coarse, maniacal laughter.

"You bitches," he gasped, trying to catch his breath. "You bitches really want a fairytale, don't you?"

Lana huffed, angry. Blinked tears. Her flushed cheeks only provoked the frog further.

"Poor Lana," Lucky mocked. "All the guys just want to fuck you. OF COURSE THEY DO, even with that little weight problem, THEY'RE STILL MEN." He laughed again. "If you don't want to be used for sex then don't fuck them! Or be a crack snacker. Guys can't use you if you don't let them. A bad murdering bitch like you? They don't have a chance anyway. What, you're waiting for a frog to turn into a prince and save you? C'mon, baby. Gimme a smooch!"

He hopped onto her lap and she swerved, shoving him back into his seat.

"Asshole!" she screamed, easing the car back into her lane.

"Yeah, I'm the asshole? Because I killed guys who acted like . . . guys? Good one princess."

She eased the car back into her lane. Then she took a hard turn that lead them to the pebble road heading to Fossil Lake. Her headlights illuminated the dark water.

"What are we doing here?" Lana asked, slamming the brakes at the edge of the trees surrounding the swamp. She hit them so hard Bart's head rolled to the floor boards, making a wet plop as it landed.

"We had a deal, and you're out of luck. Help me and I'll help you." Lucky made a kiss face with his disfigured lips. More of that pus colored drool trickled from the corner of his mouth. Then he bounded from the car and darted toward the water.

Lana snagged Bart by the hair and chased after Lucky. "What do I have to do? How can you help me?"

"I told you, kiss me and I'll turn into a prince and save you. I'll get you out of this!"

She started to roll her eyes, but heard sirens in the distance.

"What the hell! Did you call the cops?"

"Yeah, on my cell phone; it's a Cricket." Lucky uttered a sarcastic croak.

If they tracked her out here, where there was nothing except Lana, a talking frog, and whole bunch of human heads . . . She took a quick survey of her surroundings. The secret place with the heads was sort of tucked away, but nothing a few dogs wouldn't be able to sniff out. There was still a small trail of blood from the path, too, where she'd carried Bart's head earlier. Beer cans and cigarette butts, littered with her DNA, were all over the area.

And the cops were coming. The sirens were closer, and louder.

"Then what are we doing here?" she demanded. "Did you bring me here to get busted?"

"I told you. Kissing me is your only way out of this mess."

Lana inhaled deep and fast, air hissing through her teeth. The lights from the police cars flashed blue and red through the trees, but what the hell could this frog do to save her?

There was only one way to find out.

She picked up Lucky. He was fat and heavy, and weighed about as much as Bart's head, hanging in her other hand. Lana shuddered at the comparison. She felt Lucky's lumpy frog dick growing harder against her palm and fought down a dry heave.

She coughed, looked away. She looked at the lake, the woods pitch dark, but flickering with the lights of approaching trouble. Then she looked down at Lucky in all his disgusting horny glory, wondering how he could possibly help her, but inexplicably believing him. He blinked, and in that moment she thought that while he may not be cute, he might have something to offer.

Lana closed her eyes and leaned in. She could smell him. He smelled disgusting, like decay and flies and stagnant water. Instead of warmth, she sensed a wet coldness as their lips approached . . . then touched for a second.

It wasn't entirely unpleasant, but, just as she was about to pull away, Lucky shot his tongue into her mouth. The sticky part grabbed and pulled at her tongue while his lips moved against hers. She tried to break away, but she couldn't.

Finally, moaning, the frog unlatched his tongue from hers. His eyes rolled back in his head for a split second, then came back. He winked at her before leaping from her hand and landing softly in the grass, his ugly face grinning.

Lana stared, horrified, spitting, trying to get that taste out of her mouth. She realized that Lucky has also left her hand full of goo.

That moan, that wink, that hard, lumpy dick!

She tried to scream and vomit at the same time, wiping her hand on her pajamas. She fell to her knees, retching, and saw Bart's dead eyes still looking up at her.

Lucky laughed like a mental patient.

"I wish I really did have a Cricket to record this on, bitch. This is the best of the best."

She couldn't answer, she just kept dry heaving.

"And you know what the best part is?"

No answer.

"I didn't need any stupid fucking froggy cell phone. You saw that blood I splashed on your window? You really think that's all I can do?" Lucky flicked his tongue. "You dumb bitch."

Lana vomited, sick to her stomach at being tricked yet again.

"I wrote 'Fossil Lake' on the side of your house before I ever even started on your window. Bart had a lot of blood left in his neck. I can't believe you didn't see it. But you bitches never see it coming do you?"

She gagged.

"And just in case somehow you do see freedom again, here's your lesson: Frogs, men, princes, we're never who we say we are. And you bitches, well, it's all your fault."

Lana looked all around her. At Lucky, at the lake, at her vomit on the ground, at Bart's severed head. Just beyond Bart, she saw a pile of wet, mildewy, flesh-picked skulls. No doubt Lucky put them all there before he'd come to knock on her window.

For a second, she wondered just how bad Bart had been. How bad had any of them really been? Maybe they weren't such utter shits? Maybe they didn't deserve to get destroyed? Maybe she'd read the whole thing wrong, read them all wrong? Lana still didn't think so, but there was always . . . maybe.

The blue and red lights flashed across Fossil Lake. Lana heard the sirens and the screeching of tires. She heard a car door open. She heard footsteps on stones and knew that there was no way out.

A spotlight lit her up from behind.

"Thanks for the sandwich and the kiss, bitch," Lucky said hopping toward the lake. "Oh and thanks for letting me come in your hand. That was awesome. So soft. Do you use lotion? Never had a bitch let me do that before. Anyway, hope you learned something."

Lana looked at the rings that rippled from Lucky's splash and she hated him. Hated herself. Felt sick.

"Ma'am," came a voice from a bullhorn behind the open door of the police car.

She turned, shuffling awkwardly around on her knees, and looked into the light. She blinked as it blinded her. She started to raise her hands.

"On the ground, ma'am. Face down, hands behind your head. We know who you are and we suspect you of murder. Our orders are to proceed with extreme caution."

Lana stared, empty hands raised.

"On the ground, ma'am." Sterner now.

As she began to comply, she heard a fat, croaky voice chortling from the middle of the lake.

"You think this is bad, bitch? Wait until they see that pile of heads."

Gothicism on Trial
G. Preacher

"But not even the capture of The Eternal City could persuade Honorius to grant him legitimacy. Undeterred, Alaric marched south, intending to sail to North Africa, at that time the breadbasket of the entire Italian Peninsula. By controlling those grain reserves, he could starve not only Rome but the entire West. If that wouldn't get Honorius to proclaim him *Magister Militum*, nothing would."

Professor Maximillian Hastings risked a glance up from his notes. Some blank looks gazed back, from those of his students not distracted by something else. Half the classroom seemed to be focused on laptops, no doubt playing games or chatting with friends rather than taking notes. Others stared intently at the clock, as if that would somehow make the time go by faster.

His heart sank. A familiar anger kindled in his belly. Marketing, he'd been told. It was all about marketing, about selling history to the kids these days, making it exciting.

If this was what marketing got him, he'd rather lecture to an empty room.

There was a preponderance among them of pale faces, black lips and eyeliner, and attire to match. They wanted Goths, and that was what they were getting. But look at them. Just look at them.

And look at that other one, sitting in the back in the closest seat to the door. Him with his unwashed hair and torn black leather jacket over a rancid death-metal T-shirt. Him with his entitled, fuck-you attitude forever pasted on his sneering mouth. Why was *he* here? He wasn't in this class. He wasn't even enrolled.

"His plans were thwarted by a vicious storm that destroyed his fleet," the professor continued. "Alaric himself survived, only to die a short while later, near the end of the year 410, probably from disease. His successor, his brother-in-law, Ataulf or Ataulphus, took over leadership of the Gothic Confederacy, and led them north, into Gaul, where Honorius eventually granted them land and allowed them to settle as *feoderati*."

Nothing. He'd just thrown out *feoderati* for the first time and not a one of them batted an eye. They weren't listening. They weren't caring.

He raised his voice in an attempt to pull them back, to force them to listen. "The Roman response to being beaten by the Visigoths was immediate and long-lasting, and it is what we'll be examining in Monday's lecture. Which, if you've been paying attention to the syllabus, will be on St. Augustine's Concerning The City of God Against the Pagans, *De Civitate Dei Contra Paganos,* one of the ten most influential books in western civilization."

Still nothing. The dirty intruder at the back of the room smirked.

"The abridged version, assigned on the first day of class, is, of course, *required* reading. If you haven't started yet, you've got a long weekend ahead of you. Monday's class will start with a quiz on the text. Failure on the quiz equals failure of this class."

Now some of them looked worried through their masks of makeup and piercings. Others looked overconfident and smug, as if he'd just issued them a challenge.

Had *any* of them done the reading?

Why did he even bother to wonder?

Idiots. He always got stuck with the idiots. Screw the teacher-student contract. Screw them all.

"Are there any questions?" Hastings asked as the clock ticked closer to the hour.

There were none, only a general rustling of eagerness to leave. He dismissed them, then made his own quick retreat from the lecture hall.

Gothic Culture and Its Relevance Today. God, what an awful title.

"Marketing, my foot," he muttered. See what it had gotten him?

He detoured by way of the restroom and the faculty lounge, hoping – probably against hope – that if any of his students tried to seek him out at his office, they would give up and go away when he didn't arrive immediately.

Questions during class? No, never. A parade of excuses, whining pleas for extensions, and sob-stories about how unfairly overworked they were? Always.

His hopes proved only partially validated. He found two people waiting in the hall outside his door. One was a pale, slightly overweight girl of that indiscriminate college-age anywhere between seventeen and twenty-two. Her dyed-black hair was cropped in an unappealing, boyish cut. Her clothes were also black – gauzy skirt, leggings, a stretch-velvet top – except for an ill-fitting burgundy-colored corset.

The other was . . . *him.*

As Hastings approached, he heard the girl say, "– your father? Really?" His heart, already low, sank further.

"Yeah," said the other. "I'm the successful one of the family. Author, editor, publisher. That's me. Not some butt-licking burger-flipper. I do it all myself."

"Wow! So what do you write?"

"It's probably too dark for you." His eyes widened and his speech quickened. "It's too dark, transgressive and in-your-face for most people. April Derleth called me Lovecraft's heir. And Brian Keene, that hack, he just wishes –"

"Sorry to have kept you waiting," Hastings said, interrupting before he had to hear Niccolò recite his self-aggrandized resume yet again.

The girl turned toward him. "Oh, no worries, Professor. I was just talking to Nick, here. You must be so proud to have such a creative son!"

"You have no idea," he said, hiding the irony he couldn't mask by opening the office door. "What can I do for you . . . Jasmine, wasn't it?"

"Yes, sir." Now she went a bit sheepish. "I, um, see, I'm going away for the weekend . . ."

Here it was.

He raised a hand to cut her off as she launched into something about a Wiccan retreat in the mountains and how she therefore wouldn't have any time to read and couldn't she please –

"You've had the assignment for the last three weeks," he said. "Perhaps you shouldn't have left it until the last minute."

"Just an extra couple of days?" Jasmine looked tearful.

"The quiz is on Monday. For everyone."

"This is the only retreat all semester!"

"Then you have a decision to make. The spiritual advice of St. Augustine, or the Wiccans."

"But that's not fair!"

Hastings folded his hands tight atop his desk to keep them from curling into fists. Had she honestly just said that? That it wasn't fair? Not fair that the work was clearly outlined in the syllabus? Not fair that he'd stated on numerous occasions there would be no exceptions given? How was any of that unfair?

What was unfair was that he had to sit here being whined at, as if her problems were his fault. What was unfair was that he was stuck here, unable to secure his grant money, instead of in Italy! Where the river, *the* river, was at its lowest level in decades!

"Fuck, Dad," Niccolò said from the doorway. "Don't be such a shit-slinging prick about it. It's just a stupid history book."

What was also unfair was being stuck with this insane excuse for a child, who sounded like a twelve-year-old reprobate when he swore.

Doing his best to ignore that for now, he bit back his bile and frustration to concentrate on trying to help Jasmine find a solution to her 'unfair' situation. Once she'd agreed that she should be able to find at least *some* time for reading in and around her ridiculous weekend plans, she slunk timidly from the office.

Hastings, exhausted, desperately wanted a nap. But there stood his son, glaring at him with greasy petulance.

"Nice fucking work, Dad! She was into me! I was about to score, but then you had to walk up treating her like some pus-filled blister you have to lance off your ass. How the fuck am I supposed to get a girlfriend with you sabotaging me?"

"Nicco –"

"Don't fucking call me Nicco! Nobody calls me fucking Nicco, all my friends know not to call me out of name!"

"It is your name. I was there. I named you. Niccolò, after Machia –"

"My name is Nicolaus! Or Nick! Not Niccolò, that's a fag's name, do you want me to be some sort of butt-probed fag?"

Max sighed. "What do you want? Or are you just here to try and pick up girls from my class?"

"Thanks a fucking lot; I came to tell you my great news and you don't have to go and take a ripe shit on it."

"What news is that?" He did not dare to let himself dream it might be a real job, for once.

"I got a reading! For my new book, *Fossil Lake*. Those fuckstains won't know what hit them. They'll see. You'll see, too. I told you how you should give me a fucking chance to have my career."

Hastings began explaining, with as much diplomacy as he could muster, that he would be busy all weekend with analyzing and deciphering the latest images that would be transmitted during the satellite flyover of the site in –

He needn't have bothered with diplomacy.

"Fine! Don't come. Why would I want an old fuck like you there anyway? Be the asshole that I always knew you were . . . that Mom always says you are!"

With that, the storm that was Niccolò Hastings blew off as quickly as it had blown in.

Nicco's departure, however, did not signal the end of the day's troubles. Hastings was beset with ever more annoyances and inconveniences, from scheduling mix-ups to the department chair wanting to throw his weight around. It culminated with being called a selfish, domineering bastard by his own grad student.

That last stung most. He and Rob had always gotten on so well!

It wasn't as if they hadn't discussed the plan, gone over it in exacting detail more than once. Rob *knew* he'd need to get everything configured before the uplink. He knew about the time zone differences that had to be taken into account.

He also knew how much Hastings depended on him. Rob was the one who understood the programs, the software, the technical aspects of this stage of the project. Rob knew how important this was.

Why, therefore, was Hastings to blame for expecting Rob to put duty before pleasure? So he had a hot date, good for him, but a chance to 'get lucky' hardly meant ducking out on his other responsibilities.

Just as he'd told Jasmine she needed to choose between Augustine and the Wiccans, he presented a similar choice to Rob. His girl, or his thesis. He could get lucky any time, after all. An opportunity like this, like they were about to undertake, was not to be missed.

Finally, the disgruntled Rob nonetheless saw the light. Hastings was able to go home for an unsatisfying dinner of overcooked take-out and perhaps too much wine, and fall into a fitful sleep.

*   *   *

Gaius Maximius Herenus stood on the hill overlooking the works. The riverbed, dry now except for patches of mud and mire, spread out before his ever-watchful eye. The tomb itself lay in an excavated depression.

Hundreds of slaves scurried about, carrying the bricks and mortar needed to build the north and west walls of the structure. The carpenters worked in a large camp to the north, above the river bed, crafting the traditional grave offerings as well as a spectacular four-wheeled chariot that would be used to transport the body.

Or something like that, Maximius wasn't entirely sure. Upstream, his second-engineer kept the dam that diverted the Buscento under constant supervision and frequent repair. The last thing anyone needed was for the dam to break and drown everything, and everyone. That would surely mean Maximius' head. Ataulphus was not an understanding king.

"Maximius!" The call came from his scribe, Lucius.

He raised his hand in greeting.

"The king has called for you. He has bid me tell you that he wants to know when the tomb will be complete, and for you to know that he is prepared to give you great honors if you can finish in three more days."

"It can be done my friend, just barely I think. Take me to him then, and we shall see what he says."

*   *   *

His cell phone gradually woke him, the strains of *O Fortuna* rousing him from his slumber.

Fragments of the dream flashed through his waking mind and he grasped at them, desperately trying to remember as many details as he could.

In his youth, similar dreams had come to him often. Nightly, sometimes. The dreams had inspired him, given him direction for his studies, kept him going during difficult times. They'd led him to the area where he believed the remains of the tomb must be found, despite those who'd been unconvinced by his theories.

It was the wrong place, they'd said. The tomb must have been near Cosenza, not further upstream, away from the coast.

Hastings knew better, knew with every ounce of his being. He had *been* there. In person, yes . . . walking the valley of the Buscento all those years ago . . . the best times of his life . . . his young exuberance, his wonder at the world and its history, his passion, the best days of his life . . . he'd been there in the flesh as well as in his dreams. His recurrent dreams of being Gaius Maximius Herenus, engineer of Alaric's tomb.

Dreams that had made him who he was today.

But it had been years since the last one, and this time . . . this time was different.

Never before had there been a summons from Ataulphus!

Hastings yearned to go back to sleep, to pursue further revelations, but the phone rang again. He reached for the annoying object.

Soon, he would have his proof. It wouldn't be as good as being there, standing on that dry river bed, but the live satellite images and the new computer enhancement software would find traces of the tomb.

He'd be vindicated. His life's work complete. His dreams realized in every sense of the word.

Expecting it to be Rob, calling from the computer lab with an update, he answered the phone. At this ungodly hour, it had better be one hell of a good —

"Dad! About fucking time you picked up!"

The hour was even ungodlier by the time he had finished dealing with the bail bondsman and the police, and climbed back behind the wheel with Niccolò sulking in the passenger seat.

"The shriveled old cunt deserved it," he said. "Sassing me at *my* reading? Hah! She asked for what she got!"

"It was an open-mic night, not a 'reading'," Hastings said.

"She said I had a dirty mouth, and when I told her I'd make her mouth dirty, she called me no kind of Christian! Can you believe that? Who does she think she is, calling me –"

"She was a nun. A seventy-year-old nun in a wheelchair, and you slapped her."

"Fucking bitch."

Hastings sat for a moment, trying to compose his thoughts. Here he was, pissed off and tired, on what was supposed to be the eve of his greatest triumph. And his son was a fucking idiot. A fucking nun-slapping idiot.

Now he was faced with either driving Niccolò all the way across town to his tacky basement studio apartment, or take him home to the condo, which he did *not* want to do.

O Fortuna sounded again. On the other end of the line was a grouchy campus security guard, wanting to know if Hastings really needed to keep the computer lab open and empty all damn night.

"Empty?" he cried, panic surging through him. "What do you mean, empty? Rob's not there?"

"Nobody's been here," said the guard. "I could have gone home by now otherwise."

Rob and his hot date! Rob and his hormone-befuddled priorities! All their work, down the drain? Hastings' mind whirled like Hero's aeolipile.

"Don't close the lab," he told the guard. "I'll be there as soon as I can!"

The guard did not seem thrilled by this, but Hastings was beyond caring. He snapped shut the phone and roared out of the precinct parking lot faster than was advisable.

"The fuck crawled up your sour ass?" Niccolò asked as they sped toward the university.

"Rob . . . the computers . . . damn it, damn him, and damn me for not knowing anything about them!" Hastings hammered the heel of his hand on the steering wheel.

"Chill your shit already. I use computers all the fucking time. I edited *Fossil Lake* on five different word processors. Anything that fag-boy Rob can do, I can do better."

"Nicco —"

"And I told you, don't call me Nicco!"

What choice did he have? What else was there? Maybe miracles did happen, and Niccolò could get the programs to work.

He soon found out that wasn't the case.

What followed was an ordeal of anger, frustration and profanities. Niccolò ended up on the phone with the JPL technicians, screaming at them, calling them 'curry-fucking imbeciles' among other things, demanding they fix what he'd only made worse. Hastings had lost the last of his own temper in turn and told him to get the fuck out before he threw him out.

"Yeah, well, you know what?! Fuck you, Dad! Fuck you and your fucking university! You care more for your fucking dead people than you do for your own son anyway! You think you're so fucking superior to me, don't you?! We're no different, you and me! You hate all these pathetic sacks of fuck as much as I do. You're just too fucking chicken to say it. You hear that?! I'm the brave one! You're the pussy!"

He stomped out, still ranting, and Hastings sank into a chair wondering how much it would take to bribe his way back into the goodwill of anybody at JPL. Not that it mattered, if he'd missed the satellite flyover window. He might never have another chance.

The door to the computer lab banged open and Rob rushed in, babbling frantic apologies. He looked terrible, clothes torn, face bloodied, an eye swollen nearly shut.

"My God, what happened?" Hastings asked.

As it turned out, Rob had not forgotten. Neither had he blown it off in favor of his hot date. He'd had every intention of being at the lab on time, until his hot date's jealous ex showed up. Rob had defended the girl at the cost of getting the shit beat out of him.

"Would have called you but my phone got broken in the fight," he said, "and I didn't have your private number anywhere else."

He had then discharged himself from the emergency room against medical advice to make it over here in hopes of still salvaging some of the project.

Miracles, it seemed, did happen after all.

Working together, Rob at the computer and Hastings on the phone, they were able to smooth things over with the technicians. Their optimal flyover window had passed by then, but by incredible good fortune they found another satellite that could get some images of their desired coordinates a day or so later.

It wasn't ideal, but it was much better than nothing.

By Monday morning, Maximillian Hastings would either have his long-awaited discovery, or he'd know that his search had to continue.

* * *

The pavilion was enormous and grand, a palace, no mere tent. Inside, hanging white linen divided the immense space into smaller sections. The laughing of women filtered in from the back, the piercing, horse-like laugh of Galla Placidia rising above the others.

Bright Persian-style rugs covered the ground, overlapping and caked with dust, tracing a path to the room where Ataulphus held court. This large, airy space could not help but impress visitors with its splendor. Slaves, ironically wearing senatorial togas, waited on the many guests and on the king himself. He dwarfed all, seated as he was in his huge golden throne of Sassinid design. Uncomfortable, perhaps, but imposing, glittering with darts of light.

Gaius Maximius Herenus approached and dropped to one knee. It didn't bother him that his master was not a citizen, not a Roman, not even a Greek or an Etruscan. He was an architect, after all. His goal was building, and for that he needed to follow the power and the money. Ataulphus being a German didn't matter; what mattered was that the king had the resources to have a mausoleum constructed – an ambitious one at that! – and he had chosen Herenus to do it.

Well, chosen was perhaps the wrong word. The architect had been taken by the Goths during the sack of Rome, and, while he had since been able to earn himself a better position, he was still a slave.

"Tell me, builder, how progresses my sister's husband's tomb?" The king spoke terrible Latin.

"It will be completed tomorrow, as you have wished, Your Majesty. Downstream has already been prepared. Once the entombment is done, the earth may be filled back in around it. If the workers are as quick with their shovels in the burying as they were in the excavating, a day more should suffice for the dams to be torn down and the river let flow again around and over it."

"If all is in readiness as you say, Priscus Attalus will lead the burial procession tomorrow at sunset, and you will be among the guests of honor."

He bowed his head. "Yes, Your Majesty."

"You have done well, Herenus. Very well."

* * *

Between disrupted sleep patterns and the excitement of the weekend, it wasn't until he stepped into the lecture hall on Monday that Professor Hastings realized he'd entirely forgotten about the assigned quiz.

It hardly meant he would break character and let his students off the hook. No amount of tiredness or distraction could do that. He'd dragged himself away from the computer lab just as the images were beginning to come in, being able to only glance at the first few. If *he* had to suffer, why should *they* have it any easier?

He told them to get out sheets of paper as he made up questions from memory and wrote them on the board. Naturally, most of the laptop brigade didn't even have paper, which resulted in an eternity of shuffling around as they borrowed from their lower-tech, but better-prepared classmates.

The fast-food egg sandwich he'd eaten for breakfast seemed to be doing loops in his stomach, spreading discomfort through his midsection. He wished he'd thought to grab some antacids from his desk drawer.

An irate call from Nicco – same shit, different day – hadn't helped either. Nicco ranting and raving and blaming his father for him having to take the bus across town at four in the morning; as best as Hastings could decipher, a homeless person at the bus stop had either puked on Nicco, picked on Nicco, or tried to pick up on Nicco, or possibly some combination thereof.

Hastings, overwhelming tiredness finally making him snap, had told the obnoxious child to fuck off and get a life. Then he'd hung up, feeling a pang of guilt suffused by a much greater relief.

The matter of paper sorted out at last, the class went to work. He noticed Jasmine in her usual spot, brow furrowed and chewing her lip. So much for his efforts to help her find time in her plans for the reading. Good God, was even flipping through the Cliff's Notes too much to ask?

After collecting the finished quizzes, he set them aside to grade later. Partly so the students could stew in suspense, and partly because those that failed would then figure they had no reason to stay for the rest of the class, when he wasn't done with them yet.

He began lecturing on the barbarian sack of Rome and the resultant shock to the collective psyche of the entire Mediterranean world, then moved on to Augustine's interpretation of those events. In the middle of that, the side door burst open.

Dread and fury swelled in Hastings. His breath went short and his chest tight, constriction seizing his ribs. It would be Nicco, he knew. Damnable Nicco, spewing a torrent of vile abuse, making a spectacle –

It was Rob, clutching his laptop computer. "Professor Hastings! You've got to see this!"

Had he been thinking no distraction could make him let his students off

the hook? Screw that. He stopped mid-sentence, mouth dry, heart thrumming.

Rob rushed forward. He was grinning like a madman despite his bruises. Hastings peripherally noticed a curious buzz among the students – the first time the wretches had shown any interest all semester – but his eyes were only for the screen.

It showed a computer-enhanced, satellite image of a river reduced by drought to a trickle. A slightly-curved line showed where an ancient dam must have been . . . a dam perhaps built to slow the water's course and collect washed-away soil, countering erosion that might otherwise have exposed a large buried object.

And there, in the center of a wide spot, were the outlines of angles too straight and even to be anything made by nature. Suggestions of corners, a square sunk into the riverbed . . .

His legs went weak. He wore his own madman's grin, filled with such joy and triumph he could barely think straight.

Then his knees buckled. He felt himself drop to the floor. Though he saw his students, their reaction now one of alarm, he heard only the rapid-fire tattoo of his pulse thundering in his head.

People crowded around him. Kneeled over him. There was a sensation of lift.

Something about a hospital? Nonsense; he was just giddy with the thrill of the moment! So giddy that a warbling siren-sound replaced the staccato filling his ears.

Something about tests? What tests? The quizzes? Forget the quizzes; right now he'd gladly give each of them an A for the entire course!

It occurred to him that he was moving. Flat on his back, but moving. With an effort of concentration, he focused and discerned that he was in an ambulance.

"Professor? Max? Max!"

Rob's voice. Rob's battered face, wrenched with worry. Rob talking to him, random words of reassurance.

But never mind that. Never mind any of that.

"Did . . . did we . . . did we really find it?" Hastings gasped.

Emotion flooded Rob's eyes. He squeezed Hastings' hand. "Yes. Yes, Professor. We did. *You* did. You found Alaric's tomb."

A tear ran down his cheek, the last sight Hastings saw before his own eyes drifted closed.

*   *   *

In the dry riverbed, the marble tomb sat sunken belowground, a narrow ramped causeway leading down to its entrance. The plain and unadorned stonework seemed stark and too modest for its purpose, though a vital detail had not been overlooked – Alaricus Rex Gothorum *read the simple inscription above the door.*

Priscus Attalus and Gaius Maximius Herenus led the procession. Behind them came slaves herding a team of goats that pulled a four-wheeled cart of masterful construction. Carvings and inlays covered its sides, and everyone who had seen it marvelled at the speed and beauty of its craftsmanship. Upon it, in golden mail, lay the body of Alaric, wrapped in Egyptian-made cloths to help preserve the flesh.

Others followed, Alaric's personal slaves and those who had worked in the construction of the tomb. A wise man strode solemnly, bringing up the rear. He was said to be both a priest of Christ and blessed by the spirits of their ancestors.

Ataulphus and the rest of the Gothic people watched from what normally would have been the banks of the river, were it not held back by the cleverly-designed dams.

At the doorway, Priscus Attalus spoke a few words, both in Latin and in Gothic, as the goat-drawn cart was led in. Then he went to stand by Ataulphus' side. He would not be joining them in this final honor to Alaric.

The priest, shepherding the slaves forward, passed around jugs of wine. They took them, and drank, and went into the darkness..

Lucius, the scribe, had visited Maximus the night before, offering to help him escape. The only 'honor' that Ataulphus meant to bestow, he explained, was that of being sacrificed to the pagan gods. The heavy stone door would be shut upon them, sealing them in the tomb with their lord and master.

But Maximus had calmed him, and told him that he had known what was to come. That death came to all and . . .

"After a man has come to know greatness and to be truly great, what has he yet to live for? To be forever a slave? A slave to an un-understanding lord? A slave to a greatness that shall never come again? No, my friend. I shall not be brought low by pandering apprentices or disloyal and spoiled children. I have made a great thing, a wonder that will perplex those for generations to come. That it is the tomb of a great and legendary man, only makes it the greater. I shall die great, and live forever."

Then he went proudly into the tomb, his *tomb, which he had created. He drank deeply of the poisoned wine and laid himself down, content to live forever in the dreams of man but never be found on Earth.*

Finding Miss Fossie
Melany Van Every

In the early morning light, the lake is quiet and smooth as glass, reflections of trees along the shoreline darkening the surface. Fog hugs the shore in spots, hiding the shallows and creating eerie silhouettes.

Fishermen will line the banks later in the day, while fossil hunters turn over rocks hoping to find more than just the outlines of tiny, ancient shellfish. As families crowd the sandy beach, arguing over the best spot to spend the day, singles and teens will vie to catch the best rays or the eyes of the opposite sex.

The only sign of life at this hour is a light from Jericho Jake's Bait Shop. Not even the old-timers remember why it's still called that; nobody named Jake has owned it for at least fifty years. But it's been around so long, a local fixture, that none of the successors could bear to change it.

The building itself hasn't changed much either. The sign is neon now instead of painted plywood, and the cooler full of beer and sodas is brand new, but the tanks of minnows and the ancient refrigerator holding worms and leeches is the same. There's a walk-up window counter for customers who don't have to come in, and a screen door that bangs in its frame for the ones who do. Inside, a lone ceiling fan lazily circulates the fishy-smelling air.

The current owner, Tom Wilkinson, has run the place these past ten years. It isn't one of those fancy box stores they keep talking about putting up, but it does the job. Fishermen can buy their bait and basics, such as bobbers, hooks, sinkers, and a small selection of lures. There are boats that can be rented by the hour or the day. Tourists who come in looking for sunscreen,

bug spray and souvenirs tend to leave with their noses in the air.

Tom doesn't mind. He welcomes everyone to his shop, locals and tourists alike. He knows that what really brings people in is the talk. Whether it's bragging about the one that got away, or the latest crazy theories about Miss Fossie, Tom listens cheerfully. Sometimes he whistles as he fills minnow buckets or gasses up outboard motors. The tunes range from classical to contemporary, depending on his mood.

He's thirty-five, but years spent outdoors and a habit of smoking like it's going out of style make him appear older. His hair is dirty-blond and hangs to his collar. His eyes are pale green. He favors polo shirts and jean shorts; both of which tend to be covered in dirt and fish blood by the end of the day, but Tom doesn't care. He loves his job, the shop, and the lake.

This quiet morning, as he's out organizing the rack of life vests by the dockside, a commotion of splashing gets his attention. He glances up and down the shore, but the lingering fog obscures any disturbances in the shallows. Some large fish, he supposes, feeding on its smaller cousins or unlucky frogs. Sounded like a whopper, all right.

Then the first truck pulls into the parking lot, and Tom puts it out of his mind.

It's a slow day. At mid-morning, thunderstorms roll in, driving all but the hardiest fisherman off the lake. Tom ends up spending most of his time in a wobbly chair, reading a battered paperback by some guy named Brian Keene. He'd found it languishing in the lost and found box under the counter. The story is a bit far fetched, with giant night crawlers and massive flooding, but it's much better than the piece of crap that lunatic from Illinois had shoved into his hands before scuttling out of the shop a few days ago.

His most important work, he'd claimed, then gone on to mutter something about it being the book the whores and gays didn't want people to read.

Why whores or gays should give a damn about lake-monster sightings, Tom has no idea.

But then, some folks there was no reasoning with. When he wasn't talking about his books, he was demanding Tom install a computer with free internet service so he could upload his latest batch of photos – blurry pics of logs and kids, mostly. That, or complaining Tom didn't stock his favorite brand of cheap beer.

Just when he decides he might as well close up shop for the day, the door opens. It admits two dripping-wet deputies with grim looks on their faces. Town folks often jokingly call them the twins, though they aren't related. They just look very much alike, with broad shoulders, brown crew cuts, and

the builds of slightly out of shape former football players.

Danny, on the right, speaks up first. "We hate to disturb you Tom, but there's been an accident on the lake, and —"

His partner Josh interrupts, almost jittering with eagerness. "Right now we're calling it a drowning, but —"

"— in reality it appears he was attacked by an animal," Danny finishes, shooting Josh a scowl.

Tom raises his eyebrows. "An animal? Probably a momma black bear protecting her cub, then. It's the right time of year for it."

There are no customers, but Danny still looks around the empty shop before pulling something out of his pocket. It's a plastic bag, the zip-kind they use for evidence, and holds what appears to be a four-inch-long tooth.

Tom raises his eyebrows further as he wonders if the deputies decided to liven up their rainy-day boredom with a prank. Fossilized mosasaur teeth are rare, most of the finds around here being from much smaller creatures, but some still turn up every so often. They are, in fact, exactly what fuel the legends of Miss Fossie.

If they expect him to fall for it . . .

His thoughts get no further as he notices this particular tooth is no fossil. It's as white and clean as if it had been ripped fresh from the creature's mouth that very morning.

The deputies are not grinning. Tom realizes that what he mistook for eager jitters on Josh's part are the after-effects of adrenaline.

"The guy's name was Albert Campbell," Danny says. "Some kids found his body near the south shore."

"Mutilated," Josh adds. "Chunks taken out of him. Bloody goddamn mess."

Danny nods gravely.

"Campbell?" asks Tom. "Not that unpleasant fellow who's always in here going on about lake-monsters?"

"Yeah," Danny says. "From some nowhere town or another in Illinois. We'll have to ship him back."

"What's left of him," says Josh. "The pieces."

Danny shoots him another scowl. "Once the coroner's signed off on cause of death and we've closed the case, that is. You seen Campbell around here lately?"

"Not since the other day," Tom says. "Ran him off for harassing a bunch of underage girls on the beach. This tooth, though . . . you're not saying . . . you can't be saying . . ."

"Coroner says it's possible a propellor did the damage," Josh says. "Tore

him up after he drowned, maybe. We don't know on that yet. But the same kids that found the body found the tooth near the scene."

Danny turns the plastic bag over, examining the tooth from all sides. "Probably their idea of a hoax and we'll find out it's made of plaster or something. We're not going to spread this around, and we're counting on you to keep quiet. We just know you collect odd stories about the lake."

Josh squints out the shop window at the rain-swept water. Lightning flashes a ways distant, followed moments later by the dull rumble of thunder. "And if it *is* the real thing, you'll want to be careful out here."

Danny sighs. They might look as alike as brothers, but it's clear he's resisting the urge to give his more superstitious partner an elbow in the ribs. Tom thanks them for stopping by, offers them free sodas for the road and the other usual pleasantries. They exchange goodbyes. Then the deputies leave, and Tom figures his decision to close up for the rest of the day was the right one after all.

He dons a rain poncho before heading outside to check the boat moorings, lock the fuel shed, and bring in the life jackets. The poncho whips around him in the wind. The rain plasters his hair to his head. A blinding flash lights up the world, the thunderclap not following but simultaneous. The lightning strike is so close it throws Tom off his feet. He lands in the wet grass, dazed and deafened, gasping for breath. All he can think is that it was sheer luck he landed on shore instead of plunging into the water.

Tom starts getting up. A large, violent movement thrashes nearby, several yards out into the lake. Another jagged bolt splits the sky. For a stark fraction of a second, it shows him churning waves and a thick, muscular body. He glimpses a long, sinuous tail. A scream bursts from him.

In subsequent lightning flashes, he sees the creature moving across the lake. It lacks the grace of the famous monster of Loch Ness, but it has plenty of speed and power. He watches, mouth hanging open, until it dives and is gone.

＊　　＊　　＊

Tom rarely talks about what he saw that day. The few people he does tell laugh, and say it was probably just a trick of the storm, or an after effect of being almost struck by lightning.

One or two, like Josh, believe his story. But nobody is able to prove it.

If Albert Campbell had survived, he could testify that Tom speaks the truth. His final moments on Earth had been spent in extreme pain and terror, the creature charging at him, knocking him down, and proceeding to eat him

alive. It might have eaten the rest of him if the sounds of approaching humans hadn't driven it from its kill.

Visitors to Fossil Lake today can still hear stories of Miss Fossie. They can marvel at the white tooth among the collection of fossil finds in the new visitor center. They can even buy books in the gift shop about famous lake monsters . . . though nothing by the late Albert Campbell, of course.

They just aren't likely to actually spot the beast.

Perhaps it found a way to the ocean. Perhaps the storm hurt it so severely that it couldn't survive, and lies buried in the mud at the bottom of the lake. The world may never know.

Since that fateful day, Miss Fossie has never been seen again.

Arkham Arts Review
Peter Rawlik

Arkham Arts Review: *Alienation*
An Interview with Director James Romberg

Eight years ago media producer James Romberg became a sensation with his docudrama *Innsmouth*. This week he debuts his new work *Alienantion*, an account of the life of the film actor Abraham Waite. Earlier this week Mr. Romberg chattered with our own Mick Moon.

MM: Mr. Romberg, *Innsmouth* was a sweeping historical piece, and a critical and commercial success; why follow it up with an examination of someone like Abraham Waite? It seems a radical departure from your previous work.

JR: *Innsmouth* – and before that *Jermyn* – were period pieces. *Alienation* is a contemporary film, but it's still rooted in the same source, still asking the same questions. What does it mean to be different, to be fundamentally inhuman in a human world, both physically and psychologically? I could do this through fiction, but adapting history, telling the stories of these people who actually lived, I think it is much more powerful.

MM: But, in both previous films your protagonists moved from a human world into an inhuman one. In *Jermyn*, Arthur rejects his origins with tragic results, while Robert in *Innsmouth* eventually learns to accept and embrace his ancestry. Abraham Waite begins in an inhuman world and moves into the normal one, finding a place, or at least trying to. That seems to be a bold reversal of direction.

JR: Actually it's a natural progression that mimics the time and attitudes that each film was set in. *Jermyn* is an Edwardian piece, with the central character representing the dominant society, which violently rejects any revelations concerning the past that might impact their particular worldview. *Innsmouth* is purposefully a Jazz Age piece, and the response of Robert Olmstead to revelations concerning his ancestry mirrors the societal changes that were occurring during that time period. Yes, he rejects what he discovers, and reports it to the government, and the actions taken are just as violent and drastic as those portrayed in *Jermyn*. However, in the aftermath Olmstead reconsiders, his initial rejection is replaced with not only acceptance, but also a sense of outré wonder and elation. I think of *Alienation* as a commentary on post-humanism. Abraham Waite begins his journey in Innsmouth, isolated from what some would call civilization. His journey from that isolation into the spotlight of first fame, and then infamy, highlights the changes in mainstream society and the way in which it now embraces the fringe elements it once tried to deny, even destroy.

MM: But Abraham Waite is still alive, and still working in film, correct?

JR: He is. Abe has been working in film since 1962, when he first appeared in Corman's *Echidna*. He made sixteen films with Corman, including the remake of *Freaks* and the classic *Galaxy of Fear*. In 1982 he began working with Tobe Hooper, appearing first in *Tsathaggua*, and then later as the antagonist in *Warlords of Yaddith*. The failure of Romero's *Night of the Reanimator*, both critically and financially, drove Abe to take a number of minor parts, mostly as an extra or part of the special effects team. This led to him working with Carpenter on *Who Goes There?* and winning a Saturn Award for Best Supporting Actor.

MM: This was very controversial at the time.

JR: Right. There were a lot of voices, ugly voices, raised in response to Abe's appearing on network television. A coalition of actors, mostly character actors who specialized in roles that required significant amounts of make-up and prosthetics, objected saying that Abe had an unfair advantage. In the meanwhile, many people with similar characteristics suggested that Abe was catering to stereotypes. Just as ethnic groups had formed to protest the negative portrayals of Africans and Asians on film, the movement that protested Abe and similar actors became very vocal. However, while the Black Face and Yellow Face Movements worked in concert with each other, the Green Face groups found no such support and were forced to escalate their activities in order to garner national attention to their cause. Unfortunately, one radical faction chose to resort to violence to make their point.

MM: You're talking about the accident that occurred on the set of Larson's series, *Galactics.*

JR: There was nothing accidental about it. The Esoteric Order of Dagon purposefully interfered with a dangerous stunt which caused the death of six of their members. It was a reprehensible act, and psychologically scarred those cast and crew members who witnessed it.

MM: The grand jury found that the studio was not responsible for those deaths. Abraham Waite sued and won significant damages from the Order.

JR: Well he may have won the legal battle, but in many ways he lost the war.

MM: Care to elaborate?

JR: The trial was a spectacle, and it brought to light a significant amount of history, including family history, that Waite would have preferred remain out of the public eye. There was testimony about religious practices, inbreeding, genetics, even miscegenation. It was all very ugly. There was even a Congressional Committee chaired by Tipper Gore to review the legal status of residents of Innsmouth and Dunwich. Afterwards, the studio wrote Waite's character out of the series, over Larson's protests mind you, and Abe was essentially blacklisted from Hollywood.

MM: This led to his working in some questionable films.

JR: Yeah, for about ten years or so he worked with a lot of independent directors. He even did some soft-core, what was unfortunately called fish porn. Eventually, he got work with some decent directors like Raimi, Smith and del Toro. All of which eventually led to his performance in

Jackson's *Eldritch*, for which he won the Academy Award.

MM: This did not sit well with Tantamount, the parent studio of *Galactics*.

JR: They weren't happy at all, particularly with the toy line, which featured an action figure based on Waite that was almost identical to the one being marketed for the *Galactics* line. Tantamount took Abe to court claiming that he was infringing on their copyright of the character's appearance, a patently absurd tactic, but bolstered by some creative interpretation of language in the licensing clause of his contract. Waite's lawyers countersued, noting that he had only agreed to the use of his face, not his entire body, which in the series had never been fully shown. Meanwhile after reading the position taken in Tantamount's filings, the SAG union authorized a strike in support of Waite.

MM: That work stoppage lasted for six months, and eventually led to the downfall of the studio head Howard Lowe. It also changed the way studios contracted with actors and licensed their products.

JR: It also created a whole new class of actors, so called Living Effects. The portrayal of the monstrous that had spawned the Greenface opposition and groups like the Esoteric Order of Dagon, suddenly had little to complain about. MADS, the Monstrous Ant-Defamation Society, was formed, and like the ASPCA, now has a presence on any studio film. Though to be honest, the days of exploitation films like *The Blob*, *The Creature from the Black Lagoon*, or *I married a Monster from Outer Space*, are long dead. Sure there may be a few direct to video releases, but these are relatively minor films.

MM: *Humanoids from the Deep* set box office records at the Kingsport Film Festival last year. Jeff Wilmarth called it "A tour de force of cinematic sleaze that will leave you begging for more."

JR: I've seen that film, and I understand why it was so popular, and why the critics liked it. But the truth is that it possesses the same kind of nostalgic charm that things like *Madman* and *Red Hook* have. When we look at these dramas that are recreating what many see as a simpler more innocent time, what we are really doing is looking at that period and remembering it with fondness, but at the same time, we recognize that many of those behaviors and events were the product of an ignorant and bigoted society, that in retrospect can be very amusing, and yes entertaining, and therefore profitable.

But that doesn't make them significant works of art.

MM: For example?

JR: Scott's film *Extraterrestrial* was very profitable, and the critics adored it when it came out. But now twenty years later it is forgotten, the effects are sub-par, the storyline is mediocre and the acting was just bland. In contrast, *EXtro* by Burton lost money on its initial release, but has now become a cult classic and a cash cow for Dyson Pictures.

MM: Shifting back to Abraham Waite, what's his current situation?

JR: He's doing very well; he lives in Kingsport where he spends most of his time fishing and painting. He doesn't act much, though he just did a cameo in Lynch's *Devil Reef,* and he's scheduled to appear in an upcoming episode of *Professor Wyche*. He will be at the premiere on Friday.

MM: Was he involved much with the making of *Alienation?*

JR: Not as much as I would have liked. What many people don't seem to understand is that Waite is a consummate professional. The film itself relies heavily on his memoir *Monstrous,* but where Abe was really helpful was in the actual film making. He's been an actor for more than forty years, but he has also studied film and camera work. He actually has a credit in the film as a camera man. Also, Abe worked extensively with Rex Topf, the actor who played Abe in the film, to make sure that Rex had mastered Waite's very distinctive walk and cadence. This wasn't easy for Rex, he has three fewer tentacles than Abe, which we added in through digital effects, but capturing the way Abe moves was difficult for him.

MM: You told me earlier that the home release version of the film will have a bonus track, would you like to explain?

JR: Oh, absolutely, in fact we just came from the studio this morning, where I and Abe were working on the Director's commentary. So, we will actually have Abraham Waite commenting about the film of his life.

MM: That is kind of surreal.

JR: Isn't it though?

MM: James I want to thank you for joining us here at Arkham Arts Review.

JR: Always a pleasure.

MM: *Alienation*, the new film by James Romberg about the life of actor Abraham Waite premieres at Miskatonic University's Wilmarth Centre for the Arts in Arkham on Friday April 30th. Tickets are available at the box office, or online.

Following the premiere of *Alienation*, Director James Romberg, and his wife Ellen, were joined by Mr. Waite at a reception for the press. According to eyewitnesses the three were actively involved in answering questions, when Reverend Enoch Marsh, the nominal head of the Esoteric Order of Dagon in Innsmouth, approached the panelists.

Well known for his radical views in favor of racial segregation, Reverend Marsh was supposed to be barred from the reception. How he gained access is unknown. Security staff failed in their attempts to block his approach, and once Marsh reached the table, he threw himself at Mr. Waite reportedly screaming "Cthulhu fthagn!" Dr. Marsh then detonated explosives hidden underneath his coat killing himself, three security guards and the entire panel.

In light of these events Witch Hill Studios has indefinitely postponed the film's release.

Mishipishu: The Ghost Story of Penny Jaye Prufrock
Mary Pletsch

Penny sucked in one last breath as she launched her body off the dock and into the water; then the raucous noise of the other campers was gone, and she hung suspended in silence below the surface of Lake Mishipishu. She reached out and tangled her fingers in the weeds that lined the lake bottom, and opened her eyes onto a brown-green otherworld.

The flavour of the lake seeped in through her nostrils, crept under her tongue. Lake Mishipishu had its own unique taste: it was not the antiseptic chlorine of an indoor pool, nor the lively freshness of the river where she used to swim with Jessica back in fourth grade, four years and a lifetime ago when she and Jess had still been best friends. Lake Mishipishu tasted of deep, still water, and secrets half-hidden in muck and sediment.

Above her, the sun sent beams of copper light lancing through the skin of the lake's surface. A dark shape to her left might be a clump of thicker weeds, or perhaps a rock. Penny kicked out with her feet, exploring beyond the limits of sight. Her toes plowed furrows through the spongy muck; then they curled around something hard and rough-edged.

Her lungs smouldered with warning, but she folded her body like a jackknife and wrapped the fingers of her left hand around the object. She felt a sinuous tendril untwine itself from her find and slither away into the dim waters; the prize left behind was about the size of her palm, with pronounced edges not quite sharp enough to cut. She grasped it and gave her body permission to rise. Freed, her blazing lungs hoisted her skyward, a pair of

fiery balloons.

Penny breached the surface and kicked to stay afloat. Her right hand scraped her brassy hair back from her face while her left clutched the object to her chest. The thing felt like stone, smooth and flat, save for a lump on one side. She blinked water out of her eyes and examined her discovery.

The anomaly was some sort of creature – a fossilized, copper-coloured, multi-legged beastie. Penny's index finger traced the outline of ragged claws, submerged forever in stone. She wondered how many thousands of years the rock and its passenger might have lain under the surface of the lake before she found them and brought them back to the light.

The loud shrill of a whistle interrupted her musing.

"BUDDY CHECK!" yelled a counsellor as he paced back and forth on the H-shaped dock. The H-dock. anchored to the lakebed by four sets of chains, served as lifeguard station, diving platform, and outmost boundary of the Camp Zaagaigan swimming area. Penny frowned and looked around for her buddies.

Making friends at camp had been harder this year. Getting older made everything harder.

Penny had shown up at the lakefront alone and had been partnered with two girls from a different cabin. She'd given no thought to them since she entered the water; now she had to find them. What had they looked like? Where had they gone?

All around her, campers were standing together, hands clasped together and raised above their heads. The counsellor on the dock paused in his counting to frown at Penny. If she didn't find her buddies soon, the lifeguard might presume a kid was missing. All the counsellors would have to form a human chain and sweep the swimming area, while the lifeguard dove under the H-dock with a waterproof flashlight to make sure a camper wasn't tangled up in the anchor chains.

The other girls would be in trouble too for losing track of her, but they weren't flopping around in the water all alone while all the other kids stared at them. Penny's ears burned with shame. She clutched tightly to the shale in her hand.

"Over here," she heard a voice hiss at last.

The speaker, a tall blonde girl, beckoned impatiently while her shorter friend shot a poisonous look at Penny. Penny glared back as she added her hand to theirs; they were supposed to be watching out for her.

The counsellor finished his count and blew the whistle for the all clear. The taller girl drew her hand away and said, in a snotty voice, "You need to

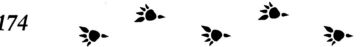

watch where we're going."

"I'm tired of swimming," Penny retorted.

She wasn't, not really, but she wasn't about to waste her time trailing after people who didn't want her. She began dog-paddling towards shore, clutching the fossil in her hand. When the lake grew shallow, she walked on her hands, kicking her legs behind her, pretending she was a creature like the one entombed in her grip.

Her belly scraped the sand. Penny rose upright like a monster from the water and lumbered the rest of the way to shore, feeling awkward and gawky on two legs.

Wrapping her towel around her shoulders, Penny wandered along the shoreline through the shadow of the boathouse and approached the semi-circle of logs ringing the fire pit. Penny's favourite time of day was sunset, when campers gathered here to perform skits and sing songs while the sun slowly slid into the lake. Then, just before they went back to the cabins to sleep, the counsellors told them a scary story.

Mid-afternoon was the wrong time of day for the telling of stories, but the fire pit was deserted now and there was no one to think it strange if a twelve year old girl sat all by herself, talking to an ugly little critter encased in stone.

Penny sat on the log nearest the fire and placed the shale on her lap. Her index finger stroked the back of her silent companion. *Now that it's here, it has to know the stories.*

"That side of the boathouse is the swimming area," Penny said as she pointed, "but *this* side is Leech Beach. We never, ever swim in that water. We launch our canoes and sailboats and then we get in as fast as we can, because there's all kinds of leeches – thousands – millions – a rare species that travels in swarms and kills its prey. If you get enough leeches on you, they'll drink your blood dry, until all that's left of you is a floppy bag of skin. Once there was a kid who flipped his canoe and had to go to the hospital for blood loss. They saved him just in time. So when we swim, we always stay on the right side of the boathouse, where we'll be safe from the . . ."

An ugly tainted flavour rose up in her throat as an idea wormed its way into her mind. What, exactly, stopped leeches from crossing over into the swimming area? How many leeches could there be in one lake? Maybe the camp just didn't want kids swimming out of bounds, or goofing off in the boat launch area. The camp didn't dredge the bottom there, either, and the waters that bordered the roped-off swimming area were peppered with sticks and sharp rocks and who knew what else. Penny clutched her fossil and wondered how many more might be out there in the leech zone.

She briefly considered climbing up on the boathouse deck and sticking her legs in the water and waiting to see if she got leeches on her.

. . . But she'd end up sorry if the leech swarms were real.

Penny stayed put, because there were still stories to tell.

She told her new friend about the knife-wielding murderers who sometimes escaped from the penitentiary on the other side of the lake. She told it about poisonous spiders the size of dinner plates that spun their webs in the old rec hall, and how those webs were big enough to catch rabbits, maybe dogs; one of the counsellors swore the spiders were bigger every year, and it was only a matter of time before some rule-breaking camper got in real trouble . . .

She told it about the Lat Monster – not that anyone was actually afraid of the Lat Monster. The Lat Monster's tale was told every summer because it was just such a disgustingly hilarious idea; and if Penny, going to the latrine in the middle of the night, sometimes paused and questioned the wisdom of sitting down atop a deep, dark, fetid hole . . . well, that wasn't entirely a foolish idea, was it? There might not be any monsters down in the stinking black, just waiting to gobble campers up bare-butt-first, but there might be earwigs, or even snakes. It never hurt to shine your flashlight down the hole before you sat. Just in case.

And with that silly story, Penny's well ran dry. She racked her brain in an attempt to exhume more tales. Surely in all these scary stories, there had to be one about ghosts; but if there was, she couldn't recall it. Camp Zaagaigan really needed a good ghost story.

Her mind lit upon an idea.

Up in the mess hall there was an Indian arrowhead mounted behind glass, allegedly found in Lake Mishipishu by a camper in the mid-70s. The Indians here had told a story of their own, the story of the Mishipishu, a being that lived under the waters of the lake that bore its name.

So Penny told her companion about the fabulous spirit called the Mishipishu, a sort of sea-serpent with a head like a cat's and brilliant copper horns. She lovingly described its fearsome fangs, as long as her fingers; its razor claws; its sinuous tail, spiked like a dinosaur's. The Mishipishu was the keeper of the copper, and when people took copper from the lake, the Mishipishu called forth water-storms, and flipped their canoes with one mighty thrash of its tail.

Then Penny fell silent, because this story had no end. Though she had looked every summer for seven years, Penny had never seen the giant footprints of a cat on the shoreline, or the glint of sun off two copper horns

176

far away on the lake's horizon. The Indians had all vanished from this place, and maybe they had taken the Mishipishu with them.

Maybe the Mishipishu, like everyone else, had grown up and moved on.

Clenching her jaw, Penny said defiantly, "And the Mishipishu lives *right in our swimming area. And* if you go into the water there, it might decide to take you home with it, down into the dark waters of the lake, for ever and *ever*."

That story was wrong. Penny sat there, in the cooling air, wondering why her story was wrong. Her eyes strayed over the boathouse, the lake, the far-off oval of Hot Dog Island where some of the trees were already touched by orange and yellow, heralds of the dying summer. There was not much time left in which to pretend that grade eight was far away, or that her father would not be coming to pick her up two days from now.

And there was the heart of it. She was scared of leeches and murderers and giant spiders. She was scared of the future that awaited her. The Mishipishu . . .

. . . She wanted it to take her away.

"This," she said quietly, "is the scariest story."

*   *   *

Once upon a time there were two best friends named Jessica and Penny who were both in first grade. They liked exploring and adventuring and telling jokes and playing together. Jessica didn't care that Penny's dad owned a funeral home, and she didn't think Penny and her dad were creepy. Jessica came over to play with Penny and not just to see if she could get a look at dead bodies.

Jessica's parents decided to go on a long vacation and wanted her to spend the summer at Camp Zaagaigan. Jessica didn't want to go alone so she asked Penny to go with her. Penny said yes and her dad said okay too. They had tons of fun. It was so great that they went back the next year and the year after that and the year after that.

Then Jessica grew up when Penny wasn't looking.

I only took my eyes off her for a week, I swear. Between the end of camp and the start of grade five, Jessica turned into someone else.

I mean . . .

Penny coughed and put her Storyteller Voice back on.

Suddenly all Jessica cared about was make-up and movie stars and trying to get the popular girls at school to like her. She didn't want to explore in the park for fear of getting dirty and she didn't want to play with toys in case someone saw her being babyish. She spent recess leaning against the brick wall of the school, acting snotty to younger kids and trying to catch the cool boys' attention. Penny played along for about a week before she got bored. She quit playing the game, and Jessica quit talking to her.

Penny was not going to let stupid Jessica ruin camp for her. Penny went to camp the next year anyway and spent the whole first day waiting for Jessica's mom's blue car to come crunching up the gravel road through the forest. And in her head she made up what she was going to say and it went like this: I'm ignoring you, Jessica, because I'm going to have fun at camp, and you can spend all your time pretending you're so cool, and I don't even care, so there.

Penny never got to use her speech because Jessica never came.

So Penny made a new friend, a girl named Ratha, and after camp they sent emails to each other all through grade six, and Penny didn't mind that she had no friends at school. Then they met up at camp again and made a new friend, Mae Wah.

Halfway through grade seven, Ratha stopped e-mailing.

Ratha's not at camp this summer. Mae Wah is, but she's all snobby now like Jessica and she told me she doesn't want to hang out with babies and nerds. She says if I want to still be her friend, I need to hurry and grow up.

Penny took a deep breath, wiped the tears from her eyes, and steadied her voice long enough to put an ending on her story.

Every year at camp there's kids crying because they want to go home. I don't know why. Home is for ex-best-friends and dads who love their dead wives more than their living daughters. If you want to cry you should cry . . .

She raked her fingernails over her cheeks.

. . . because thirteen is too old for Camp Zaagaigan . . .

Penny finished the story, but not easily.

. . . and this is my last year.

*   *   *

Human voices woke her. The other girls in the cabin were whispering and giggling while the counsellor tried to hush them. Even here, at night in her bunk, Penny could still smell the lake; it hid under her fingernails, concealed itself in her hair, and softened the edges of her scabs. She would carry it home with her like contraband, and savour it for as long as she could.

She was losing everything. Tears streaming down her cheeks, Penny rolled onto her belly and thrust her hands beneath her pillow. Her fingertips traced shale, seeking and finding the clawed creature in the rock.

She had intended to take the fossil home with her. One last souvenir of Camp Zaagaigan. A friend that she could keep in her trinket drawer and take out when she felt alone.

How would the creature fare, she wondered, so far away from Lake Mishipishu? Already it looked less substantial; the charcoal rock and copper

178

became pale grey and faint orange when they dried. She drew the stone from beneath her pillow and rubbed it against her moist face, hoping to feed it sustenance. Penny wept a lake of tears until there were no more left to cry; until the lakebed in her eyes was hard and dry.

When all moisture was gone, truth came to light.

Driven by an inevitability she did not yet understand, Penny unzipped her sleeping bag and swung her feet over the side of the bunk. She clutched her silent friend to her chest and left her flashlight behind. She walked out of the cabin and into the night alone, without even the counsellor's voice calling after her.

The halogen lamps next to the latrines screamed their illumination into the night. Penny turned away from them and headed towards the lake. The moon overhead rimed the cabins and trees with a delicate silver crust, and Lake Mishipishu was a mirror, throwing back the light like a beacon. The H-dock sat black and heavy on the silvery surface.

Penny slid into the shadows of the boathouse and wrapped them around her like a sleeping bag. The hulk of the boathouse loomed over her, clouding her reflection in the water, merging her into her surroundings. Safely subsumed, she circled the building until she stood on the deck overlooking the water.

Penny used both hands to tilt the fossil until the moon illuminated the little creature within the stone. At a certain angle, the creature appeared to be bursting free of the shale that surrounded it. Her fingers tightened on the rock; but she knew better than to be selfish. The creature, unlike her, could stay.

There was no point returning it to the swimming area for some other kid to find. Penny knelt at the deck's edge on the side overlooking Leech Beach. She had heard a lot of prayers in the funeral home and wished that even one of them could contain the words that granted release. She held the fossil over the dark waters; then, with one last look at the creature, she forced her fingers to let go.

Water slid over the stone, darkening the shape of the creature within, and for just a moment Penny thought she saw it twitch, as though something darted out of the rock and away into the night-glazed lake. The stone wobbled in the waves, and then the right end dipped and it dropped out of sight into the black.

From somewhere down in the darkness came a flash of copper.

It speared through Penny like a beacon of hope, and without thinking, she followed after. She raised her hands above her head in an arrow and let her body tumble forward off the boathouse deck.

Cold water clasped her in a tight embrace, driving the breath from her lungs. Lake Mishipeshu closed above her like a cocoon. Penny reached out her arms into the darkness, but she felt nothing, and her eyes opened onto water the colour of a night without stars. She tried not to think of leeches and wondered if perhaps the Mishipeshu might come to her if she were still. Her body conspired against her, shoving her towards the surface in quest for air.

She folded her body in half and wound her fingers into the weeds again, as she had yesterday, but here the weeds were too thin; their roots gave way, and she bobbed to the surface, clutching useless green strands. Frustrated, frightened, she looked back over her shoulder to where Camp Zaagaigan lay sleeping, its silhouette thrown into stark relief by the latrines' halogen lamps. Nobody knew she was missing, yet, but sooner or later her counsellor would question why Penny had gone to the lats without a buddy, and what was taking her so long to return.

Concerned, the counsellor checked the lats — and everywhere else a camper out alone at night might go — but Penny was nowhere to be found. Realizing her camper was missing, the counsellor sounded the alarm. Seconds later, the camp's bell began to ring its urgent warning, and sleepy campers wrapped in blankets stumbled down to the flagpole to be counted by the camp director. The counsellors formed a human chain and waded into the lake . . .

Penny would be seen as soon as the bell started ringing; she and the H-dock were the only things that broke the surface of Lake Mishipishu. Penny would be caught and she could not even count how many rules she'd broken by now. They would send her home a day early, and they would never let her come back.

She snorted, raising up bubbles when her nose dipped under the surface of the lake. She was turning thirteen this fall. She wouldn't be coming back anyway.

Her hands checked her arms and legs, just in case.

No leeches anywhere.

She looked at the old rec hall, housing the same spiders as everywhere else, and the woods where no murderers lurked. She looked at the sad, stinking, hollow lats and the cabins where traitors giggled in the dark. She thought of friends grown into strangers and fathers who loved the dead, and in the darkness, the serpentine tail with its copper spines cut through the lake between her and Camp Zaagaigan, severing heart and soul.

Penny took one last breath and went under, wrapping her hands around the tail and letting it tow her, away from the boathouse and into the swimming area, in search of an anchor more substantial than weeds. Two feeble beams of moonlight pierced the surface of the water; then she was under the H-dock and all was blackness.

She felt her body weaving in between the anchoring chains like a braided lanyard. Her copper hair swirled above her head: the tendrils of an exotic undersea plant, the Mishipishu's secret trove. She could feel some small creature zip by her ear, gently tugging on her waving strands with its ragged claws.

Penny's lungs felt like a universe waiting to implode; the pain was something she could never have imagined, having nothing to compare it to. She wondered if her friend had felt the rock closing in around it, pressing living cells into fossilized shale, and wondered if it would have hurt so much, after all, to have the years turn her heart to stone instead.

She spread her fingers and toes wide. It was inevitable that they would find her, but if she was lucky, they wouldn't find *all* of her. Penny wanted at least a few little bones to escape; to burrow down into the soft muck in search of eventual shale. It would be best, she thought, if a part of her were always in the lake.

She had seen her future and wanted no part of it.

She would rather be a ghost story.

Malicious Intimacy
by William Andre Sanders

I refuse pretending
romanticism
is chocolate truffles,
accompanying a flower bouquet.

I'd much rather prefer –
pampering you with a rodent,
victimized by road rage,
six days dead –
birthing blowflies
out of maggots.

I'd offer a bottle of Tequila,
undesirably aged.
Eat the soggy worm,
swipe its liquified innards
across my tongue,
while kissing passionately
psychotic in expression
of honorable adoration.

Most men act out
sappy sentimental charades,
in fear of not succeeding
despair in lonesomeness.

In this unsympathetic world,
scarlet madness
defines devotion.

Therefore, I've chosen
not to hide behind the deceitful
mask of assumed affection
most men cleverly sneak
into drinks on dinner dates.

Let us etch this night
together –
forever lustful in our minds
by committing our dark hearts'
desire –
low-budget pornicide.

Scream and I'll yank
strands of crimson hair
clear from hidden lacerations
streaming blood out of fresh
life-threatening fractures
scattered across your head.

Beneath
Michael Burnside

June 23, 2023

I write this in the hope that it may one day be read by the world at large. With that in mind, I hope my colleagues will forgive this journal's tendency to state things that, for them at least, are well-known facts. So it is for my readers who are unfamiliar with our endeavor that I provide some background.

Most of our world is covered by water and even in this modern age we have explored little of what lies beneath. We have all heard this simple fact, but when we hear it, most of the time our minds envision oceans. However, this applies to our lakes as well. If you have never seen one of the Great Lakes, it is understandable that you may picture a lake as a serene body of water that you can leisurely swim across in a few minutes. But the Great Lakes are inland oceans. You cannot see the far shore of any of these lakes, just an endless moving plane of dark water extending to the horizon.

The biggest of the Great Lakes is Lake Superior. It is the largest freshwater lake in the world with a surface area of over eighty-two thousand kilometers. It is over thirteen hundred feet deep in some parts. And it is from beneath its waves that I now write this.

Our foundation has lowered a habitat into the deepest depths of Lake Superior. The habitat consists of four small pods connected to a central hub. Each pod is no larger than a single car garage. The central hub is the size of a large living room. The outer pods serve as living quarters and observatories while the central hub is our primary laboratory.

There are four us living in this unusual home. Myself, Dr. Sheila Batroni, Dr. Ryan Harrington, and Dr. Leslie Walker. We are all freshwater marine biologists.

We have plenty of windows but need dozens of powerful external lights to keep the outside darkness at bay. Our home beneath the water is cramped and we have few comforts, but we are all very excited to begin our research.

I'd like to write more, but Leslie is giving me a look that says I should sign off and help her move some equipment. I probably will not be able to write more for a few days, as I suspect we will be very busy trying to organize the laboratory.

July 15th, 2023

I intended to write sooner, but the first few days down here were so busy there wasn't time. Once we had settled in, I must confess that I did not write because my disposition has become somber. I wanted this journal to serve as an inspiration to young minds and did not want my dark mood to have the opposite effect.

But now I have decided to simply tell it like it is. It's wrong of me to paint the life of a researcher as one big adventure. As with any job there are tough times. If this journal turns away students who thought this work would be easy, so be it.

I had not anticipated just how isolated it would feel down here. We are thirteen hundred feet down, which is deep in terms of water depth, but really not all that far. I am less than a city block away from the crew of our tender ship. If there were not water in between us, I could wave to them and they would see me clearly. But there is a tremendous amount of water in between us. Those who live above the water and those who live beneath it are in different worlds.

Though our habitat keeps the water at bay, my mind can still feel the water pressing down on me. I feel I could be crushed at any moment.

Perhaps I'm just working too hard in an environment that is not ideal for humans. I should be grateful that the habitat is as large as it is. It is the largest underwater habitat ever used, but I must admit, I still feel as if I am in a prison. It is cold down here and always damp. The dehumidifiers try their best but they simply cannot keep up. I can hear the motors of the dehumidifiers always whirring. There's a constant thumping sound from the compressors that move air around the habitat. Then there's the steady hum of the electrical generators and the random beeping of lab instruments.

But underneath it all is the constant sound of dripping water. Condensation gathers the water on our windows, on the pipes that run along the walls, and on duct work that hangs from the ceiling. It all runs together and drips down. The water that runs down the walls and windows just adds visually to the feeling that we are slowly drowning, but it is the water dripping from the ceiling that will drive us mad. The drips fall with a steady quiet rhythm that is almost soothing until the moment comes when a drop lands on the floor too soon or too late and your brain's sense of anticipation gets kicked in the gut.

Also the whole place smells like sweat and socks.

July 30th, 2023

It is perpetually night outside. The external lights on the habitat push back the gloom only a dozen feet. If you stare out into that darkness, you can see things move.

It's not surprising. Even at this depth, there are fish out there. Some of the fish in the Great Lakes are not the prettiest creatures. The sturgeon with its flat head and shovel-like snout is an odd-looking thing that can grow up to twelve feet long. It's creepy to see one loom out of the darkness, swim past a window, and then fade into the black again.

The sea lampreys are the worst. They are eel-like things that are usually gray or black. They are small compared to the sturgeon, but make the sturgeon seem like welcome guests. Indeed, the lampreys feed on the sturgeon. They feed on every fish that lives in the lake. Sea lampreys are water vampires. They have circular mouths that are lined with rows and rows of teeth. They swim up to other fish, bite into their sides, and hold fast. Then they take their barbed tongues and dig into the fish causing it to bleed. They'll feed on their victims like that for weeks. Once the fish they are feeding on dies, they move onto their next victim. They are simple, methodical killers.

When we bring a fish into the habitat for examination, it's not uncommon to find two or three lampreys feeding on a it. When we pull the lampreys off, they rip quarter to half-dollar size chunks of flesh off the fish. It's a horror show.

I know as a biologist I should admire the sea lamprey for its evolutionary proficiency at survival, but I simply can't stand the things. They are an invasive species, aliens from other waters. Lake Superior is infested with these vile creatures and there doesn't seem to be any easy way to stop them.

I think I'm going to start ordering mandatory trips to the surface for each member of the team. Going this long without sunlight just isn't good for any of us.

August 23, 2023

I managed to spend a few weeks topside, and the fresh air did me a world of good. I had hoped my mood would stay lifted even after I returned to the habitat, but it has darkened quickly.

We use a closed diving bell that is raised and lowered by a crane. Because of the pressures involved, it is a slow process. Going up is like ascending into heaven. The black outside the windows slowly lightens to a dark blue. The bell lets out metallic sighs as the pressure comes off it. The dark blue slowly turns clear. When the hatch opens, the stale air brought up with us from the habitat rushes out, and a sweet cool breeze sneaks in.

On the way back down, everything is reversed. The water slowly grows dark. The bell creaks as the pressure builds. The air inside the bell grows stale. It's like descending into a tomb.

Sheila and Leslie went up two days ago, leaving me down here with Ryan. We have not spoken since our return. Ryan has not done well with the isolation. I can hear him muttering to himself. He rambles about the habitat taking the same path each time. He tinkers in the lab, swears, then paces.

I hope Sheila and Leslie return soon.

September 3, 2023

Sheila and Leslie have returned and, like me, they have suffered a quick return to dreary moods. Still, I am glad they are here. They can assist me in keeping an eye on Ryan whose behavior is becoming increasingly erratic. And, though it frightens me to suggest it, perhaps they can keep an eye on me.

September 23, 2023

Walking through cramped halls, the water and darkness press in.

October 2, 2023

Bad weather has set in. Down here in the darkness, we sense nothing. Above us, the ship has departed. Without its crane, we can only return to the surface using the emergency pressure suits. That would be a long swim in the black. It is hard not to feel trapped.

October 5, 2023

This morning I awoke to screams. I threw aside the covers and bolted out of bed. I ran down the tight corridors in my socks, jumping through hatches and landing in small puddles of water on the floor. I arrived in the entrance pod to find Sheila Batroni curled up in a corner and shrieking. Sheila is not one prone to hysterics. She has far more nerve than I in dealing with the damn lampreys. I scanned the pod expecting to see some sign of catastrophe – water breaking through seals or bulkheads crumpling under pressure, but nothing seemed amiss.

I knelt down in front of Sheila and shook her by her shoulders. "What's wrong?"

She pointed at the window to the right of the main hatch. "It had a face!"

"What do you mean?" I asked. "What had a face?"

"It did!" she insisted.

I stood up and walked over to the window. The water caught in the external floodlights glimmered a sickly green that faded to black. I saw nothing in the murk.

I walked back over to Sheila and knelt down in front of her. "There's nothing there now," I told her.

"There was," she said.

"You said you saw a face?" I asked.

She nodded while pushing her blond hair back. There were dark puffy circles under her eyes. "A human face. There was a human face on something that swam up to the glass."

I thought about what she said for a moment, wondering if the isolation of this place had led her to have hallucinations. But a more plausible, more morbid, possibility entered my mind.

There have been over three hundred and fifty shipwrecks in Lake Superior and these have claimed over one thousand lives. Lake Superior does not give up her dead. In other lakes, the decay of a body will eventually cause it to rise back to the surface where the corpse may be found. But Lake Superior is so cold that it inhibits the decay process. Those who die and sink into its depths never resurface. Perhaps what Sheila saw was a body carried by water currents.

I suggested this possibility to Sheila and made clear that I believed such a sight would cause anyone to lose their composure.

She shook her head. "It swam!" she insisted. "It swam up to the window and it looked at me."

October 7, 2023
Sheila did not see a corpse.

I saw what she saw the next morning. I was reading in my cot and I felt a sinister presence in my mind. It was as if a shadow had fallen over me and I instinctively turned to see what had blocked out the sun.

I looked out the window that is alongside my bed. I peered in the green lit water and further out into the inky blackness. There was movement out in the darkness. Somehow my mind saw it before my eyes did. A huge shape slipped into the light. It had the body of a massive eel. It swam forward, its body rippling like silk in the wind. It had a human face.

It swam past the window and looked into the habitat. The thing had brown hair and hazel eyes. The skin was pallid and frayed. Its lips thin and blue. It looked at me and smiled.

October 8, 2023

It has begun speaking to us. We hear its voice in our minds. Its thoughts can reach us anywhere in the habitat, but the effect is much worse when we can see it looking at us through the windows.

We have gathered in the center hub for mutual support and because that module has the fewest windows. We have radioed that we need to be evacuated as soon as possible, but we received no answer. We have no way of knowing if our transmissions are being sent. The radio antenna is held aloft by a buoy on the surface. The storms may have ripped the buoy free. Or that thing out there may have severed the antenna.

Dr. Sheila Batroni and Dr. Leslie Walker are holding up reasonably well. They are quiet and grim-faced. Dr. Ryan Harrington appears to be breaking down quickly. He often cries out about the voice in his head and lapses into periods of prolonged sobbing. Twice now I have had to stop him from attempting to cut his head open with a lab saw. I locked the saw in a cabinet after his first attempt and cannot figure out how he managed to get ahold of it again. He has a brilliant mind. Am I supposed to outthink him as comes up with ways in which to harm himself? What am I supposed to do if Dr. Batroni and Dr. Walker also lose their grip on sanity? I am trapped down here with three geniuses who are being driven mad.

And I am quite uncertain about my own state. The voice in my head is smooth and insistent. It speaks to me as I pace back and forth. It speaks to me in my dreams. I can no longer tell if I am awake or asleep.

The voice only has one thing to say to me: *"Let me in."*

October 9th, 2023

Ryan is dead. He found something sharp and cut an artery while the rest of slept. Now there is a large dark lake of blood in the center of the hub and the small room has a strange copper smell.

I have begun to consider using the pressure suits to escape the habitat. It would mean being out in the dark water while that thing swam around us, but the pressure suits are rigid, so I don't think the thing could crush us or bite us, although it might convince us to kill ourselves by opening our suits as we ascend. But it's been trying to convince us to die for two days now, with some success. The ascent would last only hours, minutes if we decide to embrace the bends. What stops me is that I have no idea if there is a ship up there. Without a ship we'd just bob around on the surface until we ran out of air. We'd have to open the suits to breathe. The rough waters of the lake would soon drown us. Still . . . if our last few hours are free of that voice . . .

. . .

The suits have been sabotaged. Their seals have been cut. Maybe Ryan did it before he killed himself. Perhaps it was Sheila or Leslie. Maybe it was me. There are no rounds of incriminations, no accusations. None of us is certain that we have control of ourselves anymore.

I need to sleep. I will dream of the voice. Or perhaps I need to wake up, and I will think about the voice.

October 10th, 2023

I awoke with my arms wrapped around Leslie. I do not remember her lying down with me. I found myself with my hands around her waist and her back tight up against my chest. We were fully clothed. I do not think anything unprofessional had occurred, but I confess that the warmth of her body felt nice.

The voice told me that if I let it in, I could be with her forever. Her red hair was in my face. I gently brushed it aside exposing the sweat slicked skin of her neck. She smelled human. She smelled of fear.

She awoke suddenly and clambered out of the cot. She looked around with fast, spastic movements. She looked at me with wide open eyes.

"Where's Sheila?" she asked.

It's an odd thing to lose track of someone in such a small space. It was not as if Sheila had many places she could go.

Ryan is the easiest to keep track of. He is still where we found him yesterday – in his cot with his arm sliced open and hanging out over the floor. His eyes are wide open, staring at the ceiling. His mouth is open and his lips are curled back in a silent scream. His skin is an ashen white.

We found Sheila in the entrance pod. The entrance pod is connected to the flood room and the flood room is where our closed diving bell rests. When we want to use the bell, we go into the flood room, enter the bell, and use remote valves to fill the flood room with water. Then we trigger the top hatch to open and a crane on the support ship slowly lifts us up.

Sheila was standing by the hatch to the flood room. I could tell by looking at the small window in the hatch that the flood room had been filled with water. Sheila had both hands on the metal bar that would open the hatch.

There are a half-dozen safety features, both mechanical and electronic, designed to prevent the entrance pod hatch from being opened when the flood room is filled with water. Your average biologist would never figure out how to override those features. Dr. Sheila Batroni designed most of those features. I knew instantly that Sheila could open that hatch if she wanted to.

Leslie tried to rush past me. I grabbed her. I knew that if Sheila opened the entrance hatch, our only hope would be to shut the hatch to the central hub, so I held Leslie at the entrance to the pod.

Leslie squirmed and kicked. She reached out toward Sheila and screamed, "What are you doing?"

Sheila looked at us with tears streaming down her face. She said, "I'm sorry," and she opened the hatch.

The force of water at a thousand feet is something that is hard to imagine. As soon as the mechanical mechanism that held the hatch shut was clear, the door swung open and hit Sheila with such speed that she simply vanished from view. A torrent of water burst towards us like a horizontal waterfall. Leslie was struck by the water and torn from my grip. I was spun around and fell back inside the central hub. Luckily, I landed with reach of the close button. I reached up and slapped it. A motor hummed and then whined under strain as it cranked the door shut.

Leslie has suffered some cuts and bruises. Ryan remains the same. The central hub has filled with about a foot of ice cold water.

Oct 11, 2023

I've been watching the thing swim around in the entrance pod. The lights in the flooded pod have remained functional, so I have a very good view of it through the window in the central hub hatch.

The creature is about fifteen feet long. Its body is green at the tail and then blends into a shade of tan human flesh at its front. It has top and bottom fins that ripple as the creature moves. The creature is incredibly agile. It moves through the water with an eerie grace.

It has Sheila's face now. Her blond hair flows out behind it as it swims past the window. It twists and turns like a serpent and then comes around again. Her blue eyes are flat and lifeless. I hear her voice in my head.

She smiles at me.

Oct 12, 2023

This shall be my last entry.

I knew it was only a matter of time before Leslie or I broke. I considered smashing her head in with a pipe wrench, but there was no way I could be sure that she would break before me. I considered offering her the chance to smash my head in, but wasn't sure how to broach the subject. It's not the kind of conversation that you ever prepare yourself for.

Last night I went to sleep with Sheila urging me to let her back in. I awoke to find Leslie preparing to open the hatch to the entrance pod. She gave me time to get out of the central hub and close the next hatch. She waved to me and then let the water in.

Leslie managed to get out of the way as the hatch door smashed open. I watched her through the window of the last closed hatch in the habitat. The water tossed her around as it filled up the hub. She began to panic as the last of the air rushed out of the room.

The creature slid into the room. It stared at Leslie and Leslie stared back at it. For a moment they hung there motionless like two dancers in a grand outdoor ball, their hair moving about as if blown by a strong breeze. Then the thing screamed.

It could not have made a noise like that underwater. I must have heard the voice in my mind. It was Sheila's voice. I heard Sheila scream.

There was a flash of blue light from its eyes that quickly brightened to a blinding white intensity. I stumbled back and shook my head, trying to clear the strange after images that danced upon my retinas. I staggered back up to the hatch and looked through the window. I saw the thing swim by. A different shade of flesh marked its neck. The thing's body, then its tail slid past. The tail flexed and the thing arced around in a smooth turn.

The thing looked through the window at me. It had Leslie's face now. Her red hair flowed beautifully down the side of its cheeks. She smiled at me.

This endeavor began with noble intent. Its failure cannot be seen as an excuse to stop exploring. It is only with exploration that we can learn what is in the dark. I've come to accept that such knowledge can come with a high price. Someone has to walk into the pitch black room first. Sometimes we encounter things we are not prepared to face.

I have to stop writing now. I have to go let Leslie in.

Passionate in Chicago
John Goodrich

Nickolaus Passionate was the sort of man who lurked in the dark alleys and corners of Chicago, because he was a man of darkness. The landscape was forsaken as the prayers of children abandoned by their God. Trash of every sort littered the dark alley, the refuse of human refuse, where Nickolaus felt right at home.

The alley was behind a bar, next to a strip club. The air was redolent with the reek of stale beer and vomit. Used condoms squished underfoot like shelled oysters. Nickolaus was out here to take a leak.

As he was zipping up, a heap of garbage near the trash bin shifted. He stiffened. Ex-Navy, he was confident he could handle himself in a fight, but with so many people on PCP or crystal meth, sometimes the regular rules didn't apply. On the other hand, it could be someone who needed help. Or just a city-dwelling raccoon.

Nick approached what he thought was a pile of trash, scuffing his boots to keep from startling anything. The sounds of traffic and humanity were far away. Something shifted. Did he hear a moan of pain?

He squared his shoulders, ready for a crackhead to explode out of the trash. With a few steps, he was enveloped in the darkness, and his eyes adjusted to the dirty yellow light thrown by the sodium lamps. A man crouched like a frightened dog among the bags of stinking garbage. Long hair hung over his face. His shoulders were well muscled, and he wore no shirt.

"You all right there?"

The main raised his head, and for a moment, Nickolaus would have sworn it was the face of Italian model Fabio Lanzoni. But he moved his head, and the illusion was spoiled. Still, he had a bodybuilder's chest, heroic shoulders, and a chiseled jaw.

"Leave me alone." His voice was an exhausted whisper.

"What's your name?"

"Isaac Allen," he said. "Just . . . just forget you saw me."

Nickolaus looked down at the wretched face.

"I can't. You look like you're hurt, and I won't leave if you're in pain."

"No . . . No, I . . ." Isaac made a sound somewhere between a whine and a groan. "Go away."

Nick was conflicted. He respected choice. But this man seemed so wretched, so determined to be alone that his defiant streak kicked in. He would not be told what to do. A man was suffering. He wanted to help.

Isaac shifted, and something was wrong. He was hunched over, but even Quasimodo didn't have such a mass on his back. Isaac tried to re-adjust the filthy blanket that covered him, but the bulge on his back was so unwieldy that the blanket fell off, revealing pearly-white, feathered wings. Nick tried to conceal his astonishment. Was he in a Gabriel García Márquez story? How could those wings be real?

"Oh God don't look at them," Isaac said. "They're hideous. I'm deformed."

Nickolaus's eyes were wide with wonder, his hands reaching out to touch the marvelous pinions. The feathers were soft as an angel's whisper, and glowed with a clean, comforting light in the alley's dim confines.

"Not hideous. They're beautiful." As Nickolaus stroked the wings, they spread, as if through some unconscious reflex. Nearly twenty feet wide, Isaac had to turn sideways so they wouldn't touch the filthy walls that hemmed the alley. Far from being delicate, they were strong, the feathers soft but the underlying wing stiff, yet warm. Under his fingers, Nickolaus was sure he could feel the pulse of Isaac's heartbeat.

Isaac moaned and tried to pull away, folding his wings, hiding them as best he could. But Nick held onto his shoulders, not letting Isaac shut him out.

"Hey, hey." When Isaac gave up trying to escape, he rested his head on Nickolaus's chest. "Whatever is happening, it's a part of you."

Could he comfort someone so miserable, so at war with his own body? It broke Nick's heart to see someone reject themselves. Nothing good ever came from self-hate. Nickolaus stroked his hair, and Isaac's breathing calmed. Isaac's scent was musky, manly.

"I understand something about what you're going through. You feel adrift, a stranger in your own body."

Isaac said nothing, his hot tears spilling onto Nick's chest. There was nothing to do but wait for his anger to abate, to let the storm of emotional energy blow itself out. Nick promised himself that he would help this lost soul. He had once been adrift, full of hate, lashing out at everyone around him, jealous of their success. But he'd created the quiet mindfulness that allowed him to accept himself as he was, not some distorted perception others forced on him. And though his thoughts remained dark, they were a darkness of still and quiet, one that enveloped and protected. He sighed, and hoped that some of his peace would seep into Isaac.

"They're beautiful. You're beautiful," he whispered into Isaac's hair.

"I'm a freak," Isaac whispered through his tears. Despite this, his wings rose, reflecting the alley's yellow light, turning it into something softer, more pure.

"Special," Nick gently corrected him. "No one else has wings. Think of how unique and glorious that makes you. They are a wonderful gift, not something to be hidden in a dark alley." Isaac did not respond. What could Nick say? What could he do? "Accept who you are. If you let someone convince you to hate yourself, you will end up dead inside, like a fossil in a lake bed."

Isaac looked up, searching Nick's face. His eyes were a deep and soulful brown, still brimming with tears, terrible in their vulnerability.

The kiss was unexpected. Nickolaus thought about resisting, but melted into the offered heat. Isaac's mouth was warm, his tongue sensual and demanding. The sandpapery feel of his stubble added a frisson to the delight, a little discomfort that emphasized the pleasure.

The kiss grew more passionate, Nick's need surging and meeting Isaac's. His hands roamed, his fingers tracing down Isaac's sculpted pectorals, then down to his lean abdomen. Nick traced a hot line of kisses down Isaac's neck, and then the great wings arched and beat at the air as he mouthed the small, sensitive nipples. A firm erection pressed at Isaac's pants, against Nick's stomach. Nick put his hands on the front of Isaac's jeans, but soft hands stopped him.

"Not here."

They disengaged, staring at each other, the weight of their love crashing like silent thunder. Neither would be the same again.

"Never let me go." Nickolaus was not sure who said it. His heart hammered so much he feared his ribs would break.

Without a word, Isaac scooped Nickolaus up. He walked at first, and then began to run. He held Nick to him, the two sharing a heartbeat as they left the alley, and the majestic wings snapped opened. And then they were airborne. Nickolaus looked down, saw the streets of Chicago receding below. The city's lights were beautiful, a luminous carpet spreading out as far as the eye could see. Mighty wings caught the air, and they soared higher. Isaac held him tight against his warm chest, his body hot from exertion. Exultation filled Nick, buoyed by the thrill of height, and the heat of Isaac's skin.

Nothing would ever be the same, and they would be together. Forever.

Mr. Winter
Jeremy Terry

The office had been empty three minutes before when Collins stepped into his private bathroom to answer nature's call. He would have heard the outer door open; the hinges were in need of maintenance, and squealed slightly.

Yet he found a man sitting in the high backed leather chair when he returned. Collins glanced over the man's shoulder at the ornate wall clock hanging above the chair, a gift from a grateful client.

It was 12:10 P.M.

Collins frowned. Veronica never allowed anyone into his office without his first telling her to send them in, especially between noon and one when he was taking his lunch. This was all highly unusual. He looked back to the man, studying him. He was slight, barely five feet tall, with delicate features and skin as white as freshly denuded bone.

Denuded bone, thought Collins, feeling a chill run through him. *Why did I think of that?*

He looked into the man's eyes and felt he was being trapped by them. They were the blackest black, the color of midnight in Hell. They were startling, unnerving, and yet strangely beautiful. It seemed his pupils absorbed the light, devouring it so there was no shine or reflection in his eyes. They were like a void, the absence of anything.

It was very curious indeed. Collins felt compelled to speak.

"How did you get in here?"

The man did not answer.

Collins turned to his phone and pressed the button to key the intercom between his office and Veronica's desk outside, "Veronica, why did you send this man into my office? Who is he?"

Veronica didn't answer.

"Veronica?"

"She isn't there, Mr. Collins," the man said, speaking for the first time since entering. His voice was weird, high and breathy like that of an excited girl rather than a grown man.

Collins frowned. "What do you mean, 'she isn't there?'"

"I believe she has gone to lunch."

"That's not possible. She never leaves without my permission. I'm her boss."

"Oh, don't fret, Mr. Collins. Her absence gives us more time to speak."

"Excuse me, but I don't know you. Do you have an appointment?"

"Oh yes. Our appointment has been on the books for quite some time. It is a real pleasure to finally meet you."

The way he said *pleasure* creeped Collins out. He had the impression this man's idea of pleasure might be vastly different from his. Of course, Collins' own idea of pleasure was far from what would be considered normal. His mind drifted to the small room in the basement of his home. The man's lips twitched upwards as if he were about to smile and Collins felt a trickle of fear. For a moment it felt like the odd visitor knew what he was thinking.

Collins cleared his throat, "I'm not aware of any such appointment. Who are you?"

"I have many names. You may call me Mr. Winter."

"What the hell does that mean?"

Mr. Winter laughed, his girlish voice echoing off the walls, "It means just what I said. I have been called many things over the long years and while I do love the old names this is one of my favorites. Winter signifies death. It brings about the end of things so spring may come and bring new life."

"What . . . are you playing games with me?"

"I never play games, Mr. Collins."

"Then what are you doing here? What do you want?"

"You," Mr. Winter said.

"You want me?"

"Yes. I've come for you. I am *your* winter, Mr. Collins. I am *your* end."

Collins stood up quickly, sending his chair crashing into the wall behind him. "Are you fucking crazy? I've had enough of this shit! Get out of my office!"

Mr. Winter's mouth twitched up into his almost smile again and he shook his head. "No, I'm afraid not. I'm not going anywhere and neither are you."

"We'll see about that," Collins replied. He strode around the desk, making for the door.

He half expected the little man to try to stop him but Mr. Winter remained still, watching him with his flat black eyes. Collins gripped the doorknob and twisted. The knob refused to turn.

"What the hell?"

"I told you that you weren't going anywhere. It's much too late for that."

Collins turned to Mr. Winter, "What do you mean it's too late?"

"It's over, Mr. Collins. I claimed you while you stood before your bathroom mirror marveling at yourself. You belong to me now."

"I belong to nobody."

"See for yourself," said Mr. Winter. He motioned with his pale hand towards the closed bathroom door.

Terror gripped Collins. He didn't want to see for himself. He didn't want to go into the bathroom. He didn't want anything more to do with the vile little man, not now or ever again. Yet he found himself inexorably drawn to the unknown. He walked past Mr. Winter without daring to breathe and paused at the threshold. One last piece of him cried out for him to stop, to resist the madness, but the imperative would not be ignored. He reached out with trembling hand and opened the door.

Insanity crept upon him then. It was like a great blinding light threatening to burn away all he was. He fought it, seeking reason, seeking some hidden truth to explain everything and set the world straight.

There was a body on the tile floor but it couldn't be him. After all, he was standing right there. He touched his cheeks and was reassured by the solidness of his flesh, by the warmth of his skin and the roughness of his stubble. There must be an explanation and he would find it. He looked at the body again. It wore a suit like the one he wore. It wore the same shoes and the same gold watch glistened on the corpse's grey wrist. These things were disturbing but they didn't prove anything.

He needed to see the face.

The body lay on its side with one arm lying over its head, obscuring its features. Collins crossed the cold room and knelt down. He reached out and pushed the corpse onto its back.

His own dead, sightless eyes stared up at him from his dead face.

The blinding light exploded in his mind and there was no resisting it this time. Collins threw his head back and began to scream. He stood up and fled from the horror. He paused when he reached his desk. The office was empty. There was no sign of Mr. Winter save for the office door, which now stood

open before him. Collins ran through.

The reception area with Veronica's neat desk and family pictures was gone.

In its place was something that couldn't be there. Collins skidded to a halt on the smooth concrete floor. He turned, looking for the door to his office, and found a solid white wall. He turned back to the room and looked around.

There in the corner was the big wooden box he kept the children's toys in. Along the back wall ran the cabinets where he stored the candy he offered the kids, the candy laced with a sedative to make them manageable when the real fun began. His knives hung in a low row on the left wall, gleaming in the fluorescent lights like the teeth of some great beast. And there, in the center of the room was the chair. It began its existence as a simple dentist's chair but Collins had turned it into so much more. This was where he had his way with them and then cut them up.

His room, the one place he could be his true self. How had he come to be there? Had he dreamed the whole thing?

"You're not dreaming, Mr. Collins."

Collins screamed and spun, looking everywhere for Mr. Winter and not finding him. The high-pitched voice spoke again, seeming to come from everywhere and nowhere at the same time.

"This is where you brought your victims. This is where you took their innocence and then their lives. This is where you showed your true colors, the colors of a monster. You did all of this thinking no one saw you, but you were wrong. I saw you. I was in this very room as you made your cuts. I was the one who took the torn and broken children far away from you and all the hurt to a place more beautiful than the most brilliant mind can fathom. But that place is not meant for you."

Collins blinked and felt cold leather underneath him. He opened his eyes and found himself staring up at the ceiling. He tried to move and couldn't. He was bound tight in the chair, *his* chair. He began to struggle against his bonds, breaking the skin at his ankles and wrists. He felt warm blood begin to flow.

"There's a special place in Hell for people like you, Mr. Collins. It's not a lake of fire and brimstone, but a place of repetition, a place where your evil deeds are visited on you over and over and over again . . ."

There was a rustling noise and Mr. Winter came into view. The half smile was gone now, replaced by a shark's grin full of teeth much too big for the little man's face. He held one of Collins' own knives in his small hand.

"Let us begin . . ."

Impressions
Christine Morgan

"What's this nasty, grubby envelope?" the new girl asks.

Kane pokes his head up from the far side of a glass display case. "Uh-oh. Return address?"

She's behind the counter, sorting the mail. The National Parks Service sends him a new intern every season, part of a college program. This one's real name's Philippa, but she goes by Poppy.

"Um . . . Spectral Outcast Press?"

"Oh, hell." He straightens from his crouch, stretching until his spine gives a satisfying crackle.

She raises a hand. "No, wait. Sprectal Outcast. S-P-R. That can't be right."

"Typo, mistake, Freudian slip, pick one."

"Sounds like a ghost with a thing for butts. What would you even call that? A proctolergeist?"

Kane snorts. "Funny."

"Sprectal," she says. "Who fails that bad on a printed address label?"

"Believe me, that's small beans. This guy's 'published' stuff with his own name misspelled on the cover."

"Did you just make actual air-quotes at me?"

"Trust me, it's warranted."

Poppy nudges the envelope with a pen, making a face that suggests she expects something to wriggle out from under the flap. "Is this that same wackadoodle who's been writing to the *Gazette*?"

"Oh? I haven't seen any of his brand of crazy in the paper lately."

"A.J. told me. They couldn't print half of it if they wanted to."

"Ah." Kane utters a sour chuckle. "Full of ripe shits and fuck your mothers?"

"To put it mildly."

"Only a matter of time until he got around to us, I suppose. Do you know Ms. Ashton-Smith, at the county museum?"

"February? Sure."

"He's always trying to 'donate' copies of his latest crap. There, the library, even the school. Now it must be our turn. Probably wants us to carry it in the gift shop."

"Why?"

"Thinks he owns the lake. He used the same name in a story once, so therefore it's his. Or something."

She frowns. "But the lake got its name back in the 1800's. Says so in the guidebook and on the plaque right out front. It doesn't make any sense."

"You know that, I know that, everybody in town knows that, anybody who can read or has half a brain knows that. But, logic and reality, they aren't Uncle Sticky's strong points."

"Why is he called . . . on second thought, don't tell me. Please don't tell me."

He grins, but it's humorless. "Good choice."

Outside, gravel crunches under tires as the first car of the day turns into the lot. They both glance toward the windows.

"What should I do with this?" Poppy nudges the envelope again.

"Circular file."

"You don't want to open it?"

"I like my brain not vomiting itself out my eye sockets, thanks." He adjusts his uniform belt and picks up his hat. "How do I look?"

"Park Ranger Brian Kane, reporting for duty."

"Yippe-ki-yay." Slapping the hat into place, he strides out to meet the tourist-looking family. "Morning, folks. Welcome to Fossil Lake."

*   *   *

Fossil Lake.

Once part of an inland freshwater sea. Rich layers of clay caught everything that sank to the bottom – leaves, insects, worms, pine needles, fish, bits of twig, seed pods, tadpoles, ferns, feathers. More layers, settling as silt, covered them over.

As the organic matter decayed, only outlines remained, the delicate traceries of scales, leafy veins, and fibrous textures preserved in minute detail like fine sketches etched into the clay. Time and pressure took their toll, hardening the sediment into solid slabs that were eventually driven upward by tectonic forces, fractured and fragmented, scattered.

The settlers to the area, finding such relics, always hoped for some great discovery, something to rival the dinosaur bones of the Montana Badlands and put Fossil Lake on the map. Sadly, it was not meant to be. Charming though the little lake was, scenic though its surroundings, it seemed destined for a peaceful, prosperous obscurity.

Of those early pioneers, only impressions remain as well. A sole building – formerly the one-room schoolhouse – still stands, converted into a museum by the Poe County Historical Society. Kids from the Chalklines Preschool and Daycare squabble where hardy pioneer children once took their recess from lessons.

The old well at the center of the grassy village square presides over a downtown consisting of Rusty's Hardware Emporium, a Grocery Barn, the library, an internet café and arcade called GAME OVER, fine dining at Giovanni's and homestyle family fare at The Unicorn, the main offices of the *Gazette*, and shops that cater to the tourists.

Near the Visitor and Education Center run by Ranger Kane, is the campground, Mel's mini-mart, a motel with half a dozen individual cabins, and, of course, the boathouse where Ramsey's boys rent out rowboats and kayaks.

At the far end of town, past Willard and Frank's Pest Control – can't miss the place, what with that giant ant on the roof – is Not That Dark Spot, a roadhouse the summer trade tends to avoid. It's not that dark because it's darker than dark, a darkety-dark hole where the wanks and hacks hang out.

On a good night, there'll be live music from the Black Skull Death Vines, a local band. On a bad night, Peaches will have too many cans of PBR and decide to dance. It's a scary sight. Those lucky enough to not know better say it's the scariest sight ever to be seen in the vicinity.

Those who are less lucky, well, they've had occasion to run into Uncle Sticky.

And yet, amazing though it may seem, once upon a time there was something even nastier around here. The early pioneers, who'd hoped for dinosaurs, might or might not have been disappointed by what was finally discovered in the fossil record. It was no species of dinosaur, like they'd hoped for, to be sure. Still, it might indeed have put the town on the map.

But, as they say, that was then and this is now.

For now, the tourists enjoy posing for snapshots with the fiberglass replicas out in front of the Visitor and Education Center. They stick their heads into the claws, and pretend to ride astride the carapaces. They buy bumper stickers, postcards, t-shirts, plastic hand-clackers for the kids.

They don't need to see a shitfaced Peaches twerking it at the bar, or Uncle Sticky waving his stubby middle fingers while he shouts about cum-guzzling infant-rapers. Talk about making the wrong kind of impression!

Such things would detract somewhat from happy vacation memories and wholesome family fun.

Fossil Lake.

The fishing's no good – attempts at stocking the lake with trout never seem to take – but there's boating, and swimming, and sun-bathing along the beaches. Hiking trails wend through the wooded hills.

And, of course, there's the namesake activity, fossil-collecting. Most of what gets found is still ferns and worms and insects. Every now and then, the crumbling clay scree yields some more interesting prizes.

The best ones were found by a Scout troop a few summers back. Sad to say, representatives of that organization haven't returned since. That was, unfortunately, when Uncle Sticky got his moniker. Shouting senseless obscenities, sleazing around the campsites spying on teenagers in sleeping bags . . .

But, no. No. Enough of that. Please, for the sake of all that's good and holy in this world, enough of that.

The lake's the thing. Scenic, mineral-rich Fossil Lake. It isn't a geothermically-heated hot spring like at Yellowstone; the cool water seeps up from subterranean aquifers and artesian wells. Instead of sulfur compounds, it consists primarily of calcite, magnesium and iron.

It's harmless enough to drink, though it does have a distinct flavor – as well as an aftertaste and residue. For swimming, however, it provides buoyancy and a lovely, silky feel on the skin. Words such as therapeutic, invigorating and rejuvenating are frequently mentioned.

The water is crystal clear down to within about eighteen inches of the bottom, which stirs up in murky roiled clouds whenever disturbed. But few swim down so far. For one thing, it requires scuba gear. For another, there wouldn't be much to see even if not for the silt.

Usually.

If someone went down there now, equipped with mask, tank, flippers and dive-light, he or she might see something after all, something buried in the soft clay as if to hide . . . the way flatfish burrow into the sand for camouflage, peering up with a single watery eye in the shadows . . . or the houses of spiders who dig into loose desert dirt.

Imagine it there, lurking.

Lurking in the dark like some darkly lurking thing.

* * *

A tent, a cooler, some music, and three chums kicking back on canvas chairs around the fire.

Good times.

The lake glimmers under a half-moon. Ripples lap softly at the pebbled shore. A playful breeze wafts spirals of smoke this way and that. When a log splits, orange sparks whirl up from its glowing heart.

Peaceful. Relaxing.

"Nice," says Cody. Then, "Whoops, shit!" as his marshmallow ignites.

"Hold it over the coals, not the flames," Jeannie says.

Mark stretches. "Glad we got a quiet site away from the crowds."

Further down the beach, by the RV park, bonfires blaze. Silhouettes pass in front of them, people dancing or rough-housing or strolling along the boat-docks. Lights shine in a few cabin and motel-room windows.

It's just the right balance of being out in the unspoiled wilderness and being close enough to civilization that they're not totally isolated.

They talk books, agreeing that Clive Barker is brilliant, and that however skilled Orson Scott Card might be, his raving homophobic bigotry renders him utterly unreadable. The breeze shifts, bringing them the cool mineral scent of the lake and whiffs of barbecue. Stars twinkle in the blackness above.

Conversation ebbs into companionable silence. Mark pokes the fire. Jeannie opens a fresh bag of marshmallows.

"Hey, did you hear something?" Cody tilts his head.

All three of them listen. Water ripples, the wind whispers in the trees, distant strains of music and whooping voices drift over from the bonfires. A dog barks. Another burning branch cracks in the firepit, spitting sparks.

"Nope," says Jeannie. "Nothing weird, anyway."

"Okay. Must be the quiet, getting to me."

"Spooky story time?" Mark grins.

"Yeah, right," Cody says. "What, the Fossil Lake Monster?"

"The ghost of some drowned camper?" suggests Jeannie.

"A murdered maniac back from the grave," Cody adds. "Like something from a horror movie."

"Or a novel by Laymon, Ketchum or Lee. Inbred cannibal hillbilly mutants."

"Picture if you will," Mark begins, doing his Rod Serling impression. "Fossil Lake, a serene and idyllic retreat –"

Jeannie chucks marshmallows at him until he surrenders, all three of them laughing.

Then there's a heavy sort of rustle and crunch. Their laughter stops. They take uneasy glances around. The flickering firelight gives the illusion of stealthy, scurrying movement.

They wait. Nothing happens.

"Probably an animal," Jeannie says.

"What if it really is the Fossil Lake Monster?" Cody widens his eyes. "Remember those models outside the Visitor Center? What if it's one of those things, crawling out of the lake?"

"You heard what the ranger said." Jeannie chucks a marshmallow at him, too. "They went extinct millions of years ago."

"And even if they hadn't," says Mark, "they wouldn't sound like that." He makes pincers with both hands and snaps them rapidly.

The breeze shifts again.

"Oh, whew," says Cody, grimacing.

Jeannie flaps a hand in front of her nose. "God, what died?"

"A hobo in a truck stop men's room?"

The scent that hits them is not a scent but a bona fide stench, conjuring mental images of fetid basements, mouldering piles of unwashed laundry, a kitchen trash can overflowing with spoiled food and used toilet paper.

A strange chortling giggle, high-pitched but mushy, comes from somewhere past their tent.

"Who's there?" Jeannie calls.

"Yeah, quit screwing around, whoever you are." Mark stands up.

"Come on, say something," says Cody.

The reply is a slurred rush of mumbling grunts, from which a few semi-comprehensible words emerge.

". . . faggoty assfucker . . . go get raped by barn animals . . . call me a fraud? fuck you I am darkly controversial . . . all the incest abortion babies who want me to go away for not writing yaoi slash . . ."

"What the hell is it?" Cody rises from his camp chair as well.

"Creepy, whatever it is," says Mark.

Jeannie pulls a stick from the fire to serve as a torch. "Maybe someone needs help."

Another muddled mess of words spew forth like pus from an infected wound. "Why you have to be a raging bitch about it and take a big ripe steaming shit on my publications well I wish you would stick an AIDS-infected squirrel up your ass and then my whole roster can take turns taking big ripe steaming shits in your open coffin."

"Someone needs help, all right," Mark mutters.

They edge sideways around the tent until the light from the makeshift torch falls upon a pudgy, misshapen figure hunched in the bushes. Hate-filled beady little eyes squint against the glare. Long greasy tangles of hair fall in lank clumps to the collar of a grimy shirt sporting the logo of some metal band.

"Think it *is* a hobo," Cody says. "Hey! Who're you?"

"Do you have sleeeeeeeping bags?" the weirdo asks, oozing his slimy snail-trail gaze over them, licking his scabby lips. Here, unmistakably, is the source of the stench. "Tight, snug sleeping bags? Tucked in real tight and zipped shut real good so you can't move?"

All three of them take instinctive steps back. Their faces twist with revulsion.

"What is *wrong* with you?" Cody asks. "Dude! Sick!"

"I think he must be mentally defective," says Jeannie.

"Call me a retard you slutwhore I bet you are some fucking plagiarist wank, another cunt trying to sabotage –"

She brandishes the torch at him. "*What* did you call me?"

He recoils, whining. "Just because I suggested they give rim jobs to their dead relatives and suck dog-dicks, they go and try to make me a laughingstock; well, I have a crude sense of humor and am outspoken about my beliefs which the homo agenda wants me to shut up!"

"Get the fuck out of here, you creep! Before we call the ranger or kick your ass ourselves!" Mark moves a meaningful stride forward, fists clenched.

The weirdo squeals. An acrid stink of piss overpowers everything else. With a shrill, gurgling cry that is either a titter or a yelp, he makes a break for it. His clumsy, stumpy-legged excuse for a run tramples the undergrowth. Leaves don't quite wilt at his passage, but it wouldn't have been surprising.

Then he's gone. Cody, Jeannie and Mark shudder in unison. They look at each other as the smell dissipates and the normal scents of the forest once again fill the air.

"Who's for moving camp over closer to the crowds?" Cody raises his hand. "Like, immediately?"

Jeannie's and Mark's shoot up as well.

"That," says Jeannie, "or pack up and leave altogether. I don't know about you guys, but I never want to spend the night in a sleeping bag again."

*   *   *

Lloyd, A.J.'s partner at the *Gazette* as well as in other ways, bursts into the

Visitor and Education Center, wild-eyed and wild-haired, panting for breath, his rumpled clothes askew in a sexy kind of way.

"Me and A.J. . . . we were at . . . at the lake . . . we saw . . . he went to grab his camera . . . we saw . . . we saw . . ."

"What?" asks Poppy. "What did you see?"

"An unseen horror!"

"But you just said you *saw* it," she says.

He falters, blinking. Pretty, like most of A.J.'s boyfriends, but not the sharpest crayon in the box. "Unknown, then. An unknown horror."

Ranger Kane pinches the bridge of his nose and strives for patience. "So, what did it *look* like, this unknown horror?"

"It was indescribable!"

"Indescribable?"

"Like something out of a horror story!"

"Indescribable," Kane repeats dryly.

"Yeah, like from a story Stephen King, or Richard Matheson. Or an episode of *The Twi* –"

He leans across the counter to swat Lloyd upside the head. "Knock it off. You're a reporter, a writer. It's your *job* to describe things."

"Oh," Lloyd says, considering this. "Yeah . . . I guess you're right."

Before he can describe whatever it was they'd seen, however, Poppy peers out the window. "What's going on down by the mini-mart? Who's yelling?"

"We're too late!" cries Lloyd, dashing for the door again. "Ranger, you've got weapons? Guns and stuff? Hurry!"

He's gone without waiting for an answer. Poppy and Kane exchange a glance, then follow, Kane pausing only long enough to unlock a tall metal cabinet and grab a dart rifle to supplement the bear spray and taser on his belt.

Curious tourists and locals have already gathered by the time they get close to the disturbance. Among them are Angelina from the library, Ramsey and his boys looking over from the kayak rental place, a group of little Chalkliners on a park outing supervised by a teacher, the Black Skull Death Vines band members who've been having a cookout on the beach before their evening's gig, Ray from GAME OVER, others.

"I think," Kane says, "that Uncle Sticky's been trying to convince Mel to carry his crappy excuses for books."

Mel, in her smock, has chased the stumbling, disheveled figure most of the way to the lake shore. A trail of shoddy-looking paperbacks and stapled manuscripts leave a trail leading back to the mini-mart, creased pages fluttering limply in the breeze.

208

"— and stay the hell out of my store from now on, loser!" Mel finishes, hurling the last tattered sheaf of pages at him. It flaps through the air and smacks onto the rocks. Though it's about fifteen feet short, he ducks, flinches, retreats to the water's edge and cowers there, bleating that weird gibbering giggle of his.

"Loser? Who are you calling loser, skank?" He points at February Ashton-Smith. "Ask her! Her father took my books as a donation! Losers don't get books in museums! He said I was like a hybrid of a bunch of really famous scary writers so nyah!"

"Excuse me?" February raises her eyebrows. "Are you kidding? Your books aren't in the museum. Never have been."

"That's because he decided to keep them for himself instead of put them on display where all the rest of these rape-babies could pirate them, then piss on the ashes of my career like some fucking faggot terrorists who shoot up schools and give their kids X-Boxes!"

"What?" say five or six bewildered tourists.

"What does that even mean?" Poppy asks Kane.

Kane shrugs.

"Whatever my father told you," February says, "it was to humor you, to be polite, and get you to go away."

"That's a fucking lie! You say that when he liked them enough to —"

"He threw them out. He told me it was like trying to read someone doing a bad impression of a wanna-be Lovecraft ripoff. He said calling it fan-fiction would be an insult to fan-fiction."

"The fuck you know, bitchdyke cunt! Why don't you go dump a load of cum in your dead mother with your shemale cock!"

"He said bad words!" gasps a Chalkliner in a Spider-Man shirt.

"Just ignore him," the teacher says.

"But he's being mean to the nice lady!"

"Hush. It's none of your business."

"Like to see any of you write creative nonfiction true stories from your own nightmares of darkness!" Uncle Sticky rants on. "I get publicity, I put copies right in the hands of people in the goth metal scene to promote my books and they say I'm hardcore, they do devil horns at me when I meet them outside concerts!"

"Which they also throw away as soon as you're gone, like anybody with an ounce of brains in their head," says A.J., who's just arrived with camera in hand, only to find more of a spectacle than whatever he and Lloyd had expected.

"They do not do not do not!" Uncle Sticky jumps up and down, stamping his feet and shaking his dirty little fists. To either side of his ridiculously pubic patch of mangy facial hair, stubbly jowls wobble. "So shut the fuck up and let me have my readership! I have fans! I have supporters!"

"Anybody who tells you that," says Angelina, "is either trying to be nice and let you down easy, or hoping to get rid of you without you making a scene."

"Face it," says one of Ramsey's boys. "You can't write worth a damn."

"I was good enough to be in *PsychoWeenie Magazine* ten years ago, you fucking cuntfucks, how can you say I can't write? I sent a story to *Stiff Sock* too only they couldn't use it because it was too transgressive with cannibalism and other really extreme subjects too dark and gross for them to touch!"

"The only thing around here too gross to touch is *you*, princess," the Black Skull Death Vines drummer says, to a general round of agreement.

Uncle Sticky juts his chin. Or, tries to. It might have worked better if he actually *had* one. "Nuh-unh!"

"Yeah-huh!" chorus several of the Chalkliners.

"Right, that's enough," says the teacher. "Come on, children. Since you can't be polite, we're leaving. I don't want to hear any more. We'll forget all about it and pretend none of this ever happened." And, with that, they're marched off, their protests of unfairness and injustice falling on deaf ears.

Uncle Sticky, meanwhile, is all warmed up and raring to go.

"You just hate me for being the outspoken Christian conservative who won't write to the God-abominations or publish gay erotica pandering to a homo knob jockeys who want to read about men rubbing their big hard cocks together and being on their knees getting spit-roasted by sweaty slapping man-meat and swallowing gallons of each others' creamy loads while getting ass-pounded up the ass with giant cocks pounding in their asses yeah pumping their asses full of hot thick spunkjuice!"

Everyone only stares.

A.J. nudges Lloyd and murmurs, "This is him *not* liking gay porn?"

"For someone who claims that, he sure knows a lot about it."

He rounds on them. "Shut the fuck up you cockgobblers, I'd like to see your balls on video! I mean, see you have the balls to expose yourself on video, why don't you do that with your real name A.J. not hiding behind faceless initials like some faggot with your trash piece of shit tabloid-purpose newspaper! Why can't you show your dick I mean why do you have to be a dick and not give it to me?"

"Someone's got a crush," Lloyd lilts in a singsong.

"Ohhh-mygawd." A.J. holds up both hands with palms out. "Eew."

"Go molest a goat wrapped in a flaming rainbow pride flag! I am not gay, I like the ladies, natural-born ladies not fake tranny fag hags, so quit making me out to be some cum-gulper and sabotaging me getting a girlfriend!"

"Yeah, the women are lining up for the chance," says the Black Skull Death Vines lead singer. "Who wouldn't want a piece of that?" She turns aside and mimes poking a finger down her throat.

"Raging cunt, I wish someone should rape you and get you pregnant —"

Kane heaves a sigh. "Yeah, okay, we've had enough of this." In a single smooth motion, he unshoulders the dart rifle and fires.

"Hurk!" Uncle Sticky staggers back, heels splashing into the shallows. Clutching at his leg where the needle of the ballistic syringe has pierced his filth-encrusted jeans, he sputters, "Cocksucker! You . . . fuck you . . . fucking fucker . . ."

He totters another few steps, sways, reels, and takes the full-on Nestea plunge. An oilslick of grime, grease and scum forms, spreading around him as he lolls like a bloated, floating corpse. His eyelids twitch. Foamy drool dribbles from the corner of his mouth.

When the applause and cheering die down, a somber thoughtfulness descends over the assembled crowd.

"I suppose we ought to dredge him out before he drowns," February says.

"Or pollutes the lake," says A.J. "He's leaving a bathtub ring already."

"Glurrrr . . ." mumbles Uncle Sticky, struggling toward semi-sentience.

Then the surface of the water surges up in a sudden bulge beneath him, as Lloyd's indescribable unknown horror rises from the depths.

It's just like a scene from a movie, like that scene in *Aliens* where the alien queen impales that guy and rips him in half. Just like that, only more graphic and surreal with extreme horror!

Uncle Sticky screeches, blowing bubbles of blood and curds of spit, gaping goggle-eyed at the barbed point sticking through the metal band logo on his grubby shirt. His limbs thrash in a wild, useless flailing. What comes next isn't a *ripping* in half so much as a *cutting*, a *chopping* . . . as an enormous claw with serrated edges comes up, seizes the flabby torso, and closes with a single hard snap of powerful tendons.

KLAK!

His lower portion, legs kicking in spasmodic reflex, plop down amid a shower of bilious bodily fluids. The monstrous scorpionoid tail flexes, waving Uncle Sticky's upper half in a triumphant flourish. Unraveling gut-loops swing in slippery sausage ropes from the ragged bisection. A knobbly length of spine sticks out.

Moderate pandemonium erupts. People stand stunned, or rush screaming toward town. The thing in the lake submerges again, taking its grisly trophy with it. Water churns and seethes in its wake. The other chunks of Uncle Sticky slowly sink.

"See?" Lloyd says after a while. "I told you."

A.J. belatedly remembers the camera he holds, and swears.

"Well." One of Ramsey's boys hooks his thumbs in his belt loops. "That made a hell of an impression on the tourists."

"Made a hell of an impression on *me*," says Mel. She wedges her toe under a manuscript and kicks it into the lake.

"This is going to complicate the rest of the season, isn't it?" Poppy asks.

Kane removes his hat, wipes his brow and puts it on again. "Yeah," he says. "Yeah, it is."

There they stay, watching until the last of the frothy scum and greasy hair tangles melt away, and Fossil Lake is calm once more.

Make Me Something Scary
Patrick Tumblety

Ghosts are always white. Sometimes on the cartoons they are see-through, or their clothes are colored, like the green jackets on the three brothers that chase Mickey, but their bodies are still white. Sometimes ghosts wear sheets, but the sheets are white, too.

Should she have used the white crayon? That didn't make much sense to her, but maybe that's what she should have done . . .

The door to the teacher's office clicked open, and Annie snapped to attention, standing up from the hallway linoleum and brushing her wrinkled dress down with the palms of her hands.

"Annie," Mr. Beakman called from inside the office, "You can come in, now."

Annie deflated when she saw that her mother's lips were pursed and her arms and legs were crossed. She lifted herself into an empty chair and kept her head lowered. The picture of the ghost lay on the desk in front of them, its top corner fluttering from the chilly breeze through the open window.

Mr. Beakman set a finger down on the paper. "Annie, can you tell me why you didn't complete the assignment?" he asked.

Annie didn't understand how to answer the question, because she thought she *had* completed the assignment.

"Annie, please answer me," Mr. Beakman said, more forcefully, almost angrily, "Why didn't you color in the ghost?"

The teacher's skin was turning a shade of red, the same color her father turned when she had done something wrong. Her mother's silence was terrible enough, but Mr. Beakman had scared her since the first day of school. He was very loud, very forceful, and never particularly nice to any of his kids.

When she was coloring the picture and thinking about ghosts and monsters and things that were scary on Halloween, she thought that nothing could scare her more than Mr. Beakman. As Annie concentrated on coloring, she wished that a ghost would haunt Mr. Beakman and scare him this Halloween.

"Ghosts are white," she whispered, almost inaudibly.

Mr. Beakman breathed in deeply and the color in his face darkened. "Are you mad at me, Annie?"

Why would she be mad at him? What did he do wrong?

"You colored everything but the ghost, Annie. I can't help but think that you did this on purpose."

Annie had taken the brown, orange, red, and yellow crayons and applied each color one after the other to fill the empty space. Then, with her thumb, she rubbed across the lines where each color met in order to blend them together. When she was finished, the ghost was floating in the autumn dusk that Annie had seen above her house the night before.

"I colored the outside, because the ghost is white, and the paper would be blank if I didn't add color to the outside. So I colored it like the outside. Like a Halloween sky."

"Are you happy now?" Her mother's loud scolding voice made Annie flinch. But when she looked up, she found her mother's punishment face staring at the teacher. Was she not in trouble?

"Your daughter failed the assignment, Mrs. Reese, and this isn't the first time she took liberties with assignments."

"Took liberties? She's in Kindergarten."

"And is showing early signs of behavioral inconsistencies. I think it would be beneficial to everyone if you allowed the guidance counselor to evaluate her for potential withholding from graduating to the first grade."

"All because she thought outside of the box? Aren't you supposed to encourage that kind of thinking?"

"The project wasn't about artistic ingenuity, Mrs. Reese, it was about following instruction. Your daughter failed."

"I'll be talking to Principal Anders about this." Annie's mother picked up her purse from the floor and stood. She took the ghost off of the desk and handed the paper to Annie. "And I'll be putting this on the fridge when she gets home. I don't know how your previous school nurtured children, but here we expand their minds, not force them to color inside the lines."

Annie didn't want the picture to go on the fridge. Only good work went on the fridge, and that paper had a big, ugly red F stabbing through the ghost she thought was supposed to be white.

She tried to avoid eye contact with her teacher as he escorted her back to the classroom. As she navigated through the rows of wooden desks he grabbed a stack of papers from the work closet. He began to place a single sheet in front of each student, moving slowly from row to row. When he reached her, he slapped the paper down so hard that she almost tipped her chair back when her body jumped involuntarily.

He must have been waiting for her to meet his gaze because he paused and hovered above her before moving to Jimmy's desk. The students noticed the hostility, and they all exchanged glances and smirks at the possible trouble Annie had caused.

"I want you to make me something scary to hang in the gymnasium for the Halloween party on Friday. You have one hour." Mr. Beakman sat down at his desk and flipped open a notebook as the students slid open their drawers and took out their crayons and colored pencils.

Annie was still upset, and she couldn't take her eyes off of Mr. Beakman. It was like he was a big dog she had to watch just in case he decided to pounce. The teacher looked up from his notebook as though he could feel her stare. His face turned red, and he looked like he was about to shout. Instead, he looked back down at his notebook and stared at it as his hands clenched into fists. Annie didn't take her eyes off of the man until the red drained from his face and he began scribbling in his notebook.

She slid out her desk drawer slowly, carefully, silently, and placed her coloring tools on top of her desk. She plucked her orange crayon from its box. On the bus ride to school she saw a lot of houses had Jack O' Lanterns on their porches. The smiles carved into them were creepy, but not too scary, so drawing one was safe. She started by scrawling a big orange circle in the center of the paper. She was about to outline the placement of the eyes and mouth inside the surrounding orange line, but the image of the white circle cautioned her to think about what she was making.

She had colored the ghost wrong the day before, and her teacher was furious. If she failed again, what would he do?

Annie's hands trembled; what was she expected to do? She could feel her eyes welling with water and her fear threatening to collapse her body onto the desk and weep. If she showed how afraid she was of doing the assignment wrong, then surely Mr. Beakman would be even more mad. Mr. Beakman had once refused Christopher from going to the bathroom in the middle of class. Annie had never seen an adult yell that loudly. Mr. Beakman had been her teacher only for a month and a half, but he got upset more often than any adult she had ever known.

So what would happen to her if she failed or cried again?

Annie's mother taught her to learn from her mistakes, so she concentrated on discovering what she had done wrong the first time. Mr. Beakman said to "color the ghost," and he was mad because she "colored everything but the ghost."

This time, Mr. Beakman said to make something scary – that's it! Mr. Beakman never said to draw anything, but to "make" something. It was a test just for her, to make up for not following directions the first time. Her fear was pushed away by excitement; while the other kids wrongly scribbled and colored on the paper, she would complete the assignment exactly how her teacher wanted. He would like her so much for being a good listener that it would make up for her previous failure.

She peeled off the crayon's covering and frantically filled all of the white space with orange. She slid open her drawer once again and pulled out a pair of scissors. She used the scissors to round out the edges of the paper and poked holes for the eyes and mouth, then carefully snipped until she created triangle eyes and rectangle teeth. When she was satisfied, she proudly lifted the paper Jack O' Lantern up to the ceiling to let the light shine through the face she had created . . .

Mr. Beakman's eyes filled the Jack O' Lanterns', and the paper fell from Annie's fingertips and fluttered toward the desk like fall leaves from a tree.

"What do you think you're doing?" Mr. Beakman asked, his face again the color of apples.

"I made you something scary out of the paper," Annie said proudly, and managed a smile despite her nervousness.

Mr. Beakman lifted quivering hands and hid his face as though he were about to play peek-a-boo with a baby.

Had she not made the paper scary enough?

Her teacher lowered his hands and closed his eyes, breathing heavily as though he was snoring.

"Class," he said calmly, "how many of you are done with your assignment?"

Some of the students raised a hand while some raised their paper.

"For those of you who have correctly completed your assignment, I want you to take a piece of tape and hang it up in the coat closet."

Though every child was confused by the request, they sheepishly and silently complied, moving all of the coats to one side and taping their monsters around the corner of the closet, covering the back and side walls until the tiny space was filled white with speckles of color on top.

Annie tried to pick up her creature from the desk, but the moment she touched the paper, Mr. Beakman slapped it against the wood with great force and ferociously screamed, "Don't you move!"

All of the students looked frightened. Annie was sure that she failed again, and so she cried. That seemed to enrage Mr. Beakman more, because he grabbed her tightly around the arm and continued onto the back of the room toward the closet. The force pulled her out of the chair and a sharp pain stung her shoulder. Her teacher dragged her across the dirty floor and then pulled her forward, sliding her into the closet. He slammed the doors, and Annie found herself in darkness. Only a sliver of light from where the closet doors met bled through, and then she heard the door latch.

"Think about your behavior, Annie," said Mr. Beakman's voice, muffled through the wooden doors, "and study what you were supposed to make."

Annie crawled backward and huddled in the corner. She cried until the bell rang for lunch, and then she cried some more when she heard her classmates leave the room and the classroom door shut without her teacher letting her out of the dark closet filled with monsters. She peered through the small slit in between the doors, but she couldn't see Mr. Beakman either. She felt better being closer to the light, so she stayed sitting against the door.

With the little light that came through she could see the different creatures lining the walls – a Frankenstein, a zombie, a vampire – one with bloody fangs and one that sparkled. After a while of staring at those pictures in the dark, silent and alone, Annie no longer saw them as children's drawings, but actual nightmares staring back at her, mocking her for failing so miserably. She was being punished, but wished she knew what she had done. She had followed her teacher's instructions to the word.

"Don't be afraid," a child's voice whispered to her, and she immediately turned toward the light to peek through and see who had come back. She pivoted her head against the door as though she were trying to squeeze through the thin opening and tried to look around the classroom. Her Jack O' Lantern slid underneath the door.

"I can't see you," Annie cried out, desperately, "where are you?"

"Behind you," the child answered, and Annie could hear that the voice was truly coming from behind, within the closet.

Annie turned, screaming, using her feet to push her back against the wooden doors that buckled under her desperate retreat.

A boy was kneeling in front of her, holding his hands in the air and smiling.

"Don't be afraid, Annie, I'm a friend, and I know you don't want to get

your teacher's attention."

The little boy seemed friendly, and he was right, she didn't want to get Mr. Beakman even more upset with her crying and yelling. If the boy didn't want to upset the teacher, than he must be a nice boy. However, the longer she stared at the boy's face the more she realized that she could see the pictures of the monsters behind him, through his face.

"It's okay, Annie. I'm a ghost but I'm not scary."

Annie's body shook with fright and she felt another welling of fear threatening to belt out of her throat.

"I used to be normal, like you. Look at my shirt!"

Annie looked down at the boy's shirt that she hadn't noticed he was wearing until he mentioned it. It was bright blue and had the Teenage Mutant Ninja Turtles eating pizza on the front. That made Annie smile, but she was still a tiny bit afraid, because the shirt, too, was see-through.

"Have you seen the cartoon where Mickey, Donald, and Goofy, are being chased by the three ghosts? You could see their clothes too even though they were almost invisible! But in the end they were friendly too, weren't they?"

Annie nodded. The boy was right. Her tension eased slightly, though she was still very nervous.

"I'm Annie," she said.

"I'm Michael. That Mr. Beakman is a bad man, isn't he?"

Annie thought about it, but ended up shrugging. Adults got mad when kids didn't do things right, so it wasn't his fault she had to be punished. "I did the assignment wrong."

"No, Annie," said the boy, and for the first time he looked angry, making Annie push backward slightly against the doors again. "You didn't do anything wrong."

Michael looked away and when his face returned to her, he was smiling pleasantly.

"Adults shouldn't hurt children like that, no matter what they do wrong," he said. "And you didn't do anything wrong by using your imagination." He pointed a translucent finger toward the arm where her teacher had grabbed her, and she could see a dark mark across her skin.

"Mom and Dad said not to let anyone hurt me, or I should tell them. But Mr. Beakman's a teacher, he's supposed to be my friend, too."

The boy nodded his head, his jovial expression becoming sad. "Yes, Annie, but sometimes adults can be bad, even if they're supposed to be our friends. Your teacher is a bad man, and he's hurt other children, too." He moved the same finger upward, and though his form was barely visible,

Annie saw a dark blue mark circling the boy's pale neck.

"Should I tell on him?" Annie asked, cautiously. Her parents have told her about strangers and other adults that might want to harm her, but a teacher?

"I know, it's confusing, but telling on him didn't work before. No one believes a child over an adult."

"But what if he hurts me again?"

He smiled, and from below his feet slid out her picture of the white ghost with the autumn background.

Annie picked up the paper. "I did this wrong."

"No, you did it exactly the way you wanted to do it, and because of that it's beautiful. That's why I'm here. You wished for a ghost to haunt your teacher this Halloween, and I was sent here to make your wish come true."

Annie wasn't sure about scaring an adult, even if he was a bad man. But if he was a bad man, he deserved to be scared. If he was hurting children, he deserved to be scared.

"That's right, Annie. You need to stop him from hurting other children."

"How do I do that?" Annie asked, a little uneasy.

A box of crayons slid forward from beneath the boy.

"Turn the paper around and complete the assignment exactly as your teacher asked. Make Mr. Beakman something scary."

Annie finally understood! Mr. Beakman didn't want her to make the paper into something scary, he wanted her to make *him* something scary.

She plucked a red crayon out of the box and made an outline of her teacher's body. She drew the body like a box, like a normal person's body, but then twisted the legs and arms into strange angles, like he was a giant spider, bent into a non-human form. She then drew one curly line from the body and to the left, ending it with a circle making his head and neck a balloon blowing in the wind. On the head-balloon she drew two x's as eyes and a jagged line for a mouth. Mr. Beakman looked creepy, no, scary, and she knew she had done it right this time. She finished the picture by coloring the scenery behind the scary teacher with red crayon, making the adult man look even more menacing.

"How is this?" Annie asked, pleading for approval.

"It's perfect, Annie. You did it exactly right." Michael smiled at her, and it warmed her heart. "Now, I need you to take two of these warm jackets and push them up against your ears. Your teacher is about to come in, and he's going to get in trouble for hurting you."

"Is someone going to yell at him?" Annie asked, thinking that maybe the boy would alert the principal or her mother and told them what Mr. Beakman had done.

"Yes. There will be screaming."

Annie did what she was told, because she always tried to be a good listener. After a long while, a gust of wind brushed across her body, so she looked up from the jackets she had been pushing against her ears.

The closet doors were open and every student stood gathered around the middle of the classroom, staring down at the floor with a confused expression on each of their faces. Annie pushed to her feet and patted her wrinkled and dusty dress down with the palm of her hands. She picked up her drawing and moved forward, pushing through the group of children until she made her way to the front.

On the floor lay Mr. Beakman. His arms and legs were twisted and broken and his head hanging to the side, held on only by one thick line of skin, and the color of red surrounded the body, just as she had created.

Annie was shocked and confused at the sight, but then realized something wonderful as she compared what she was seeing to the picture in her hand.

She had finally completed the assignment!

Annie made Mr. Beakman something scary.

Though there was something incomplete about the scene, Annie thought, and she lifted the paper up so that she could look over both images side-by-side. What was wrong?

Oh! She discovered what was missing, but she wasn't worried, it was a quick fix. On the paper she never colored in Mr. Beakman's skin, so now his new form was completely white to match how she had drawn him.

If there was anything that her teacher had taught her, it was that ghosts weren't always white, and he must be a ghost, because he was surely dead. She couldn't just leave his skin blank as she had done with the ghost.

Annie moved toward the new form on the floor. She knelt and studied her teacher's face. She needed to complete the assignment exactly how she was told to, however, she didn't have a big enough pink or brown crayon to color in her teacher's skin. She hadn't colored the ghost, and Mr. Beakman got mad, so how mad would he get if she left him blank?

He would get so mad he would turn red again –

Red! Mr. Beakman was always turning red! Annie grabbed the color from of the background and began to fill in the colorless space.

The Day Lloyd Campbell's Mama Came To Town
Scott Colbert

"I'll take a steaming shit in your mother's cuntsack!"

Trickles of foam bubbled from the corners of his girlish mouth, making the greasy goatee shine even more. Alby stamped his hairy, clubbed-looking feet for emphasis, as his tiny fists flitted through the air as if he were swatting flies (though in reality it was what passed for punches). He'd just read the email his now-ex-boyfriend had sent breaking up with him.

"Alby,

It's not me, it's you. Your greasy hair, lack of hygiene, temper tantrums aside, it's your lack of respect for my mother that forces my hand. The names you called her - I can't bear to think of them - and threatening to piss on her fresh grave, it was the last straw. It was fun for awhile, but no one insults a son's love for their mother and gets away with it.

Lloyd"

Alby stepped back from his nicotine-stained laptop, with the non-working track pad. He tripped on an empty energy drink can and went careening on his ass. As he fell back, he hit his head on the edge of a particle board book case, sending a dozen of his self-published books (the only ones that had ever been purchased), crashing down on him.

His vision blurred while blood began flowing from the gash in his head, matting the clumped hair even further. His consciousness waxed and waned to the incessant bleat of a smoke alarm until Alby passed out.

". . . Albert, can you hear me? Albert?" It was a sweet voice in spite of a noticeable Brooklyn accent. He could smell the sachet that contained a flowery

potpourri with an underlying hint of something . . . darker. When he was able to focus a bit, Alby opened his eyes and confusion washed over him.

"Where am I?" he asked.

The woman smiled at him. "Why, Lake Fossil Diner of course. It's your favorite place."

"I've never been here! And who the fuck are you? Some fandom wank trying to scare me? It ain't gonna work! I scared a preacher's wife once!" Alby said.

In spite of his bravado, the quivering tone in his high pitched, whiny voice gave his pants-shitting fear away. He looked around, his too-small mouth opening and closing like a suffocating fish. Human heads were mounted on the wall, all in various states of decomposition. Underneath were tarnished brass nameplates; the closest to him that he could read was A.J. Poe.

"But this is the same diner you write about in all of your stories, isn't it?" The old woman continued gazing at Alby's unkempt appearance. The concert t-shirt of some obscure metal band was stained with beer, and ketchup. A thin crust of grime encircled his neck, and she couldn't help but notice the copious amounts of dirt beneath his fingernails.

"No it's not! I don't have the heads of my characters mounted on the walls!"

"But they aren't your characters, sweetie." She took a sip of her tea that she'd been letting cool. All the while her smile didn't leave her face. For others, her grin would have been reassuring. For Alby it offered nothing but discomfort and fuel for his anger. "You never created a character; they are all based on real people." She looked down, swallowed hard and brushed away a tear with one arthritic finger. "Sadly, they all committed suicide rather than be associated with you."

"Stupid horse fuckers!"

"Such language!"

"Fuck you, lady! I don't even know you!" He tried to pound the table with a pudgy fist, yet it contained all the force of a fly fart.

She held her hand out, and introduced herself. "I'm Lloyd Campbell's Mama."

Alby shrank back in the booth, getting as far away from the hand as possible. "You're dead!"

Mama Campbell shrugged. "You say tomato, I say tomahto. Dead is a relative term. I mean what is death, really? Do you know Alby? You write about it, but you don't comprehend it."

Alby tried to speak, but his throat began to constrict, choking off anything he could possibly say to defend himself. Mama Campbell meanwhile, reached into her blouse and pulled out the sachet. It was a flowery leather pouch on a

222

necklace of fine gold. With a bit of effort she opened the pouch, and Alby's own voice poured out of it.

"I'll take a steaming shit in your mother's cuntsack!"

Mama Campbell gave Alby a look of disappointment, and tsked-tsked at him. "Is that what you want? Is that really what you desire? To shit in my cuntsack?" Her jovial blue eyes dimmed while veins began to pop from her forehead. Slowly, and with the effort only a geriatric with arthritic hips can muster, Mama slid out of the booth, and stood by Alby's side, blocking him in.

She slowly began to push down her slacks, her eyes now a black void which seemed to swirl ever so slightly. The throbbing veins began moving, snakelike across her forehead and temple. Tendrils of smoke issued from her nostrils, and when she opened her mouth to speak, a long forked tongue whipped out and smacked Alby between the legs.

Alby screamed and promptly wet himself. Mama Campbell stepped out of her slacks, and started to pull down her peach colored panties. "No! Stop!" he pleaded.

"Not until you . . . SHIT IN MY CUNTSACK!" The voice was not that of the old lady, but an old God. It sounded of sawing wood and breaking rock.

Those twisting veins began to erupt from her face, revealing themselves as tentacles. They whipped themselves around her head, Medusa-like as they reached out and gripped Alby by the ankles. The heads on the wall became a Greek chorus, chanting "cunt-sack! cunt-sack!" in unison.

With a deftness and agility that was more shocking than her transformation, Mama Campbell leaped up on the table, legs spread and facing Alby. One of the tentacles that had grabbed his ankles now slithered up his pants and invaded his rectum, forcing him up until his face was level with her crotch.

Her vagina opened, revealing a maw of glistening teeth. Row upon row of sharp, porcelain daggers greeted Alby. The tentacles pushed him forward into the fleshy morass.

Alby's scream was cut short as the teeth ripped at his face and neck. It continued eating and gnawing at his flaccid body, until there was nothing left. Not even his dirty clothes.

Six weeks later, Alby's Uncle Ronny ventured into the basement and found it empty.

Alby's body was never found, and he was never missed.

The Rack
Mike Meroney

There I lay tied-
spread on the rack-
screaming to the dark
with no turning back.
Next came a shuffle-
followed by light-
the whisper of a man-
"It's gonna be a long night."
A mask on his face-
all I saw were his eyes-
staring into mine
as if I were a prize.
He told me to scream-
encouraged with delight-
but instead I laid still-
paralyzed by my fright.
A knife in my face-
"You see this here blade?
It's time you were acquainted."
Then gashes were made-
into my flesh-
so intense it did slide-
ripping and tearing-
I could feel it inside.
Gouging so gory-
no time to befuddle-
my senses scraped raw-
as the blood dripped to puddle.
Pouring from wounds-
too many to count-
I lapsed into shock
as the terror did mount.

Then burning on skin-
patches now thinning-
acid to boil
and it's just the beginning.
Next came the laughter
and the glint of a sword-
screaming came after-
"Hope you're not growing bored."
The slice of the blade
slew the meat of my thigh-
slit up to the groin-
as if cutting a pie.
Right about then-
catapulting with shock-
quivering and bleeding-
the butcher, the block.
Screaming so fierce-
I then lost my voice
but the torture kept going-
as if I had a choice.
Next there were tongs-
on nipples with twist-
ripped off like paper-
then smashed on my wrist.
Bones now were broken-
left and then right.
My insides were burning
from the heat of the night.
The man held a pencil
with the menace of a spear-
his cackling would soften
as it jabbed in my ear.
I felt like my head
was going to explode.
The pencil broke off-
but the pain never slowed.
Praying for death-
my resulting behavior-
as the branding iron touched me-

there would be no savior.
Molten hot lava
that scorched all my flesh-
the stench of cooked meat
in my nostrils so fresh.
Next came the cuts
having skill of a laser-
slicing under my balls
with the edge of a razor.
To the top of my cock-
flayed like a steak-
no more dancing or romancing-
for this decapitated snake.
My head it was spinning-
as then I was released-
passed out from blood loss
like dead meat for a beast.
The nightmare not over
as it started again-
muffled voice in my good ear-
not really sure when-
and there was a face
staring right into mine.
I felt as if needles
were pricking my spine.
"Do you know who I am?"
The man over me said.
I just shook my head
because soon I'd be dead.
Muffled and wretched-
grotesque and with spite-
tears erupted from red eyes-
scorching skin that was white.
"You killed my boy-
he was tortured I'm told.
I showed you no mercy.
He was just nine years old.
We can't bring him back-
there's no need to repent-

but I'll feel so much better
'cuz to Hell you'll be sent.
Guided by hands
that helped raise my boy-
now I can sleep better
these hands helped destroy-
the one who crushed life-
that once felt so new-
took my reason to live-
that one it was you."
There was nothing to do
but lie there and bleed.
Even if I had wanted
there was no way I could plead-
for he cut out my tongue-
now I'm choking on plasma-
my lungs filling up-
hacking like I have asthma-
and as he stood crying-
I bled and I choked-
my being was scorched
from this man I provoked.
You see, I was a teacher
and his boy was my student.
I got carried away
with acts far from prudent.
First there was touching-
then screaming in pain-
it felt rather good-
you won't hear me complain.
But what can I say?
No harm there was meant.
Still I went overboard-
with most curious intent.
Mutilated and tortured
this poor fucker's son-
and somehow he knew
that I was the one.
David was his name-

so young and so sweet.
A smile just like candy
that I longed to eat.
So yeah, deserve death?
I guess that I did.
Just throw me in a box
and nail shut the lid.
Now as I slip away
into torrid abyss-
the flames lick my soul-
as I'm greeted by kiss-
for now Hell is my home
and here I shall dwell-
the cracking of my bones-
most uncomfortable knell-
and wrapped there in flames-
forever lay screaming-
maybe I'll see David.
Ah, but I'm dreaming.
But this is no dream-
an eternal nightmare.
My life reeked of Hell-
now forever I'm there.
My only redemption
is there's no turning back-
my reward is my death
for a life drenched in black.
Slaved by desire-
I was fit to be tied-
now here I expire-
on this rack where I died.
Left now to rot-
from the sins of the past-
David wasn't my first-
but he would be my last.

Beautiful
John Claude Smith

"Everything has its beauty but not everyone sees it." – *Confucius*

We are beautiful.

We of nine limbs and three pleasant smiles. We, with we one great silver eye and many large breasts. We, one of a kind and special because of it.

We are beautiful.

They, male they and female they, sit across from we, ugly in they gray and navy blue fabric, ashamed of they naked flesh. We understand they shame, though. Two arms, two legs, two eyes, two of they, everything so uniform. Just like all the rest of they.

Not special like we.

Granmama made we clothing before we born, sewed shirts and pants, but we did not fit those clothes. We are different. Special. Granmama still made clothing, for hobby, in Granmama's sewing room. But we always naked to show off we beautiful we.

They, male they and female they, are sent to we from social services, as Granmama said they would be. Initially, social services wanted to take we from we home in the heart of a city we have never walked. We have only seen out we one window and not often. It so disgusts we. They so disgust we.

This apartment, all we have ever known. Ever since Granmama died, it is as if in discovering we, all of they scrunch they noses and crinkle they faces in repulsion of such beauty. Granmama warned we they would not understand we.

But Granmama left we well off, apartment paid for years, we only issue, missing Granmama and Granmama's stories. So, social services sent the male they and female they to help we.

Granmama used to entertain we with stories of we kind. We beautiful we. Now, we have no idea about how to handle these things. Granmama made sure social services understood this much. Made sure we would get help. But because we cannot speak, they think we stupid. We are not stupid, we just cannot speak. At least not in a language as minor as they language.

We can think and we can listen and we can listen deeper into they minds. That is we language, within.

We of nine limbs and three pleasant smiles and one great silver eye and many large breasts, we are special and they are not.

Listening:

"There's no way I'm staying here with that freak, Dan," the female they says. "Can you actually tell me you want to look at it every day for who knows how long? Can you really comprehend such an anatomical atrocity? I mean, what the hell is it? It's as if God tossed three, four . . . how many people into a blender and set it on mix and spat it out and . . ."

"She's not deaf, y'know?" the male they who the female they calls Dan says.

"She? You gotta be kidding me. She's about as much a woman as you are. Hell, no way is she . . . is it even human." We watch the female they fidget, wringing hands as if dirty. "I'll quit first if Broggs thinks I'm cleaning shit from that thing's ass. I'll quit if he thinks I'm going to feed that thing. Those drooling mouths . . ." With we one great silver eye, we watch the female they face contort. So ugly is they.

"They can . . . she can feed herself." Dan holds up papers as they say this. "It says here, she can feed herself."

The female they shakes head again and again.

"Look. It's the job. I need the money. Don't bail on this one, Sarah. Don't bail on me."

"I'm not bailing on you. Just on that thing." Staring at we again, yet not trying to. "Fuck! Doesn't it ever blink?"

"Broggs'll have your ass —"

"Screw Broggs. I'm out of here. This is one caregiver position I don't care about."

"Sarah . . ."

"No. No way. You can't talk me into splitting shifts with you and *that*." The female they who Dan calls Sarah shakes Sarah's head some more and we watch Sarah rise swiftly from the hardback chair, glance at we with Sarah's face twisted, and slam the door as Sarah leaves.

We watch Dan pull out Dan's cell phone from Dan's pants pocket, like Granmama's cell phone that Granmama rarely used, and call they who is Broggs.

Listening:

"Sarah's outta here. What? Yes . . . Yes, I'll do the job." Glancing at we, we smile. Dan's look confuses we, so we listen deeper:

I can't lose this job, but why her. Why her? But I need the money. Can't just walk away. Can't. Tracy'll kill me. But look at her. Look at her!

We know Dan's confusion must be inspired by we beautiful we. Dan has a partner, the they he calls Tracy, and Dan must sense the strain being with we for twelve hours a day might impact on Dan's relationship. Because we beauty is so overwhelming, even to ugly they. Even if they do not understand. Yet.

We watch Dan flip cell phone closed and Dan turns to we and says, "Well, according to the schedule, it should be time for your lunch."

We smile with we three pleasant smiles and Dan's face does what Sarah's did. Dan must already be sensing the tension of being around we beautiful we. We spread we five arms out, an invitation for a hug we might find disgusting, but it is how we attempt to let Dan know it is all right. We also know we have taken a big step as Granmama said we would have to, in order to let they know we just want to be friend, even if they ugly. Granmama told we it was the only way we would be able to get along when Granmama gone. So we try for Granmama.

We will become friend to Dan.

After three weeks, we have grown accustomed to Dan. They other assistant, a female they called Doris, not so much. But Doris is mostly around while we sleep, only here to get we breakfast and help clean we in the morning. Dan shows up soon thereafter and spends the waking hours with we. Dan is dutiful and courteous. Dan even call we by we name, Belladonna. Doris grunts and has a face of dark clouds. Dan smiles.

Yes, we like Dan.

On this day, though, Dan is sad. Dan's face is dark clouds as Doris's face, but different dark clouds.

We listen deeper:

How could you leave me, Tracy? How could you go? I thought we were building a life together. I thought we were good to go.

And empty space. We listen deeper and sense empty space. We sad for Dan. We do not know how to help Dan, but think perhaps now a hug would help. We spread we five arms wide and welcome him into we embrace. He smiles but it is not a smile.

We listen deeper:

Empty space.

Later, Dan receives a phone call. We listen:

"I really can't stay here tonight, Doris. Look . . . no, you look. You call Broggs. Have him send somebody down here now." And pause, face shifting, clouds still dark. "Look, you know I normally would, but . . ." And pause, face shifting, clouds still dark, angry. Then awash in nothing, as if empty again. Or still.

We listen deeper:

Why argue with her? Going home isn't going home? It's no longer a home. It's my private hell. Why not stay? Because you want to get plastered and bury your misery in the drink, that's why? Your usual way out, Danny-boy. Fucking pathetic asshole!

We listen:

"Fine." Shaking empty face. "Fine. But you need to be here tomorrow, and early."

Dan closes his cell phone and sighs heavily.

"Aw, Belladonna," Dan says, looking at we with empty eyes.

We roll on we many limbs behind Dan as Dan goes into the kitchen.

"It's not dinner time yet," Dan says.

We not thinking about dinner. We just want Dan to be happy.

We watch as Dan goes through cabinets up high. Dan brightens up. Dan's face like sun breaking through dark clouds. Dan pulls down two bottles. We do not know what is in bottles, but Dan seems happy to have found them, so we happy for Dan.

Later, after dinner and when we are to go to bed, Dan helps we up into bed, tucks we in. Just like Granmama used to do. Dan turns off the light when Dan leaves, closes door, but not all the way. We feel anxious. Dan's face so sad, but we do not know what to do to help Dan. Dan is we friend.

We lie in bed and listen:

We hear the rarely used television, voices, nothing more.

Time passes and sleep is near, when we keen ear holes hear Dan sobbing.

We quietly slide out of bed and roll into the room with the television. The lights are off, but the light from the television shines on Dan's face. Dan is lying on the sofa and sobbing between swigs of whatever is in the bottle. One bottle is on the floor next to the sofa. It is on its side. Dan has already drunk that entire one. We wonder why Dan drinks from the bottles if it does not make Dan happy, as we initially thought they would.

We listen deeper:

Such clutter, such confusion. No clarity.

We enter the room, but Dan seems oblivious to we presence.

We approach Dan slowly. We do not know what to do but to try and be supportive. Let Dan know we know Dan sad and we sad for Dan. We want to help.

We step in front of the television. Light passes through we webbing between limbs. We are so beautiful.

Dan moans something we cannot make out and reaches up with Dan's left hand to touch one of we many large breasts and moans again.

We not sure what to do, but Dan almost smiles. Perhaps this will make Dan happy. To admire we beautiful we. To finally understand we beautiful we.

Dan sits up and reaches out with both hands and touches one, two, and then all of we many large breasts. We feel blood rushing through we. We feel strange wetness in we vagina, which trickles down into we belly button. We do not understand, but now Dan seems happier and we want Dan happy. But this feels wrong. Not wrong, just different. Different.

We not sure what is going on.

We listen deeper:

We cannot hear Dan at all.

We breath grows rapid.

Dan rises up and with eyes that do not look like Dan's eyes, smiles. We confused. We do not understand what we are feeling and why we cannot listen deeper.

Dan pulls Dan's shirt over Dan's head and shows us Dan's nakedness. We are repulsed. We want no more of this.

Dan unzips Dan's pants and slips out of them. Dan slides down Dan's other, smaller pants. Dan is completely naked and not ashamed as Dan should be. So ugly. So ugly. We want to leave but Dan moves closer, hands caressing we many large breasts. We are confused. We do not understand sensations. Dan's body is hard against us. Dan wants hug now, but we do not want hug now. Something wrong. Something different. *No, something wrong.*

Then Dan pushes we to sofa and as Dan massages too roughly now we many large breasts, Dan seems in a frenzy as Dan puts Dan's penis in we vagina.

We many limbs try to push Dan away, but then in we confusion, we feel something different. Something so different.

We do not know what this feeling is, but Dan seems to feel it, too. All of a sudden, we feel as dark clouds pouring rain sunlight burning silver like we one great eye and Dan screams and we feel within we Dan wet, too. Wet with force. Hot within we vagina. We feel we —

– changing.

We flesh begins to melt. We many limbs and many large breasts feel liquid. We vagina clenches Dan's penis and Dan screams even louder, a sound like nothing we have ever heard. Dan seems hurt. Yet Dan seems to want more hurt. We cannot help we body. We have no control. We continue to clench Dan's penis but we body is changing, melting, melting away . . .

"Oh, my God," Dan says. We reach up to push Dan away even as we vagina holds on to Dan's penis. We reach up to push Dan away and only two arms push Dan.

Dan smiles in a way we have never seen.

We listen deeper:

We hear nothing still.

What is going on?

We finally pull we body from Dan, Dan's penis still erect as it has been since Dan's intrusion. Dan's trespass. We stand and look down on we and see two arms, two legs, two breasts . . .

We scream, a sound never emitted from we. We scream and it is a scream of anguish. Of rage.

"What have Dan done to we?"

"Belladonna, you can talk!"

Dan seems happy about this, too. Dan seems so happy now. We not happy, though. We not happy at all. We feel so wrong.

"What have Dan done to we?"

Dan reaches up to we, standing now, hands touching we on sides. Eyes taking in we ugliness.

We scream again and run to kitchen.

"This cannot be, Dan. We are no longer beautiful."

Dan chases us into the kitchen.

"Beautiful? Oh, Belladonna, you are the most beautiful woman I have ever seen."

"We are not beautiful women. We are repugnant. We want we back," we say, as we turn and shove knife into Dan's chest.

Dan stumbles backward, falls. The look on Dan's face is shock. This is what we feel, so perhaps Dan understands we sadness. Perhaps Dan understands what Dan has done to we.

"Belladonna," Dan says, gurgling and spitting blood from Dan's mouth as blood gushes from Dan's chest.

"We are not we beautiful we anymore. And we need to be we beautiful we again, Dan," we say, as we drag Dan to Granmama's sewing room, even as Dan squirms defenseless below we.

But we do not care if Dan understands or not. For what Dan has done to we, making we ugly, we do not care if Dan understands or not.

Afterward, we are not the same, but we try. We try to be we beautiful we.

Doris shows up as we sit on the sofa, television still on from last night. They nonsense. We sit up proud as Doris turns to face we and lets out a tiny scream of surprise.

We must have succeeded. Perhaps we are even more beautiful than before.

Doris approaches we slowly. Doris's always dark clouds face is now contorted much as Sarah's had been distorted when Sarah left. Doris glances away from we, around the apartment, and sees the open door to Granmama's sewing room, where we left the remains of Dan.

We did not need all of Dan.

"What have you done?"

We smile we one remaining pleasant smile and one stitched on pleasant smile.

"What have you done?"

Doris takes out Doris's cell phone with shaking hand.

We listen:

"Broggs. You need to come to Belladonna's apartment now. No, Broggs. No. She's . . . Dan's dead. What? She . . . She cut him up. She killed him and cut him up. She's different, not the same. What? She's . . . It's as if something happened and . . ." And pause, listening to Broggs. "She's sitting in front of me, on the sofa. She's got Dan's arms and legs stitched to slits in her flesh at her shoulders and hips. She's got . . . she's . . ." Pause again, speechless. We beauty must make Doris speechless. "She's like . . . like a Frankenstein's monster version of who she was. Of what she was. You need to get here now. Get somebody here, now. What? No, not long. I can't stay here long, goddamnit. Haven't you been listening to me? *Get somebody here, now!*"

Doris closes Doris's cell phone and backs away toward the front door. Doris places Doris's hand on the door handle. Doris must be eager for Broggs to show up. To show Broggs we beautiful we. Doris stares at us with strange look in Doris's eyes.

We listen deeper:

Oh, my God. Oh, my God. Oh, my God.

We must inspire awe now. God-like. We stand and open we two functioning arms and two Dan arms toward Doris, to offer Doris a hug. Doris leans away from we, back pressed to the door. We understand Doris's apprehension. Doris has never seen such beauty.

We are beautiful. So beautiful. More beautiful than before.

The most beautiful thing in the world.

"There is no exquisite beauty . . . without some strangeness in the proportion." *– Edgar Allan Poe.*

The Last Revelation of Gla'aki,
An Excerpt
Ramsey Campbell

Sandra hadn't even let Fairman finish telling her what he knew about Deepfall Water, although it wasn't a great deal. He'd found none of it worth mentioning in the essay that had ended up online.

Had a cult ever really made its home beside the unfrequented lake? In the 1960s the notion had been revived after Thomas Cartwright, a minor artist specialising in fantastic and occult themes, moved into one of the lakeside houses and died as the result of some kind of attack. A police investigation had proved inconclusive, and a family who were supposed to have abandoned the house before Cartwright took it over had never been tracked down. If the houses had at some stage been served by a private graveyard, no identifiable trace was found, though some tales suggested that the stone tombs had been pulverised beyond recognition. *We Pass from View*, an occult book by local author Roland Franklyn, even claimed that they'd been destroyed by the police.

Fairman had thought this unsuitable for mentioning in *Book Hunter Monthly*, and Sandra hadn't wanted to hear any more. She would have liked his other anecdotes even less – schoolboy stupidity, he imagined she would call them. They dated from his days at Brichester High, a quarter of a century after the Cartwright business. The lake had become a place you dared your friends to visit after dark, and he'd assumed his fellow pupils had borrowed the idea from films, though the originator of the challenge had lived on the edge of Brichester nearest the lake. Those who ventured there brought back increasingly extreme stories: the lake had begun to throb like an enormous heart, or a

procession of figures as stiff as bones had been glimpsed among the trees on the far side of the water, or a globular growth on a stalk in the middle of the lake had turned so as to keep a party of teenagers in sight, and they'd realised it was an eye. How could any of this have been visible at night? At the time Fairman hadn't been surprised that the adventurers had ended up with nightmares, but once the headmaster learned of the visits to the lake he'd forbidden them. Apparently his fierceness was daunting enough, since the lake reverted to the status of a rumour. Since then, so far as Fairman knew, it had been visited mostly by the kind of people who tried to plumb the depths of Loch Ness, and they'd found just as little evidence of anything unnatural.

He didn't think he would ever tell Sandra that he'd visited Deepfall Water. He'd hoped to bring his essay more to life, but perhaps he also meant to prove that he wasn't quite the bookish introverted fellow his schoolmates had thought him. He could see no reason to go at night, and even on a February afternoon the place had seemed unnecessarily dark, no doubt because of the trees that stooped close to the unpaved track from the main road as well as surrounding the lake. They overshadowed the row of three-storey houses that huddled alongside a cobblestone pavement at the edge of the water. All six roofs had caved in, and some of the floors were so rotten that they'd collapsed under the weight of debris. Great leaves of blackened wallpaper drooped off the walls of a house in the middle of the terrace, and Fairman had wondered if this was the one most recently occupied, nearly half a century ago. None of the windows contained even a fragment of glass, and he suspected his old schoolmates might have been at least partly responsible. The buildings seemed to gape at the expanse of water like masks lined up to demonstrate they had no identity of their own. He'd found the thought oddly disturbing as he went to the edge of the lake.

The murky water stretched perhaps half a mile to the trees where some of his schoolfellows had claimed to see a procession that shouldn't have been walking. He doubted you could see that even with a flashlight, given how close together the trees grew. The depths of the lake were even harder to distinguish. It was fringed by large ferns, but he'd made out just a few inches of the stalks beneath the surface, which was so nearly opaque that he might have imagined the mud was being stirred up by some activity in the lake. In fact the water had been absolutely stagnant, and he'd peered harder into it as though he was compelled to find some reason to have visited Deepfall Water. He'd had the odd impression that around it all the trees were craning to imitate him, enclosing the lake with an iris of darkness that was capable of shrinking the sky overhead. That must have been an effect of his concentration, along with the idea that his scrutiny could waken some presence in the depths; in fact, a sluggish ripple had begun to spread from the middle of the lake, followed by another and another. They'd advanced so slowly that their lethargy had seemed to take hold of him; he could have fancied that the waves of his brain had been reduced to the pace of the hypnotic ripples. The thought had jerked him back to consciousness, not least of the unnaturally premature dark. As the ripples grew audible he'd turned his back and retreated to his car. He'd heard water splashing the edge of the pavement by the time he'd succeeded in starting the engine. Of course the ripples must have been caused by a wind, since all the trees around the lake had bent towards the water.

Besides these impressions, he'd seemed to take something else home. Like Sandra, for whom it was a reason to be proud of her rationality and control, he didn't dream or at least never remembered having done so, but for some nights after visiting Deepfall Water he'd been troubled by wakeful thoughts. Whenever he drifted close to sleep he'd found himself thinking of the investigators who had tried to search the lake. The notion of sounding it had brought to mind a disconcertingly vivid image of a vast shape burrowing deeper into the bed of the lake, raising a cloud of mud so thick that it blotted out the denizen. No doubt this betrayed how preoccupied he was with the impossibly rare book, but he'd been assailed by the vision several times a night, until he'd begun almost to dread attempting to sleep. If dreaming was like that, it wasn't for him.

Excerpt from: "The Last Revelation of Gla'aki," 2013

About the Contributors

Jerrod Balzer

In addition to a horror target, Jerrod Balzer is the co-founder of Skullvines Press, and he's the website/ebook tech and cover designer for its umbrella company, KHP Publishers, Inc. He rarely behaves but even at his grumpiest, he won't turn down a good laugh. Look for him at jerrodbalzer.com and wherever else Jerrod-Balzers can be found.

*   *   *

Doug Blakeslee

The author lives in the Pacific Northwest and spends his time writing, cooking, gaming, and following the local WHL hockey team. His interest in books and reading started early thanks to his parents, though his serious attempts at writing only started a few years ago. From time to time he blogs about writing and other related topics at The Simms Project at http://thesimmsproject.blogspot.com/. His current project is an urban fantasy novella featuring a group of changelings in the modern world. He can be reached on Facebook or simms.doug@gmail.com.

Michael Burnside

Michael Burnside is a graduate of Ohio University whose inquisitive nature has led him to study and work in a wide variety of fields. His interests include gaming, science, computer technology, history, politics, and, of course, writing.

Michael is the creator of the role playing games Space Conspiracy and World War Two Roleplay. He is now branching out into fiction writing, specializing in the steampunk and horror genres. Read more nice things about him, as well as some free stories, at www.michaelburnside.com.

* * *

Ramsey Campbell

The *Oxford Companion to English Literature* describes Ramsey Campbell as "Britain's most respected living horror writer". He has been given more awards than any other writer in the field, including the Grand Master Award of the World Horror Convention, the Lifetime Achievement Award of the Horror Writers Association and the Living Legend Award of the International Horror Guild. Among his novels are *The Face That Must Die, Incarnate, Midnight Sun, The Count of Eleven, Silent Children, The Darkest Part of the Woods, The Overnight, Secret Story, The Grin of the Dark, Thieving Fear, Creatures of the Pool, The Seven Days of Cain, Ghosts Know* and *The Kind Folk.* Forthcoming are *Bad Thoughts* and *Thirteen Days at Sunset Beach. The Last Revelation of Gla'aki* and *The Pretence* are novellas. His collections include *Holes for Faces, Waking Nightmares, Alone with the Horrors, Ghosts and Grisly Things, Told by the Dead* and *Just Behind You,* and his non-fiction is collected as *Ramsey Campbell, Probably.* His novels *The Nameless* and *Pact of the Fathers* have been filmed in Spain. His regular columns appear in *Prism, Dead Reckonings* and *Video Watchdog.* He is the President of the Society of Fantastic Films.

Ramsey Campbell lives on Merseyside with his wife Jenny. His pleasures include classical music, good food and wine, and whatever's in that pipe. His web site is at www.ramseycampbell.com.

Spencer Carvalho

Spencer Carvalho has written short stories for various literary magazines and anthologies. Revolver Concert was previously published in the Barcelona Review issue 70 2010, Litter Box Magazine, issue 9 Sept. 2010, ken*again Summer 2011, Inner Sins issue 4 Dec. 2012, Fever Dreams Ezine Issue 1 January-March 2013, Allegory Volume 21/48 Spring 2013, and eRomance volume 1 no. 6 June 2013. His stories have also appeared in the anthologies Certain Circuits Volume 1, Another Wild West, Remembrances of Wars Past: A War Veterans Anthology, and Tales of the Undead-Suffer Eternal: Volume 3.

*   *   *

Stinky Cat

Stinky Cat is a long-haired grey domestic feline suffering from hyperthyroidism and chronic diarrhea. Stinky's hobbies include excessive purring, table jumping and eating other cats' food. Stinky's birthplace and age remain unknown.

*   *   *

Scott Colbert

Scott Colbert is the author of the horror novella Barbed Wire Kisses and the short story sampler Detritus. He is also a contributor and editor for the movie website www.talkbacker.com. Scott resides in Phoenix, AZ with his cat Odetta and can be reached at www.scottcolbert.com.

*   *   *

Joshua Dobson

Joshua Dobson likes to make his own fun some of which can be seen at http://joshuadobson.deviantart.com/

Deb Eskie

Deb Eskie is a resident of Somerville, MA and has an M.Ed in creative arts education. With a background in women's studies, her focus as a writer is to expose the woman's experience through unsettling tales that highlight the dilemma of sexual repression and oppression. By combining the genres of feminist and horror fiction she aims to not only disturb readers, but deliver a message that is informative and thought provoking.

In 2005 Deb's play, Tell Me About Love, was featured in the Provincetown Playwright Festival. She has been featured in online magazines such as Deadman's Tome, Bad Moon Rising, Death Head Grin, and 69 Flavors of Paranoia. Deb has also had a number of short stories published through Pill Hill Press, Post Mortem Press, Cruentus Libri Press, and Short Scary Tales Publications.

*　　*　　*

Tony Flynn

A filmmaker & writer of short stories, poetry and screenplays, Tony is fantastically afraid of most everything, and therefore has a particular interest in the Horror genre. Previously his work has been published by wordlegs.com, Mocha Memoirs Press, Horrified Press and Sirens Call Publications. Other works in writing and film can be found via http://tonywritesstuff.tumblr.com and http://vimeo.com/tonyflynn
Twitter: @Tony_Flynn_

*　　*　　*

Carl Thomas Fox

Carl Thomas Fox Lives in Swansea with his fiancé, Samantha Smith, and their two daughters, Amelia and Nevaeh. Carl is a teaching assistant in the Reception area of a Primary School. Primarily a writer of horror, but also of thrillers, science fiction, sword and sorcery and fantasy and children's novels and picture books. A pagan with a deep interest in the occult and ancient mythologies, all of his work will all be part of what is known as the Wellworlds mythology, with invented languages. You can find him on Facebook at carl.fox.5454@facebook.com.

Ken Goldman

Ken Goldman, former Philadelphia teacher and an affiliate member of the Horror Writers Association, has homes on the Main Line in Pennsylvania and at the Jersey shore depending upon his need for a tan. His stories have appeared in over 680 independent press publications with over twenty due in 2014. Ken's tales have received seven honorable mentions in The Year's Best Fantasy & Horror. He has written four books: YOU HAD ME AT ARRGH!! (Sam's Dot Publishers); DONNY DOESN'T LIVE HERE ANYMORE (A/A Productions), STAR-CROSSED (Vampires 2 Publishers), and DESIREE, (Damnation books). His novel, . . . OF A FEATHER, is due in late 2013 or early 2014 (Horrific Tales Publishers). Ken would be famous except for the fact nobody seems to know who he is. Visit Ken's Facebook page at : http://www.facebook.com/kenneth.goldman1

*   *   *

John Goodrich

John Goodrich has never enjoyed the company of monkeys. Something to do with their manners.

*   *   *

Wesley D. Gray

Wesley D. Gray is an author of fiction and poetry. His work is difficult to classify, as he writes words of darkness and light, things both beautiful and grotesque. That is to say, his writing is diverse. He doesn't easily adhere to one particular genre, although much of his published work can be found in the speculative realms of fantasy, sci-fi, and horror. He currently resides in Florida with his wife and two children. Visit Wesley and learn more about his writing on his website, www.wesdgray.com.

*   *   *

Meagan Hightower

Meagan Hightower is a writer and music producer from Japan and North Carolina. Her work has published in the *Peace College Prism* magazine and in the *Peace Times* newspaper. When she is not writing, she can be found playing with voice synths and other virtual instruments.

*   *   *

Mathias Jansson

Mathias Jansson is a Swedish art critic and poet. He has been published in such magazines as The Horror Zine Magazine, Dark Eclipse, Schlock, The Sirens Call and The Poetry Box. He has also contributed to several anthologies from Horrified Press and James Ward Kirk Fiction as Suffer Eternal anthology Volume 1-3, Hell Whore Anthology Volume 1-3, Barnyard Horror and Serial Killers Tres Tria.
Homepage: http://mathiasjansson72.blogspot.se/

*   *   *

Melanie-Jo Lee

Melanie-Jo was born at Women's Pavilion Hospital in Winnipeg Manitoba, July 28th, 1982. Both parents were at the birth, and dogged her with their common sense and watchful eyes until she left home to wander the country at 18. She currently resides somewhere in the valleys of Manitoba, and writes about her two favorite places, the Pembina Valley and Snow Valley. If you happen to see some of her work, whether you like it or not, she'd love to hear from you at melaniejo.lee@gmail.com.

*   *   *

Kerry Lipp and Emily Meier

Emily and Kerry are an unlikely pair who found a bond over hating the same skanks, liking the same beers, and ignoring 90% of what the other says. Kerry spends his days in Dayton writing and getting turned down by women, and Emily resides in Cincinnati with her son, who will never be allowed to read this story. Links would be @kerrylipp on Twitter and New World Horror - Kerry G.S. Lipp on Facebook. Emily doesn't have/want any links included.

Mike Meroney

Mike Meroney has been writing stories and poetry since the age of 8. He is his own genre and writes for both children and adults. He finds particular comfort in dark writing, loves coffee and thinks that dogs are better than humans. His writing can be found at his own blog site (http://thatmanitouguy.blogspot.com/) as well as a horror themed blog that he shares with his wife (http://deadbydawn66.blogspot.com/)

*   *   *

Christine Morgan

Christine Morgan is so terribly afraid of being exposed as a fandom hack that she's written over two million words of fanfiction since 1996 and posted it all online under her own real name in hopes that nobody will ever ever ever find out. She's also the author of about twenty novels and has had dozens of stories published in anthologies and magazines. Visit her at http://www.christine-morgan.org/

*   *   *

Russell Nayle

For reasons that will be self-evident to those in the know, this contributor chooses to remain as anonymous as such a name allows.

*   *   *

Tanya Nehmelman

Tanya Nehmelman, although has always been a bigger fan of horror, is a graduate of the Institute of Children's Literature. In spare time, when not working on adult horror, she enjoys writing, and illustrating children's books. You can find one of her short, horror stories entitled, "Every Time I Close My Eyes", in the anthology entitled, "Dead Men and Women Walking" A collection of short stories, "Nighty Nightmares" is available at authorhouse.com. Updates for her recent work/events can be found at facebook.com/tanyanehmelmanauthorpage.

Mark Orr

Mark Orr resides in the wilds of Middle Tennessee, out past Gemütlichkeit and well on the way to La Dolce Vita, with his wife of thirty-two years, three daughters, one granddaughter, and roughly 10,000 books. His current work in progress is a comprehensive history of the horror genre in every medium imaginable, spanning the years 1890 to 1980. He is also working on devising a workable tango solo, disproving the old saying about it taking two to you-know-what.

*   *   *

Mary Pletsch

Mary Pletsch is a glider pilot, toy collector and graduate of the University of Huron College, the Royal Military College of Canada and Dalhousie University. Her short stories have been published in "When the Hero Comes Home 2" by Dragon Moon Press, "Dark Bits" by Apokrupha and "Steamed Up" by Dreamspinner Press. "Mishipishu: The Ghost Story of Penny Jaye Prufrock" was inspired by summer camp nostalgia, Bon Echo Provincial Park and T.S. Eliot read after midnight. Administrator by day, writer by night, she stays up late to indulge the voices in her head, powered by the lunar tides and too much caffeine. She currently lives in Ottawa with Dylan Blacquiere and their four cats. Visit her online at www.fictorians.com

*   *   *

G. Preacher

G. Preacher is a world traveler and renaissance man whose hobbies include music, mayhem and meditation. He is an historian by trade, specializing in the Gothic subculture, and has been in more museums than he can count. It is his great pleasure to be able to bring his love for the past, his immersion in academia and the literary arts together in this anthology.

Peter Rawlik

In the beginning there were the books, and Pete Rawlik loved them. Through the years they grew, some were lost, some were replaced, but the collection and the books themselves grew. They filled his room, and then his apartment. The apartment gave way to a house, but even that the books filled. They grew bigger, and smarter, wiser, more difficult to understand, and handle. Rawlik tried to stop them, he sold them, he gave them away, he burned them. They found ways to return, and in the end they consumed him, filled him up, until all that was left were the words pouring out of him and onto the page.

*　　*　　*

William Andre Sanders

William Andre Sanders resides in Narrows, VA with his wife and two children. He has had three short stories and over two dozen poems published. Right now, he is committed to completing the final touches on the first draft of what he hopes will become his debut horror novel. Feel free to contact him on facebook at http://www.facebook.com/dre6380, or by email at william_a_sanders@yahoo.com.

*　　*　　*

Michael Shimek

Michael Shimek currently resides in Minnesota where he writes horror, fantasy, and science-fiction. Some of his stories can be found in the anthologies *Grave Robbers, Barnyard Horror, ZOMBIE:Lockdown, Blood & Roses,* and *Tales of the Undead: Suffer Eternal - volume II,* along with more on the way. He also posts random free stories on his blog: michaelshimek.blogspot.com

John Claude Smith

John Claude Smith has had one book published, a collection called, The Dark Is Light Enough For Me. He will have a second book released in 2014—details coming soon. He is currently writng a novel, while shopping around another one, and putting together a second collection. Busy is good. He splits his time between the SF Bay Area and Rome, Italy.

Blog: http://thewildernesswithinbyjohnclaudesmith.blogspot.com/
Email: jcsmith0919@yahoo.com

* * *

Jeremy Terry

Jeremy Terry is the author of the apocalyptic horror novel Dreams of the Dead from Damnation Books and Mirror, Mirror from SSTPublications. His short fiction has appeared in anthologies and magazines from Nightscape Press, Azure Keep Quarterly, and SSTpublications. He lives in the Florida Panhandle with his wife, three boys, and Great Dane named Max. You can follow him on the web at www.facebook.com/jeremyterrywrites/

* * *

Patrick Tumblety

Patrick Tumblety is a multimedia artist and writer. This fall his work has appeared in Tales of Jack the Ripper, by **Word Horde Press**, as well as issues of **Dark Moon Digest** and **Sirens Call Publications**. In 2012, he released Dark Passages, an anthology of thrillers currently available on Amazon.com. That year he was also published in **Infinity's Kitchen**, an experimental narrative magazine, and received an honorable mention from **Writer's Digest** for short format storytelling. Patrick currently resides in Dover, Delaware with his wife, Kathleen, and their cat, Dusty. He would love to hear feedback from you at SpeakerPatrick@gmail.com.

D.J. Tyrer

DJ Tyrer is the person behind *Atlantean Publishing* and has been widely published in anthologies and magazines in the UK, USA and elsewhere, most recently *Cthulhu Haiku and Other Mythos Madness* (Popcorn Press), *Sorcery & Sanctity: A Homage to Arthur Machen* (Hieroglyphics Press), *All Hallow's Evil* (Mystery & Horror LLC) and *Strange Lucky Hallowe'en* (Whortleberry Press), and the well-received, sold-out limited-edition novella, *The Yellow House* (Dynatox Ministries).

DJ Tyrer's website is at http://djtyrer.blogspot.co.uk/. The Atlantean Publishing website is at http://atlanteanpublishing.blogspot.co.uk/. He can be reached at atlanteanpublishing@hotmail.com

*   *   *

Lewis Unknown

Lewis Unknown went to University to discover he knew nothing, he now spends his time as his elderly father's full time carer and dreams of becoming a Viking, or a wealthy alcoholic. In the meantime however he writes the odd story for the entertainment of others.
pandaswahey.blogspot.com

*   *   *

Melany Van Every

When not trying to save the small Iowa town she lives in from Cthulhu and heavy metal groupies one country song at a time, Melany Van Every can often be found hanging out at local restaurants or the town's one screen movie theater. Inspiration for her writing comes from such authors as Stephen King and Jim Butcher as well as the worst of the monster movies that cable television has to offer and wildlife documentaries. This is her first time being published.

Dana Wright

Dana Wright has always had a fascination with things that go bump in the night. She is often found playing at local bookstores, trying not to maim herself with crochet hooks or knitting needles, watching monster movies with her husband and furry kids or blogging about books. More commonly, she is chained to her computers, writing like a woman possessed. She is currently working on several children's works, young adult fiction and horror short stories and is trying her hand at poety. She is a contributing author to several e-zines and anthologies.

Twitter: @dana19018

http://danawrightwordscribe.wordpress.com/

email: dana19018@gmail.com

*   *   *

The MageLore & ElfLore Trilogy
Also by Christine Morgan

Curse of the Shadow Beasts – MageLore Book I

They come from beyond the walls of nightmare, hideous creatures bent on seeking and slaughtering, leaving only death and misery in their wake.

Arien Mirida knows them only too well. He has faced them before and witnessed their evil, and fears that their hunger can never be stopped.

Cat Sabledrake is about to meet the horror, when a deadly dream becomes deadlier reality.

$11.95 • 1-56315-188-X • 182 pages

Dark of the Elvenwood – MageLore Book II

They are the Morvalan, elves in the service of a god of destruction. To further their war against humanity, they have joined forces with the minotaur wizard Solarrin. Together, they have hatched a plot to bring about the downfall of the Northlands.

Four reunited companions are all that stand between the Morvalan and success. But as Cat, Arien, Greyquin and Alphonse brave the dangers of the woodlands, a worse peril threatens the very home that they left to save.

$11.95 • 0-9702189-0-7 • 272 pages

Archmage of the Universe – MageLore Book III

He is Solarrin. Once his body was as twisted as his mind. Now inhabiting the form of a minotaur, his physical and magical prowesses are without equal.

The young Highlord is his pawn. The city of Thanis is under his control. His next move will plunge the Northlands into war.

The only ones who will stand a chance against him fled on a foolish quest – to bring his predecessor back from the dead.

$11.95 • 0-9702189-1-5 • 292 pages

The ElfLore Trilogy – All 3 books in 1 volume

Set 20 years after the MageLore books, the ElfLore Trilogy follows the story of the next generation as they seek to find their place in a world recovering from a devastating war.

Caught up in the scheming of manipulative elves and the plots of dark warriors, Ariana Mirida and Mischa Narrin are forced to fight for their lives as they get caught up in the struggles for the Emerinian throne.

$39.95 • 0-9771005-1-0 • 636 page hardback

Horror Novels
by Christine Morgan

Black Roses – Trinity Bay Book I

He is the man of their dreams – literally. He feeds on the sleeping minds of the women of Trinity Bay, making them believe their most forbidden fantasies are coming true. Now he has chosen the one woman he intends to be his, no matter how many people must die. Theresa Zane, newly returned to her childhood home, is drawn into a century-old mystery of sex, death, and the ominous haunting of the power behind the black roses.

$14.95 • 0-9702189-5-8 • 300 pages

Gifted Children – Trinity Bay Book II

The children of Trinity Bay are like any other American kids. Lora Blake has a way with animals. Toby Edwards is the class brain. Jenny Forrester can talk her friends into anything. But in the innocent gifts of these children and others like them, someone has seen a gift of terrifying potential. Seacliff, the house on the hill, has a new secret.

$16.95 • 0-9702189-9-0 • 372 pages

Changeling Moon – Trinity Bay Book III

For thousands of years, they have lived among us. Their abilities have given rise to our oldest legends and our deepest fears.

They are changelings. Shape-shifters. Hunters. Creatures of the night. Ruled by the moon, and by their own savage hungers.

To them, we are prey.

Now they have come to Trinity Bay, where one troubled young woman will be caught in the midst of their deadly conflict.

$14.95 • 0-9771005-0-2 • 284 pages

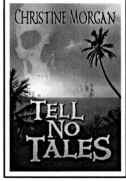

Tell No Tales

The latest hot reality television program is in the works, blending historical re-creation with physical challenges, mental strategy, and emotional manipulation. On the Caribbean island of Veradoga, a dozen contestants and the show's production team get more than they bargain for when world events and the island's haunted history combine to make it anything but a game.

$15.95 • 0-9771005-3-7 • 304 pages

Roleplaying Games

Naughty & Dice: An Adult Gamer's Guide to Sexual Situations

Naughty & Dice takes a light-hearted yet serious look at the topic of sex in RPGs. The tone of the book is centered around themes of tolerance and respect. It is recommended for mature readers, and is easily adaptable to any roleplaying game system.

Naughty & Dice includes chapters on:
- instructions for factoring a character's "Sexuality" statistic.
- rules for sexual gifts, drawbacks and abilities.
- character types and adventure ideas.
- pregnancy, contraception and sexually transmitted diseases.
- enchanted items, spells, potions, and types of sex-related magic.
- an overview of sex in history, mythology and folklore.
- genre-specific looks at horror, aliens and fantasy races.
- OGL conversions, feats and classes.
- and much more!

Christine & Tim Morgan

$19.95
• 0-9702189-6-6 •
108 pages

Ellis: A Kingdom in Turmoil

Good King Heinrich is dead, betrayed by his closest advisor. His three sons, quarrelsome to the end, have vowed that only one of them shall rule. How many thousands will die before a king is chosen?

Rumors tell of unrest in the border-lands, and among the recently subjugated Cordovans. Will they sit idly by while civil war rages throughout kingdom?

Religious zealots speak of the end times and whip themselves into a frenzy. Heresy is stirring right under the noses of the clergy, while church leaders bicker amongst themselves.

This is your character's world and it is crumbling down. What will you do? What will you fight for? What is worth saving and what needs to change? Who can you trust? To what lengths will you go to save a kingdom in turmoil?

A Pen-and-Paper Roleplaying Game of Low-Fantasy, High-Roleplaying

$49.95 • 978-0-9844032-1-9 • 604 pages

SCOOT

CHRISTINE MORGAN

Print: $14.95 • 978-0-9844032-2-6 • 220 pages
Kindle: $0.99 • 978-0-9844032-2-6 • 489KB

An assassin who's just accepted her latest contract, complete with target, weapon, and half her fee up front.

A skateboarding purse-snatcher, cruising along, always on the lookout for the next opportunistic score.

When their paths cross, it"s bad news for both. Lives in danger. Livelihoods on the line.

Can't go to the police.

What would YOU do?

SCOOT!

CPSIA information can be obtained at www.ICGtesting.com
Printed in the USA
BVOW05s0918280414

351834BV00008B/17/P